HEIST OF HEARTS

E. A. WINTERS

*To Seth Ring and Eric Ugland
For their incredible continued kindness, generosity, and support,
without whom I may never have had the guts to figure out dictation.*

*Heist of Hearts represents my eleventh written fantasy novel and my
first fully dictated novel.*

*To my husband, who found himself walking into my office with me
in noise cancelling headphones saying all sorts of crazy things with no
idea he was standing there.
And to that one time he came in to tell me something the kids were
doing, to which I unknowingly but convincingly responded,
"You're lying."*

SOCIAL MEDIA

Connect with me on social media! [1]

- Website and newsletter: eawinters.com
- Facebook: facebook.com/eawintersnovels
- TikTok: @eawinters
- Instagram: @e.a.winters

---

1. Warning: connecting on social media may lead to exclusive content, behind the scenes snapshots, and joining a community that is way more fun than your daily to-do list. Engage with caution.

CHAPTER ONE

GRIGG

Twisted. Bent. Folded into whichever shape he envisioned. Onkar lifted the green paper siren in his hands and examined it against the haze of early morning as the first rays of sun fell across the ship's deck. At least, that's what anyone else would see. Ship captain Onkar Dhoka, sporting his signature teal jacket with its polished brass buttons, leaning bored as a boat in a bucket against the mizzenmast of the *Mermaid's Menace.*

He'd had to trade out ships several times over the past few years. This one wasn't quite as fast as the *Wraithweaver* had been, but it came close—and after his latest seafaring ventures, the rumors around the captain who'd conquered Ghosts' Gorge had nearly sprouted legs and run away with themselves.

Which is why he'd miss playing Onkar. The notoriety he'd built up, the work put into an established alias—all about to end. He couldn't go to the next stop on his list as himself, of course. He twisted the paper mermaid in his fingers again, then tucked it into a pocket in the inside lining of his jacket. He'd have to get a new ship, but that was just as well. This *Menace* had barely made it into harbor and needed repairs anyway.

Movement caught his eye, and Grigg shoved off the mast as a twig-thin dusty-blond man skirted into view in tattered clothes and leathered skin more crinkled than the folded paper in Grigg's fingers.

Grigg—or rather, Onkar, as he slipped into the captain's persona—shook his head and sucked his teeth as the scrawny man slipped onto the ship's deck. "By the gallows, Rakesh, have you seen a ghost? I thought I hired you for your robust constitution."

"That's funny. I thought you hired me for my good looks." The man's face split into a wide smile, showing off three missing teeth and a crooked nose. He was easily the richest man on the east end, largely due to commission jobs he took for Grigg. He didn't know Grigg's real name, of course. No one did. He didn't remember how many years it had been since he'd said the name Grigglor out loud. It'd been so long since Grigg had heard it, he could've forgotten it himself. At least, that's what he told himself.

But as the man's anxious smile faded away and he reached for a bundle from under the tattered shade of his cloak, Grigg winced as his full name burned like a scalding branding iron in the back of his mind.

Grigg spun one of the polished golden buttons between two fingers. It had come halfway loose along the latest journey. If he hadn't been planning on ditching it tonight, he would've had it mended, but as it was …

He pursed his lips at Rakesh. "Don't be a fool. You can't bring that out here, in the open."

"I don't want this with me any longer than necessary."

Grigg clapped the man on the back, and the splinter of a human staggered back under the weight of his firm hand. "It's almost adorable that after all this time, you still believe I would do anything unnecessary."

He steered the man across the deck and down a flight of stairs into a dark pit of a room where he'd set out a single wooden carved chair. Hamza, the beefy Keketi crestbreaker Onkar had most recently brought on as a bodyguard, emerged from the shadows of the quarterdeck and followed them down the stairs. He took up his position to one side of the chair, folded his arms, and drilled Rakesh with an unfeeling stare.

Grigg may not have been a melder himself—with abilities to manipulate rock and soil like quakemakers, water like crestbreakers, wind like windcallers, or fire like firebloods—but keeping plenty in his employ had been at least as good as having abilities himself. Hamza, for example, had been worth his substantial weight in gold. For obvious reasons, crestbreakers were even more important when traveling by sea.

Below deck, Grigg strode to the chair, spun with a flourish, and plopped down, offering a low hay bale the height of an old worn-out shoe as seating for his guest.

"Oh, I'm not staying long enough to need any of that." Rakesh wrung trembling hands and reached for the bundle again. "May I?"

"That depends. Do you plan on unwrapping it, running up the stairs, holding it over your head and screaming, 'Look at the magical golden egg' to all who will listen, so that I'm forced to send you swimming with the fishies?"

Rakesh gulped. He shook his head.

Grigg spread his hands and offered an easy smile. "Then you may deliver the object."

"This thing isn't just magical, Mr. Onkar, sir. It's possessed."

Grigg clapped his hands in mock delight. "You *have* seen a ghost, then. What fun. I've never met a ghost."

Rakesh was a few teeth shy of a mouthful, in more ways than one—which made him perfect for Onkar's uses. Usually. Smart enough to keep his mouth shut, dumb enough that he couldn't cause much trouble if he tried. But he'd never seen the man this freaked out.

Grigg leaned forward in his chair, as if about to share conspiratorial secrets. "Did the ghost speak to you?"

Rakesh shook his head so hard, his scraggly brown hair threatened to fly free of his scalp. "No, sir, but it near killed me."

Grigg sank back in the chair again, regarding the man. No, Rakesh was a weasel, not a shaken leaf. What had him so uptight?

He gestured to the man to get on with it, and Rakesh reached for an object from his pack, careful to keep a layer of cloth between his fingers and the object as he unwrapped it.

It was large for an egg, perhaps the size of a pakshi egg or a cannonball. Delicate designs ran across the egg in swirling, mesmerizing lines across a metallic golden shell.

This was it. After seven years, this was it. His life, his death, his curse. Grigg wasn't sure at first whether to kiss Rakesh or hurl him into the depths of the sea. He hadn't realized he'd moved until he was standing, heart pounding out the hoofbeats of the horses of death, staring at the egg in Rakesh's hands.

Then his heart nearly stopped. A long, thin crack ran across its surface. "What did you do? Drop it?"

Now Rakesh nearly *did* drop it. He blanched white as cooked flounder, the whites of his eyes almost comically large around his irises as he gaped back at Grigg in horror. "No, sir, no. The shell is harder than solid gold. Nothing can penetrate it."

"How would you know? What did you do?"

"Nothing. Nothing, sir. I'm just saying. It's not received even a dent from me. Please, sir, take it. I need to get out of here."

Grigg reached out a hesitant hand. His finger lightly touched the smooth, cold surface of the egg.

Blinding light shot out, searing as the sun. A rough hand knocked him sideways as Hamza shoved himself between Grigg and the egg. Grigg rocketed backward, and the world went black.

But the world did not remain dark. Though he didn't open his eyes, Grigg found himself standing on the edge of a moonlit lake. A ring of trees surrounded the lake, illuminated with glowing white-and-blue flower bulbs the size of irises, bursting in voluminous blossoms like shimmering pearl and carnelian, soft as melted silk. The perfect circular ring of trees shed their light on the bank of the lake where he stood, a full moon casting silver kisses to the ink-black waters below.

A dark object plummeted down from the sky straight at his head. Grigg threw his hands up to protect himself from what looked like a great dive-bombing bird. That's when he noticed—he wore nothing but a loose tunic and basic trousers, without any accoutrement or accessory in sight. No jacket, no dagger, no pockets, no nothing. That fact alone was enough to tell him this place was not fully real.

At the last second, Grigg altered course and instead of protecting his head, thrust the blade of his forearm up toward the beak of the bird. But the feathers of its wingtip merely grazed his arm and brushed over the top of his head before alighting on the surface of the water—a magnificent black swan, its beak ruby red, feathers dark as death. But as soon as he registered the nature of the bird, it was gone. And after a swirl of ebony feathers obscured the creature, there stood in its place a woman.

Thick dark hair draped over one shoulder in a long gray-streaked braid, leaving only a few stray wisps to frame her face. High cheekbones and intense brown eyes sharp as an executioner's axe set in a canvas of glowing bronze. She was decked in animal hide, dyed black as the depths of the lake in which she stood. An embroidered ruby-red collar draped across her shoulders, its pattern complemented by beaded necklaces falling from the woman's neck. Her animal-skin clothes were simple, save for the fringe along the collar and hem, and black swan feathers dangled from her ears. Her face, illuminated by the cold silver of the moon, looked as unmoving as stone, and ageless as the same.

The maturity of her face, the gray in her hair, and the ghost of lines in her features implied she might be in her fifties, though something about her whispered of a longer existence. Perhaps it was the keenness of her eyes, the way her gaze cut into the soul as though hers was as endless as the seas.

She hadn't come to him for months. He'd first seen her the day of The Return, when magic was unleashed upon the world from its dormant state seven years ago. When all the melderbloods were waking to electrifying new powers overnight, Grigg was afflicted with fresh nightmares of the woman who'd sentenced him and his family to a fractured, cursed existence. Since then, she had come only rarely to prod at wounds refusing to heal into scars, a flash in the night, a dose of lemon on a fresh gash, to edge his bleak gray into a deeper dark.

"Did you miss me, Sergei?"

Grigg held back a grimace at the use of his ancestor's name. He hadn't figured out if she did it to needle him for being related to the man she so despised, or because she truly conflated the two of them.

"Maybe he *would* miss you, if he hadn't died six hundred years ago. Or if you hadn't cursed him and all his descendants."

Her lips curved into a thin, cruel smile. "All his *male* descendants."

She swept from the lake in slow, deliberate steps that left a trail of disturbed ripples in her wake. It was indicative of everything she touched—Giovanna, the Black Swan Mage.

She reached for his face and dragged a finger gently across his cheek. Needles of ice worked their way between his shoulder blades and down his spine at her touch. He stiffened, but didn't move.

"Sergei lives on in you. And he did not suffer as he should have." She shook her head as if dejected over some inconvenience, like an unwanted houseguest, or having spilled wine on a favorite dress—though he'd only ever seen her in the garb she wore now. "Unfortunate that those four fools weakened my power for so long. But as long as I've been alive, the world still manages to surprise me. I never thought I would offer a break to the curse. I never thought there would be anything you could do that could earn my good favor. And here we are."

She caressed his cheek, and it was all he could do not to thrust his fist into her stomach. It would do no good. He'd tried it before, and the outcome wasn't one he wished to repeat. The mage smiled again, a joyless expression that didn't reach her eyes.

"Now that you've retrieved the egg, only one thing remains."

Grigg clenched his jaw. "You mean three things. Three Hearts."

Her hand stalled on his cheek. She popped him on the side of his face as if he were a petulant child, then dropped her hand. "Don't get smart with me. *One* thing. With three ingredients. You consider yourself very clever."

She walked her hand in an eerie spider crawl, finger by finger, down his neck and across his chest over his heart. "So in case you have any ideas of grandeur, I've added something to help you stay on track. Getting the egg was a critical first step, but the egg will continue to crack. Consider it a sand timer. Once the egg breaks apart, your time is up. If you do what I want, all will be well, and I'll remove the curse. But if you have not gathered the three Hearts by then—if you have not completed my instructions to the letter —you will die. And I'll ensure it's just the sort of death Sergei should have died."

Her serene face never changed as the palms of her hands thrust hard and fast against his chest in a powerful strike that shot him backward. The next moment, he hurtled back into his waking body. Grigg wrenched himself off the floor with a gasp. His breath came ragged, the blood rushing through him full tilt as if he could rid the world of the mage by sheer terror.

He had to get a hold of himself. Nobody rattled him. What was wrong with him?

The room was dark and utterly silent save for the lap of the water against the hull of the ship and the faint creak of wood beneath his feet. Grigg's chest burned as he straightened, as if a funeral pyre had been trapped in his ribcage, and her strike had dumped oil on the kindling. He tugged away his teal jacket and yanked down the top of his pressed white tunic. The black mark over his heart had been there since birth—proof of a curse more real than legend. But now, for the first time, it had expanded. Ribbons of cracked onyx fled from the site like rivulets of blood from a wound. Or messengers sent from a great queen to do her bidding, carrying out the sentence of the curse.

When magic had lain dormant, the power of the curse had been muted. Now that it was back, so were its effects. And it grew stronger every day.

Goosebumps rippled along his skin. Panic welled in his chest. The egg. What had happened to it? He whirled to find Rakesh and Hamza sprawled on the floor, unmoving. He checked their pulses, but he needn't have bothered. They were dead. And laying just beyond the reach of Rakesh's spindly white fingertips, the golden egg lay with a fresh crack winding up its side.

Grigg took the cloth on the floor, wrapped the egg carefully inside it, and moved in a daze up the stairs to the main deck. He didn't so much mind the loss of Rakesh, but losing Hamza was a shame. His next heist was a two-man job.

His boots fell heavy on each creaking wooden stair as he made his way back up to the main deck. He stumbled to the rail as if in a daze.

People came and went. Nobody stayed long, whether by death or desertion, or falling for the lie that a different kind of life would bring smoother seas.

Grigg had known little about the egg when he commissioned a high-end thief to steal it for him. He'd set up a string of couriers to get the egg from the thief to his hands, all the while doing everything he could to learn more about the object. But he hadn't known it could kill.

The mage had conveniently left that little piece of information out of their conversation.

Hamza's death wasn't Grigg's fault. Rakesh's death hadn't been his fault either. Rakesh was an idiot, and Grigg hadn't liked him, but he hadn't deserved to die. Even so, the mage's instructions had been clear: he would get the egg or die trying. Literally. He hadn't had a choice.

Grigg didn't like not having choices.

He dipped a finger into the bucket of pitch that had been left out from resealing the wooden planks of the deck and swiped a streak of the stuff on the railing. Grigg stared at the mark on the railing for a moment, then he shook himself from a bitter reverie, fished the paper siren out of his jacket pocket, and set it into the glue to dry. He needed a meeting. The right person would see his signal and know what it meant.

It was time for Onkar Dhoka to die.

And it was time to go to the place he swore he'd never return: home.

CHAPTER TWO

Adelina tipped her head back and shook her canteen, but the last drops of water clung stubbornly to the sides as if they knew the laws of nature declared she could never quite get what she wanted. She tossed the canteen down with a huff, which would have felt more dramatic if it had landed on the forest floor three meters below her with a satisfying *thunk,* instead of swinging helplessly from her belt after a short drop.

She swung her legs from the tree branch, popped up one leg, and sank her chin on her knee, eyes still locked on the house at the bottom of the hill. It wasn't that *nobody* had gotten what they wanted from life. Pietro Palladino, for example, seemed to have gotten it all.

Three small children ran squealing through the parlor. She couldn't hear them, but she imagined she could, seeing the wide laughing smiles and eager outstretched hands as they fled from their father's playful chase. Pietro lunged after the slowest of the children, catching a little girl with cascading blonde curls and tossing her up into the air. His wife stepped into view just behind him, running her hand across his back in a warm, familiar gesture.

Pietro flipped the girl upside down, held her by her ankles, and let the child walk on the floor with her hands like a wheelbarrow as he held her feet with one hand and wrapped his free arm around the waist of his wife, pulling her in for a kiss.

He was good. He was kind. He loved his family, and his family loved him. Adelina's mother had lied.

Adelina smiled a sad sort of smile—the sort born of betrayal, heartbreak, and hope, all mingled together and twisted into a tonic she drank every time she came here. Yet she still hadn't seen the person she expected this evening.

Pietro released his daughter and wrapped his wife in his arms. The little girl scampered off into the arms of another young man across the room. Adelina snapped her gaping mouth shut. He'd come after all. The younger brother, the children's uncle. He had a five-year-old boy under one arm and another dangling off his back, but he still managed, with one free hand, to scoop up the little girl. A moment later, he tossed them all onto the sage-green sofa with a mighty heave.

The sofa was probably once a vibrant forest green, lush as the jungle around her, bright with an unspent future, but stiff and not yet broken in. Now, as the joys of happy childhood collided with years of wear, stains and marks of fading time tracked across its soft stitching. Adelina had never owned a home. Not a real one. But she imagined if she ever did, this was the sort of sofa she would want inside it. Not a stiff, perfect one, but a messy one, with the marks of a life lived. And not just lived, but shared.

The young man, Pietro's brother Sebastian, fended off an attack from the oldest boy but failed to see the second rambunctious punch as he tripped over the baby of the family to keep from knocking her to the ground by mistake. His fancy blue-and-gold embroidered jacket didn't keep him from engaging the children in their games, but only accentuated the playfulness in his matching ocean-blue eyes. The man ran a hand through blond waves that rivaled those of his niece and spun the girl in a dancing twirl.

Sebastian, too, was good. He, too, was kind. A man motivated to protect rather than destroy. The kind of man worth falling in love with. The kind of man who might make a good father one day —as good a father as his brother was.

If Adelina were ever to have a child, she would want the child to have a father. She'd never known hers, but she knew they weren't all bad. And if she had a child, even if she had a son, she would protect him with all her heart.

Because her mother had lied.

Adelina sighed and leaned back against the trunk of the tree, the concoction of bittersweet unmet hopes still at war within her aching chest. She shifted against the tree to keep the bow and quiver at her back from digging into her skin, plucked a fresh leaf from the nearest branch, and twisted it into the stem of a second, absentmindedly weaving a bracelet for nobody. It's not like she had anyone to make them for.

But her job wasn't to be happy. Or to watch other people be happy. Her job was to protect the jungle, to protect the mountain housing a great skein of magic.

It had been easy enough when magic was presumed dead, but now that magic had returned, interest in old legends was reviving. Apparently, not everyone had forgotten about the secrets of the mountain. Secrets were easier to keep when no one knew there were secrets to begin with.

But there would always be threats, and the mountain could never be left unprotected. That was the one truth she could rely on from her mother's teachings. Sure as the sunrise, constant as the breath in her lungs, unfading as the mountain itself, some secrets required a keeper. High callings always required sacrifice. Who was she to question hers? She might not be able to fill the chasm inside her, but she could fulfill her purpose.

And with that old boring reminder, as she always did, she

released the view of the happy family in the house at the bottom of the hill and leaned forward, preparing to jump down to the jungle floor. But just as she did, a new figure caught her eye through the window.

The newcomer walked in with all the confidence of a noble, as if he were a peer to the Palladino family. But he didn't look like any noble she'd ever seen. And she knew all the nobles in Smŭrttata. Brown hair framed an attractive face, decadent locks short enough to be neat but long enough to run a hand through and for a single curl to fall across his forehead. He turned a smile to one of the kids who'd stuffed a pillow beneath the couch and peered out from beneath the sofa as if the pillow were the gate to an impenetrable domain.

The man's maroon vest was pressed to perfection, but open enough to reveal an off-white shirt rolled to the elbows, showing off muscled forearms. He extended an arm to clasp Sebastian in greeting, or in farewell, and extended another to Pietro, who turned from his wife to acknowledge him.

But why had she never seen him before? Adelina shook her head. It was none of her business. Just because she spied on the Palladinos didn't mean she had any right to details in their lives. It was a nice escape from her own life, but it was never intended to last for long.

She trailed a finger over the lines of the tribal tattoo on her upper arm. Running from who she was would be about as effective as closing her eyes and expecting the tattoo to really be gone just because she could no longer see it.

Adelina jumped to the jungle floor and took off down the slope fast as a falcon who'd caught sight of a mouse. Or maybe *she* was the mouse, the wings of a bird of prey closing in like a shadow of a cloud hanging over her head ...

It was time to go home.

CHAPTER THREE

Grigg

Grigg slapped the table with a too-loud guffaw at the story the military man beside him had been telling for the past fifteen minutes. The other man, Igor, tossed back the rest of his ale, quite the feat considering how full the tankard had been a moment ago. If the guy could tell a story as fast as he could drink, Grigg may have been able to escape the idiot's laughter at his own terrible jokes. Grigg let out another boisterous laugh to drown out Igor's and hailed the barkeep, ordering his companion another drink.

"The guy was sound asleep 'til mornin'." Igor snorted ale out of his nose and shook a finger in Grigg's direction, promising a punchline yet to come. "The commander called on 'im to report. Didn't even notice 'is own missing britches, *or* the tattooed mustache, 'til the commander flew into a tailspin. Never looked us in the eye again, no sirree, but 'e never messed with us either."

The man chortled as if that'd been a punchline worth waiting for and clapped Grigg on the shoulder. "Where'd you say you were from again, sonny?"

"Same place as you, ole boy." Grigg had matched accents with the man the instant he'd walked in the door. Igor wasn't from Smŭrttata, but definitely had a Bulgor dialect. Northern, if Grigg had to guess. But that wasn't what Grigg was interested in this evening. He needed to slip Igor false intel that the Guerrori were pushing the limits of the treaty, not chat about the good old days Grigg never had. He dropped his voice low. "Which is why I was so concerned when I 'eard 'bout the Guerrori doin' all those drills closer an' closer to the Morturi border."

The other man reared his head back and cocked a sideways eye at Grigg. "What's that you say?"

The Guerrori, the fierce all-female tribe, had kept a death grip on control of the jungle known as Dead Man's Folly for hundreds of years. Their greatest rival, the tribe known as the Morturi, was led by a man named Nico Caruso and his son, Frederico. The Morturi had pushed in toward the jungle with varying success over the years. The treaty currently in place allowed the Morturi a closer border than ever before, while still restricting them to the fringes of the forest.

Grigg glanced this way and that and leaned in closer. "You know ... the drills the Guerrori have been doin'. They're pressin' closer each day to Morturi territory, an' they've started partnerin' with Morturi suppliers, too. If you ask me, they're lookin' to force weapons dealers an' craftsmen to choose a side—an' pilfer any already workin' with Morturi 'til they've got nobody left. I'll bet the Carusos won't take too kindly to that."

Igor gaped at him. Grigg let a trail of the drink dribble down his chin and wiped at it sloppily with the back of his hand before taking another messy sip and waving off his own assertion, as though it were nothing of significance. "But who am I talkin' to? This ain't any news to you. What do *you* think it all means? Are the Guerrori really bold 'nough to steal Morturi suppliers an' informants? It sounds like they're gearin' up for war."

Igor drew himself up tall on his stool, reclaiming a semblance of respectability and confidence, as if he hadn't just shared his favorite juvenile hazing story. "You can bet your britches the Morturi won't take kindly to that at all. That's why I'm 'ere, sonny. Just had a meetin' with the big boss 'imself to consult, I did."

Grigg ballooned his eyes out big. "You really are as top brass as they say. I wondered what coulda brought a man like you down this far. But I gotta ask for family, you understand. My uncle has lived in Smŭrttata all 'is life. Pays the fee, business protected by the Morturi, the whole kit an' caboodle. What happens to 'im if the Guerrori decide the jungle's not enough, and they push into town? What if the Morturi can't hold 'em?"

"They'll hold 'em, all right. The Guerrori are brazen, but their tactics are outdated." Igor reached for the tankard and missed. Grigg stabilized the cup, and the man got a hold of it on the second try, with a nod of acknowledgment for Grigg's assistance. "The Morturi need fresh eyes on the situation, with modern strategies to get this ancient little hole of a town up to snuff with the new age. The Guerrori won't be a problem. Don't you worry."

"Whew! That takes a load off my mind, it does!" Grigg grinned wide, then gasped as though suddenly remembering something important. "Which reminds me, you swore two stories ago that you could woo a woman in five minutes or less. I'd like to see you prove it."

"That I did, my man, that I did." Igor laughed and slipped from his stool, waving in an exaggerated gesture toward the barkeep, who hadn't moved far enough away to need to be flagged down. "Another for the lady."

The barkeep scanned the tavern, stuffed with laughing and drinking humanity of all sorts. "Which lady?"

"Whoever is lucky 'nough to accept it first." Igor grinned and dug in his pocket for his coin purse, then grunted and started patting down his pockets.

Grigg cocked an eyebrow. "That doesn't bode well for your evenin' with the ladies."

"I've got it here somewhere. I was talkin' to you ... Boyan came up and asked me to spot 'im a drink ... I told 'im to buzz off, but popped 'im a coin an' put the purse back in my—" His brow furrowed, and he cast a glance across the room. The top of his coin purse still stuck out of the pocket of the younger man's jacket. "That knave stole my money and didn't even put it away properly."

The man sniffed and took another long draft of his drink. It came crashing down on the table a moment later with a slosh of spilled ale. Grigg leaned away and brushed the droplets from the back of his hand and sleeve.

Igor dug his elbow into Grigg's ribs. "I'll teach you more than how to handle women tonight, sonny."

With that, the broad-shouldered man staggered off toward the thief—or away from the thief, really, since Grigg was the one who stole the money purse and planted it on Boyan. But since Grigg wasn't the one who was going to be knocking teeth from mouths, he couldn't really be counted as the problem here, could he?

Grigg lifted his own drink in silent salute to the man as Igor disappeared through the tavern's crowded room toward his target. With a final sip, Grigg left his drink on the bar, nodded goodnight to the barkeep, and slipped up the stairs toward the guest rooms.

Now that the consultant was occupied, his room would be empty. According to his sources, the tavern had increased security over the last few years with expensive new locks. Somebody had to break them in. How else would the establishment learn whether they'd made a good investment?

Grigg pulled out his lock-pick set, felt for the pins inside the lock of the third door down, and a moment later stood inside a single-bed room with earth-brown and sunset-yellow tapestries on one side, and a wood-carved bench on the other. Igor's travel bag dumped unceremoniously on the bed served as the only evidence anyone had rented the room.

He lifted the bag's carrying handle and ran his hand along the seam. One gray thread interrupted the black in the threading.

Grigg pressed the tip of his lock pick over the gray thread. Something hard, about the size of his thumb, met his instrument. He skirted the tip of the instrument along the hard surface until he felt a divot. He pressed and twisted in the indentation, and a cloth tab that had been hidden before popped out from behind the thick cloth of the bag's handle. He made a mental note to reward his informant.

Grigg tugged on the tab, and a small, stiff panel slid out. Fabric covered what might have been a thin steel or iron plate, a Bulgor military insignia-seal ring with stripes on the sides to indicate his rank. Or previous rank. Grigg wasn't sure if the man was ex-military or freelancing in his free time, but either way, Igor would be giving up more than a night's rent tonight. Grigg slipped the ring into a pocket hidden in the inner lining of his vest, slid the panel back into the handle, and left the way he'd come. He exited the door, crossed the hall in two short strides, and disappeared into his own rented room.

The room was untouched, save for a tall hat on the end of the bed and a thin gray cloak he'd placed there upon checking into his room earlier that evening. Grigg folded the cloak and carefully connected the three hooks he'd attached to it that morning, so that it became a circle of cloth, then he slipped his head and one arm through it so it sat diagonally across his torso. Grigg snatched the hat from the foot of the bed, flipped it onto his head with a flourish, crossed to open the window, and slipped out onto the narrow window ledge.

Chill night air bit at his face as if to awaken the new personality he'd inhabited since arriving in the forsaken little town. Nobody cared about the valley in Smŭrttata, forgotten in the midst of the churning development of the surrounding cities—just as nobody had cared about him when he lived here. Grigg slid the window shut behind him, dropped with a roll to the ground below, and slipped his arm into the makeshift sling he'd created. The moment his arm was in place, he stumbled sideways into the torchlight of the tavern's alley, singing the off-key tune of the ballad of sprites and satyrs.

Just because he was clear of the tavern didn't mean nobody would notice him, and he intended to ensure anyone walking by would describe the man leaving the tavern as a drunk fellow with an injured arm. Keeping a low profile wasn't just about being quiet. Sometimes it meant shifting the profile of the most recently inhabited alias into something noticeably different.

Grigg fumbled down three more streets, ramming his shoulder into two of the walls lining the alley and swearing under his breath more than once before he let the song die away. The moment he did, he unclipped the mantle, stuffed it under his arm, and doubled back in a zigzag pattern through the streets, dropping his cloak on the gate of a blacksmith's yard on his way. The owner waited for him to pass before looking up from his work, taking the cloak, and clipping it around himself without a word before returning to work.

In the blink of an eye, Grigg had rolled his shoulders back, pulled himself up to his full height, slipped the ring from his pocket and onto his finger, and was striding toward a young stableboy at the end of the lane. The gregarious loud-laugher personality was *so* three minutes ago. Not to mention annoying. But it was also memorable, as was the down-on-his-luck drunken moron from one minute ago, unsteadily making his way toward nowhere in particular.

Grigg snagged the waiting horse from the boy and walked the bay mare several paces forward before swinging a leg up and over his new mount, smoothly inhabiting his third personality in as many minutes. He clicked his tongue to the horse and set off, a sliver of relief working through his taut muscles as he left the buildings behind.

It wasn't that the town was too quaint for his taste, though it was. It wasn't that the governor was a pawn for the nobles with the biggest purse strings. Or that Smŭrttata was a forgotten hole, like a snag in a sock in desperate need of darning, but the sock had been stuffed so far back in the recesses of the drawer that one would really have to *want* that particular old sock to find it again. It wasn't even that Smŭrttata had the misfortune of neighboring the thriving city of Vodkra, where Grigg had actually grown up.

Smŭrttata, with its primitive, primeval lack of development and flurry of gossip. With its older people who used to spend time on their porches talking into the night, now ushered indoors by the skulking shadows of entitled wannabe gangsters creating trouble where there had been none before. There was no finesse anymore, no artistry in anything in Smŭrttata. No one worth his time, no one interesting in a town that never aged, save for the crumbling foundations of old, neglected houses.

But the biggest problem was that in an ageless town like this one, legends lived when they should've died, and memories clung to oral traditions when distractions should've left certain truths long buried in the dust. Families never moved, businesses passed generation to generation, and none but the smartest and brightest —those who might actually have had what it took to revitalize the town—ever managed to escape its borders.

Grigg had been smart enough to leave once and abandon his name while he was at it. Coming back was like stuffing his feet in old shoes four sizes too small, with sharp stones stuffing through the holes in the toe and poking the soles of his feet with every step, promising an onslaught of blisters by morning.

He'd learned, as a child, the legends of the jungle and the single mysterious mountain within it. But he'd never dared cross the edge of the jungle back then, because children were stupid, and they did what they were told and believed what they were taught. And when they didn't do what they were told, they didn't disobey very effectively, and they got caught. But Grigg wasn't a child anymore, and he needed to get as far into the jungle toward the Heart of the Mountain as possible.

He kicked his horse into a canter. Poorly maintained cobbled streets dissolved into dirt paths until anything reasonably called a path had given up entirely. The only sign of civilization lived on in a flickering torch from an old Morturi outpost. He ignored the shouts at first. They'd stop him, of course, but that was the point.

Men dropped from the trees, their metal collars rimmed with feathers set over a leather breastplate or bare skin. Thick belts wrapped thick waists embellished by strapping over it all manner of weaponry under the sun—or, in this case, under the moon. Grigg's horse slowed at his touch, and he lifted a hand to the men. At least fifty men surrounded him now, though he knew there were more at other outposts along the border.

The torchlight of the first Morturi warrior glinted off the metal ridges of the ring on his finger as Grigg lifted his voice for all to hear. "I've come with word. It's the Guerrori. They've crossed the river."

The foremost man, holding the torch, laughed. "They haven't crossed the river in years, and no one gets past us without identification."

Grigg rolled his eyes. "Don't you know what this is?" He rotated his hand to give them all a good view of the ring. "The boss has a problem, and I'm his solution. Igor Hristov, military consultant. I consulted with your boss just this evening. If you keep me from doing my job, I still get paid, but *you'll* be the boss's problem instead." He crossed his arms over the neck of his mount and drilled the first man with a hard stare. "The Guerrori are crossing the river, which breaks the treaty. You're going to stop them. Since they've made the first move, you're well within your rights to use lethal force. Or, if you'd prefer, you can sit around and wait for them to attack first."

"You're out of your—"

Grigg held up a hand and inhaled long and deep. He sniffed at the air. "Is ... is something burning?" Grigg tugged the reins. Lightly. Ever so lightly. The mare stepped obediently backward. "Now, I'd recommend—"

Boom.

The ground shook. Land at the base of the outpost collapsed into itself, and the two-story structure fell with a crash. Shouts filled the air.

"Quakemaker!"

"The Guerrori!"

The men spun to assess their attackers as smoke billowed up into the night sky and the fallen outpost burst into flames. Grigg took that as his cue and dug his heels into his horse, flying through the mass of confused Morturi warriors.

"This way," he shouted. "They're just across the gulch."

Grigg tore northward, veering just enough eastward to travel along the border. The edge of the gulch dropped four stories below. His horse was a good one, her hooves pounding the underbrush into chaff as she galloped full tilt down the slope. He crashed through the forest with all the finesse of a hammer slung at newly thrown glasswork still hot from the furnace.

Seconds ticked by as he hurtled through the jungle trees with all the subtlety of a scream in the night. The height of the gulch cliff barrier dropped with every hoofbeat. Below him, at the base of the cliff, the river burbled—just audible now over the frothing huff of his horse, the thrash of branches as they passed, and the shouts of warriors in hot pursuit behind them.

His horse slipped in the soft ground, still wet from last night's rain. The mare tried to skid, to halt, but she was going too fast. The next thing Grigg knew, he was flying through the air toward the boulders on the riverbank. Airborne. Tumbling. Falling.

A blink of darkness.

A burst of pain.

But he never landed on the riverbank. At least, not that he could tell. One minute, he was pitched off his horse and flying through the air, and the next, he stood on the shore of a glassy lake. The dark swan of his dreams descended and materialized into a woman before him once more.

He must have been knocked out. Why else would he be standing here, on the edge of the lake, with *her*? Absently, Grigg hoped his body would be decently neglected until he came to himself again.

The Black Swan Mage struck him in the throat without warning, and he staggered back, blackness edging his vision. Could he black out in a dream when he was already blacked out in real life?

Even in the dream, her voice hissed through a clouded mist rolling over the surface of the tar-black lake. "You'll never earn the success you seek. You'll never know true power. Anyone who falls in love with you will die. And now, if you do not gather my Hearts by the time the egg opens, you will join the corpses at my feet."

CHAPTER FOUR

It had been a week since she'd seen the stranger in the vest at the Palladino house. Tonight, Pietro Palladino and his family had played games after dinner, but his brother Sebastian didn't come. And, as always, time ran its course, and she had to return home to reality. This time, reality came crashing down with the sound of rock-splitting explosions.

The silver light of the crescent moon snaked its way down through a canopy of lush-green jungle leaves splayed over her head. It was the finest ceiling she'd ever had the pleasure of walking under, and beneath her pounding feet lay the richest of carpets to match. The little town of Smŭrttata knew the legendary jungle forest as only *La fallia del'uomo morto*, or Dead Man's Folly. But to her, and to all the Guerrori with her, the jungle was Nascosta, meaning *hidden*—hidden from prying eyes, from dangers, from undiscovered secrets. The wind whispered of long-forgotten memories and kept confidences as it rustled through the leaves, each hollow and shadow promising a safe hiding place from predators.

But today, Adelina was not the one hiding. Nor did she walk. She'd dropped from her perch and sprinted for home the moment she'd heard the explosions. She was chieftess of the Guerrori, and *she* was the predator.

The sound had come from the border, where the enemy tribe, the Morturi, patrolled the edges of their territory. But if the Morturi thought they could break the treaty and cross over the gulch without her notice, they could think again.

"Adelina!"

Adelina looked up as a young woman of about twenty-two burst into view from twenty paces off, breathing hard. "The Morturi. They're halfway to Splinter Creek."

Lucia found Adelina on her way back into the jungle to warn her of the rival tribe's breach, but Adelina could already hear the crash in the brush up ahead. The Morturi were strong warriors, capable of silent movement in the forest. What did such a brazen approach mean? An open challenge like this, not even concealing their movements, could only mean a ruse. A distraction.

Adelina leaped across a dip in the ground as she joined Lucia in a dead sprint. "Where are the closest horses?"

"Just across the gorge on this side. I brought you Velocina."

Adelina jumped to catch an overhanging branch, not bothering to nod. Lucia mirrored her movements, spidering up on top of a thick limb beside hers and disappearing with a whoosh of air ahead of her. Adelina shook her head. Lucia was the best scout they'd ever had. Nobody ran like she did. She was the wind itself, there one minute and gone the next.

Adelina took three running steps across the limb and vaulted into the air. Thick leafy vines met her fingers, living, breathing cords of the jungle fitting into her cloth-wrapped palms as if made just for her. She hooked one leg around the trailing length of the vine and swung out over a dizzying expanse falling so far below her that even the moonlight dared not touch its base.

Six stories above the rocks of the gulch and the rush of the river below, she flew. She couldn't see the landing, but she could feel it —the extension of the vine as it swung out over the abyss, the kiss of the wind against her cheeks tugging through her hair and inviting her to play. She didn't need a home or a well-worn sofa. Not when she had this.

Adelina released the vine at just the right moment, as always, twirled through the air, and landed with a roll on the opposite side. Bursts of red and orange flame interrupted the serenity of the night a hundred meters off. A shuddering crash sounded as crestbreakers commanded the river to leave its banks and assault warriors far below—but whose crestbreakers controlled the water? Hers or theirs?

She gathered her feet and took off down the hill through the trees to the closest staging area, and sure enough, Lucia was there, already mounted on her bay horse. Lucia loosely held the reins of the midnight mare next to her, a sleek onyx animal with a white snip down her forehead and one white sock defying the wholeness of her dark coat. Velocina.

Adelina only remembered leaping into the saddle, urging Velocina down the slope, and notching the first arrow on the string, as she reminded herself to breathe. She couldn't recall exactly when it happened, though it certainly had, and she couldn't remember asking her body to do it.

She pulled the bowstring back to her cheek. Her thighs pressed her to the horse as securely as if she'd been lashed down, her body moving with Velocina's rolling gallop as if she were as one with the horse as a centaur. Silhouettes of invaders shot across slivers of moonlight, drifting to the forest floor a hundred paces off. Broad masculine shoulders with tied-back hair, collars draping chests, and leather armor. With a flick of her wrist, the tip of her arrow ignited into flame.

Thwip. Her first arrow hit its mark. A shadowy figure fell. *Thwip.* Another fell. *Thwip.* This time, her arrow sank into the bark of a tree as her opponent whirled, deflecting the arrow with a wave of his hand.

Adelina ducked low against Velocina's neck as the windcaller's gale of wind swept over them. It had been years since she or her women had seen real combat. But Velocina and Adelina had both trained for this, the two of them one unit. She ducked her head and bobbed to one side; the power of the gust slowed but didn't stop the forward drive of the horse.

She'd never expected to hold the element of surprise for long. Now they knew where she was, and it was time to switch gears. Another blast of wind slammed against her, this one targeted not at the horse but at her center mass. The shot knocked her off her seat. Adelina slid down the side of her horse, one arm and one foot still draped over Velocina's back and neck as Velocina pounded into the fray, hoof after hoof.

To her left, the jungle exploded outward with a thousand varieties of trees, its beauty defiled by female Guerrori warriors throwing blasts of air and fire toward Morturi men dressed for war, answering with missiles of fire and wind of their own. To the right, the river swept through the Nascosta, coursing against the rocky face of the cliff wall of the gulch rising on its far side.

Adelina hauled herself back onto the back of her horse, adjusted her grip on the bow in her left hand, and threw the palm of her right out toward Cassio, a Morturi fireblood she recognized. Flames shot from his hands, the orange-red light glistening off his bald head and casting an eerie glow over the flesh of his open-mouthed, crooked smile. He had about as much regard for the sanctity of the forest—or the sanctity of life in general—as he'd had for his nonexistent hair.

Screams mingled with the burst of fire and water. The crash of wind ripped through branches overhead and whipped the trees into an unnatural storm. Arrows flew. Figures sprinted through the night. But Adelina was focused on only one thing.

Her palm glowed with heat, but she didn't let it go. The power in her blood boiled white hot, its energy mounting with every second she held it in.

Victory is not a brawl, but a dance. Her mother's words snaked into the back of her mind in unbidden instruction. The ghost of her teaching, the feel of her mother's careful arms guiding her body through the motions of combat in the heart of the warrior, settling over her like a garment, wrapping her in knowledge and confidence.

Cassio's fire burst from his hands, a ball of blazing light crackling in the air as it shot toward her face. Still, Adelina waited, just a half beat more, before releasing her own shot. Not a ball, but a shield of flame. Embers showered a Guerrori and Morturi fighting pair to one side, but Adelina didn't take the chance to see the damage. Time was too precious, and Cassio still stood on the Guerrori side of the river.

The wide wall of fire from her shield left a halo of light for any who had stared at the brightness against the backdrop of night. Anyone who had not turned their head away into the shadows like Adelina had would have their night-adjusted vision destroyed by the burst. In the next instant, night vision retained, her arrow cut through the last of the embers toward Cassio's underarm, where his extended hand left a vulnerability. If she hit the brachial artery, he would die in seconds.

But he didn't die. Cassio was suddenly a meter higher than he had been before, and the arrow grazed the side of the leather armor just above the man's hip before falling into the water beyond him.

Adelina's Guerrori warriors were scattered, some in pairs, some in trios, and some all alone, thrashing about in chaos rather than order. Adelina flashed a series of fireballs, three short volleys into the air overhead in bursts. Her Guerrori warriors responded to the signal without a word, reminded of their training. Her crestbreakers surged forward in pairs, their fireblood attachments blocking any flaming missiles from the enemy as they fell back into a structured formation.

A wall of the river escaped its bounds, capturing Cassio's legs and dragging him into it. Lucia dropped her hand as the river dutifully tossed Cassio beneath its foaming surface. Lucia was a valuable sprinter, but she was also a disciplined crestbreaker with the power to manipulate water. Adelina had selected her as her own personal crestbreaker pairing three years ago, and it was one of the best position appointment decisions she'd ever made.

Three more Morturi, foolish enough to stand close to the bank, were captured by her influence as Adelina focused on pressing back the boldest of the warriors on this side of the gorge.

A booming voice cut across the sound of crackling fire, rushing wind, and crashing water. "Give me Adelina."

No sooner did the words ring out, than a Morturi windcaller knocked a Guerrori fireblood back, causing her blasts to go high. Fire caught in the branches overhead. Adelina jerked her head up as her jungle was infiltrated by a volley of flame, assaulted by a cadre of liars, with no right to the Nascosta or its sacred secrets.

But glancing up at the blaze was a mistake. The ground beneath her bucked. Velocina stumbled beneath her, a hoof swallowed by the ground. A distressed whinny cut to Adelina's heart as another tremor rocked the ground. Her horse toppled sideways as the ground released the animal's trapped hoof, and Adelina fell. Lucia cried out behind her.

The river surged up into the air and back and forth in towers of water, in an invisible tug-of-war between magical melders on either side. A few stray bolts of water reached the treetops of the expanding flames, but it wasn't enough. The Morturi didn't have many quakemakers, and Adelina only permitted her own few quakemakers to operate in limited short bursts—to protect the jungle, the paths of the ground they knew so well, the homes of the animals in the trees and the underbrush, the history of their home as they knew it.

A burning fury overpowered a winding vine of panic working its way up through Adelina's stomach. This was Frederico's doing. Frederico Caruso served as both prince of the Morturi and their strongest quakemaker. He wouldn't fight at the forefront among his warriors like she did. He would want the high ground to look down his nose on the fight. His power was in rock and dirt, but he didn't have to get his hands dirty to shed blood. Not that he was averse to blood when the time came.

A swath of ground beneath her feet shot upward and slanted, sending her skidding down the newly made rocky slope amid an avalanche of rock and roots ripped from the soil. Adelina turned her head from the blaze, begging her vision to adjust to the dark again in time to see him. Again, her arrow was on the string, two fingers against her chin and cheek, the string drawn back, her left hand outstretched and strong as an oak, eyes piercing the night for her mark.

And then she saw him, standing regal as the self-proclaimed prince he was, on a rocky dais along the cliff face that had not been there this morning. A feathered headdress crowned his head, a single enlarged eagle's talon reaching down over his brow. War paint marked his face. A jeweled metal collar accented with feathers draped over his bare chest, and long dark hair flowed back over his shoulders.

Frederico Caruso, son of Chief Nico Caruso, chief of nothing and no one—since the Morturi was little more than a rebellious militia with no true right to Nascosta. They were bullies in the city, violent criminals with their hands in every influential pocket of Smŭrttata, with political aspirations higher than the proud feathers of his headdress.

The Caruso clan's sights had been set on Nascosta for generations, but they'd kept an uneasy peace with the Guerrori for years. Until now.

Adelina released her arrow on an exhale. If the arrow struck, the fallout of the Caruso family would be upon her and her people by daybreak. Life as they knew it would be over. Peace, a distant memory.

But she was not the one who had broken the treaty. She was not the one who had crossed the gorge. None of her women had taken a step past the gulch. And here the Morturi were, sweeping in with murder and greed in their eyes like a spreading infection.

And if Nico wouldn't stop the infection, Adelina would do what she must. The rock beneath her feet slipped again, and her shot nudged off center just as the arrow launched from the string. A tendril of water surged up the rock, wrapped around her waist, and pulled her backward. Lucia, trying to save her from the rock beneath her speeding toward the cliff.

Adelina fell off the moving rock, falling, falling into the arms of the river controlled by her friend. The next moment, a whistle of wind and the crack of splitting rock sent a chill down Adelina's spine that had nothing to do with the ice-cold water of the river. Lucia's hold on her vanished. Three waves of water rushed upon her at once, seizing her in their hold and dragging her in a tower of water across the river toward their melders' master.

The next second, Adelina smashed into a solid chest with all the force of the burning sun. The hold of the river released her so suddenly that she lost her balance. Her bow slipped from her fingers, and she plunged after it, her hand seizing the weapon just as a pair of strong arms wrenched her back upright. His oily-smooth voice met her ears like sharpened reeds stabbed under the beds of her nails.

"Am I to take this as a no to my proposal, then?"

She struck him in the diaphragm with her right fist and swung a hook at his head with her left hand, still clenched around her bow. But instead of shoving her off the narrow rocky dais into the river depths, he wound an arm around her slender body, hooking iron fingers around the crook of her hip so that her free hand was trapped between their chests. Her hook still landed with a satisfying hit to his temple against the side of his helm. Landing the hit was her only consolation to a situation that flushed her cheeks with heat and set her blood to boil. She could only assume she was bleeding, but it was worth it.

Her fist glowed in the space between them, but as quick as the light leaped to her palm, her heels dropped a hand's breadth deeper into the rock beneath her feet, exaggerating the height difference between them as the stone swallowed her up to the ankle. His lips twisted in a half smile, but no mirth reached his eyes.

"I said time was running out to accept my deal, but your breaking the treaty is going too far. What did you expect would happen? Call off your dogs."

"*My* dogs?" Adelina lifted her chin. "I never broke the treaty. We've kept the terms of your father's ridiculous, entitled agreement. You're the one who came crashing into the forest like a bear after her stolen cubs. But we've stolen nothing, and you and your men are out of line."

He captured her chin so fast she never saw his hand, tugging her face toward his until their noses nearly touched. "Your forest burns. What can hide in a wasteland? What is Nascosta without its trees and secrets? Who's the fool now?"

The booming crackle of a consuming fire eating away at the trees on the Guerrori side of the river *tick-tick-tick*ed away the time she had to negotiate before the blaze spread too far from the river to control. She wrenched at her feet, but the stone still captured them as firmly as if she were a tree hoping to rip free of its roots with only the help of a wistful breeze.

Adelina clenched her jaw. "What do you want?"

"I told you, I want the forest and all that is in it, from *Il fiume di luce* to *La cascata vivente,* as is the birthright your ancestors robbed from mine. And if you have any aspirations of keeping your head attached to your shoulders, you'll marry me to show a united front and minimize the bloodshed. We'll negotiate the terms of our merger. You've broken our treaty, so it's only fitting you have less time to accept my generous offer than before. You will treat with me in four days' time, or you and your women will die—but not before you watch the jungle burn."

Adelina wrenched her free hand out to the side. His arm tightened around her at the movement, pressing their bodies closer together, but her hand was free to signal her women. One short burst, and two showers of embers, like flaming rain, fell from her fingers over the river. A blast of wind knocked so hard against the cliff that bits of fractured rock showered down around them. Frederico tottered on his feet, and the cliff released her feet. It was all the time she needed.

Adelina hurled backward in a high arcing flip over the water, where Lucia and the other crestbreakers caught her in the river and swept her to the Guerrori side of the bank. The river released her dripping wet on her feet in the midst of her warriors. A piercing whistle cut through the air, a staccato series the Morturi often used to communicate. The rushing river piled up high, and Adelina sent her orders to the crestbreakers with short light signals from her fingertips.

Crestbreakers on both sides worked together to pile up water upon water in a tower three stories high. Firebloods tugged at the flames in the trees. Wind callers formed buffers around the flames to starve the flame and snuff it out among the leaves, and a torrent of water tossed into the treetops, snuffing out the flame like a candle before the heavy drop of water of the weight of the river fell down on the Guerrori women like pig slop in a muddy pen. The force of it knocked Adelina to the ground, and she wasn't the only one. Warrior after warrior collapsed under the tremendous weight, some swept into the river, others sliding down the bank, using any powers at their disposal to stop their descent.

Adelina gathered her feet and glared after Frederico. The

snickers of his men echoed through the chill night air. The breeze sent goosebumps along her skin, wicking at the cold, wet animal skin wrapped around her chest and waist. He may have left feeling like a king with the upper hand, but he was still retreating.

Pursuit now would do little good. She ordered her women to focus on small outbreaks of flames skittering to the fringes of where the fight had been. Once the fire was out, her crestbreakers would draw the Morturi fallen warriors to the river and send them upstream and out on the bank on the Morturi side. Let them bury their own dead in the way they saw fit.

On the Guerrori side, five or six women were wounded with burns or gashes from the blunt-force trauma of being whipped about and smashed against trees or rocks or the blade of an enemy. But injured as they may have been, they were quick, and they knew their footing better than their adversaries. Compared to the Morturi side, the Guerrori had not sustained heavy losses. But as she scanned the battlefield, one of her windcallers, Caterina, let out an anguished scream and fell to her knees over the body of a young woman with two arrows to the chest on the bank of the river.

A lump surged to Adelina's throat, her tongue thick in her mouth. It was Rosa, Caterina's baby sister. Her bronzed skin was already drained of its normal color. Dead. Adelina had started forward when three more women called to her through the forest at her back.

"We've got something, Chieftess."

Adelina blinked back the tears pricking her eyes. There would be time for mourning later. Right now, she would leave the moment to the girl's sister and fulfill the role she was born to fill. But as she turned to the three women, her jaw nearly dropped.

They'd taken a hostage, but the unconscious man, bound by his hands and dragged behind a roan stallion, was no Morturi warrior. He wasn't a warrior at all.

His maroon vest was caked with mud, and brown locks of his

hair were plastered to his forehead from the spray of the river. His once-white shirt was wrinkled and marred by snags and holes, but the sleeves were still rolled to the elbows as they had been earlier that evening. It was the stranger she'd seen in the Palladino house.

CHAPTER FIVE

The mage woman, Giovanna, strode from the black water at the edge of the lake. If it had been *his* dream, he should have been able to change portions of it, as he did with normal sleeping dreams. But though his body was unconscious, his mind was awake, hosting this dream run by someone else. He existed in a hijacked realm of his consciousness, a reality between waking and sleeping, where his mind was more vulnerable—and where she could push in and take hold.

Her power had nursed a six-hundred-year curse that did not wane with time, and her bitterness over Sergei's betrayal had only grown. Grigg never knew Sergei, but he was beginning to hate him, if only for his terrible judgment in women. If the idiot had left Giovanna alone, Grigg wouldn't be cursed.

Grigg needed something to turn the tables. A way to destroy her once the curse was lifted. It was hard to imagine she'd really let him go once he gathered her three Hearts. But if he didn't first get what she wanted, he'd be dead before he had the chance to extricate himself from her hold. The egg was already breaking. How long before its long crack worked its way across the rest of the shell and broke it apart?

The shadow of a wicked smile flashed across her features so fast he almost missed it. And then the woman was gone. A massive, sleek, shimmering swan appeared in her place, diving straight for his face. Something twined around his chest from behind, as if a thousand hands seized him in the back of his shirt and yanked him so hard he fell out of the dream.

Grigg awoke as a force cold as a thousand winters smashed into him, drenching him head to toe. His body convulsed in protest to the icy water running down through his clothes and along his skin, as if looking for one last dry piece of him to infiltrate. It needn't have bothered. He was soaked to the skin.

A throb in his head warned of a possible concussion, and the aches of his muscles hinted at a less-than-gentle landing after being thrown from the horse. But his head hadn't been smashed open on boulders, and he wasn't near the river anymore at all. That was two wins to one loss. He'd take those odds any day.

Grigg stifled a groan and tore his eyes open. The sight before him was a haunting sort of beautiful, like the threads of a ghost story spun at just the right pace. Shadows of wide, green ferns cast reaching fingers in every direction under cool moonlight drifting in through thick greenery overhead. This contrasted sharply with the warm tones of crackling fire from torch light casting oranges, yellows, and perilous reds into orchids, vines, and strangler fig trees.

It had been years since he'd seen a strangler fig. One of the oddest staples of the jungle, the tree looked like a thousand threads of unwoven yarn calcified straight down in falling rain roots. The tree with perfectly straight threads making up its vertical trunk stood beside another, completely different strangler, standing in a cacophony of seemingly hazard-weaving spiderweb bark, wrapping around a thick chunk of another tree, cutting into the flesh of the victim tree. It would strangle the tree into submission, kill it, and let it decay, until one day all that would be left was the webbing—the hollow spaces between its hundreds of weaving bark arms hugging the empty cavern of a phantom tree.

Heliconia flowers echoed the reds and yellows of the flames, striking yet harsh all at once, their pointed lobster-claw-shaped petals bursting out in color at the spiky ends of its plant. The figures of women dotted the scene like blossoms, and he couldn't shake the feeling that they fit the jungle exquisitely. Not just because of the untamed wildness in their eyes. Their primitive animal-skin coverings had an exotic beauty, tantalizing and perilous, as if the strangler fig and heliconia had gotten together and created a personified version of themselves. Stunning, yet deadly; brutal, yet lovely.

Four of them stood with flames dancing in their palms, north, south, east, and west of him, standing sentinel as human torches. Firebloods. He hadn't noticed it at first as he'd come to, but these were the flames he'd seen dancing across the foliage.

At least fifteen female warriors dangled from branches or crouched at the edge of the jungle. Only three stood within the bounds of the four torchlight sentinels, staring down at him with eyes sharp as a parrot's beak.

Grigg lay on his back on the jungle floor. He reached up to wipe the cold water from his face. He didn't see the river. If the crestbreakers had doused him with water, how far had they transported the water? Or was there another source nearby that he hadn't yet seen? As he reached up to wipe his eyes with one hand, his other hand came with it. Grigg squinted at his wrists and realized that he was bound hand and foot. A rope ran from his wrists down along the underbrush of the jungle floor. He trailed the line of it as far as it would go in the light of the moon and the fire.

At the edge of the darkness, he could just make out the rump of a horse. He'd probably been dragged here by the horse. That would explain the body aches. Okay, so maybe he had two wins and two losses.

Before him, the first of the women stood like a vision of dreams and dares. Her chest and waist were wrapped in animal skin, with a strap over one shoulder, leaving her long, bronze, shapely legs glowing in the firelight. She took a silent step forward, and his gaze traveled up from her leather footwear to the hide skirt cutting a diagonal from mid-thigh on one side to above the knee on the other. Her curves were in all the right places as a woman, accented with the leather arm guards on her forearms and bow and quiver at her back marking her as a warrior.

She had enough tone on her body to look like she vaulted over rocks and swung from one side of the jungle to the other as a leisurely workout before breakfast every day. It was, in fact, probable that this was precisely the case.

Long black hair flowed in a thick braid down her back to the waist. She and the other warrior women with her were also soaked to the skin, their clothes pressed tighter by the water-logged fabric. Dirt and bloodstains confirmed his hypothesis about the vaulting over rocks. Although, tonight, she'd probably been vaulting Morturi bodies. Tendrils of damp hair clung to the sides of her face as she skewered him with golden-brown eyes that spoke of a sharp wit beyond the intoxicatingly flawless exterior. Apparently, warmth and smiling had not been emphasized in her daily rituals.

It took Grigg a moment to realize he was staring—or more accurately, gaping. He liked the look of a beautiful woman as much as the next man, but he was rarely overcome by them anymore.

Clearly, he'd fallen into the hands of the famed Guerrori. No need to let them feel more in control by realizing his fascination. No need to let *her* feel more powerful. And she already was, with her warriors at her side and him bound at her feet.

Grigg tilted his head to one side and peered up at her from the ground. "This is the best dream I've had in weeks. Surrounded by beguiling women, their eyes all fastened on me." He flashed an impish grin. "Is anyone going to search me for weapons? If I'd expected this, I would have been sure to bring some."

The woman in the center didn't move, but the warrior to her left whirled a double-headed battleaxe. Her animal-skin top wrapped crisscross over her torso instead of one shoulder, and her hair was tied back in severe tight braids from her scalp to halfway down her back. She gripped the axe hard enough to whiten her knuckles. If she'd been a tree, she'd be the strangler, and the axe would've been long dead.

"We should kill him."

The woman in the center responded in an even tone, her eyes never leaving Grigg. "You want to kill everybody."

The girl with the axe worked her jaw, and from the glare she shot at the center woman, this was not the first time the two had suffered a disagreement.

Grigg pursed his lips. "Are you sure you don't want to search me for weapons first?"

In the next breath, Axe Woman broke past the invisible barrier just behind her leader and swung the axe in a high arc. The next thing he knew, the rope at his wrists lurched, and his body swung sideways half a meter just as the axe buried itself precisely where his head had been.

Warrior women dropped from the trees like bats flying out from a cave to feed. Grigg spun back to face his assailant. The first woman had the rope from his wrists in one hand and had looped the axe woman around the waist with the other, hauling her back in a smooth motion. She must have yanked him out of the way by the rope at his wrists, which had moved him just in time for the axe to bury itself in the ground instead of his skull.

The leader set Axe Woman on her feet so hard the girl stumbled back. The four firebloods with flames in their hands had burst forward but hesitated as they looked to their leader for direction.

The first woman dropped her voice so low Grigg had to strain to hear what she said: "You shouldn't be here. Go take a break."

The axe spun in the other woman's hands again. Her lip curled in a snarl, derision rolling off her in waves. She fastened a murderous look on Grigg that nearly made his cold heart stop.

"I'll take a break when I know everything there is to know about what happened tonight. Everything that led to what happened to Rosa. Anyone bearing a fraction of responsibility for her death will die."

The leader woman let out a long breath that spoke more of fatigue than fury. She rolled her shoulders back and spoke again— this time not soft, but firm and strong. "Take a break. Now. I'll tell you what I learn."

The other woman didn't move. Four bursts and a shower of embers shot from the leader's fingertips in what must have been a signal, because as soon as the flames danced out into the air, two of the fireblood living torches and two of the women from the shadowed fringes stepped forward to march the axe girl away.

But though they'd come to carry out orders, the interaction was less stiff than it could have been, as one of the warriors slung her arm around the axe girl's shoulders and pressed their foreheads together in a silent moment of human comfort.

A familiar twist wrenched at Grigg's stomach, the one that meant he was responsible for the grief, but also that his plan had worked. He chewed on the interaction and the knowledge it brought him. The Morturi had indeed taken Grigg's bait and invaded Guerrori territory. They'd fought just as Grigg predicted, resulting in at least one casualty—a girl named Rosa.

The air seemed to thin as the four warriors escorted their tribe sister away from the scene. Each remaining warrior angled their body toward their leader, adopting the disciplined posture of a soldier awaiting further orders.

Grigg returned his attention to the chieftess, taking in what he'd gathered of the woman so far. She was tough, but she cared about her warriors, and they respected her for it. Or at least they pretended to in her presence.

Grigg mentally ticked off the pain points to exploit: a bleeding heart of care for her women; a fractured trust within the Guerrori tribe, as evidenced by Axe Woman's remarks; stress from a sudden invasion; blame for a recent loss. He could work with that.

His eyes locked with hers. She appeared to be in her mid-twenties, maybe five years younger than himself, but something in her demeanor exuded confidence, obligation, and honor. It rolled out before her footsteps like a red carpet before a queen. Yet there was something else there too, something less refined, like the backside of a tapestry—a chaotic opposite to the presentation. An untamed beast, restrained by a chain around its neck.

What was the chain around her neck? Perhaps the Carusos, the Morturi leadership family that Grigg had ensured would attack tonight.

Grigg dipped his head. "An honor to meet you, Chieftess. I'd shake your hand"— he waved his bound wrists in a flourish —"but under the circumstances, I do hope you'll understand."

She made no move toward him. The lines of her face neither tightened nor relaxed under his scrutiny. "You'll understand that your dramatics won't keep us from a search."

Her voice was lower than typical for a woman. If she'd been a singer, she would have taken up the lower register part of a song. It made her feel somehow stronger and steadier, in combination with the fact that she spoke to him as if tying up strange men behind horses and dragging them through the jungle was an activity she carried out regularly. Maybe swinging through the jungle and vaulting boulders was only her exercise on Mondays and Wednesdays, and tying up men and hauling them around provided some variety for workouts on Tuesdays and Thursdays.

He looked her up and down in as pointed and obnoxiously ogling a manner as he could muster. Which wasn't hard, considering she was a sight for any pair of eyes—sore eyes. Tired eyes. Sunflower bright and healthy eyes.

"Gilded gallows, go right ahead. Who am I to stand in the way of thoroughness?"

The chieftess ignored him and nodded at someone in the shadows. The beefy frame of a Guerrori warrior, with a silhouette closer to Hamza than to the gorgeous specimens around him, strode forward. Her arms were at least as big as Grigg's, and that was saying something. She looked like she'd swallowed a two-hundred-pound wrestler whose muscles had been absorbed rather than digested, and now rebelled against its new host by bursting out from every direction on her body.

He glanced back at the chieftess. "And here I was thinking you didn't have a sense of humor."

The corner of her lips twitched. "Don't worry. I'm sure Umbra will be just as thorough as you had hoped."

Umbra grinned, more like he was a grape tomato she could squish between her fingers than anything else.

Okay, so the chieftess was unflappable so far. But he'd already identified weak points. Right now, she was surrounded by her women warriors. The Carusos had withdrawn. Her body was flooded with adrenaline, she had the proverbial high ground, and he wasn't high on her list of problems yet.

Plenty of time to change each and every one of those variables.

Except the adrenaline. Everything on his to-do list involved plenty of adrenaline for both of them.

Umbra patted him down head to toe, shoving him onto his stomach to repeat the process down his back, and rolling him again to face the chieftess when she was done. She'd missed the hidden compartments in the heel of each of his boots, and the secret pocket on the inside slit of his waistband. But she did manage to retrieve the knife that had miraculously stayed in place inside his boot on his galloping journey down the slope and flying fall from the back of his horse. She also found and took the ring he'd taken from Igor.

Umbra handed the objects to the chieftess. She took the

knife. Twirled it in her hands. Tossed it up over her head, shot a glare at Grigg, and caught it on its descent without breaking eye contact.

He waggled his eyebrows at her. "I'm glad to have made enough of an impression on you to warrant your showing off."

She knelt beside him close enough that he might hear any whisper, but far enough away that he wouldn't be able to take a swipe at her with his bound hands.

"Tell me your name."

It wasn't a question.

His neck ached from craning it, and he didn't particularly love the vulnerable feeling of lying down while negotiating. Grigg adjusted his back against the prickle of leaves and grasses on the nape of his neck, then pressed his lips together. In a swift move, he lurched forward, his head nearly ramming into her forehead as he sat up and popped a bent knee up toward the sky.

"Igor Hristov." He draped an elbow over his knee. "I was in the area and had never seen the legendary Dead Man's Folly for myself. I've heard it's worth seeing."

"It's not worth seeing if it's the last thing you ever see." The chieftess turned the knife in her hands, twisting the end into the pad of one of her fingertips. "Igor, an ex-military turned bandit, was discharged less than honorably. Yesterday, he consulted with people who had no business being in the forest. He's lawless, more brute than brains, and he's surrounded himself with worthless scoundrels. I can see why you might relate to him. But that is not your name."

Grigg took care to keep his face neutral. He'd known she was intelligent, but she was more informed than he'd expected. As isolated as everyone said the Guerrori were, living in the jungle, she clearly had a network of informants of her own to keep abreast of movements in Smŭrttata.

"If you don't like that name, I can give you another one. And if you don't like that one, I could give you more. We could go on and on, but I'm not really sure which names you like, so it might save time if you picked a name for me instead."

The chieftess pressed her lips together. It was the first significant show of emotion she'd allowed herself. "Igor doesn't even talk like you. If you're going to be good at using lots of names, you should have enough voices to go with them."

Grigg nearly choked on a snort. "Too true. If only that were a skill set I had developed. Ah, well." He shrugged. "Whoever I am, you know I'm not a commander, and I'm not a Morturi, and I'm not from around here. And it seems to me you have bigger problems on your hands than me. How much time do you think it will take for you to decide that Rosa's death was your fault?"

The chieftess blanched, a wounded chink in her quickly hammered-out armor. She looked less surprised by the concept, and more shocked that he was the one to have voiced it—or perhaps it was simply that her own thoughts had been spoken out loud for the first time, and they seemed corroborated and more real than they'd been a moment ago.

"It sounds like what you need is a problem solver." Grigg plucked a leaf from the forest floor and twirled it in his fingers, watching a flicker of the fireblood's palm torches play on the rich color of green fading into the crinkled brown of discarded life, of hope lost, of death threatening to overtake the rest of the stubborn sage.

The leader's eyes followed it, and he knew he had her. No one was watching what he did with his other hand at the rope at his feet.

"You need a problem solver," he said again. *And I need time.*

She snatched the leaf from his hands between her forefinger and thumb and tore it in two. "No, what you need is my favor. And you don't have it. If you know so much about Rosa, you're welcome to join her. Or you can give me verifiable information right now."

"Do you underestimate all of your hostages, or just me?" Grigg clucked his tongue. "If I give you information now, I give up my leverage. That doesn't sound very intelligent of a move for me, considering you've just threatened my death."

The chieftess just shrugged. "Maybe you're the dumbest hostage I've ever had."

"I must be your first, then. Which means I'm also your smartest." Grigg gave a dramatic sigh and scanned the jungle around them. He snagged another leaf with his right hand. His left hand brushed the heel of his boot, found the hidden notch, and pressed.

"They say there is a temple in this jungle." He swept his gaze over the ferns, the heliconia, the vines hanging like robes off the neighboring trees. He dropped his voice and leaned in as if he were telling them the secret, rather than speaking to the keeper of secrets. "They say it is sacred. They say that any man who sees it will die. They say ..." He scanned the area again, catching glimpses of the expressions of the watching warriors around him. He pretended to focus more on the trees than on the women, as if looking hard enough would show him the direction of the temple. Though the landmarks all looked the same in the dark, in the thick of the jungle. It was the women's expressions and reactions that would lead him.

"They say it is west of the gulch, and that after you cross its border, you are closer than any would have you believe. That is why the Bulgor are so afraid of a Morturi being right there at the river Il flume di luce." He brought his gaze back to the chieftess. Her breathing remained even. She blinked once as she regarded him, unmoving, unconcerned. Silent.

It made sense his prattle had not impressed her. He'd made it up. He had no idea where the temple was. But he knew it was close to the thing he sought, and that his stab at *west* wasn't the right answer. Time to turn another direction.

Grigg leaned forward over his propped-up knee, bringing his face closer to hers. She stiffened just a hair, a rigidity so slight he might have missed it had he not been looking. "But I think they are wrong," he whispered. His left hand tugged out the compartment in the heel of his boot. "I think the temple, the heart of Guerrori civilization, lies to the east in the direction of the water. It's a series of waterfalls, really. At least that's what they say. La cascata vivente. The temple is positioned at the mountain."

Three blinks in close succession served as the only indication his words carried any impact. But no one could control their blink rate. If he could get her to respond ...

But she was already responding. She adjusted her weight in her crouch in the jungle underbrush and twisted her lips into a dismissive smile, as if he were a petulant child. "People have guessed at the location of the legendary temple for years. No one even knows that it exists." She lifted one shoulder and dropped it. "These are mere legends. They are not real. You are trespassing. And you should know that aside from an obsession with fairy tales, the best legend hunters have only one thing in common. They fail to maintain boundaries with danger, and they die."

One-sided shoulder shrug on the phrase *no one*. Lack of contraction on they *are not* instead of they *aren't*. Indicators of possible deception. Of course, he hadn't established much baseline. Perhaps she didn't use contractions often anyway. But he already knew she was lying.

The temple was east—or, at least, closer to the east than the west. He'd wager his father's inheritance that the mountain met the water somewhere, and the temple was nearby them both.

Then again, his father's father had failed at every endeavor he ever tried, so his father's inheritance was a pittance. Grigg's own father, Aleksander Frizzletwerf, was a criminal who had gotten his mother pregnant in a meaningless hook-up. But then he tried to be noble and be a present father, and he fell in love with Grigg's mother. Not long after, Grigg's mother fell ill. After she died, Aleksander shut down and gambled every last gold coin before kicking the can himself. Grigg's only real inheritance was the curse on his family name.

Grigg flashed the chieftess a fresh grin. "What can I say? We legend hunters are an impulsive sort."

Grigg slid the first of two small vials from the heel of his boot. He popped the cork with his index finger and thumb and poured it onto the knot of rope between his ankles. If he did it right, he would break the bonds between his feet. If he did it wrong, part of his heel would explode. He winced.

The chieftess misread his expression and smiled. "Perhaps you'll be more useful in the morning." She jerked her head at a warrior behind her. The other woman moved to the horse. If the horse started moving before he freed his feet ...

His mouth went dry. Grigg slid the other vial from his heel, a tiny thing shorter than the length of his pinky finger. He popped the cork and dumped the second substance over the first.

White smoke burst from a miniature explosion at his feet, and a pop of heat and a sliver of pain ran across his ankle, just above the top of his boot, where the rope had begun to chafe. But the rope binding his feet melted, weakened, and fell away.

Grigg surged to his feet, wrists still bound, but he wasn't fast enough. The horse shied at the loud sound and bolted into the night, dragging a rag-doll Grigg bouncing along behind it.

CHAPTER SIX

One minute, Adelina was dealing with the aftermath of an invasion, the death of one of her warriors, and a mysterious man serving as her one shot at unlocking clues to the events of the evening. The next minute, she had nothing.

The man with the velvet vest and once finely pressed white shirt had been snatched away as swiftly as a mouse ripped up into the air by an eagle. Only in this case, the eagle was a terrified horse, and the mouse was a strange man. He was calm enough to be arrogant while being held hostage, knowledgeable enough about the affairs of her enemy to be threatening, and crazy enough to enter the jungle without being part of either the Guerrori or Morturi tribes. And he was her only chance at salvaging a win for the night.

Oh, and he and the horse, Spavento, were headed straight for the rocky stream. If the horse dragged him through there, his head would be split open on the rocks before she had the chance to properly motivate him to spill whatever information he had.

Adelina shouted orders and sprinted after the man all at once. "A squad to the border of the gulch. Make sure no more Morturi investigate the sound and breach a second time! Lucia, cut off the horse in case he banks left before the stream. Umbra, contain Caterina and check on Rosa."

Shapes of fern and flower. The outline of root and rock. The cut of a path through the jungle. The soles of Adelina's feet pounded into the earth, chasing the thundering crash of the galloping horse up ahead. Adelina whistled. Velocina was still nearby, and the mare would respond to the call.

A moment later, there she was, a shooting star to bless the night. Hoofbeats struck the earth with the steady huff of the horse's breath as Velocina cantered up beside her. Adelina reached up for a hanging vine, shoved off the bark of a tree, and swung up off the ground and straight into her seat on the back of the black mare.

Adelina gripped the horse with her legs and leaned forward over her neck. One hand buried in Velocina's mane, she extended the other into the darkness and called for the fire. Flame blazed from her palm like a living torch lighting the way.

If the man in the vest was bumping along somewhere up ahead behind Spavento, it would do no good to trample him under Velocina in the dark. At the same time, incinerating him with a ball of fire or spooking the other horse further wouldn't do either. Adelina shook her head.

They'd taken Spavento off normal drill duties because he was too skittish and needed more training. He was a liability in a fight, but something as innocuous as plodding along to drag a hostage somewhere was a simple enough task. Mostly, all he'd had to do was walk, carry things, and stand still. After this, she'd have to rethink his training regimen with the primary horse trainer of the Guerrori.

Leaves crinkled under Velocina's hooves. Wind brushed Adelina's braid behind her back, messy and half-undone by now. The cool of the air wicked at the still-damp garments wrapping around her body. She could hear Spavento crashing through the brush somewhere ahead but hadn't yet laid eyes on him. Until—there, through a break in the trees, a glimpse of the horse frothing at the mouth and glistening with sweat.

And behind him, the man in the vest, wrists still bound with a rope tied to the harness of the horse. But he wasn't as far behind Spavento as she would've expected. Was he climbing? His hands moved with purpose and looked as though he was gathering slack, climbing hand over hand, even while his body slung into a tree and raked across the jungle floor. If he pulled in too much of the rope, he would get himself crushed beneath the horse's hooves. But if he failed to free himself before Adelina got to him and they reached the river, he would die on the rocks.

Adelina urged Velocina faster, turning the mare to cut off the gelding at the next turn. Adelina reached the next bit of path just as Spavento careened into view. She turned her glowing palm toward the rear of the horse, but though the harness and its flailing rope were there, the man in the vest was missing.

Panic seized her chest, and the adrenaline of the chase spun her mind into a torrent of images. Images of her failure to protect the Guerrori, and her failure to take the one lead, the one advantage they'd gained that night, and turn it into something useful. Her failure to protect the secrets of the mountain.

The gelding splashed into the river, forging ahead as though rabid wolves had chased it there. Her hopes dashed to the rocks just as surely as the man in the vest had likely been.

Adelina didn't know where the pop or the smoke had come from. She'd heard it, and knew the man had done something, but it wasn't a magic she was familiar with, and his hands and feet had been bound. What was it, and how did he do it? She shook off the thought. It wouldn't matter if he was dead. But maybe he was only half dead. She could work with that. She had to find the place where the rope had come unfastened from his wrists and follow the trail to his body.

Spavento knew the way home, and the other women would find him soon enough. She had to get to the man in the vest. Adelina turned Velocina's head down the path, lit palm outstretched, searching the cacophony of cracked twigs and crushed underbrush. The gelding had definitely gone down this way. The terrain wouldn't have allowed much opportunity for a body to roll. There were few hills steep enough to carry a man away from the path the gelding had taken. He was likely injured and could only—

A solid mass of muscle, dead weight, and velvet knocked her—bow, quiver, and all—from the back of her horse just as she wheeled back toward the river. The prickly leaves of a traitorous vine brushed across her face as it swung back to its position. The vines were supposed to be for her and her women, not pretty men in vests with stupid smiles and asinine remarks.

Pain rocked her body on impact. She didn't have time to think before a thick arm slithered around her neck from behind. Adelina snapped her chin down to block access to her airway, but he was faster, working the crook of his elbow under the tip of her chin and against the tender, vulnerable skin of her throat. A second arm snaked its way behind her head, pressing her head forward, intensifying the pressure on her airway.

She gagged and flailed, and now *she* was the one being dragged off the path into the dark, toward the burbling of the stream splintering off from the main river. It was little more than a creek, waist high, filled with rocks the size of her fist.

The mass of her bow dug into her back. She hoped it made it hard for the man to get a good grip on her throat, but from the feel of him around her, his capture of her had been as easy as the eagle's had been of the mouse.

Adelina cursed herself for wasting time flailing, held by the crook of his elbow. She knew better. Adelina stomped down at his ankle, and a grunt told her she hit it—and it hurt more than it should have. Maybe he was injured after all. The vest man stumbled, and she got half a breath before his grip secured again.

She shot her elbow straight back into the man's gut, then drove the fingers of her right hand up into the face of her assailant, feeling about for her target. Mouth. Nose. Eyes.

There.

Adelina plunged her thumb straight back into the eye socket. His hold loosened, and she shoved the fingers of her left hand further between her chin and the man's arm around her throat just before his hold cinched tight again.

Her palms burst with heat as she called to the fire. But just before it burst forth to scorch his skin, her body plunged beneath ice-cold moving water. She struck at him, but he held her tight. Her chest constricted. Her lungs burned. She couldn't breathe. A wave of dizziness rocked her, and her knees began to give. At the last second, he ripped her up above the surface again. Desperate, gasping drags of air sucked down her windpipe.

His elbow still secured her throat, and in the next moment, his other arm trapped her right arm to her torso. He hissed a warning low in her ear.

"I love to play games, Fireblood, but do that again, and you'll lose more than this battle. I've come with a message."

She flared her palms with fire again, and down she went as promised. Smooth icy current coursed over her face, water swirling around her arms and legs. This time when he brought her up, the man in the vest dropped his weight so they were both submerged in water up to the neck, their legs entwined as they collided with each other and the stones at the bottom of the river. Adelina kicked, but his arms held her fast, her palms completely enveloped in the water.

Fury bubbled up from her belly and ripped from her throat in a guttural yell that was more snarl than scream.

She considered a headbutt backward, but if he was on his

game, he'd use the opportunity when she arched her neck back to gain more control over her throat. But the man was a talker. Maybe he'd let her talk.

Adelina dug her nails into the man's forearm and gathered enough of a breath to scrape out a sentence or two.

"If you wanted to die, you didn't have to run. You could have just asked."

He slipped on the rocks, and she wormed her right arm free. In a flash, she had an arrow from her quiver, the arrowhead in the palm of her hand. She wrenched out from the crook of his elbow and twisted toward him. An instant later and the cold sharp edge of the arrowhead pressed against the man's jugular.

The vest man hooked her leg under the water and yanked her off balance, and she was falling. Adelina thrust the arrow forward, but he caught her arm and doubled it back behind her in a single fluid motion. His other hand shot out and twined into her hair. With one arm, he tugged her against him, and with the other, he ripped her head back. She could feel her pulse hammering against the smooth skin of her neck, naked to the night, to his touch, to any weapon he might drive into it to silence her for good.

Instead, the man in the vest dropped his lips to her ear. His breath tickled her neck as he murmured against her hair. "I can get rid of your Caruso problem. They're planning a coup. And they won't settle for your head on a platter. Maybe you think you know what he wants. Maybe you think you can overpower him. But you're wrong on both counts. You've relied on your melders long enough."

Adelina writhed in his hold, but his arms were iron, though his nose and mouth were soft as silk on her neck and earlobe.

"Melders against melders only cancel out, Chieftess. You may have a good defensive position now, but the winds are changing. So if you want more out of me, or another opportunity to kill me ... I'm offering you an opportunity. Meet me tomorrow night.

Midnight, on the roof of the canary house a street over from the shoemaker with the blue door."

He'd attacked her to invite her to a meeting? She nearly forgot to fight him. What was this man after?

But he was already talking again. Had Vest Man ever gone a full hour without running his mouth?

"Unfortunately, I don't trust you further than I can throw you, and I can't throw you far enough that you won't catch up. I won't hurt you, but I can't have you following me either." The arm at her back moved in a blink and recaptured her throat. The hand in her hair tilted her head back further as the elbow completely encircled her neck. "I won't ask you not to struggle. But I only need you to black out. And I hope it goes without saying, but when you come to the meet, come alone."

No!

Adelina shot an arm free of his hold. Flames exploded. Her palm swung backward toward his face. Her feet struck out for his legs, but her limbs moved slow as molasses in the water, when she only had a fraction of a second to spare. She missed.

The man let her blazing arm flail and focused instead on her windpipe. Pressure. More pressure. A boa constructor around her throat, crushing and squeezing every last shred of ... she couldn't think. Her vision swam. The soft tissues of her throat screamed in pain. She fought to keep her eyes open. Her sharp elbow found his abdomen, and she struck him hard, but it wasn't hard enough.

The world went dark.

The flame winked out.

The next thing she knew, she was lying just beyond the edge of the river, its tranquil water bumping up against the soles of her feet as it burbled by. Cicadas sang their usual droning song, undeterred by the low staccato calls of the frogs and toads taking up residence along the bank.

It wouldn't have taken long for the jungle's smaller inhabitants to continue their activities after a disturbance, but it would take more than a few seconds. If the man in the vest had let go as soon as she lost consciousness, she'd only have been out for a few seconds. But if the frogs and insects were already back to their songs ...

Adelina shoved up off the bank. He'd held onto the choke after she passed out, which meant she could've been out for a couple of minutes. The world spun at her sudden movement. Bad idea. She grimaced.

He already had a head start, and she didn't know where he was going. But chances were he didn't know where he was going either. He'd probably get lost in the woods, and she could use more bodies to cover more area. If she did find him, she had no interest in repeating the encounter she'd just had.

She'd underestimated him. Yes, she could handle it on her own. If she saw him again, chances were high she could put an arrow through his chest at a distance rather than need to rely on hand-to-hand combat. And she was a fireblood, after all. But if she killed him, she'd never learn what he knew. It was time to pull in more of her warriors and work as a unit.

Adelina let out a soft whistle. A rustle of leaves and a crunch of twigs later, and Velocina's soft velvety nose bumped into her hand. Adelina ran her hand down the animal's nose and slowly stood. She scratched her horse behind the ears, swung up into her seat, and retraced their steps back to the place where Vest had been when he escaped.

The area was abandoned, as expected. Her warriors had jumped to follow her directives, spreading out to cover the gulch and return to base to check on Caterina and guard Rosa's body.

Adelina slid from Velocina's back, lit a fire in one palm to illuminate her path, and crouched on the ground. An indent in the soil and leaves marked the place where Vest's body had lain. A divot of broken earth remembered Caterina's axe. Bits of frayed rope littered the natural path.

She picked up the rope with her non-blazing hand and turned

it over in her fingers. He hadn't loosened the coils, undid the knots, or even worked his feet free of their bonds. He hadn't even cut through it. The edges pooled together and mingled into a solid mass, melted yet blackened at the ends as if charred.

The sheen of reflective glass caught her eye from halfway under a leaf, reflecting bouncing flame from her palm on its surface. She picked it up. It was a vial. Small, only about as long as her horse's eye, and barely the width of her pinky finger. Adelina brushed through the leaves, moving her fingers along the soil. Were there more?

After a moment's search, she was rewarded with a second vial. Both were empty. The leaves beneath where the rope had been were also blackened, burned away as if by fire.

She'd seen the smoke, heard the pop. Adelina sniffed the bottles but couldn't identify the scents. What had he used to do this, and how had these vials escaped Umbra's notice? Even if he'd managed to keep her from finding these vials, how had he accessed them and mixed them together, right under their noses, with her and her women watching him?

How had he known so much about the Morturi? How had he known where the temple was? He must not know exactly, or he would never have asked the question. He likely asked in hopes she would give away its precise location, but if he thought she would give away critical info as easily as that, she wasn't the only one who'd underestimated tonight.

But he knew more than he should have.

She tried to shake the lingering sensation of his strong arms around her body, the low rumble of his voice haunting her thoughts. The last thing she needed was a reminder of how close he'd gotten to her. How he could have killed her.

Insufferable idiot.

But he wasn't an idiot. He wasn't a Morturi warrior. And he wasn't a commander. And yet he'd shown up. At precisely the same time the Morturi had.

And what had he been doing in the Palladino estate just seven days ago? If he knew more about the temple than most, and he'd known about the Morturi attack before it happened, but he wasn't with them, what was he there for?

A niggling vine of gaping fear wormed its way through her stomach and clutched at her chest. What if he was right about Caterina and the women? About her being to blame for Rosa's death?

One of her warriors had died on her watch. She'd had one chance to make her death mean something and gain information, and she'd failed.

What did it mean about her that she couldn't take one man surrounded by trained warriors and make him worth his while? The women that had gathered back at base by now, what did they really think? What were they saying?

Adelina rocketed to her feet so fast Velocina's head snapped up in surprise. "Home, Velocina," she ordered. "Go home." The mare tossed her head and cantered off alone.

Adelina took off through the forest by foot at a dead sprint. Branches snapped against her cheeks as she tore through the jungle. The roar of a howler monkey protested somewhere in the distance, but she didn't care. She had to get back to base, alone, and fast. She had to know.

Tears stung at her eyes, blurring her vision, but it didn't matter. She'd run these paths since childhood. She'd been carried through the jungle since her mother had run through it with Adelina still in the womb, and Adelina knew the Nascosta better than she knew most people.

Though its leaves might change, though its trees might grow, though branches might snap, and the wind might howl, the jungle was always home. Changing yet unchanging. Full of dangers, yet safe. Safer than people, safer than her own mind. Familiar as the open sky, sure as the coming of the sun each day.

She didn't know what awaited her at base, but she was home. And she would do anything to protect it.

The swell in her chest shifted into an ache, but she crushed the feeling underfoot like dead leaves. Not now. Not today.

She didn't have time for a wave of emotion to catch her. She never had time. She couldn't afford to fall apart. Not as a Guerrori warrior, and never as chieftess. As guardian of the Heart of the Mountain.

By the time Adelina reached base, the wind had dried her tears against her cheeks. The pounding of her own running footsteps had mercifully drowned out the swirling thoughts that would have left her paralyzed had she given in.

Adelina shifted from a thunderous sprint to light-footed, silent movements, quiet as a deer, untraceable as the wings of a night owl. She climbed the exposed skeleton of a strangler fig fifty meters off from base, approaching from overhead as she swung vine to vine, branch to branch, creeping from canopy to canopy until she crouched on the thick branch of a tree right at the edge of base.

A web of thick mossy branches spread out before her like highways in every direction. Mushrooms popped up to peer at her over a bed of slick moss, a miniature forest in their own right, there on a single branch.

Two torches illuminated a stone structure down below through the interlocking branches of the trees where she hid. A series of stone archways concealed themselves in the thickest of the foliage, one archway after another set around stone steps leading down to a circular meeting area. The Guerrori kept the steps clean and the inner sides of the arches free of overgrowth, but Adelina had allowed vines to crawl up the pillars, and greenery to grow thick with ferns, vines, and heliconia on the outer sides of the structure to hide it from the outside looking in.

The structures were impressive, but impressive was harder to hide, and the foliage offered concealment. This wasn't the temple, but it was close enough that she didn't need to draw any attention here. The center meeting space opened up to the canopy of branches where Adelina had swung in to overhear her women from above.

A symbol emblazoned in black marble stood out on the center of the stone floor of the meeting space—the same symbol tattooed on each of their arms. Graceful swirling line art depicted the outline of a swan's head and neck, flowing into a series of sweeping lines that made up an extended swan's wing. A swooping symbol branched out from wingtip all along the wing's edge and could easily have served to represent either feathers or flame. In the center of the wing, captured in an almost teardrop shape, stars hung in a sky over a mountain meeting water at its base. The emblem dripped down past the edge of the swan into two elegant arrows hanging like icicles from the rest of the design.

Adelina's left arm moved to touch the upper arm on her right side. She couldn't see the tattoo in the dark, but the Guerrori touched the mark in a respect ritual so often she hardly thought about it anymore. She just did it.

The torches on either side of the pillars allowed limited light for the group of Guerrori women down below but saved the fire-bloods from using any extra energy to keep the flame alive.

Rosa's body was already wrapped in the finest animal fur, as though bundled for the cold, leaving only her face exposed. Her long hair was braided in the *treccia di riposo,* the traditional braid of rest. Heliconia flowers worked into three thick braids, weaving through the remaining free-falling tresses before wrapping all together at the base.

Adelina's breath hitched. Caterina hadn't even waited for her for the ceremony. Sure, they had not yet sent her off, but the braiding was important. She should have been there. Then again, maybe something as important as the braiding was the only way the other girls could keep Caterina from running off and doing something stupid.

Rosa lay on her back, eyes closed forever. Fifteen Guerrori

warriors knelt around her in a circle, knees together, sitting on their feet—not a crouch for a swift response to peril, but a full kneel, in solidarity with the dead. Rosa would not be able to leap up at the first sign of danger. Her danger was past.

Caterina sniffed and wiped her hand across her nose. "'Someone *contain* Caterina.' She actually said that? I don't need contained." Her last word spat like poison.

Umbra extended both arms over Rosa, palms down in a protective gesture, and looked Caterina in the eye. "Not like this. Not here."

A tense disquiet filled the air. Somewhere in the branches to Adelina's left, a bird fled from the bitter taste of the new strain in the atmosphere. Caterina spun to one side, away from the body. She would not defile the rest they had planned for Rosa. But she wouldn't let go of the conversation either.

The other women gathered around Caterina in a new circle, backs turned to the body on the ground. Umbra was the first to speak.

"She wants to make sure that when we strike, we do it right. That we are effective. You cannot be effective when you are blind with grief and rage. You know this."

Yes. The slow, building ache in her chest and the spiral of thoughts chasing each other like squirrels eased. Umbra understood her. It was obvious, wasn't it?

But the next moment, another girl, Letizia, spoke up. "Adelina should never have allowed the Morturi to set up their guard towers so close. She is so focused on peace that she prepares us to lose battles before they begin. An invasion was bound to happen at some point. It would have been better if we had struck first."

Any reprieve Adelina had felt from Umbra's words evaporated in a whoosh.

Below, Lucia shook her head. "Those towers have been there longer than Adelina's tenure as chieftess."

Another of the warriors, a broad-shouldered woman in her

forties named Paloma, crossed her arms. "No, they began building them prior to her tenure, but they were completed after Adelina became chieftess."

Lucia threw up her hands. "What does it matter? If the Morturi break in, we will be guardians of nothing."

Caterina gritted her teeth. "If the Morturi break in, they will pay. But … they've already broken in. They need to pay *now*."

Paloma tapped a finger against her arm, brows knitted together in thought. "Perhaps peace isn't the wrong way to go. Frederico has been wanting to marry Adelina, and maybe that's not such a bad idea. I wouldn't envy her a position as his wife, but it could keep more lives from being lost."

To Adelina's horror, a few nodding heads agreed.

Caterina snorted. "Adelina knows less about men than any woman alive. Tonight, she had to speak to two men in one evening —Frederico Caruso and the hostage. It probably about killed her. She's reclusive. She refuses meetings with men for almost anything. At this rate, she'll never bear an heir. We'll have no more chieftess in the line of Accardi."

Murmurs. Frowns. Caterina pressed on. "Without an heir, we'll be forced to establish new leadership. Perhaps it would be better to put that in place sooner rather than later, so we're not torn to shreds when the time comes. Men are *useful*. We don't need to ally with them, but we do need to negotiate with them and use them for children. It has been the way of the Guerrori for generations."

Up in the tree, Adelina felt as though each of the warriors down below had taken an axe and lodged it deep in her chest. Her women were always permitted to leave the jungle to engage with men for trade, or for the necessary trysts that would result in carrying on the mission with new warriors to defend the mountain. But if any got too attached to life beyond the Nascosta, they could leave. Only Adelina and her mother, and her mother, and every daughter after her, bore the full weight of the secrets of the mountain.

"I think it's been a long night, and we should sleep on it. We need a clear head before disrupting our world so completely."

Lucia. Bless her. She was trying to bide time without taking Adelina's side too strongly and they stopped listening to her.

But Caterina leveled Lucia with a hard glare. "Our world? What about *Rosa's* world? What about the treaty that they don't come into the Nascosta? What about the hostage? Where is he? What information have we learned from him? If Adelina comes back with information from the hostage, very good, we take our time to decide. But if she doesn't—if she lets him go—perhaps we consider this as evidence toward a vote of no confidence. Perhaps the line of Accardi no longer deserves to reign as supreme keepers of the Heart of the Mountain. Perhaps new leadership is in order."

Long, fractured fingers of ice twisted through Adelina's soul and wrung at her heart. New leadership? They didn't even know what she knew about the Heart of the Mountain. No one but an Accardi could carry that knowledge. They couldn't replace her. Not really.

But it was true what they said about her and men.

They didn't know about the curse. It was only true of her and her line. The other women were exempt from the curse, and men who loved them were betrayed by the women, but not killed. Generations of their Guerrori ancestors before them had ensured that hatred of men, that wariness, was deeply entrenched in them from the start—even if the Accardi chieftess line alone bore the wrath of the curse for any who dared break the code.

Men were to be used for the bearing of children but never permitted into the jungle or into the Heart. The heart was the gateway for betrayal. The heart was a first step into a steep sliding slope of misplaced trust and breaking the bonds of the warrior sisterhood of the Guerrori.

But those bonds were more fragile than ever in this moment.

The Carusos were not going to stop, and something told her the man in the vest wouldn't either. He was right that the Guerrori had begun to rely on their melders, and that the Morturi had strong melders now, too. The winds were changing.

Adelina pulled the empty vial from the small pouch hanging from the belt at her waist. She turned it over in her hands. The man in the vest had weapons. *New* weapons. The kind that the Carusos had never heard of.

If she didn't come up with new resources soon, the shaken confidence her people had in her could be torn completely asunder. It was time to turn some tables of her own.

And she would start with the man in the vest.

CHAPTER SEVEN

Grigg drummed his fingers on the arm of his chair and peered down his nose at the squirmy little man before him. The man's long brown beard trembled as he worked his lip, and he was still huffing from climbing the ladder up to the rooftop where Grigg had set up an elaborate meeting space.

Getting out of the Nascosta jungle the night before had been enough thrill for the evening. Rigging the Morturi outpost with explosives ahead of time to make them think the Guerrori's quake-makers were upon them, and arranging for his horse to step on the trigger, had been child's play. But that was simple chemistry. Predictable and beautiful. Escaping the Guerrori had been something else entirely.

Grigg couldn't remember the last time he'd been so acutely aware that his normal tools were not enough—that if the Guerrori caught him, he'd likely be a dead man. Dead Man's Folly. How many centuries had men entered the forest, never to return?

Grigg had relied on a good old-fashioned compass and three exit strategies placed at different points along the jungle's border in hopes that he'd make it out alive, but each of the strategies had required him to make it to the border in the first place. He'd done it, but it had been closer than he'd liked. Whatever had happened after he left her on the bank must have worked to his advantage, because he hadn't been pursued, and he should've been. Or had the Guerrori chieftess decided to take him up on his offer?

The thrill of an uncertain outcome wove through the threads of a gentle night breeze. An ornate red rug filled most of the square rooftop. Four lanterns hung from poles standing at each corner, shining light on gilded trunks and tables. They were decorated with platters of fine food, trays of expensive bottles, and a display of a few choice weapons. Candles added a soft warm light to the veritable feast.

And it was almost midnight.

Grigg sat in a high-backed armchair in the center of the room, across from an empty stuffed loveseat. A low table stood between the chair and the loveseat, holding a bottle of fine wine and two sparkling goblets. Darian, the unfortunate soul in front of Grigg, shifted his weight and pulled in long drafts of air to catch his breath, but refused to sit. Grigg waved the apple in his hand at the man.

"Care for an apple? Perhaps a bite of something to eat would steady your nerves."

The other man's rotund face burgeoned into bold new shades of red, transforming into a decent representation of the apple.

"I wouldn't need to steady my nerves if you hadn't popped up out of the blue with your creepy little folded papers dropped in places they shouldn't be, like my bed pillow. How did you get in? How did you ..." Darian swallowed and licked his lips. He eyed the full wine goblets on the table. "Perhaps I do need to steady my nerves."

He reached for one of the goblets.

Grigg leaned forward, lightning fast, eyes fastened hard on the shaking man. "That's not for you."

Darian hesitated. He clenched his jaw, then straightened, resigned to the wishes of his host. Abandoning the goblet, he reached into the satchel over his shoulder instead and pulled out a somewhat crumpled little folded paper display, small enough to fit easily in the palm of his pudgy hand.

"What is this?"

Grigg sprawled back against his wood-carved, throne-like chair again, running his arm along the back of the chair. "Please, I had to use more than one sheet of paper for this one. The least you can do is acknowledge that you can clearly see the yellow custard and berries."

Darian pursed his lips. "Yes, I know *what* it is. What is it supposed to *mean*?"

Something churned in Grigg's gut. He'd scheduled this meeting with Darian just before midnight on purpose, but it was boring. Important, but boring.

And now Darian was wasting time asking stupid questions with his stupid little beady eyes and questionable constitution when all Grigg wanted to do was find out whether the chieftess had decided to come to the meet. Which meant *this* meeting needed to be short and effective before Grigg sent Darian scurrying back down the ladder and out of sight.

Was she out there now, watching? He'd assumed she would be. That was why he'd scheduled the meeting for now. Had he done it for nothing? Maybe he'd misread her. Maybe she trusted her women too much for him to drive a wedge between them so quickly. Maybe she would bring not one, not two, but every last one of them to surround the house and break in at dawn or wait until he left and trail him to more neutral territory.

Grigg ran a weary hand over his face. "It's not nearly as much fun if I have to explain it. Who do you know that's involved with a bakery? Maybe one that's famous for a yellow custard dish served with red berries that looks precisely like this." He gestured at the paper ensemble in the man's hand.

A somewhat tardy flicker of understanding danced across the man's eyes. Ahhh, there it was. Slack jaw, more visible whites of the eyes, a pinch of horror. Yes, he'd gotten the message.

But Grigg was in a hurry. He leaned forward in his chair, drilling Darian with a cool stare. "That's right. Your father-in-law. Shame he's never liked you. Personally, I think you're a stand-up fellow, except for the times when you're lying down with other people's wives, of course. He'll be murderously angry if he discovers you've gone astray again. Which is why you're going to sleep with Mira again tomorrow."

Now the poor maladroit fellow went from slack jaw to full gape. How could sleeping with one of his previous flings precipitate favor with his wife's father?

Grigg took a bite out of the apple. "While you're with her, you're going to let it slip that there's something valuable at the Caruso estate, and it's going to be on display the night of the Lovers' Ball. You're going to tell her that Nico consulted with a military commander recently, specifically because he's decided Stoyan is a bug who needs to be squished. And that the Carusos are about to make a move on the jungle. If Stoyan has any aspirations at all of making his mark as a legitimate rival, he's going to have to do it soon."

Darian's hand crumpled into a fist, crushing Grigg's little creation. The man blanched, winced, hesitated—then swallowed. Resignation. "That's not exactly pillow talk. How am I supposed to bring all that up?"

Grigg waved him off. "I've taken care of it. I've dropped a few breadcrumbs of my own, and Mira will be the one asking *you* for information. You're going to resist, then regretfully let some details slip and swear her to secrecy. In return, I will forget your marital indiscretions and let your awkward family dinners with your wife and father-in-law continue without giving him a reason to bash your head in."

Here, Grigg made an exaggerated grimace and held up a finger.

"Correction. Without giving him *further* reason to bash your head in."

Darian let out a sound that might have been mistaken for the high squeak of a rat pressed into a corner. It was fitting, really. Darian opened his mouth again and closed it, a move he'd repeated enough since getting to the rooftop that Grigg had begun to wonder if he was part codfish.

Grigg stuck his face forward and arched both eyebrows. "Have I been unclear?"

Darian's knuckles went white around the destroyed bits of shaped paper in his hand. Sweat beaded on his brow. He shook his head.

"Then what are you still doing here? Head home to your gracious, loving wife, whom you do not deserve, and arrange a tryst with Mira tomorrow. Get out of here before I decide to talk to your father-in-law sooner rather than later."

Darian paled, spun on his heel, and scrambled back to the ladder without a word.

Grigg tossed the apple in his hands up in the air, watching the candlelight play off its red shades as it completed a tall arc. It took four tosses of the apple for Darian to muddle his way through adjusting the satchel on his back and getting safely on the ladder, and another several tosses for the fool to make it down the ladder without toppling off it.

And now, the wait. Grigg turned the apple over and over in his hands before tossing it up again. He tossed it higher, caught it, and tossed it higher still. Was she there, or was he sitting alone on a rooftop? It was elaborately decorated and prepared, all to see what would draw her focus. All to impress or distract—except for one item hidden inside one of the trunks.

He didn't like the urgent need he felt to keep the egg nearby, to check it constantly for cracks. Twice in the night, Grigg had gotten up to examine it, once after a particularly hostile dream-state interaction with Giovanna. So far, no more cracks had presented themselves on its smooth golden shell.

But who was to say the cracks, when they came, would be small? What if only two more cracks were enough to break open the shell? On the other hand, perhaps it would be slow, and a hairline-fracture-sized crack would work its way slowly around the side. Looking was useless, but he still couldn't help himself. Grigg resisted the urge to check it now.

Minutes ticked by at the speed of growing grass. Midnight had passed. Was punctuality an important value for the Guerrori?

But it was likely, if the chieftess did come, that she would want to watch from some place she felt safe. The residence he'd chosen had a rooftop at the end of a row of homes on the outskirts of town, facing bits of forest that jutted out from the Nascosta, but really belonged to the more innocuous Verde Forest, a far less contested area frequently used for basic hunting by the people of Smŭrttata. But it butted up against the Nascosta jungle, which meant Adelina could travel close to his location without sacrificing a sense of cover and comfort that she would need to feel good about a meet.

The area was civilian, with small shops bringing in modest revenue at best. It was too far from the main square and thus offered poor real estate for shops like the unfortunate shoemaker with the blue door, who couldn't hope to gain as much foot traffic as his competitors. Most of those living out here were people living quiet lives away from the bustle, surviving the best they could, and ignored by the powerful. They simply weren't worth the time it would take to focus or care about the inhabitants on this end. Which made it perfect for Grigg—particularly the rooftop bordering the town on one side and the forest on the other.

The question was, Was it enough? He'd torn through Guerrori territory and trespassed on contested land in the middle of a literal firefight, though being unconscious, he certainly hadn't appeared a threat at the time. He'd upped the ante by taunting, threatening, and ultimately attacking the Guerrori chieftess. He could only hope he'd created a desperation in her for new tactics and a drive to understand what possible answers he might have to her problems.

One way or another, lives were lost on both sides the previous night, and the status quo was ruptured for good. Things would never be the same as they were before, and the treaty had been torn to shreds. It was just that each side believed the other had breached it first, and neither knew *he* had been the instigator. He just needed—

Thwip.

Grigg snapped back in his chair so fast it nearly toppled over, as an arrow whizzed by his face, skewered the apple in his hands, and hit the base of the lantern before dropping to the rooftop. *Plink.*

Grigg whipped his head in the direction the archer must have occupied. He saw nothing in the dark, but if the archer had wanted him dead, he would've been. Grigg turned slowly to regard the arrow on the floor. It had pierced the apple's core soundly enough, but it was the piece of paper rolled up and bound to the rear of the arrow shaft that caught his attention.

The angle of the shot had to be just right not only to hit the apple as he held it in his hands, but to hit the lantern so the arrow would drop to the rooftop instead of soaring over the short wall and winding up meters away where he would have no chance to see, much less read, the note attached to the missile.

A tingling sensation washed over him from head to toe, though from the thrill of an excellent shot, the near brush with death, or excitement over his invitation apparently being accepted, he couldn't say. Slowly, Grigg stood, turned in the direction of where the archer must be, and offered the invisible woman in the shadows a long stare of acknowledgment—and courage, or stupidity—as he opened himself up clearly for another shot before moving to the arrow lying on the corner of the rooftop.

Would it be a threat, a denial, a list of demands? Perhaps it would tell him she didn't negotiate with intruders or foreign enemies. Perhaps it was a stall tactic to relocate him on the roof for some reason. Or perhaps ...

Grigg tugged on the string binding the parchment to the arrow shaft and unrolled the paper. Two simple words greeted him.

Come down.

She didn't like the roof. He couldn't blame her. There was only one ladder up to access the roof, and it was open to a street on one side and connected to more buildings on another, lit with lanterns and candles where she could be seen and he could observe her approach from the high ground. He'd expected her to be on one of the neighboring rooftops rather than in the more obvious choice of the forest. She would assume he was prepared with all the tools he wanted up on the roof, and less so if he removed himself from his optimal position. After all, he knew what was on the roof, and she didn't.

Grigg's heart thundered in his chest. He could almost picture her standing ramrod straight in the dark forest beyond his view—feet a shoulder-width apart, hand on her bow, eyes sharp as blades. She knew what she was doing in combat. She'd clearly faced her share of idiots wandering into the forest. But here she was. She'd come.

The question was, Could he cut an agreement with her? Had she come alone? Would he end the night with a blackmailed, reluctant agreement, or with an arrow in his back? The uncertainty of it all made his head spin. Interactions with people like Darian were boring. He always knew how they would go, but he genuinely *hadn't* known whether or not the chieftess would show up tonight. And he hadn't expected a message via an arrow shooting an apple out of his hands.

She wasn't just confident. She was bold and unafraid. Or did she only *project* that confidence, the way he had when he'd been in the belly of the jungle with his hands and feet tied behind a horse, surrounded by her warriors and impenetrable gaze?

Grigg swallowed. When had his mouth gone so dry?

She could have killed him, but she hadn't, which meant she was willing to have a conversation. He had to show he was willing to play ball for the conversation to start.

So he'd begin by a concession: coming down the ladder. Then he'd persuade her to move to the roof. Grigg lifted the parchment in his hands and gave it a little wave over his head in the direction he guessed she must be watching from. He smiled and gave an exaggerated bow before tucking the note away in a pocket of his sky-blue fitted vest.

He strode to the ladder and dropped down to street level, facing the forest. Grigg stepped off the ladder and moved forward into the empty space where his silhouette should still be seen before the soft glow of lantern light faded into obscurity.

He waited. Nothing.

Grigg steeled himself to stay calm. Perhaps she was waiting in order to test him, to make him anxious. If so, it was working. But he couldn't let her think so. He spread his hands in an open, welcoming gesture.

His only answer came in the rustle of leaves as a gentle breeze played through the branches of the trees. He shifted his weight. A leaf crunched. Then a soft scraping from behind him caught his ear. He spun back toward the rooftop. She was there, on the roof, in his space—fast as lightning and quiet as a fox.

How long had she been up there?

Grigg's heart lurched into his throat. *No, no, no.* He ran for the ladder. Her head popped into view over the low wall just as he reached for it. She flashed him a devastating grin before shoving the ladder off the roof. It fell to the ground with a crash.

CHAPTER EIGHT

The previous twenty-four hours had been about as much fun as having her toenails ripped off. The Morturi had broken the treaty regarding the border of the Nascosta jungle for the first time in years. The status quo had been incinerated faster than flame took to a dry leaf. The trust of her women had begun to crumble, and she'd lost the weirdest hostage she could have dreamed up.

But Adelina still held a few advantages. One, her unnamed ex-hostage wanted something from her, which meant she had leverage. Two, she still had loyal women. Lucia, for example.

Dear Lucia. When Adelina had pulled her aside and told her about the meet with the man in the vest, she'd been alarmed, then skeptical, then begrudgingly willing to come help cover the meet. After all, the only thing dumber than Adelina going to the meet was her going alone.

Adelina had told the women she'd been able to get some information out of the man, but that she needed to confirm the truth of it before sharing too much. That had drawn some side eyes between Caterina and her sympathizers, but Adelina hoped it walked the line between Adelina returning with nothing and potentially having useful intel. The best she could hope for was buying time so that she could build back lost trust.

She'd paid her respects to Rosa, performing her own solo version of the *treccia di riposo* ceremony without actually touching the braid Caterina and the others had already completed. Lucia and Umbra had joined her in solidarity. Paloma had looked like she wanted to, but wound up standing awkwardly off to one side instead, probably not wanting to seem too close to Adelina with the undercurrent of distrust rocketing through the rest of the group.

Adelina would have preferred to confront the Caterina problem head on, but she didn't yet know what cards she might hold. If she told them about the meet and it went badly, she'd lose any tenuous trust they still had. If it went well, she could come back with proof she still deserved to be their chieftess, then deal with Caterina from a position of power. Off the heels of a win, rather than a loss.

Adelina had wondered if the man in the vest would actually be at the meeting or only hiding somewhere nearby, hoping for an ambush. But he'd been there, meeting with a man made of pudding and a poor constitution, easily visible from the forest from which she'd observed the exchange. He'd likely scheduled this meeting for now on purpose, hoping she would see it, which made him calculating. But he'd also chosen an idiot to make himself look powerful. If he had to compare himself with people like that to feel confident, Adelina questioned his ability as a worthwhile adversary.

Then again, he'd managed to subdue her in the river without using a single melder power. Was he a melder and choosing to hide his ability to retain the element of surprise, or was he not a melder at all?

Lucia and Adelina had come up with their strategy while the man in the vest intimidated his target, and as the terrified man scuttled away down the ladder and off into the night, Lucia had remained in the fringes of the forest while Adelina circled around to the other side. Without a ladder or any other clear access point to the roof, the man in the vest wouldn't be expecting her to approach from there.

The moment his feet touched the ground, Adelina sprinted for the wall with all she had, bow and quiver on her back, hands free, launching up the wall in a practiced move. The building joined a wider building beside it, creating a corner she could use to her advantage. She ran up the wall, pushing off the corner, and her hands caught hold of the lip of the low wall. The wall was perhaps only knee high, running the perimeter of the rooftop.

She'd scanned the roof in half a second, taking in the lavish spread on the long table, audacious jewels begging a greedy person to snatch one—or three—and the weapons display containing nothing small enough to hide on her person, but large weapons like a mace, a lance, a war hammer, a spear, and even a crossbow.

Adelina ran her hands over the smooth wood of the crossbow. Gorgeous carvings ran the length of the tiller, ornate patterns that looked like they belonged in a palace or hanging on a wall with richly colored tapestries rather than used as a weapon of war. Technically, the weapon was an arbalest, with a steel bow assembly capable of piercing armor. She nearly reached for it then and there but stopped herself. Now was not the time.

Had he set this here just to bait her? What kind of mind games was he playing, inviting her to a rooftop stocked with weaponry like this? Was it a museum, a threat, or a meeting? The more she saw of this man, the more convinced she was that he was purposeful in all he did—deliberate and premeditating.

The question was, What sort of mistakes had he made? He likely had expected to be up on the rooftop *with* her to direct her focus where he wanted it. Where had he slipped up?

She crossed to look under the tables of food. Nothing. She examined the weapons for booby traps and snares, then turned them over to check for hidden compartments or hollowed out items. More nothing. Next, she moved on to the trunks.

Two heavy trunks sat against the short wall at the edge of the rooftop, one open, one shut. Which one was she meant to explore? The closed lid practically screamed of secrets to be uncovered. The other promised that what she saw was what she got, declaring its contents openly.

But she had a feeling the man in the vest wasn't the sort who made honest promises. She crouched before the open trunk. Arbalest ammunition bolts sat inside on one end, nestled in a box between a pair of high-end machetes and various field equipment gear. A pile of cloth covered the left side, maybe hammocks or ponchos or something of that sort.

Adelina pulled out the stack of cloth and set it aside before feeling along the bottom of the trunk. She did the same with the other equipment, pulling the items out and placing them on the floor beside her before pulling out boxes of bolts. There were three large boxes of bulky ammunition, but when she opened the fourth, her hand slipped.

The box scraped the floor. Her mouth went dry. The man in the vest would have heard it. And she was running out of time.

Adelina lurched forward to poke her head over the roof, and there was the man in the vest, staring back at her, eyes wide. She'd caught him off guard. He was genuinely surprised, maybe even fully panicked. Good. It was about time she saw something real on his face.

She flashed him an insolent grin before shoving the ladder off the roof. It clattered to the ground close enough to him that he had to jump to the side to avoid getting hit. That bought her an extra few seconds while he repositioned the ladder.

Adelina spun to the last box of bolt ammunition. She probably shouldn't waste her time on it, but she just had this feeling ...

Her hands brushed the latch. She lifted the lid, and her breath caught. A shining golden egg, about the size of a human skull, glittered back at her under the lantern light.

It couldn't be. It couldn't be *the* egg. It couldn't belong to *her* —to the woman responsible for the curse all Accardi women bore. Hands trembling, Adelina reached for it, then hesitated. Her fingers hovered over its golden surface.

Don't touch it. Danger. Death. Deception.

It couldn't be real. And yet, there was a magical quality about it she couldn't deny.

On a whim, she flipped the lid shut, shut the lids of the other three bolt boxes, shoved the egg box under the carved armchair in the middle of the rooftop, and perched on the edge of the chair just as the man in the vest scaled the ladder, vaulted the short wall, and landed light on his feet three paces away.

Just like that, there he was, looking every inch the strange foreign aristocrat she'd seen shaking hands with the Palladino brothers. The man who'd infiltrated a house of safety, a warm family, with a smile and a nod.

She wondered again what he'd been doing at the Palladino estate. It wasn't any of her business. The Palladinos didn't know she existed, as far as she knew. Surely, they'd heard of her tribe, but they would know nothing of her as a person. There was no reason for her to be possessive of their sunshiny family dynamic.

But the man in the vest who had taunted her in the jungle and choked her in the river didn't belong in the same *sentence*, let alone the same room, as the happy childhood and trusting family of the Palladino house.

The man in the vest eyed her, chest heaving, nostrils flared, eyes sweeping over the scene. His arms flexed, and his jaw clenched, and for a moment, Adelina feared he would rush her. She had the time to string an arrow and lodge it in his chest, but she didn't want to. And if she did, she'd never get the answers she came for.

But in the space of a long, measured breath, he seemed to gain control of himself. Fists at his sides relaxed into open hands, the pressed shirt and fitted blue vest softening as he relaxed his shoulders. He inclined his head gently toward the box under the chair. "That's not yours."

She cocked her head. "How do you know? It certainly isn't yours."

He stepped forward. She stiffened. Another step, and she wouldn't have time to draw the bow if he decided to lunge for her.

He stepped again. But it was okay. She was a fireblood. She was a chieftess. She could handle this.

The man in the vest reached forward, and she shot out of her chair to meet him on her feet. But just as her feet hit the cold stone of the rooftop, his hand wrapped around what he'd been reaching for—one of the two goblets on a tray between them.

He swirled the dark liquid in the goblet and eyed her over the rim. "I was talking about the chair."

The glint in his eye told her he was enjoying this. And she was pretty sure he had *not* been talking about the chair. She decided to ignore the remark for now. She waved a hand at the table overflowing with food.

"The feast is quite a gesture, but I'm not hungry."

He reached forward and captured the other goblet in his free hand. "Not to worry. Good wine with a beautiful woman and interesting conversation is far more rewarding than stuffing my mouth anyway."

His gaze lingered a second too long on her lips when he said the word "mouth." "I'm much more interested in yours." He cleared his throat. "More interested in you, I mean. Than the feast."

Adelina smothered a smile. For all his bravado, she made him nervous. And that fact brought her no small satisfaction. After all, the rooftop was meant to be *his* high ground. His turf.

She lifted her chin. "I'm not thirsty either."

The man in the vest arched an eyebrow. "Worried I've

poisoned it? Isn't it obvious after last night that if I wanted you dead, you would be?"

Adelina sent a whisper of heat through her palm until tiny candlelight-sized flames danced across her glowing skin. She shot a small ball of fire into the corner where Lucia's arrow still skewered the apple on the floor. The apple caught fire, and she let her mouth twist up at the corners.

"Isn't it equally obvious that if *I* wanted *you* dead, it would be you lying at my feet rather than the apple?"

He waited a beat, then shrugged in concession. "So we both want each other alive. All the more reason to toast our common ground."

The man lifted a goblet to his lips and took a small sip, then switched goblets with a flourish and took a sip of the other. "See? Not poisoned. Come now, I simply must enjoy a good drink while we chat. And I refuse to drink alone. Besides, sharing a drink is better than a traditional handshake. Too many people are left-handed."

It was a roguish peace offering, but a peace offering nonetheless. Maybe he was right, and threats were not the best way to start the evening. If she wanted him to spill secrets, a few concessions to keep him comfortable and believing he was in control might not be a bad idea.

Come on, Adelina. Don't let your ego change the status quo. Get him comfortable. Get him talking.

She picked up the goblet and cradled it delicately in her fingers.

He raised his cup. "To those we love and must protect."

She cocked her head, examining him. She hadn't noticed the blue of his eyes before, like the depths of the ocean after a storm, dancing with rays of rebel sunlight. Who did he love? Who was *he* protecting?

Adelina touched her goblet to his, and both took a drink. He smiled, an easy smile that released a tautness in his face she hadn't noticed was there until it was gone.

"Now. Isn't that better?"

He took her hand gingerly, spun her around, and offered an elegant bow, brushing his lips to her fingers, before seating himself like a king on the carved chair.

Her jaw dropped. "You stole my seat!"

And he'd maneuvered her away from it without her even realizing he had done it. Her stomach burst with angry butterflies, furious that they existed at all inside her, and anxious to get out at any cost.

He grinned a beautiful impish smile. "Did I?"

Seated, the man in the vest was shorter than she as she stood before him. So how did he still seem to be laughing *down* at her rather than up?

He held up a hand in defense and gestured toward the cushioned short sofa across from him. "Please, I insist."

The undercurrent of his words wrapped her body in the unshakable memory of his iron-strong arms around her waist in the river. *There's no need for tonight's interaction to be like our last.* Her gaze dropped to the cords of his forearms, the lines of the hands that had twined themselves in her hair. He'd toyed with her while bound, then managed to free himself, knock her from her horse, and drag her to the river before she lit her hands on fire. And now, he invited her to chat on a candlelit rooftop with wine and cushioned seats.

Was accepting his offer weakness? Was refusing too stubborn and egotistical? She sat. Her nerves were on fire. Maybe she did need the wine after all. She took another sip. "What do you want with me?"

He leaned back and rested his arm along the top of the chair at his back as though lounging with a crew of his closest friends. If he had any. "The question, dearest, is what *you* should want from *me*."

She let out a breath. "I hate riddles, and I'm not in the mood. Spit it out."

He swirled the wine in his glass, watched it trail down the inside of the goblet, and glanced up at her. "You know, for as stressful a position as you have, it wouldn't kill you to loosen up a bit. I find life far more worth living that way."

Except that loosening up might in fact kill her. That's why she avoided it at all costs. If she slipped up, people died.

The previous night was a case in point. She should never have gone to the Palladino estate. It was frivolous, wasteful, and treated her mind to perilous fantasies that borrowed the Palladino's sense of safety when she hadn't earned any safety of her own. She lived on the edge of a knife, not on worn green sofas, and pretending otherwise could get people killed.

Adelina gritted her teeth. She looked him in the face and slowly poured the wine goblet out on the floor. "I'm not here to play games. I'm not here to waste time."

Okay, so that may have been childish. But she didn't want to play his little chitchat gambit. She wanted answers. She set the empty goblet on the tray. "Why do you need me?"

He steadied her for a moment. "Maybe I just like pretty things."

On second thought, maybe she didn't make him nervous. Maybe he'd pretended even that, to make her feel in control. To make her feel powerful. Maybe everything about this was a game to him.

She stood and strode for the ladder. "This has been a mistake."

"Suit yourself. I'm sure the Carusos will be more than happy to take the konnolan I have on offer. Pompous Frederico won't need to marry you. He and his men can take their time slitting your throats one by one, as you retch helplessly into the dirt."

The hair on the back of her neck stood up. Her mind spun with a thousand colliding thoughts at once. "What did you say to me?"

Her eyes flicked to the box under the chair. The box that shouldn't have been there. It was supposed to have been destroyed in some far corner of the world long ago. Not here, close enough to touch. Intact, with an air of magic thick as morning fog rolling in off the river.

The egg was neither destroyed nor far away. An epiphany struck her. She'd thought the mage who bound her family had died, and the curse was on her forever, without the curse giver to lift it. But what if it could be lifted? What if the curse was tied to the dead mage's power, housed in the egg, and if she could destroy it, the curse would die with it?

And why did this man have it? Did he know what it was? If he did, why would he bring it here, of all places?

In the span of twenty-four hours, the man in the vest had gone from moron trespasser to formidable fighter to the most dangerous man in the known universe.

And he'd done it with a smile.

Why did he care about her?

He'd just threatened to sell some sort of tool to the Carusos, and he knew Frederico wanted to marry her. He had tools she hadn't even heard of. But she didn't want to sound stupid by admitting she had no idea what konnolan was.

What he'd said was intended to instill fear. If the goosebumps ravaging every square inch of her skin were any indication, he'd pulled it off with wild success. He had the power to kill her. Maybe even her whole tribe. And if he was connected with the wicked mage that had cursed Adelina and all the mothers in her line going back six hundred years, he was already worse than Frederico could ever hope to be.

She had to figure out what he really wanted and make a deal to use this konnolan herself, whatever it was, or stall long enough to figure out a way to get the egg.

Or you can make him fall in love with you.

The voice was thin and flew feather light into the edges of her consciousness. It was a ridiculous suggestion.

Yes, if he fell in love with her, that would kill him. But that would take too long, and he didn't look particularly enamored by her.

He considered himself the eagle and her the mouse. Every compliment he tossed her way was a taunt, a tease—nothing genuine or warm.

And she didn't want to kill him like that if there was another way. She'd promised herself she'd never use the curse on her to curse someone else's happiness. Killing murderous invaders in defense of the Heart of the Mountain was one thing, but manipulating someone and killing them when their only crime was loving her? That was another.

Then again, that tactic would also require that she was lovable to begin with. That men wouldn't just like her face or her body but actually experience a truer love for her as a person. The likelihood of that happening was even smaller than the possibility of the golden egg having survived the past six hundred years when it was supposed to have been destroyed.

No, she couldn't use the curse. But the man in the vest was an egotist. She could use that.

Adelina glanced up at him as if with renewed interest. "Frederico wants to marry me because he's a coward. He knows he'll never take the Nascosta while I'm alive. He knows an all-out war would mean losing so many Morturi lives that his people would rebel against him in protest before they made it three steps past the river."

"If you're so confident, why are you here?" The man in the vest set down his goblet and leaned forward. "The truth is, I need your help."

He had to be kidding.

"My help?"

"Yes. The Carusos have something I want. There's an event coming up, and that's when we'll get it. You're going to help me."

The edge in his voice felt like silk laced with glass shards. His face was soft. His tone warm. Warm like the too-hot flame of a fire about to consume its target completely.

She ran her thumbnail lightly along the inside of her middle finger. His suggestion was outlandish. "You want me to help you in a robbery?"

He grimaced. "It all sounds so sophomoric when you say it like that. I want you to be my accomplice in a heist. And honestly, I wouldn't trust you with any of the important parts."

Adelina arched a skeptical brow. "You're suggesting that with tensions higher than they've ever been between the Guerrori and the Morturi, that I waltz into the Carusos' home and steal something they think is important."

He nodded once. "Yes."

She leaned back in her chair. "And why would I do that?"

"You don't know what konnolan is, do you?"

Adlina fixed him with an even gaze, but no retort came.

He offered a small, sympathetic smile. "Don't worry, I expected as much. I've arranged for a demonstration."

The man in the vest stood and offered her his arm. She ignored it and rose to her feet of her own accord. He jerked his head toward the edge of the rooftop and strode in that direction. She took several cautious steps after him, careful to place herself between the man in the vest and the box with the egg in it still under his chair.

"Konnolan is a substance that, when it explodes, completely nullifies melderblood powers. Crestbreakers, quakemakers, wind-callers, firebloods—all of them relegated to nothing. The effects are temporary, but strong."

He lifted two fingers to his mouth, and a piercing whistle cut through the night. Fifty meters off, two large bonfires lit at once, flooding the empty field between the edge of the forest and the rooftop with flickering orange and red light.

Boom. The explosion cracked the air.

She jumped. Then she saw it. Two shadowy figures between the pillars of flame, dragging a female body from the forest.

Lucia. Compassionate Lucia, defending Adelina to others, yet always pushing her to slow down and make the wise choice when they were alone. Soft, caring Lucia, who'd followed Adelina straight into a trap. Adelina's stomach ripped open wide and swallowed her whole.

The man in the vest turned toward her. "Konnolan doesn't just mute melderblood powers, Chieftess. It has considerable adverse effects as well, including dizziness, disorientation, muscle weakness, nausea. Your friend can hardly walk on her own."

He gestured toward Lucia, who looked like she might be trying to pull free of the two men. She should have been using her wind-calling. She should have blasted them backward. She should have shot them with a powerful gust of air that knocked them into the fire and shot an arrow through their hearts in the span of a single breath.

Instead, she toppled sideways, so one of the captors had to catch her as she retched into the grass, precisely as the man in the vest had suggested.

This was her fault. First Rosa, and now Lucia. Thick black sludge seeped into Adelina's chest, heavy and impenetrable. She couldn't move. She couldn't breathe.

The man in the vest returned her gaping horror with sickening businesslike neutrality. "Do we have a deal?"

Adelina never felt herself move. After the paralyzing terror of what she'd seen seized her, she hadn't been aware she still could. Adelina threw up her hands and called to the fire, bursting forward toward the man. She'd incinerate him then and there. She'd scorch him to ash.

But the fire never came. Her flameless fist connected with his broad chest like a sparrow on a windowpane. He parried her next blow, spun and half-shoved, half-threw her back against the table of food.

Bowls and apples clattered to the ground. Her quiver flew up her back as her body went airborne, and the edge of the table bit into the base of her spine as she slammed down again. Pain exploded along the back of her head and shot down her torso.

And then the man in the vest was there, all power and pain and muscle. The reflection of candlelight danced in eyes no longer playful, but dark as tar, arms around her like a vise. He captured both of her wrists in one large hand and shoved them up over her head onto the table. She writhed in his grip, her weight awkwardly slanted against the quiver at her back as her feet cycled in the air off the floor.

Adelina kicked at his hip. He grunted, dropped his elbow in her stomach, and leaned forward until his nose brushed hers. She jerked her head sideways, chest heaving, rebelling against his closeness.

How dare he touch her?

How dare he hurt Lucia?

How dare he threaten everything she loved?

Why did he have the golden egg?

His breath fell hot against her cheek. "Your power is not working because of the magna I put in the wine."

Viper's breath. The wine! She knew she shouldn't have taken it. Adelina called to the fire again, but he was right—her call was empty and useless.

The man in the vest continued. "The wind is blowing our direction, carrying the konnolan with it. If not for the magna, you'd be in the same condition as your friend, but as it neutralizes your power, it also neutralizes any effect konnolan would have on you."

Adelina brought her knee up sharply, but whatever part of him she hit, it wasn't hard enough. His grip only tightened, and the elbow in her stomach dug deeper.

"I prefer we work amicably together, Chieftess. In return, I'll keep your friend safe and release her when we're done. I won't let Frederico marry you, and I'll toss in the konnolan for good measure if you do well. So I'm going to ask you again ... do we have a deal?"

Maybe she did need to make him fall in love with her. If the man knew what the egg was, and brought it here on purpose, he was more dangerous than anyone she'd ever known.

Or maybe she just needed to play along long enough to find a way to free Lucia and get some of this magna and konnolan for herself. If she had the magna, she could protect her women and use the konnolan on the Morturi if they dared cross the gorge again. She'd confirm her effectiveness as a leader and keep this new weapon out of the hands of her enemies.

And she might be able to buy enough time to destroy the egg.

She nodded once. "We have a deal."

CHAPTER NINE

To say the transition from terrifying fear-monger captor to cooperative business partner was awkward was an understatement. Grigg couldn't be too friendly too fast, exactly, but he'd also done more hand-to-hand combat in the last twenty-four hours than he had in a number of years.

Sure, he was capable, and he kept up his skills, but Grigg preferred to let employees do the heavy lifting while he did the blackmailing and threatening. He'd already ruined one shirt along with his maroon vest. There was no need for more wardrobe carnage.

Grigg had eased the chieftess off the table, offering a hand to steady her as her feet found the rooftop once more. He'd taken her bow and quiver of arrows with assurances he would keep them safe and in good condition until their business was complete. Grigg kept hold of her as he pulled back the rug and let her down the trapdoor under the rug on the roof into the small house.

He hadn't spared the box under the chair a second glance.

The trapdoor dropped them straight into the living room via a climbing rope. A threadbare sofa and two wooden chairs made up the living area. Several box crates lined the back wall next to a bookcase, which served as the only decoration on the walls. Similarly, the furniture sat on a plain wood plank floor.

The entire place was only two rooms, one with a food preparation area at one end and a living area at the other, and a single adjoining bedroom. Beyond the living room, a square table held an oil lantern that illuminated the modest dwelling. A counter ran the length of the wall from the table to the far corner of the house, the counter sporting two old buckets, a water pitcher, cups, a stack of clean plates, and a few sacks of food supplies.

The front door to the house was positioned in the living area opposite the bookshelves and crates, leading out to the side of the house that would spill into the street facing the town. Two windows faced the same direction, and none looked out toward the forest. A closed door on the living room end of the house led to the single bedroom.

Grigg glanced at the woman beside him. Every fiber of her body was tensed like a cat about to spring. But now that she'd agreed to the deal, as long as she remained cooperative, there was no reason for him to remain unpleasant.

He cleared his throat and nodded toward the pitcher on the counter. "Glass of water?"

The chieftess gave him a look but said nothing. A fair reaction, under the circumstances.

"I get it. The last thing I offered you was drugged. But if I hadn't, you'd be in the same condition as your friend—who will be fine, by the way. The boys are bringing her in now, and I do intend to keep you both dosed on magna until our business is complete. Because it's hard for me to get what I want if I'm dead, and if looks could kill ..." He let his voice trail off, met her severe gaze, and flashed a smile. "Well, you know."

Her lips pressed together. She glanced at the door.

Grigg adjusted his grip on her arm and dipped his head. "They'll be in shortly. They may have to pause for her to puke some more, and they might end up carrying her inside. She'll be staying here, in the basement. She'll be fine."

Any sane person in her situation would think he was a monster. Of course, that had been half the point. For her to do what he wanted, she had to be afraid of him and recognize that he posed real danger.

He'd intimidated hundreds of people in his life without batting an eye. So why did her stiffness bother him? His chest tightened, as though the walls around his heart had begun to compress—pressing in with a steady, persistent pressure.

"I won't put my hands on you again, if you're worried about that. Not so long as you cooperate. Now that you've agreed to our partnership, things can be rather civil."

She arched an eyebrow, jerked her chin down to shoot an icy glare at his hand wrapping her upper arm, and stared back at him, eyes teeming with scrutiny as though she were a stern schoolmaster and he an unruly pupil.

"So far, you've attacked me, choked me, and thrown me onto a table. Now you're telling me you won't touch me—while your hand is *still* on me."

Grigg offered a conciliatory, dramatic grimace. "I admit that doesn't sound great. But in my defense, you're hardly helpless, even without fireblood powers. It's only by sheer luck that I escaped you in the jungle. And you surprised me again this evening. Great entry, by the way. I really didn't see that coming."

He waited a beat, but she said nothing, so he forged ahead. "Your combat skills are more than impressive, and I'm not entirely convinced you're human. It would be reasonable of you to want me dead. So I'll be taking minimal precautions for self-preservation. I hope you'll forgive me for it. But then again, if you don't forgive me, I'll need to protect myself all the more, won't I?"

The door opened, and Trifon and Boris, the two melder guards he'd hired, came in carrying a young Guerrori woman between them. Her head had dropped to her chest, and each guard held one of her arms over their shoulders as her feet dragged on the ground. Sweat beaded her brow. Her head bobbed up to take in her new surroundings, recognition registering in her face as her gaze landed on the chieftess. It flickered to him next, along with the way he held her chieftess' arm.

The weakened girl lurched forward then, as if to lunge at Grigg, but the sudden motion only made her sick. She moaned, swallowed hard against probable bile surging up her throat, and slumped again against a wave of dizziness.

Grigg dipped his head toward the guards in acknowledgment. "Take her downstairs, boys."

They grunted an answer and moved one of the crates by the bookcase to reveal another trapdoor, this one leading to a staircase down to the basement. The chieftess moved to follow, but Grigg tugged her back as Trifon and Boris disappeared down the stairs with their charge.

She turned to face him. "I want to see where Lucia is staying."

Grigg shook his head. "Not a chance."

The chieftess crossed her arms, ignoring his hold on her. "How long is all this going to take? The event you're talking about is days away, isn't it? You're going to keep her down there for *days*, and not even let me see where she's going to be? Does she have a bed? What about food? Are you humane?"

Grigg rolled his eyes. "I don't like this situation any more than you do. Probably less. But I'm a businessman. The item we're after is important. I will retrieve it at any cost. But though there's certainly been the odd mishap ..."

He bobbed his head as he considered the phrasing. Okay, so mishaps had been more frequent when he started out, before he was as good at negotiation and blackmail. When his reputation preceded him, he didn't need to use muscle as often.

Grigg sighed. "On the whole, I prefer a sophisticated life without harming anyone unnecessarily. We may disagree on when it's necessary, but it isn't your life, is it? So you don't get to decide.

You saw all that food up there on the rooftop. I can't eat it all by myself. Obviously, we have plenty to go around, and she'll be taken care of."

The woman's eyes narrowed. "She'll be comfortable? You have a bed?"

"There's a cot."

"Not just for the bodyguards. For her too."

Of course there were—he hesitated. He'd gotten cots. But how many had he brought? There was definitely at least one. With one guard on duty at any given time, the other would use the cot. He liked to treat his guards as well as he could.

He wasn't against treating prisoners well either, especially since he didn't mind being on decent terms with the chieftess during their arrangement. But now that he thought about it, it was entirely possible he'd forgotten to arrange for a second cot.

The chieftess groaned. "How can I work with you if you treat her like this? For all the impressive skills you want me to believe you have, are you telling me you can't *count*?"

Grigg sucked his teeth. He had forgotten the other cot. He was sure of it. He'd been discussing it with the vendor, arranged for the one to be delivered, and planned to haggle for some other supplies before asking the vendor to toss in the second cot for free once he put more pressure on the man. But he'd closed the deal before asking for the second cot.

Giovanna was showing up more nights than not. His sleep deprivation was getting worse and worse.

Grigg ran a hand over his face. The fatigue was getting to him. He glanced around the room. There was no way the loveseat from the rooftop was going to fit down the trapdoor. It had been a nightmare to get it up there to begin with. It was also out of the question to let Lucia sleep in the living area, where he was planning to tie up the chieftess for the night. Letting two accomplished Guerrori warriors stay in the same place was a terrible idea. The basement would be safest by a long run.

But offering the sick girl some small comforts was an acceptable request. The poor girl's only crime had been loyalty, after all, and loyalty should be rewarded. A lantern was already down there, along with water, and the cot for the bodyguard. There were two blankets. He'd remembered to procure the right number of those.

His gaze landed on the sofa. Grigg held up a finger and pulled his hostage with him toward one of the buckets on the counter. He reached into the first of the buckets and pulled out a coil of thin rope.

"I'll tie your wrists, and I'll even let you keep them in front of you. Because I'm a gentleman. Once that's secure, I'll toss the couch cushions down to the basement, and the boys can arrange them for your friend's bed. If you attack me, she dies. Understood?"

The chieftess chewed on her lip, then gave a slow nod. "Fine."

Grigg tugged her back with him toward the living area and gestured for her to sit in one of the wooden chairs. Miracle of miracles, she did it.

Grigg slid his hand from her upper arm to her wrist and tensed for any first blow she might throw. Headbutt, elbow to the face, full-on tackle—he'd expected her to try something. But she didn't. She only watched him intensely as he secured one wrist first, separately from the second to prevent her easily worming her way out, and then bound the two together.

He held up both hands defensively as if to say, *See? I only held on when I had to.* Grigg backed away slowly, keeping his gaze fixed on her, and called down through the trapdoor. "I'm tossing cushions down for you to make a bed for the girl. And an extra blanket. Make sure one goes over the cushions so she doesn't throw up on them if she keeps upchucking."

An assenting response came up from the basement, and Grigg plucked the cushions one after another off the sofa and threw them down the stairs to the basement, along with the blanket draped over the back of the couch.

Grigg turned back from the basement stairs and frowned at the chieftess. Seeing her sit there, calm yet resolute, peaceful yet determined, he realized that fire wasn't just her melder ability. She was flame itself—danger one minute, and tranquil dancing light the next.

When Grigg had been *her* hostage, he intentionally rattled her by taunting and teasing and being obnoxious. Now that she was *his* hostage, she kept quiet, offering him nothing but the blazing fire of an unquenchable spirit.

Nothing about her straight-back poise signaled that she'd given up. If anything, she looked more determined than ever, as if this was a normal occurrence in her life. Though, based on everything he'd heard about her, this was *not* a common occurrence.

Why wasn't she struggling more? Why wasn't she bargaining? A woman with her skill set and unquenchable spirit, and she planned to go along with him quietly?

He didn't buy it, and the incongruence made him nervous. If his taunting bothered her in the jungle, she'd made little indication of it. But now that the tables were turned, her silence shrouded her in more secrets than ever and fed a growing unease in Grigg. He may not have made an impact on her, but she made an impact on him.

It wasn't fair. What was it with this woman?

"What?"

Grigg jolted from his thoughts and blinked at her. He'd been staring. Again. He swallowed and glanced around the room. "I had planned on tying you to the couch, but there aren't great places to secure the ties in here, and now the couch doesn't have any cushions."

Her lips pressed together, as if disappointed by his novice preparations. "What if I'd brought ten warriors to back me up? Where would you have kept them all?"

Grigg shrugged. "I would've figured out something. Maybe I wouldn't care so much about offering cushions."

The chieftess scanned the room with an analytical gaze. "You're right, there's not much here. The biggest post is the table leg, and that moves. Did you just wake up one day and decide to kidnap a tribal chieftess?"

"Yes, but that day wasn't today."

Truth be told, he'd gotten the idea after Hamza died, when he'd had to reconfigure his plans to get the Heart of the Stars. It had taken time to lay the groundwork with new contacts and refresh his knowledge of Smŭrttata and the surrounding area. He hadn't been home in years and had avoided anything to do with it for the bulk of his life.

She laughed. Actually laughed. "Could have fooled me."

Fooling her had worked pretty well in the jungle. That's how he'd redirected her attention enough to free his feet. He didn't mention that.

She continued. "If we're both tied up and drugged with this magna you talk about, I don't see why you couldn't keep me where Lucia is."

"Because you're far more formidable than most of my hostages. The basement is out of the question."

The chieftess pulled back a hair, surprise flitting across her features. Not at his assessment, he didn't think. They both knew she was more skilled than most. Perhaps it was his willingness to say it out loud. She recovered and tried again. "Where are *you* sleeping?"

Grigg nodded to the closed door to his left, the one that shared a wall with the living area. "There's a bedroom in there."

She cocked her head. "You could be a gentleman and give me the bed."

He crossed his arms. "I'm not giving you the bed. You live in a jungle. You could probably sleep just fine on a pile of rocks. So could your friend."

He paused, then glanced at the bedroom door. He would *not* be giving her his bed. He deserved a good night's rest. But there *was* a place in the bedroom that afforded a decent way to secure restraints.

He gestured for her to stand, grabbed the rope between her wrists, and hauled her with him to the door. Grigg opened it and brought her inside.

The room was simple; a large four-post bed with a wooden canopy took up most of the modest space and was the first visible thing in the room, placed straight ahead from the door. A three-drawer dresser stood to the right. To the left, a writing desk and two large wooden chests lined the wall. Apart from the carved bedframe and canopy, exposed beams served as the only visually interesting part of the room. The walls were bare, and the floor was composed of unforgiving gray slate.

The chieftess took it all in at a glance. "For all the extravagance of the rooftop, you're living in relative squalor. Is that why you need whatever you're trying to steal? To keep up an exorbitant lifestyle?"

He ignored her and tugged her toward the bedpost at the foot of the bed. The posts were thick, nearly the size of his thigh, with light carvings running up and down their pillars and across the wooden canopy over top. Even the head and footboards were taste-fully carved, but still sturdy. If she stayed dosed on magna, the solid wood would keep her well secured.

On the other hand, if the magna ran out, she could set the bed on fire with him in it. She hadn't finished her glass of wine on the rooftop. He'd have to have her drink more magna before bed.

Grigg held her hands up to the post, slid them down as far as they would go before meeting the mattress, and gestured at the slate floor.

"How far to the ground can you get if your hands are tied here?"

She arched an eyebrow. "Not very. I wouldn't be able to lie down."

A voice in the back of his mind told him it didn't matter. So what if she couldn't lie down? She could sleep sitting up, with her head against the footboard. Again, she'd probably slept just fine against a tree trunk plenty of times in her jungle life, and the wood of the footboard was far smoother and more comfortable than rough bark would be.

Which is why Grigg hardly understood himself when he heard his next words spill out of his mouth. He gestured at the big trunk set against the wall. "What if we move the big trunk to the foot of the bed and you sleep on that? The rope for your hands will be shorter, so you won't be able to reach me to kill me, but you could lie down."

She glanced from the trunk to the slate floor and back at him. "Are you serious? That's not large enough to sleep on."

He assessed the trunk again. "Why not? You're petite."

She gave him a look that said, *Really?*

Okay, so she was probably right. It wasn't much room. But why had he offered it at all? Hadn't he heard himself thinking through how hostages didn't need to be comfortable to sleep at night? It wasn't even required that she sleep at all. He was a moron even to consider—

"Fine, you can sleep on the bed. But you have to drink a full glass of what I give you, and you have to stay on *this* end of the bed."

He was tying her hands to the bedpost before he could process what he'd said out loud. He really was a moron. What was wrong with him? Grigg secured her ties so she could pivot around the post, but her wrists were touching it at all times, giving her no leeway to move an inch in any direction.

The chieftess tugged on the ropes meaningfully and tossed him another sardonic look. "Where else would I go, exactly?"

He pointed a finger at her as if doing so would restore his dignity. "You're drinking the *full* glass of what I give you."

"Are you scared of me?" Her voice took on a lilting quality he'd never heard from her before, and he did a double take.

"Afraid of you murdering me in my sleep? Yes."

The corner of her lips tipped up, but she said nothing.

He frowned. "I'll have you know that was good wine you poured out on the rooftop. I'm getting you another glass with cheaper stuff. If you don't drink it all, Lucia loses a finger, and at that point I don't think she'll care whether she has cushions to sleep on or not."

With that, Grigg turned and fled from the room. No, not fled. He *marched*—assertively, with purpose. Yes, that was it.

He climbed the rope from the trapdoor to the roof and made a beeline for the box under the chair.

Maybe it wasn't what he thought, what he feared. Maybe she'd simply planned to steal the crossbow and some ammunition.

He dropped to his knees and slid the box out from under the chair. His hands trembled as they pushed open the lid. His stomach soured, and he rocked back on his heels as the smooth glistening surface of the golden egg shone up at him in the candlelight.

She'd found the egg.

Had she known he had it the whole time? Is that why she agreed to the meet? What did she know of it? Maybe she'd merely found it while searching the rooftop, assumed it was valuable, and—

He shook himself. The egg originated from the Nascosta. It came from here. Perhaps some old legend from the jungle had survived this long, and she knew of it that way. Was this why she'd really agreed to help him? Is this why she maintained such composure? Because she knew something he didn't? Because she wanted access to the egg?

A tremor rolled him, and he fell back, barely catching himself against the floor of the rooftop. Grigg slapped himself in the face as if to wake himself from a stupor. If this chieftess really did know about the egg, it was all the better that he had her in his grasp. He would need to keep her close, not just for this job, but until everything was done. He couldn't have her stealing the egg or interfering with anything until he'd gathered all three Hearts for Giovanna. He couldn't risk anyone damaging it.

Grigg used the cloth folded beneath the egg and picked it up, turning it slowly in his fingers. The two cracks that had been there that morning remained, but now one of the cracks had branched off from the main line in another direction.

For the first time in a long time, his heart stopped. Breath refused to come. Grigg's throat seemed to close, as if his body were shutting down in response to the fracturing egg. But isn't that precisely what was happening? And by the time it broke apart alto-gether, he would be dead.

Grigg shut the lid to the box, grabbed a fresh bottle of wine from the table, and the chieftess' discarded goblet. He would mix her drink, re-hide the egg, and make sure she never touched it. More than that, he would ensure she never knew he'd discovered her discovery. She had to believe she had the upper hand. And if her chasing the egg kept her cooperative, he could use that to his advantage.

He sucked in a pained breath and turned back to the trapdoor.

CHAPTER TEN

The man in the vest had shut the door on his way out, taking the lantern with him and sealing Adelina inside in the dark.

She'd been right before. She was sure of it. He *had* seen the box under the chair. He'd known what she found. And he was running now to get it.

Why else would he shut her in a room with the door closed? He would want to hear everything in a room with his hostage inside. Unless there was something *he* was doing that he didn't want her to see.

Adelina focused on her breathing to calm her racing heart. *Inhale, exhale, inhale, exhale.* What could she hear?

Faint motion through the floor from the basement or maybe coming up through the open trapdoor. The guards were shuffling around. A retching sound informed her the konnolan was still doing a number on Lucia, but she was alive, with no other sound of distress or injury.

Adelina should have asked the man in the vest how long it would take for the konnolan to get out of Lucia's system. On the other hand, she had no reason to believe whatever he told her.

Beyond the sounds from the basement, she heard nothing. No footsteps on the main floor. No movement—not the wind of the night air or the chorus of locusts and frogs she was accustomed to lulling her to sleep at night.

The room really was bare. Nothing on the walls, not even a tapestry. The slate floor felt cool against the thin soles of her leather footwear, with not even a rug to protect against its harshness. No windows.

She couldn't see the trunks against the wall anymore after he'd removed the lantern, but she remembered them being beyond her reach. The only thing relatively nearby in the room was the bed she was tied to and the three-drawer dresser against the other wall. But she'd been tied to the post closest to the center of the room, not the post closer to the dresser.

Adelina stretched as far as she could and struck a leg out toward the top drawer. Her foot swung uselessly in the air. She tried again, this time lying belly down on the bed and inching backward away from the bedpost as far as she could manage. She swung her toes out toward where the dresser should be.

Her toes brushed solid wood. *There.* If she could open one of the drawers, maybe she could find something to loosen her bonds. Another cord of rope, even a shirt, to work through the bindings of the rope and apply pressure to loosen the ties.

She swung her foot further, and her toes hit something round. The drawer pull. She tried to hook it with her toes, but her foot fell as it lost purchase. Adelina tried again, and on her third try, caught the edge of the drawer pull. She tugged the drawer. It jostled, but didn't move. She went for it once more, and this time the drawer shifted half an inch in her favor, but it wasn't enough to open the drawer. Adelina let her foot fall.

Maybe if she could work on the ropes between her hands, even if she didn't get free, she could get *just* enough leeway ...

Adelina scooted forward on the bed so that her elbows could bend again and reached for the tie winding itself around the end of her messy braid. How had she not thought of it before? Adelina yanked the tie loose from her hair, placed one end of the tie between her teeth, and fed the other end between the cords of the rope between her hands. But it wouldn't quite poke through to the other side. It wasn't stiff enough, and the ties were too tight.

She steeled herself for another attempt. This time she aimed not for the ties between her hands, but at one of the loops around her left wrist. *Success.* The tie slipped between, but she wouldn't be able to pull hard enough with her teeth.

Adelina kicked off her shoes and pulled her feet under her. Next, she planted one foot against the thick bedpost, trapping one end of the hair-tie twine against the bedpost and holding the other end firmly with her right hand. The thread wound through the loop securing her left wrist.

If she could apply enough pressure, she might be able to loosen the bonds enough for her arm to slip free. As long as she could wiggle back into it to keep the man in the vest from suspecting what she'd done, she could even wait till he was asleep in the middle of the night, search the house at her leisure, get Lucia, and go.

No matter what tools he had, she could cut a new deal with the egg as leverage. But she'd never let him actually have it. Again, she wondered if he really knew what it could do, what power it held—the power of the mage who cursed her. How could anyone who understood its power source align themselves with that power? He didn't have melder abilities. Did he think that by helping the mage, she would grant him powers of his own?

She shook off the thought and focused on her work. Adelina took a breath and shoved off the bedpost, pressing, pressing, pressing. The twine between her foot and her grip went taut. The end of the twine slipped a little between her fingers. Her mouth went dry. She couldn't lose it. Adelina paused to adjust her grip and tried again.

Something shifted. It was working. *As long as it didn't break.*

The door opened. She jumped. *Snap.* The twine broke against the sudden pressure, and the pieces of the twine fell to the slate floor. Her stomach dropped. *No.*

The man in the vest stepped inside, a satchel under his arm, with a lantern in one hand and a filled goblet in the other.

She couldn't believe it. She'd ruined her shot. Adelina dropped her foot from the bedpost and stuffed it under her so that one foot folded beneath her body and the other dangled off the edge of the bed as he approached.

Her mind still raced. Had the string broken in the middle, or off to one side? There was no way either end of it would be long enough to use again ... was there? Would he find the pieces that fell to the floor? The lantern was only so bright. If she could keep his attention away from the floor long enough, maybe she could ...

The man sidestepped away from her, opened one of the trunks, and placed the satchel inside. *The egg.* The satchel was about the right size. Was he holding the egg right now, or was he holding a dummy? Something to make her *think* he had the egg in here. Something to redirect her focus.

He closed the trunk, locked it, and came to stand in front of her. His gaze slowly raked over her messy dark hair, only half-contained in the remnants of her braid. Slowly, he took in her bare feet and shifted the lantern to look for her shoes. A moment later, the light of the lantern fell on her shoes and—curse of curses—on the scraps of twine on the slate tile floor.

Keeping himself out of reach, the man in the vest placed the toe of his shoe over the two pieces of twine and pulled them toward himself well beyond her range of movement. He crouched on the floor, set down the lantern, and picked up the pieces. He glanced up at her. "Your hair. That's what this is from, isn't it?" He pursed his lips. "Smart."

Adelina swallowed. He scanned the room again, and this time, his gaze fell on the drawer just slightly askew in the dresser. He turned back to her.

"I know some people are very hung up on precision in words. Did I need to clarify that attacking me was not the only thing that could lose your friend a finger … or worse?"

She shook her head. "I've not done anything against our agreement."

The words fell flat, but she couldn't think of anything better. From the look on the man's face, he wasn't impressed. He picked up the lantern and placed it out of reach on the floor, then crossed to the dresser and shoved his weight against it so that it scraped a full half a meter down the wall, where she could never hope to reach it.

"I would never have expected you to take this lightly. But I do expect you to be smart. I may have gotten your friend cushions …" His eyes grew cold, and his tone measured, but firm. "But don't mistake that kindness for softness."

Adelina balked at his threat. What would he do if pressed? Would he really kill Lucia? Considering he had the egg, he probably would.

The man took in a deep breath, and when he let it out, the tension that had built up in his body since discovering the twine and the shifted drawer melted away like wax. As if nothing unusual had occurred in the last five minutes. As though he were almost a different person entirely, completely at ease.

He stepped forward with a face so serene she nearly choked on the lie of it. His quietness was far more terrifying than a yell would have been. A yell would have told her she'd rattled him. A yell would have signified his loss of control.

He held nothing now but the goblet of wine in one hand. He lifted it up toward her mouth. "If you would be so kind."

She gritted her teeth. The goblet was too far from her tied hands to use them to drink. She'd have to accept his help to do what he asked, and he knew it.

Adelina bit back a retort and gave him a short, curt nod. He brought the goblet to her lips and tipped it up slowly, but did not remove it until she'd downed the full glass.

The man wiped an errant drop of red wine from her lips with a swipe of his thumb, then stepped to the side to set the goblet on top of the dresser.

"Don't do anything stupid. I'm going to check your hair for more thread. Sometimes, you people have elaborate hairstyles ... and all sorts of different ties and accessories in there."

You people. What an odd way to describe women.

She shifted away from him. "Do I look like the type to stuff baubles in my hair?"

He didn't meet her gaze as he reached to loosen her hair where it still wound about itself where the braid had been. "You look like the type of person I shouldn't be letting sleep on my bed. Remind me to rent a house with a dungeon in it next time."

"I'm still not convinced the basement isn't one. You haven't let me see it."

His hands ran whisper soft through her hair, his touch sending light tingles across her scalp as his fingers drew through her dark tresses piece by piece. Something in her gut flopped about, and she couldn't decide if she wanted the sensation to go away. But she *did* want *him* to go away.

The man's response came in just as sweet and gentle a tone as his touch had been: "And let those unpleasant thoughts motivate you to act more cooperatively."

She opened her mouth, then shut it again.

The man let the last section of hair fall, then froze. He brushed her hair behind her bare shoulder and stared. "How did I miss this?"

He'd said it more to himself than to her, half under his breath. She waited to see what he was talking about.

He set his jaw. A muscle in his neck twitched. He gestured at her arm. "What is that?"

Adelina craned her neck to stare down at her arm. "Do you mean my tattoo?" She shrugged. "It's just a tribal tattoo. All of the Guerrori have this."

He fell back a step as if he were a burn victim and she a cauldron of boiling water.

She quirked an eyebrow. "You know tattoos aren't contagious, right?"

He said nothing. And then he turned on his heel and left without a word.

This man had the golden egg that housed the power of the mage who cursed Adelina, but he was surprised and terrified by her tattoo. What was so odd about the marking?

None of it made sense. Neither did the fact that he acted so weird around her—that he'd been cold and threatening on the rooftop, but gentle with her hair. That he'd transitioned from powerful enemy to awkward man standing in his bedroom with a woman, as if he had no idea how to proceed in such a scenario.

When threatened, the powerful adversary returned until he slid away again into a soft persona built to set her at ease. But the awkwardness he'd had when they first entered the bedroom had seemed real—raw, unplanned, like he was embarrassed to have revealed a vulnerable part of himself.

If that were true, and she did unnerve him, it meant he would slip up. And if she was supposed to work with him to go to this event only days away, to do whatever she was supposed to do in his heist adventure, he'd have to untie her at some point.

The longer she waited, the more comfortable he would get, and the more opportunities she would have to make her move. Adelina curled onto the foot of the bed and lay her head on the edge of the mattress.

Sooner or later, he would make a mistake. And she would be there when he did.

CHAPTER ELEVEN

GRIGG

Grigg's head spun as he fled from his own bedroom for the second time in under an hour. He'd tried to talk himself down from the cascading worries bursting from the sight of her sitting on his chair on the rooftop, as if she were the queen of the world—with the box beneath her chair.

Correction. Beneath *his* chair. Just because she *looked* like she owned the thing didn't mean she did.

He'd tried to tell himself she was taking the crossbow bolts, but that hadn't been true. He'd tried to tell himself that, when she stumbled across the golden egg, it had been a legitimate stumble—that she'd seen something unique that looked valuable and wanted to hold on to it. If the egg had been solid gold all the way through, it would have been worth a pretty penny. Enough to pay for extravagant new weapon systems or other supplies for the Guerrori.

But the chieftess didn't strike him as a petty thief. She seemed more measured and specific than roving for the odd treasure. And why had she agreed so readily to his deal? Yes, he had blackmail over her head, but she wasn't the giving-in type.

And now, after seeing the tattoo on her shoulder, the tattoo of a swan ...

He'd known the Black Swan Mage had roots in Smŭrttata, just as his ancestors did. Sergei, the man Giovanna had fallen in love with over six hundred years ago, had been from here too.

Had Giovanna been Guerrori? Was the tribe even old enough for her to have been a part of it?

Smŭrttata had been more built up back then. And Sergei Frizzletwerf, the man who'd so destroyed Giovanna's trust in men, had owned most of it. Wildly successful and extravagantly wealthy, he'd captured her heart before things went south. Of course, the story was six hundred years old now, and certain details were unclear. Like whether Sergei ever loved her in return.

Grigg shut the door behind him and lurched forward on unsteady feet. His thoughts hardly formed words—save for one, over and over, reverberating through his skull:

Swan. Swan. Swan.

It couldn't be a coincidence. If the chieftess knew something about the egg, she was far more dangerous than he had given her credit for. Was she working for the Black Swan Mage? Was Giovanna in contact with her as well? Was that why the chieftess had agreed to his deal? Perhaps she only *wanted* him to think he was in charge, while *she* held all the cards.

He wondered absently if the fact that Sergei and Giovanna were both from this area was why two of the three Hearts he had to steal were here. The Heart of the Sea had been a horrendous mission that took many lives in the effort to gain it, but he'd done it. And he'd managed to bring the massive statue of the siren here, holding it in a safe place along the river.

Did she know about the Heart of the Sea? Did she want the Heart of the Stars for herself?

Grigg ripped off his vest and shrugged out of his shirt, tossing the clothing over the couch as he half-ran to the light of the lantern on the table to examine the mark on his chest. When had the new crack on the egg appeared? Did it coincide with the expansion of the black mark on his flesh?

He ran a hand over the blackened place on his chest, where dark long-reaching fingers spread across his skin in hungry cracks. A deep-seated ache dwelled there, just beneath the skin. The pain of it swelled like a wave about to break as he traced the splintering lines of the growing dark.

There was no water, but he was drowning. There was no quicksand, but he was sinking. And the black veins across his chest were spreading.

He traced a trembling finger over a black vein-like line working its way across his pectoral muscle. It was reaching up toward his shoulder, still hidden by tunics, but definitely longer than it had been.

No man in his line had experienced the full weight of the curse since Sergei, the ancestor Giovanna had fallen in love with. When the four elemental melders had destroyed magic six hundred years ago—or *thought* they had destroyed magic—the effects of the curse had been muted.

But magic had returned in full force seven years ago, and with it the pain in his chest had grown worse with each passing year. It could only be alleviated by love, but if a woman were stupid enough to love him, she would die.

Grigg raked a hand through his hair and spun away from the table, grateful for the shadows hiding his condition. He thought of the raw fear he'd seen just for a moment in the chieftess' eyes before rage had taken hold of her as he threw her on the table. He'd hurt her, and she'd been afraid of him, whether or not she wanted to admit it.

What would it be like to be a man free to make his own name, not slave to the reputation of another's misdeeds? To be free to live the simplistic life of an honest man, rather than forced to steal names, personas, and riches just to survive?

You'll never earn the success you seek.

Anyone who falls in love with you will die.

That first day after magic returned full strength in the world, when those thousands upon thousands with once-dormant melder blood were waking to new powers, Grigg had found himself face to face in a nightmare with Giovanna. That was the first time she'd appeared to him. She'd come intermittently over the years, slowly increasing since then. Now, it was almost nightly.

Grigg clenched his fists and snatched the tunic off the back of the couch. He tossed it on, covering the mark on his chest, and paced the floor of the small abode. He had to get the upper hand over Giovanna. Once he did what she wanted, and she lifted the curse, he had to find a way to destroy her.

He paced. He sat. He paced some more. He dropped his head in his hands. Grigg wasn't sure how long he alternated between these, but eventually fatigue tugged at his mind and dragged at his body. He would not get *more* creative by depriving himself of sleep night after night.

So, finally, he slipped off his boots and set them neatly to one side of the bedroom door. At last, he crept into the bedroom where his hostage lay: the woman with the swan tattoo.

She looked peaceful lying there, eyes closed, breath deep. What types of dreams did *she* have? Maybe one day, after the curse was lifted, his only dreams would be those dictated by the sort of day he had, or whether he'd accidentally eaten undercooked food.

Grigg tiptoed around the side of the bed, blew out the lantern on the dresser, and eased his weight onto the mattress on the furthest side away from the woman.

Two large pillows leaned against the headboard, with a third decorative pillow centered over them. He took the decorative pillow and one of the regular ones and set them along the bed at the chieftess' back as a barrier between the two of them.

He started to lie down, then hesitated, glancing at her bare arms and shoulders, her bronze waist and long legs, open to the cool night air. Surely, even in the jungle they had blankets.

Grigg sighed and got up, crossed to the dresser, and pulled open the dresser drawer she'd tried to open on her own. He retrieved a blanket, shook it out from its neat folding, and eased it over her sleeping form.

It was good to start a cooperative relationship. They'd have to work together, after all, no matter what she might know about the egg. And if he wanted her to open up, he'd have to show some good faith.

That's why he'd done it. And that's why he'd let her on the bed to begin with. It was strategic.

At least, that's what he continued to tell himself, as he climbed into bed and slipped under the covers.

He lay down on the single remaining pillow and stretched his legs out. Or tried to. Every time he began to stretch out properly, his feet bumped into the pillow barrier he'd set up between him and her. He flopped this way and that before finally landing on an awkward diagonal position with his feet separated from hers only by the pillow wall, and his head in the opposite corner of the bed.

Tomorrow, they would start training. They didn't have much time, and he needed to be on his game. Which meant he needed sleep.

But sleep was the most terrifying part of his day. He might be a walking nightmare for others, but *his* worst nightmares came at night.

When he finally did manage to drift off, his nightmares awoke just as he'd feared, and he was standing again by that cursed black lake with its cursed mage mistress presiding over it.

The black swan swooped down over the glassy surface of the lake, its wingtip grazing the surface just enough to leave tiny cascading ripples in its wake. The graceful lines of its long curved neck perfectly mimicked the chieftess' tattoo.

A moment later, the black swan transformed before him into the ageless woman Giovanna—and for the first time in seven years, he was grateful to see her human rather than as a swan.

He didn't need any more reminders of the connection he'd discovered.

Giovanna appeared in the same animal-hide attire as always, with the red embroidered collar, beaded jewelry, feather earrings, her gray-streaked, dark braid draped over it all. The similarities between her appearance and the cultural clothing of the Guerrori warriors were impossible to miss, but were they simply from similar tribes?

He grimaced. Every time he'd tried to keep himself from believing the worst lately, he'd been wrong.

Giovanna took five steps forward from the lake until she stood before him, as always.

This time, it was Grigg who spoke first. "Did you ever love Sergei?"

Something in her eyes pooled in a depth of emotion she'd guarded for hundreds of years, yet never quite resolved. Her expression sprung back to stony flint, then dropped into a neutral state devoid of any feeling at all. "If I had not loved him, we would not be here together."

Grigg shook his head. "I don't think that's true. If you'd truly loved him, you wouldn't have wanted him to die a torturous death. You wouldn't have punished innocent people in the name of love. Sergei may have lied to you—broken your trust—but it's you who've lied most. You've become every bit the person you hated in Sergei, even more so."

She stared back at him so evenly, his breath hitched. She was going to reach into his chest, rip his heart out, and crush it in her hands. She'd done it before. His actual heart, ripped free of his ribcage, and she'd begun to squeeze. He'd fallen to his knees, screaming in pain, before she shoved the vital organ back in his chest—all without breaking a sweat, without showing an iota of emotion. His heart hammered within him even now, as if remembering the naked experience.

"I never said I still loved him." She lifted her chin just a hair. "I am not the person you need to be concerned about. You've retrieved only one of the three Hearts. I've been more than generous with your timeline, but it's coming to a close. Your time is running out, and who are you to judge me? Surely, you remember Sofia Isakov."

Grigg hadn't spoken her name aloud since he was ten years old, when he worked as an apprentice for Sofia's father. When he'd still hoped—hoped he could live an honest life, believed he could learn a profession and live like everyone else in the world. When he'd thought the curse was a legend, an excuse for his father to be absent and worthless at the beginning of his life. After all, the only person who'd loved Grigglor as a child had been his mother, and if the legend was real, she should've been dead before he gained memories. As it was, she hadn't died until Grigglor was five.

Sofia had been the first girl Grigglor ever truly loved. He'd spent time with her every spare minute, sneaking up to her bedroom window after lights out, just to talk for hours from the tree outside her window. He'd danced with her in the barn and left notes on her pillow for when she woke before he went about his duties. But then she'd fallen ill, and orphan Grigglor began to understand that the mark on his chest was real, and the curse was real as well.

Grigg's father, Aleksander, had had a meaningless hookup that resulted in pregnancy with Grigglor, and Grigglor experienced genuine love from his mother for several years before his father decided to do the noble thing and be around for his son. Grigglor's mother lived while Aleksander didn't love her. But when Aleksander reconnected with his son, he also bonded with Grigglor's mother, and the two fell in love. Both started to fall sick.

Because Grigglor's father didn't fall in love with his mother until after he was born, his mother lived long enough for Grigglor to have those memories—beautiful memories that burned when he thought about them. Yet another curse to carry, and yet he wouldn't give them up for all the world.

He'd once thought his mother surviving until Grigglor was five was evidence the curse was fake, and the dark spot over his heart was an unrelated birthmark oddity. But after Sofia, he realized the truth. His mother had lived because she never really loved Aleksander, either. He'd been as meaningless to her as she had been to him. Until finally he wooed and won her.

And Grigglor was the one to lose.

His tongue stuck to the roof of his mouth. He swallowed. "I left Sofia because I had to. Because you made me."

Giovanna clucked her tongue. "Now, now, don't be like that. I didn't *make* you do anything. You knew the consequences of falling in love. You knew the consequences of making a girl love you."

His hands clenched into fists. He took a breath. "I abandoned her when she needed me most. If I'd stayed, she would've died."

"She realized you weren't worth loving. That's what kept her alive. I did her a favor. She'll carry that lesson about men with her forever, unlike your other trysts."

Giovanna's eyes widened, and her mouth twisted into a cruel smile. "It felt good, didn't it, when they loved you? It eased the ache."

She placed a firm hand over his heart, and he flinched away. Her reptilian smile deepened. "If magic had not been bound, the girl would've died without hope of recovery. The other women who have loved you, Inaya, Desislava, Rositsa. So many of them were not as wise as Sofia. So stupid. So unfortunate. All dead, and you didn't even give them the courtesy of loving them in return. If anyone falls in love with you now, they will die so much faster. The pain will be just as severe, only compressed into a shorter period of time."

It was all Grigg could do to keep his hands balled into fists at his sides. His breath was ragged, his chest heaving. *Get a hold of yourself, Grigg.*

He let out a long breath and forced his muscles to relax. "Mistakes of a younger man. I swore ten years ago not to make any woman fall in love with me. I pull a lot of cons, but that's no longer one of them."

"Is that so? Inaya was only six years ago."

"Yes, but Inaya was insane. I did everything I could to push her away. She brought that on herself. It wasn't my doing."

She laughed, a laugh as lilting as glass shards. "Oh, look at you. The noble, principled knight."

The image of the chieftess' tattoo flashed back to mind. How closely were the two women connected? What could he learn if he pressed?

Grigg pursed his lips. "I've tried not to kill anyone that didn't deserve to die. But with the amount of pressure you've put on me, perhaps I'll break my oath. I met a woman just last evening that I've forced to work with me. I'll start with her."

Giovanna laughed. Or attempted to imitate laughter, anyway. How likely was it that Giovanna experienced joy? "If she's intelligent, she won't fall for you. If she's stupid, it is better she dies than lives a life loving you."

Grigg tensed reflexively at the slap of her words. He'd gotten used to them, but that didn't mean they had no sting. He crossed his arms. "And here I thought you considered yourself a champion of women. If she falls in love with me and she dies, her blood will be on *your* head, not mine."

"Games will not buy you time, Grigglor."

Grigg recoiled from her use of his real name. He typically imagined he would prefer the mage call him Grigglor than Sergei, if only to show she *did* know he was distinct from his ancestor. But hearing it on her lips now, he took it all back.

Giovanna smiled up at him, and his stomach shredded like cheese through a grater. "Magic is back, and your father's curse is on the clock. Time is running out. When the golden egg breaks apart, I will be free, and I will take the rest of your life force as penance for your failures. The punishment of your line will be complete."

She ran a hand through his hair. He locked his knees and tensed his body to keep from jerking away from her touch as she spoke.

"The curse was never meant to live this long, because your line was never meant to survive this long. This is not my fault. Take it up with those four rebels that tried to kill magic all those years ago. Morons, all of them. Magic so central to the fabric of the world cannot be removed without destroying all life. But when the magic was bound, so was the power of the curse. Now that it's back and my power is returning, you don't have long. Do what I tell you, or you won't make it to your next birthday."

Grigg tilted his head. "How do you know? Maybe my birthday is next month."

She smiled again. "You might not see the end of the month."

Grigg shrugged. "I hate birthdays anyway."

"Do you like being alive?"

"I'm not convinced I do."

"Die then, without an heir, driving your family line to obscurity like your father was meant to."

The veins across his heart pulsed as if driven by a madman charioteer. His chest constricted, his life force held in her vengeful hands, the black mark of his chest spreading outward to cover more and more of his skin.

"You mean my father's father's father's ... well, however many there have been in the last six hundred years? Because my father was Aleksander, not Sergei. And Sergei was not Aleksander's father, either."

Giovanna shook her head, dismissing him with a wave as if tired of his nonsense. "I told your father there would be consequences. Meet my demands, or blood will be spilled. Your father's blood. Sergei's blood. The blood of a Frizzletwerf."

Grigg pursed his lips. "Wasn't a name like Frizzletwerf enough of a curse?"

Giovanna arched an eyebrow. "*I* didn't name your father. That wasn't part of the curse."

"Sure, but I didn't name myself either. What did I do as a newborn to deserve such a surname?"

She ignored him in favor of more favorable topics. "If the girl you found falls in love with you, she dies."

Grigg paused. This was it. This was his chance to press against the boundaries. To test her.

His heart burned in the empty chasm of his chest, begging him not to do it. Begging him not to do anything that might make her rip it from its mooring in his chest. He forged ahead before he lost his resolve.

"This one wears a swan emblem. Flames along the wingtip. Arrows dripping down from the swan. She knows something about the egg. She's from the same place you're from."

Five blinks in quick succession. Victory flooded Grigg's every vein. Giovanna reached toward her face, then adjusted her braid instead, fiddling with the ends before tossing it over her shoulder. She was nervous. Her expression was even, neutral, unconcerned, but she'd already given herself away.

Grigg stepped forward. "Maybe after all this time of you killing my family, I finally have the chance to take out one of yours."

Giovanna froze. The six hundred and sixty-something-year-old mage was *nervous*. Because of him. Apparently, not even high-powered ageless individuals could control their blink rate.

The air in Grigg's mouth tasted like ash. What would she do with her stress? But there, in that fraction of a second, he knew he had her. He'd been right about a connection.

Giovanna's shock melted from her features, but it was too late. "It's a tribal marker." The same words the chieftess had used to describe it. Giovanna dismissed him with a wave of her hand. "There are thousands of us. I don't care for the girl."

Grigg flashed a debonair smile. "Then maybe I'll enjoy pretending to fall in love. One last time."

CHAPTER TWELVE

Morning came without wind, without songbirds, without Lucia joining her for a morning hunt, or Umbra offering to skin the game. It came without horses. It came without fires. It came without her women practicing sparring, building new shelters, or weaving new baskets.

Pale gray light snuck in through the crack under the bedroom door. The day was cooler than the previous one had been, and she found herself wishing she'd brought heavier garments. The animal skin wrapping her chest and up over one shoulder, and from her waist halfway down one thigh on one side and reaching down to the knee on the other, wasn't quite enough for the chill in the air.

Adelina moved to sit up and toppled off the edge of the bed with a harsh thump. Her bare knees collided with the hard slate as her body fell, but her wrists were still caught at the bedpost over her head. A light blanket tangled around her calves. She had no memory of a blanket. The man in the vest must have covered her with a blanket after she'd fallen asleep.

Another note of oddity about the man. Hostage taker, or gentleman? Definitely the former. Any kindness he offered served an angle. Nothing else made sense.

The door creaked open, and Adelina lurched to her feet. The man in the vest stood in the doorway, this time sporting a sage-green vest with polished gold buttons over his trademark white shirt rolled to the elbows, showing off the form of his arms. His brown hair was neat, with a vague tussled look about the long locks in the front that fell over his forehead on one side. Neatly trimmed facial hair shaded his face beneath high cheekbones. His blue eyes widened to find her tangled on the floor in the blanket, struggling to rise from where she'd been on the floor.

"If you wanted to sleep on the floor so badly, you could have just asked."

She stifled a grimace and lifted her chin. "The mattress is more suitable. Thank you."

He spread his hands. "As you wish." The man gave a mock little bow, and when he came back up, a goblet of wine was in his hand. How had he done that? She was almost certain it hadn't been there before.

"I'd like to untie you for breakfast, but before I do"—he lifted the goblet in her direction as if in a toast—"I'd like assurances you won't burn me to a crisp."

She rolled her eyes. "We made a deal, and you have Lucia. Where is she, by the way? I'll be needing my own assurances."

"She's in the basement, where she'll be every time you ask this question, until our business is complete. Last I checked, she was asleep. You can yell and wake her up or let her sleep off the rest of the effects of the konnolan from last night. Have breakfast with me, and get your proof of life when she wakes. She'll be treated to the same morning meal as we are, but she won't be eating with us."

He leaned lazily against the doorframe, swirling the wine in the goblet as he watched her. No sign of hesitation, no evidence of deception that she could find. Was his relaxed manner because he felt in control, or because he was telling the truth? Maybe he was so practiced a liar that he was comfortable with all untruths on his tongue. Regardless, she'd made a deal. And Lucia was still in the basement, and the man in the vest still had the golden egg.

She gave a nod. "Hand it to me."

He stepped forward and handed her the goblet, allowing her to manage the drink herself by standing close to the bedpost where her wrists could reach her mouth. She downed the drink and held up the goblet. He took it, set it aside on the dresser, and withdrew a knife from his pocket.

"You still promise not to kill me, right?"

She shrugged. "For now."

"Good, because we have a busy day. Today, you learn the art of the lift."

"The lift?"

He worked the knife between the cords binding her wrists and began to saw through the fibers. "Yes. By the time I'm done with you, you'll be an excellent pickpocket and maybe even a decent grifter."

"The thing you want so badly is going to be in someone's pocket?"

The knife tugged free, and the ropes fell away. She rubbed her wrists. He turned and led her out of the bedroom into the living room, turning his head to answer over his shoulder. "I never said that. But you will be using the skills I give you. Details later."

He rubbed his hands together and walked to the kitchen. After pulling out a chair for her, he crossed to the opposite side of the table and took a seat where two plates stacked with fruit, sliced meat, and bread awaited them. Adelina's mouth watered. Had she had dinner last night? No, she didn't think she had.

She sat and waited for him to take the first bite. He dug in unconcerned, stacking the meat on the bread and chomping into it with vigor. Adelina knew he must need her alive, but somehow it still made her feel better that he'd gone first. Slowly, she followed suit, rolling the meat in her fingers and eating it first, then the bread, then the fruit. It was weird eating meat killed by someone she didn't know.

The man in the vest took another bite of bread, finished it, and dusted his hands on a napkin. He glanced up at her. "So far, I've been calling you *Scary Jungle Woman* in my head. It's just too clunky a name. What should I call you?"

Wasn't he the captor and she the hostage in this scenario? Still, no harm in encouraging a little wariness on his part. She pressed her lips together. "Scary Jungle Woman is appropriate."

He laughed. "That's hardly fair unless you have a similar name for me."

She popped a grape into her mouth.

His jaw dropped. "Baron's backside. You have one, don't you? What have you been calling me?"

She shrugged. "The man in the vest. Vest man. Vest." Adelina nodded toward the sage-green number over his shirt. "You have an obsession."

He ran a hand over the fine cloth of the tailored vest of the day and grinned. "There are worse accusations than being well dressed."

Adelina stiffened. Accurate ones, too. Like trespassing, assault, no concern for violence against others, hostage taking ...

The man winced. "Gold and gumption, I deserve that."

"Deserve what?"

"Whatever you're thinking. I'm sure it's not nice, but I probably do deserve it. Still, I think it would be much easier if we used a name for each other instead of an entire phrase. What do you say?"

Adelina hesitated. There were so few things she felt in control of in this moment. Part of her wanted to withhold her name just for the sake of holding back something that he wanted. But she was playing the long game, and he could get her name from anyone. It's not like she was a low-profile person in the area. She popped another grape into her mouth, relishing the sweet juice before answering. "Adelina."

He smiled. Had he known her name already? Had this been another test? The man dipped his head. "It's a pleasure, Adelina. You can call me Grigg."

He tensed for just a second after he said the name, as if suddenly unsure of himself. He hadn't said that *was* his name. He'd only said that's what she could *call* him.

Adelina cocked her head. "Is that your name?"

The man who'd told her to call him Grigg shrugged. "I've had lots of names. This is one of them."

Then why was he being weird about it? She folded her hands in her lap. "All right then, Grigg. Why do I need to be a pickpocket? What are we stealing?"

Grigg took a sip of water and leaned forward on the table. "We're going to the Caruso mansion, where I will be stealing a necklace worth more than three kingdoms. You will be strategically placing several objects around the room, as well as drawing attention to keep the Carusos busy. I need a distraction, and I can't think of a better one than you."

Curling wisps of dread worked their way through every fiber of her body. Sure, there was danger in providing a distraction for her most dangerous adversaries, but it was another phrase that caught her attention.

A necklace worth more than three kingdoms.

The man in the vest wasn't just here for the egg, and he wasn't here for money. He was here for the Heart of the Stars. Rumor had it the Carusos were in possession of the magical necklace of old, one of a set of three Hearts of various types. But rumor also had it that the Heart of the Stars was a key, not a necklace, and that a dragon had snatched it away hundreds of years ago. So she didn't put too much stock in the rumors. They were only hearsay, after all—with little believable substance.

The Guerrori tribe's primary purpose was to protect the Heart of the Mountain, but part of the Guerrori's mission since the inception of the tribe had also been to protect any of the three Hearts they could. Although what they did, exactly, remained a bit of a mystery. She knew more about the Heart of the Mountain and the skein of magic running through the ground from it. But little information had been passed down about what the magic could be used for.

Grigg smiled at her again, his gaze lingering in a way that made her squirm in her chair. After a moment, he seemed to shake himself and then gestured toward the living room. Grigg took her empty plate, stacked it on his, and placed them neatly on the counter before sweeping into the adjoining room. He pulled a crate off the stack against the wall, opened it, and retrieved what looked like a scarecrow that fit atop a stand. But with bells hanging from a well-to-do jacket, this scarecrow was dressed more for a fancy dinner than a farmer's field. The entire ensemble rang as he arranged it, then settled into silence, standing alone in front of the sofa.

Next, Grigg reached into the crate and pulled out a series of folded papers in squares, plus several coins. Last, he retrieved six small glass vials of powder and three potted plants and set them on the wooden chair to one side.

"This is our task for today." He tossed a coin in the air, caught it, and dropped it into the pocket of the scarecrow. "Get it out without alerting our friend here."

Adelina eyed the scarecrow, with its blank stuffed-linen face topped with a brimmed hat.

What does he want with the Heart of the Stars?

She stepped toward the scarecrow and slipped her hand toward the pocket.

Where was the golden egg?

She'd barely even touched the jacket before the bells chimed.

Grigg leaned on the arm of the sofa, observing her progress.

"The heart of this exercise is nuance. Less is more. Slow is smooth, and smooth is fast. Take your time."

Adelina pressed her lips together and tried again. This time she got to the first knuckle of her finger, but the jacket still rang alarm bells at her touch. She tried five more times with the same result before Grigg stopped her.

"Nuance is nothing without technique." He stepped up to the scarecrow, and she stepped back to give him room. He lifted his hand and pinched his thumb and index finger, the same fingers she'd been using, to emphasize which two he was utilizing before reaching for the jacket again. The bells rang. He lifted his hand and tapped his thumb and index finger together again.

"These are the two fingers everyone tries to use, but look how my hand is forced to take up more room by using these two. The thumb is clunky and too short compared to the index finger, forcing a full circle to let the fingers meet."

He held up his hand again, this time lifting only the index and middle finger of his hand. "These two are neighbors, similar height —subtle. The thumb can now be tucked in close to the hand at any angle."

Grigg dropped his hand into the pocket. He dropped just those two fingers into the pocket, and when he withdrew it, the coin sparkled between his fingers. The bells never made a sound. He repeated the motion to drop the coin back in and retrieved it again using his middle and ring fingers instead.

"These two can also be used. You may find you have a preference." He replaced the coin for her practice and gestured to the dummy. "Try again."

Adelina sucked in a breath and bent all her focus on stillness and intuition. Her hand reached further into the pocket this time, using the technique Grigg described, before the bells rang. But they did ring, and before she found the coin inside the pocket.

They worked for an hour before she made her first successful lift. A thrill ran through her at her victory. She stared at the coin between her fingers. She'd done it, and the bells were none the wiser.

He clapped his hands. "Well done, Adelina. Now do it again. Fifty times. But first ..." He sidestepped five steps over toward the basement hatch and opened the top. Her heart jumped in her chest. She took half a step forward, then stopped.

Lucia.

Grigg called down to the guards. "Is the girl awake?"

A gruff voice floated back to them. "Affirmative."

"Excellent. Lucia, Adelina has been practicing to set you free. You'll be with us for only three days, and then you will be returned to the jungle to attempt to exact your revenge or whatever else you'd like to do. Please say something so she knows you're alive, and she and I can continue working together."

Adelina held her breath. She wasn't sure what she was expecting. But when the familiar voice came up from the floor, it felt like storm clouds finally shifting to let the light in.

"Adelina? Are you all right?"

Adelina swallowed and lifted her voice to call back to her friend. "I'm fine, you?"

"I ... I can't feel the wind."

Her stomach twisted. "Yes, I know. He's mixed something into our drinks. It's temporary."

Grigg held up a hand to Adelina and turned back to the hole. "Lucia, we have a deal up here. If Adelina doesn't attack me, you get to keep all your fingers. I'm offering the same deal to you. Adelina does need fingers for our work together, but she doesn't need all of them. Please control yourself so we can have as pleasant an experience together as possible, and we'll all be on our way quicker than you can say Dead Man's Folly. Capiche?"

He didn't wait for an answer. "Boris, come make yourselves plates. We've got a feast up here, and I'd hate for it to go to waste."

Boris, one of the two guards Grigg had in the basement, came up the creaking stairs a moment later. He assembled three plates of the food laid out on the counter and disappeared with them back down into the basement.

As soon as this was done, Grigg closed the hatch to the basement and turned back to Adelina. "Now, back to work. I assume your heart rate is up, but that's fine. You'll need to be effective in high-stress situations as well. Do it again, until you can do it ten times in a row without jingling the bells."

Adelina steeled herself. *Be a good student. Keep him comfortable. Keep an eye out for the egg. He'll slip up eventually.*

He had no reason to hurt Lucia while she cooperated.

Adelina nodded and stepped toward the jacketed scarecrow again. "How did you learn all this anyway?"

Grigg strode back to the kitchen and poured two glasses of wine from the counter. It was the first time he'd turned his back on her since cutting her hands free. That was progress already, wasn't it?

He turned back toward her and approached to watch her progress. "I practically rappelled out of my mother's womb with a lock-pick set."

The bells rang. Adelina withdrew her hand and tried again. She arched an eyebrow at Grigg. "That's gross. Didn't the lock picks cut her up from the inside?"

Adelina retrieved the coin. Grigg handed her one of the glasses of wine and arranged his face in mock sorrow to respond. "It was tragic. She really locked down my father when she picked him. Opened a lot of new doors for her. Her loss really did a number on my father."

Adelina blinked. Her lips twitched. She didn't know whether to laugh at his awful puns or stare.

He sank into the couch cushion, laid his arm across the back, and took another sip of wine, a twinkle in his eye. "She stole his diary when they were dating. Some people say it isn't manly for a man to have a journal, but he kept one diligently for years. His thoughts were with her when she died."

Adelina snorted wine out of her nose. She caught herself too late and wiped her face with the back of her hand. "Your first ones were better."

He pulled back as if affronted. "I disagree. The second one has more nuance."

Adelina shook her head and set the glass down to return to the scarecrow. She reached for the jacket. *Ding, ding.* Adelina cursed. "Viper's breath. Why can't we just use fire or some other type of distraction?"

"Because we can't be well-rounded individuals if we only rely on our current skill set. You can't use fire for everything, Adelina, and you won't always be backed up by fifty of your closest warrior friends."

He took yet another sip of wine. "The room will be crowded, and you are already a person of interest. Announcing your location with fire rates pretty low on the subtlety scale. It's okay if people look at you as long as we tell them where to look. But before we get to that, we practice this. The basic lift. Go again."

"What if I get caught pickpocketing?"

"Well, you'll be in the Caruso mansion, and they think you broke the treaty."

"Which we didn't."

"Be that as it may, multiple of their men are dead. It'll take some restraint for them not to kill you on sight. Frederico wants to marry you for a merger in a power play, and his father would rather make a poor-faith deal or remove you altogether. If you get caught pickpocketing in their house, I imagine the debate will be over. The only remaining question will be whether you die quickly or slowly."

"You're not making this sound very motivating, Vest Man."

"Really? I assumed you wanted to live. You only die if you get caught." He nodded at the scarecrow. "Again."

They worked all morning. As much as she hated to admit it, Grigg was an excellent teacher. He showed her how to angle her hand, why this footing or that footing was best, and how to find the mark inside the pocket quickly without sounding the bells. She wasn't nearly as practiced as he was after several hours, but she'd gotten a decent feel for it. He applauded her efforts and let her know she was doing well.

Over lunch, he surprised her with a new question. "How good are you with that bow of yours?"

Adelina stopped mid-chew and looked up at him. Was he suggesting she carry a weapon into the Caruso mansion? Did he trust her with instruments of death one day after capturing her? She lifted her chin. "I could beat you shooting with my feet."

He laughed. "I'd love to see it. Unfortunately, I'm not much of an archer myself, so that may very well be true. After dinner tonight, I'll let you show me just how good you are."

This was by far the strangest thing he'd said to her to date, and he'd said some pretty odd things. But offering her a chance to hold her preferred weapon, in the same room as him, with the opportunity to put an arrow in his heart? That was something she couldn't make sense of.

It was curious. As a teacher, he was firm, challenging, but encouraging. As a captor, he threatened to kill Lucia or chop off her fingers one by one. And yet he'd covered Adelina with a blanket while she slept. Who was this man?

The cursed thought came to her again more than once throughout the morning: *Make him fall in love with you. He'll get sick. He'll get weak. He'll be easy to overpower.*

But as much as she tried to muster a familiar air around him, the best she could manage was a moderately friendly dynamic where they talked, and he taught, and she listened and learned. She was a quick study, and he seemed impressed by her efforts, but as soon as she achieved one milestone, he pushed her for the next, reminding her of her imminent death in the Caruso house should she miss the mark.

Afternoon wore on into evening. Dinner came and went, and

the light faded from the windows until they were forced to light lanterns to continue their work.

"You've gotten smoother. Now, you need to be able to do it to me while I'm watching you."

"Is that how you did what you did in the jungle?"

"Excellent catch. Yes. I was spinning the leaf and spewing nonsense. You watched the leaf, and you watched my face, and you listened to my words, but you didn't see my second hand getting the vials out from the compartment in my shoe. You saw what I wanted you to see. You paid attention to what I wanted you to pay attention to. So ..."

Grigg crossed to the scarecrow, took the jacket off the dummy, and slipped into it like a second skin. A roguish smile spread across his face. "Distract me."

Adelina could almost feel the color draining from her face. "And how do you suggest I do that?"

"Use your imagination."

"If we wait for the magna to wear off, and I use fireballs. People tend to watch those pretty closely."

Grigg groaned. "Scratch that. Do *not* use your imagination. Your imagination is abysmal." He shrugged out of the jacket, and the next second, he was close—too close. Grigg lifted her right wrist and slipped the sleeve of the jacket over it, then held it up for her to put her other arm through the opposite sleeve.

"You're not charging in with a bludgeon, Adelina. You are *directing* with a gentle hand. Let them think *they* have charge of where their eyes roam, while all the while it is *you* encouraging their focus in one direction ... or another."

He tugged the jacket closed in the front and lifted a hand. Light as feathers, he trailed his hand around to the nape of her neck and brought her hair out from under the jacket, arranging it over her shoulder and stepping back slowly, letting her dark brown tresses fall bit by bit from his fingers until at last he released the final lock of hair.

Adelina swallowed hard, as if the action could ward off the warm tingle spreading across her scalp and down her body at his caress. This version of him was the most infuriating—the one that existed between the teasing and taunting and threats. The one where his eyes turned into deep pools of ocean blue, soft and open, rich as plush carpet, yet for a moment so vulnerable she imagined them transparent as gossamer. A window to a deeply human soul beneath a casually perilous exterior.

But he was a con man, and she was his mark. And when the moment expired, the softness would be gone, conflated by laughing eyes or a tense, threatening frame with a face of flint.

She noticed too late that she'd parted her lips as she took him in, and that he was watching her like a hawk. The sharp watchfulness was back. The tenderness nearly extinguished, if not completely.

Grigg gestured at her pocket. "Check it."

She did, and her fingers froze around the solid circle of a coin.

The edge of his mouth quirked up in a ghost of a modest smile. "The other side, too."

Adelina slipped her hand into the other pocket. When she withdrew it, a square folded paper sat in her palm. "How did you ...?"

But she knew how he'd done it. He'd had plenty of time, touching her arm, her shoulder, anywhere except her pockets. Helping her into her jacket, arranging her hair, tugging the jacket toward the front, so that even when she'd known he was up to something, she still hadn't noticed the drops themselves.

He motioned for her to hand over the jacket. "Your turn."

Adelina slipped out of the jacket and tossed it to him. He caught it and slipped it on in a smooth motion.

What could distract *him*? What had made him feel so uncomfortable around her before?

Make him fall in love with you.

She'd rather try skinning a cat with a blade of grass. But maybe if she looked like she was *trying* to flirt, she could do just enough. She tried to remember the last time she attempted to flirt and drew a complete blank.

Adelina avoided men, except for basic interactions with store clerks on her rather infrequent trips into town. She occasionally visited her grandmother in Smŭrttata, but those visits, too, were short-lived. And her grandmother lived alone.

She sucked in a breath and let it out. And again. And again. Trying to force her muscles to relax as she'd seen Grigg do when *he* let out a breath. How did a single breath relax him so much? She'd just taken three, and she felt just as pent up as before.

Adelina stalked away from Grigg, snatched at the bottle of wine and poured the dark-red liquid nearly to the brim of the crystal glass. She closed her eyes and tried to envision she was back in the jungle, treading lightly across the jungle floor, tracking dirt paths, an errant breeze in her hair.

This was for Lucia. This was for Rosa.

She turned to face him. His eyes flicked to the crystal glass, then back up at her expectantly.

She shifted her weight. "I don't think this is a good idea."

He spread his hands. "You've got to learn somehow."

Adelina pursed her lips and took a long sip of wine.

Last night on the rooftop when she'd first seen him stumble, it had been when he'd seen the egg box under the chair. She'd claimed his chair as her own, oozing confidence like a boa constrictor slinking its way around a strangler tree.

The egg being out of place had thrown him off his game, but so had she. What if it wasn't just an angle that had made his transition from captor to awkward host feel so strange?

It was time to reach beyond the game to play the man.

Adelina lifted her chin and strode forward, locking eyes with Grigg, never breaking his gaze as she tipped the goblet back and downed half the glass. His eyebrows rose just a hair, and she caught his eyes drift to her lips and throat just for a moment before returning to her sharp eyes.

She tilted her head slowly, and his cocked just a hair in return, mirroring her movement. She had his attention, though she imagined he still kept a wary, close awareness on her hands, on her hand placement.

"No, you're not understanding me. This isn't going to work, because you're not here for card tricks and coins."

The coin burned between the index and middle finger of her hand holding the goblet, but she wasn't sure if Grigg knew it. She'd made the switch while pouring the wine with her back toward him.

Grigg stood stock still in his bell-adorned jacket, the shadow of a smile still dancing across the lines of his lips. "What am I here for, then?"

She swallowed bitter pride and ran her free hand along the shoulder of his jacket, picking off invisible lint before letting her palm slide down his chest.

"You're here for magic. And you think you can use me to get it."

No sooner had she said the words than Adelina splashed the rest of the wine in her glass at his face. The second her right wrist moved in the throw, she dropped the crystal. In a fraction of a second, her left hand caught the glass as it fell, and her right hand opened and slapped him across the face.

Her left hand dropped just at the edge of his right jacket pocket. His hand shot out and caught her wrist. The bells complained of his movement with a harsh *ding ding ding!*

Grigg wiped his face free of the wine with his free hand. A vein on his neck bulged. A blaze turned his blue eyes to foaming dark seas. "You'll have to do better than that, love."

She stepped back, and he let her go. Adelina jutted her chin toward his other pocket, the one Grigg had left exposed when he moved to block her throw and to wipe his face.

"Check it."

He held her gaze with a long look, the wine still dripping down the rest of his face and soaking into his white shirt. Slowly, he dropped two fingers into his own pocket and lifted out the coin.

She'd never targeted the pocket on her left, where he'd caught her wrist. But she *had* created an opening for herself in the pocket on the right. And she'd managed to test his reaction to her hypothesis about his true purpose here, too.

Magic. The Heart of the Stars. The golden egg.

Grigg wanted power. And if he could gather the secrets of two enemy tribes, waltz into the Nascosta, escape unscathed, kidnap her, and pit her against his mark with nothing but a few powders and sleight-of-hand tricks ... Adelina shuddered to think what he could do with real power.

Which is why she could never let him truly have it. It belonged with the Guerrori. With the Keepers of the Mountain. It deserved to be respected—to be protected and hidden in the Nascosta.

Getting the egg wasn't enough. She would learn all Grigg's tricks and use them against him to take back the Heart of the Stars.

She would take the Heart of the Stars herself.

CHAPTER THIRTEEN

You're here for magic.

Her words rang in his skull like a thousand bells tripped all at once.

You're here for magic.

And if she knew about the egg, so was she.

Grigg had stumbled away from her before marching off to the bedroom to change his shirt, only to turn on his heel and come back to grab her wrist and tug her into the room after him. He couldn't leave her unattended in the living room. What was he thinking?

She'd been creative, but she'd cheated. Then again, that's exactly the sort of thing he would have done. He was typically proud of pupils showing that sort of initiative.

She'd found his weakness and played it like a stringed instrument. She'd gotten in his head.

It was bad enough that he'd told her his real name. It flowed off the tip of his tongue like a well-practiced alias. Something about being home must be throwing him off. This house wasn't his, of course. He'd rented it for an excellent price for the whole month. But being here in Smŭrttata, so close to where he was born —being near the jungle again, hearing the accents of the people walking the streets—it turned him upside down.

He jabbed a finger at the trunk farthest away from him and almost in the corner. "Go! Sit!"

His jacket jingled like a jester's too-loud, too-colorful performance as he moved his arm, making a mockery of his firm command. Grigg ripped the jacket off and tossed it onto the bed. It clanged in protest and then fell silent.

Adelina didn't move. "What's your problem? I did what you asked me to do. I redirected your focus. I thought you wanted me to get good at this."

He clenched his jaw and jerked his head toward the trunk again. The one on the end had a creaky lid. If she sat on it, it would creak and would creak again if her weight shifted to get up. He wasn't changing his pants, so it wasn't insane to let her watch him change his shirt, but he'd have to turn his back to her to keep her from seeing the mark on his chest.

"You can sit, or I can tie you to the bedpost."

She lifted her hands defensively, palms out, eyebrows raised as if to say, *Wow, dramatic much?* But she did as he asked and crossed to the trunk. A small creak confirmed her weight transferred to the trunk's lid. She glanced down at the trunk, and then back at him, realizing why he'd placed her there.

Satisfied, Grigg spun to the dresser and tugged open the second drawer. *You're here for magic.* He ripped a fresh tunic from the second drawer, chucked it on top of the dresser, and glanced over his shoulder to make sure she was still behaving. She sat demure as a noblewoman on the wooden trunk, eyeing him with open curiosity.

You're here for magic.

Grigg undid the buttons of his vest and tossed it on the bed. "You cheated."

He saw her throw her hands up out of the corner of his eye. "What rule did I break?"

"You don't get to dump wine on people at the ball. How many times will that work? Once, maybe? And you ruined a good shirt." He ripped off his wine-stained tunic. "That's two shirts in two days. This is getting wasteful."

"The first one was not my fault. That shirt looked like it was destroyed long before I met you. It's not my fault you don't know how to ride a horse."

He gritted his teeth. "Stupid thing threw me."

Grigg had wanted to get captured by the Guerrori and had planned to stage his knockout. But he hadn't wanted to *actually* lose consciousness. He'd played the scenario too close to reality, and the horse really had slipped, and he really had fallen and gotten knocked out.

Grigg ran a hand over the smooth lines of his chest as he faced the wall, tracing the latest extensions of the black veins just beneath the skin. Each spreading black vine burned like fire. His chest hurt. It had hurt when he got up and had stayed that way all morning. The curse was growing stronger, and he was getting worse. Had the cracks on the egg expanded too?

He tugged the fresh tunic over his head and spun to face her. She had her eye on the trunk beside her, as if determining how to open it without his noticing.

She glanced up as he turned. "I need some new clothes too. I hadn't expected to stay in these so long."

"You live in a jungle. Who cares how long you wear those clothes?" The words spewed forth before he could catch them, but the moment they were out and he saw her face, he nearly wished the floor would open up and swallow him whole.

Grigg rolled his eyes and passed a hand over his face. "You're not being smart. You're supposed to be smart."

"What are you talking about?"

Something in his chest stung. Was she progressing slower than he'd like, or was he embarrassed she got to him?

No. She'd lost sight of the bigger picture. Of the mission. And losing sight, losing perspective, was dangerous. He worked his jaw. "I might like explosions, but do I use them for every single thing? No. I do not. Because that would be asinine."

"What's your point?"

"You were so focused on beating me, on winning, that you lost sight of the bigger picture. You're supposed to win by *nuance*, by skill. Not by a stroke of luck. What you just pulled will only work one time. What are you going to do? Splash wine on everyone?"

She set her jaw, but didn't answer. Grigg decided to take that as acknowledgment he was right. "I have clothes for you. We're going into town tomorrow, and you're going to need them to blend in. Because you're going to get yourself invited to the Caruso mansion for peace talks."

Adelina's eyes widened. Then she laughed. "Is this a joke?"

"Not in the slightest."

Grigg grabbed the soiled tunic from his bed and toweled off the rest of the wet wine from his hair. He dumped a clean sleeve from the soiled tunic into the pitcher of water by the bed and went over his hair again to rinse it out.

Adelina's tone dropped from jovial to flat. "He'll never accept. Frederico wants me to marry him and claims that's the only avenue to peace. That or our complete surrender."

Grigg had heard of Frederico's play for marriage. Frederico hadn't exactly played it close to the vest, as it were, and several of the Carusos' guards and suppliers had gabbed about it. Frederico himself had made a joke about it to Pietro Palladino, for example— Frederico's wine supplier for the big event.

He nodded. "Yes, I know. That's why you're not going to Frederico to get invited. You're going to the father."

Surprise lit her face. "Nico?"

"That's right. He's got a passionate but overreaching son.

You've got a solution to his son's impulsivity. Frederico is about to get a lot of people killed, and you're going to solve it by offering up land in a deal he can't refuse."

Adelina shot up off the trunk. "That's ridiculous."

Grigg held up a hand and motioned for her to sit again. Reluctantly, she did.

"You don't have to *keep* the deal. You just have to entertain Nico enough to get invited to the ball. Tell him you want in, and you'll discuss the terms then."

Shadows invaded her dark eyes, the lines of her face taut with tension. "He's a melder, but I don't know what type. There's no way to prepare for a meeting with him, and he'll bring guards. He'll kill me."

"Maybe he's bluffing. Maybe he doesn't have any power at all." Grigg was similar. He had no power of his own, but he surrounded himself with well-paid melder guards and leaned into weapons of chemistry to control anyone who got out of hand.

Adelina shook her head. "Even if he isn't a melder, his guards are."

"Then we won't have you go in person. We can write him for an invitation, so he'll only see you in a crowded ballroom full of witnesses."

"If I make a deal and break it, they'll set the forest on fire and kill us all. They've got triple the manpower we do. If they're well organized, they might be able to win."

"No, they won't. Because we're going to rig the forest with konnolan, and your women can drink magna and take care of things the old-fashioned way."

Grigg let the silence stretch as the reality of his suggestion settled over her.

Adelina leveled him with a defiant glare. "We aren't murderers."

Grigg pulled open the third dresser drawer and pulled out the set of clothes that seemed best to suit her size. He'd gotten three sets of various options in preparation for this particular venture. Grigg closed the drawer and crossed the room to stand in front of her. She rose to meet him on her feet, chin high, eyes dark.

He peered down at her. "What a crass term. You're *defenders*. And what are you defenders of again?"

For an instant, she didn't move. Maybe forgot to breathe. She crossed her arms. "I don't know what you're talking about."

Fast blinks. Defensive posture. *Liar.*

He quirked a smile. "Defend it. Or don't. And then your forest burns, your tribe is dismantled, your women die, and the city, along with the man you stalk on Tuesday nights, falls into the hands of the Carusos."

He thrust the bundle of clothes toward her. She caught it reflexively, and his hand brushed hers as he drew away. Her top lip gave the shadow of a curled snarl. "I don't stalk anyone."

Grigg shot her a knowing look. "Sure. I just threatened your forest, your tribe, and your women, but what are we defensive about? The man you definitely do *not* stalk on Tuesdays."

Catching wind of the Guerrori warrior who'd fallen in love with a man from the city had been a stroke of priceless luck for Grigg in the months leading up to kidnapping the chieftess. The lovestruck girl had known a lot, too, and though she trusted her newfound love, as forbidden as the love may have been, the man she so trusted wagged his tongue a little more freely than she. With the right motivation, of course.

It had taken Grigg months of work to set up his angle. Less than he wanted, but hopefully just enough to get the job done. The girl had followed her chieftess once to see where Adelina slipped off to each week, like clockwork—and voilà, Grigg established a pattern for his mark.

Which meant, naturally, that Tuesday evenings would offer the best times for the Morturi to break the treaty.

Adelina was still glaring daggers at him. "I don't stalk anyone."

She'd repeated the same words, as if they would be more

convincing the second time. Now would be a good time to lean in, to prove he held the upper hand. That he knew more than she thought he did.

He laughed. "So for the record, you do *not* leave the forest on Tuesday nights to watch the Palladino estate through the windows?"

Her mouth gaped open, slammed shut, then opened again. "Are you following me? Who's stalking who now?"

"So you *do* watch the Palladinos through the windows!"

Her eyes blazed white-hot fire. Her shoulders tensed, and a hand curled into fists at her side. She threw a hook, and he caught it in the palm of his hand. He grinned. "What do you want with them, anyway?"

"What do you want with the Heart of the Stars?"

He froze, and she yanked her fist free of his hand. She didn't just know about the egg. She knew about the Hearts too.

How much did she know?

Grigg shrugged. "I like shiny things."

"That's a terrible reason."

Adelina threw an uppercut.

He blocked. "People have terrible reasons for all sorts of things. The Heart of the Stars is also enormously expensive, and gold is shiny too."

"You're threatening hundreds of people to get it."

Grigg scrunched his nose as if the mention of humanity reminded him of the smell of rotten eggs. "I don't really like people."

"They're good people."

Interesting that she so readily defended the people of the town. Adelina, chieftess of the reclusive woman-only Guerrori tribe, supposedly deeply anti-man. The Carusos called them black widows, and they weren't far off. The Guerrori were concerned with their mountain and their jungle, and little else. What did she care about the people of Smŭrttata?

Grigg arched an eyebrow. "I sincerely doubt it. Nobody's good. Not really."

"And it's your job to judge them?"

"I'm not judging them. I'm robbing them. You're the one who's judging."

She shook her head. "You won't get away with this."

The pain in his chest flared into searing agony. His hand flew up to clutch at his heart, but he couldn't let her see—couldn't let her know what was really going on inside him. His hands shook. His heart burned with an unquenchable ache that threatened to buckle him at the knees. Grigg swung for her, half for balance and half for intimidation, and yanked her toward him.

She gasped at his sudden onslaught and threw another punch. This one landed right in his gut. Adelina followed it up with a knee strike to the groin.

Intolerable pain in his chest exploded to match her blow. He couldn't move. He couldn't breathe. He was going to fall.

Grigg let out a yell and stumbled forward. She was strong for her size, but he was still heavier. He started to fall and tripped his way forward toward the wall.

She swung again, and he slugged her once in the stomach to keep her at bay before the two of them collided into the corner of the room. Her body smashed into the wall between his weight and the border of the house. He seized both of her hands, shoved them behind her back, and captured both of her wrists in one hand, his weight still driving into her. He wasn't convinced he wouldn't fall if he removed it.

Grigg withdrew the dagger from his waist and slipped it along the bare skin of her lower back, up under the binding of animal hide wrapping her chest. Her skin was smooth and warm to his touch, a stark contrast to the cool of the blade driving goosebumps along its path.

An iota of control returned to him, but his breath still came in ragged drags. It took everything in him to throw out a veneer of strength. "I get away with everything, darling. Who will you run to? Who do you think is so untouchable in this city?"

She grimaced, jutting her chin stubbornly up into his face, pretending not to be affected by his crushing weight. "I'll tell the governor what you're doing. He'll kick you out of the city."

Grigg laughed, tightening his hold on her hands and digging the knife edge deep enough that it threatened to break the skin. "I'll have you know the governor is having an affair with Mira, the wife of young, over-ambitious Stoyan Mironov. He fancies himself as the head of a gang with potential to rival the Carusos. Anyway, the governor's done a few unsavory favors for his mistress—favors he wouldn't want getting out."

Her brows knitted together. She hadn't known of his infidelity. "What are you going to do—expose the governor? What would that accomplish?"

For one, it would stop him from trying to throw Grigg out of the city. But that was too obvious. He ignored the question and worked the blade up between her shoulder blades. "I don't expose people just for fun. I do it for a reason. I like having something over the governor, but he's not a threat right now."

"What, then? You'll tell this Mira girl's husband and get him angry enough to kick up some dust? Distract the Carusos?"

Grigg shook his head. "Oh, Stoyan already knows. The Carusos have a grip on the city that Stoyan wants for himself. With the Carusos so focused on your jungle, Stoyan sees an opportunity. He sends his wife to sleep with people for blackmail and information—a respectable endeavor. One can never hold too many secrets over someone else's head. But right now, he needs a way up the ladder, a way to gain notoriety, so more people will join his burgeoning clan against the Carusos. You and I are going to pay Stoyan a visit, but not before we chat with his wife."

"You ... we're going to interrogate her?"

"I was planning on going tomorrow, but after our enlightening conversation this evening, I think we'll go now. Mira should be getting home soon. But before we go, you should know—if Stoyan thinks you aren't under my protection, you'll never leave the house alive. So whatever I do in there, be a doll and play along."

Every action he made put a damper on his threat to Giovanna that he would make Adelina fall in love with him. But she was impossible. And making her love him hadn't been realistic anyway. What he needed most was not for Adelina to love him, but to fear him enough to do what he needed—to respect him enough not to try anything stupid.

The burn in his heart subsided to a stable ache so that at last he was steady on his feet once again. Grigg ripped the dagger through the last shreds of the animal hide wrapping Adelina's chest and stepped away, still breathing hard. She screeched half a girlish squeal, half the feral scream of a wild animal, as she realized what he'd done and clutched the bundle of clothes he'd given her tightly in front of her.

Fury still lined every muscle in his body. Her own ire blazed back at him from his stunt with her clothes, though a part of him felt justified to have evened the score. She now felt what he felt. It was only fair.

So why did a niggling, uneasy guilt poke and prod at him like a constant *drip drippp drippppping* sound he couldn't escape? He'd humiliated her. But hadn't she humiliated him first?

Drip. Drip.

He'd gone too far. It was unnecessary.

She's your hostage! You've been more than generous!

Grigg clenched his jaw and jerked his chin at the bundle of clothes in her arms. "Get dressed. We're going to visit Stoyan tonight."

CHAPTER FOURTEEN

Adelina

Grigg, or whatever his real name was, was clearly insane. Every time Adelina had tried to pretend otherwise, it had come back to bite her. Her plan to knock him off his game had worked exceptionally well. Too well. What if the next time she claimed a victory, he slit her throat instead of her clothing?

Adelina had insisted on changing with privacy, which Grigg had flatly denied. She had countered with a request to change behind the bed in the opposite corner from where he stood. This he had granted, and once she had crossed the room to stand with the dresser on her left and the corner of the wall on her right, the bed between them, he had turned his back so he could hear her and retained full view of the two trunks.

Where the egg probably was.

She had changed quickly from the thick animal hide she was used to, though it covered less skin, to the far thinner garments that covered more skin but allowed more airflow. What he'd provided fit her perfectly—or nearly so. The tunic was a bit over-sized but had a lace-up front that she could tighten a bit. Adelina tugged on the loose-fitting brown trousers next, pulled the hem of the long tunic over the waist, and cinched the waist with the thick leather belt he'd provided. She never wore socks, but he'd given her some, so she put them on to pair with lace-up boots that came halfway up her calf.

Adelina wasn't exactly sure where this Stoyan lived, or what he was expecting, but as she believed that Grigg could kill her in a bad mood, she could easily believe that the people he was dealing with were just as volatile and violent, if not more so. Adelina left her shredded animal-skin top on the bed next to the hide skirt she'd been wearing with it and cleared her throat for Grigg to turn around. He'd regarded her with cruel indifference, looking her over from head to toe, before giving a sharp nod and jerking his head out the door. *Time to go.*

He'd spoken briefly with Trifon, one of the men guarding Lucia—probably about instructions on what to do should Grigg not return. Her stomach twisted, and she swallowed hard against the bile rising in her throat.

It was dark by the time they stepped out onto the streets. Apparently, Grigg had no intention of breaking their streak of interacting with one another solely at night—outside the house, at least. He'd strode off into the darkness with a flint expression and long strides that swept him off so fast she had to jog to keep up.

At the end of a row two alleys down, Grigg nodded to a stableboy sitting in the doorway of the first residence large enough to have a stable. The boy disappeared without a word and returned with a single horse—a sleek bay with four white socks. The socks made Adelina think of Velocina, and a pang twisted at her heart. She missed the beautiful mare.

Adelina had been gone far longer than she'd planned. What would her women make of her absence? Would they look for her? Where would they look? Would they think she'd gone off to make a deal with Frederico? Would Caterina spew lies to turn them in her favor? Once Adelina finally got free of Grigg, what exactly would she be facing at home?

The horse was tacked in the Bulgar style of saddle and bridle—a far stiffer way to ride than Adelina was used to. Grigg offered her a hand. She ignored him and mounted the horse, hoping her small act of defiance wouldn't set him off again. But his expression never changed as he swung up behind her, his body nestling close to hers as he wrapped his arms around her to reach the reins.

She fought the urge to elbow him in his stomach. Why hadn't he managed to get two horses? But the answer was obvious. If she had a horse, she could take it where she wanted. Far too much freedom. And if their positions were reversed, she wouldn't exactly want her combative hostage behind her back either.

Adelina let her body roll with the motions of the horse, the familiarity of a mount underneath her working like a salve within her soul. She tried to ignore Grigg's warm chest on her back and his arms reaching around her torso to direct the horse. She forced herself to relax and focus on the steady rhythm of the horse's hooves as the mare traveled down street after street, walking through cobbled squares and cantering down dirt pathways.

Maybe her women were right. If all else failed, she *could* make Frederico fall in love with her, and he would die. But that notion was even dumber than the idea of making Grigg fall for her, and besides, being married didn't make people fall in love. Plenty of loveless marriages resulted in tortured souls worse off together than they ever would have been alone. Her curse only worked on men who fell in love with her, not men who made commitments based on political aspirations.

Before long, Grigg brought the horse to a stop outside a house with the common red-tile roofs of most of the city. The home was two stories and fit along a line of homes so that it was hard to tell precisely when one house ended and another began. Two broad-shouldered gentlemen—or men, anyway—lurked in the street outside, one lounging against the wall next to a glossy black door, the other playing with the flame of a torch lighting the street from the opposite side.

The fireblood's outstretched hand was half a meter below the flame of the torch. He seemed to be practicing his abilities, shifting the flame of the torch so that it narrowed at the base and reached up high or fell squat and wide, alternating between the two every few seconds. He snatched his hand down as they approached on the horse.

Grigg acknowledged the fireblood by name, slipped off the horse, and embraced him. His palm lingered just barely against the other man's hand, and the guard slipped something into his pocket. Grigg clapped him on the back.

"How is the baby? What is he now, six months?"

The man's stoic expression lit like sunflowers in spring. "He is the joy of my life. Just figured out how to roll from his belly to his back last week, and it's his new favorite trick. Yesterday I hung my belt over a chair when I got home, and he rolled his way two meters across the floor to grab my knife sheath. Gave the wife a fright."

The mention of a two-parent home sent a jolt of curiosity and grief through Adelina, the two emotions mingling until they nearly melded into one for how fast the thoughts came.

What would her childhood have been like if she'd had both a mother and a father? Would they have feared for her as she grew and reached for dangerous things? Would they have worked together to raise her and disagreed on what was funny and what was dangerous, like this man and his amusement over his wife's worry?

Grigg laughed along with the man. "He'll be running circles around you before you know it! If he's half the bodyguard you are, Stoyan's going to have to up his fee to keep you both on staff."

The man bobbed his head and cackled. "That he will; that he will!"

Grigg jerked his head in the direction of the black door. "She home?"

A nod. "Not five minutes ago."

Grigg clasped him by the arm in thanks, then repeated the gesture with the second guard. Something metal glinted in the man's fingers as Grigg withdrew. Coins.

"We won't be long."

Grigg offered Adelina his hand to dismount. Taking his hand after being forced to sit so close to him already was about as high on her to-do list as sitting on a hill full of stinging fire ants. She hesitated.

You're cooperating for the egg and the Heart of the Stars. Sell it.

Her slender hand slipped into his larger one, and his hold felt like coaches and footmen and forbidden lifestyles. Adelina couldn't bring herself to place any weight on him as she slipped from the mare's back and landed lightly on her feet. She began to pull away, but Grigg caught her hand and moved it to the crook of his arm before she could.

He strode forward, all charisma and smiles, with a swagger that would have demanded the attention of anyone in a two-block radius despite the empty street. Her heart lurched to her dry throat. She was betraying the way of the Guerrori by walking with him, by being with him at all.

Adelina's mother would roll in her grave. But what did she care of her mother? Her mother had lied. Even the guard, with all his excitement over his baby, proved it.

Grigg opened the door to the house and let Adelina inside, as if the home were a palace rather than a slightly above-average dwelling in an outskirts area of the city. Pulled curtains and shades caused the light of a candle somewhere deeper in the house to shine all the brighter in contrast. The space to the left felt large, and she could see the shapes of sitting-room furniture. But Grigg had no interest in sitting. He moved through the house like a sweeping wave, drawing her with him on his arm.

He exited the foyer, moved down the hall, and opened a door with a faint flickering light glowing from within. Grigg plucked Adelina's hand from his elbow as they entered and left her in the doorway of what appeared to be a small study. A woman stood with her back to the door, dark curls cascading down her back as she leaned over a journal or ledger of some kind, pen in hand, the *scritch-scratch* of the pen working its way across the page. Heavy boots in a woman's size sat on the floor beside the desk, and her bare feet just barely poked out from the hem of her skirt as she examined her work.

Grigg came up behind her in three long strides and tapped her lightly on the shoulder. Mira jumped half out of her skin with a half gasp, half squeal as she spun toward him, bumping into Grigg, who stood too close. The corseted bodice of her dress cinched her waist tight and pushed up her chest, though Adelina hardly thought the woman needed the enhancement. Little skin was left to the imagination, with a plunging neckline and a bosom spilling out the top of her corset. Flowing sleeves draped off her shoulders, landing at her arm instead.

Impossibly red lips parted in surprise as she turned, but the color was wrong—smeared off the lines of her lips onto her cheek and chin. Her expression moved from startled to a flat wariness as she took in the stranger standing in front of her. "Who are you, and what are you doing in my house?"

Grigg flashed a dashing smile that promised morning regrets and spoke with a silken voice that churned Adelina's stomach like sour milk. "Oh, come now, I heard you did favors for knowledge-able men."

If Grigg's advance on the woman made Adelina squeamish, the way Mira responded made Adelina nearly want to throw up.

Her expression changed in an instant, sliding into a persona as easily as Grigg had done. She slinked toward him—but they were already standing close. How her hips managed to sway that much in the span of a single step, Adelina would never know. Mira's expression transformed from rigidity to fluid lines and smooth oil, to seduction and trysts and salacious nights wrapped in secrets.

She tipped her chin up to Grigg. "Only the important ones. How important are you?"

Adelina shifted her weight. Was she completely invisible? Did she have to be here for this?

Grigg trailed his finger across Mira's collarbone and along her exposed shoulder, then reached up to muss her hair. Then Adelina saw his other hand drop something down Mira's corset.

Distraction. Whose attention was easier to redirect than a woman who spent all her time distracting men? He played the role of her next prey, and she became what he'd set her up for without a second thought.

It was all strategic, and he clearly hadn't brought Adelina along to actually be involved in anything with Mira. So why did her mouth still taste like rot?

He offered Mira a smile. She moved to wrap her arm around his neck, but he pressed two fingers to her collarbone at the base of her throat and pushed her away from him. "Today, however, the favor I need is from your husband."

Adelina's satisfaction at Mira's staggering backward step was probably stronger than necessary.

Heavy boots stormed down the hall, and the door burst wide. Mira's initial squeal was bound to have drawn attention. Adelina jumped to the side just in time for a burly man to rush into the room, a club in his hand.

Grigg spread his hands in welcome and swept toward the man, easily creating space between himself and Mira as if she'd ceased to exist. "Ah, the happy husband! Just the man I wanted to see. Tell me, does Mira ever look like this for you, or only for the men you send her out to?"

The already-destroyed lip color ... the newly mussed hair, thanks to Grigg ... the bare feet ... if Grigg planned to get out of here alive, he had a strange way of showing it.

Both Mira's and Stoyan's brows knit like mirrors of confusion mingled with shock. Mira shot an uncertain look in Adelina's direction, clearly surprised to find a woman in the room, followed by an immediate refocus on her husband's reaction.

Stoyan took in the sight of his wife's tousled hair, smeared lip color, and demanding attire in a cursory glance, as if he were checking a horse's mouth for good quality stock. He fixed his gaze back on Grigg, knuckles whitening around the handle of the club. "Tell me why you're here before I have my men gut you like a fish."

"Do you mean the new father outside? Delightful fellow. Did you know the baby just learned to roll over? Such an exciting time."

Grigg pulled a handful of something out of his pocket—small brown oblong shapes. He popped one in his mouth, and it crunched when he bit down. "At least that's what I hear. Never had kids myself."

Had he brought walnuts? Grigg snagged another one and rolled it between his fingers. Definitely a walnut. What was with him and eating during every meet with people? Weren't they only going to be here a few minutes?

Mira took a hesitant sidestep closer to her husband, and Grigg pretended not to notice, enraptured in the taste of his snack.

Stoyan adjusted his grip on the club and gave it a light practice swing. "Who are you, and why are you here?"

Grigg returned Stoyan's glare with an even gaze as he wordlessly popped another walnut into his mouth, taking his time with it as he savored it in his mouth, chewed, and swallowed.

He spread his hands. "I'm the best thing that's happened to you all day—unless you decide to give your wife the attention she's been sleeping with everyone else to get in hopes you'll give her the same one day. That experience may just top what I have on offer—at least, that's the word on the street."

Adelina grimaced. If he was trying to de-escalate the situation, that would—

Stoyan lunged, but not at Grigg. He seized Adelina's arm and yanked her toward him. "What if I take yours instead?"

Adelina whirled in an arc and smashed her elbow into Stoyan's nose. He rocked backward, but she grabbed him by the shoulder with her right hand, her left arm wrapping his biceps as she yanked him down to her level and drove a knee into his groin. Stoyan let out some composite of a pained grunt and an enraged yell and swung the club at her, but she was too close for a mid-range weapon. She stripped the club from his hands and stepped back, leaving the man holding his bleeding nose, and with his mouth flopped open like a fish dropped on a dock.

What had Stoyan planned to do with her if she hadn't been able to fight back?

Grigg popped another walnut into his mouth and shook a disappointed head at Stoyan. "Don't you recognize her? You married a pawn. I borrowed a chieftess. By the knife in my back, at this rate, you'll never rise above the status of a squishable bug under Nico's shoe. And you'll never get into the dance."

Stoyan drew a bloody hand back from his nose, examined the crimson dripping down his hand, and returned it to his nose with a groan. Mira fumbled in the desk, found a cloth napkin, and passed it to her husband. He smacked her hand away so fast Adelina didn't think he had time to consider what she was offering. Was this his knee-jerk reaction to anything the woman handed him? The next instant, he thought better of it, took the kerchief, and applied it to his nose.

He cleared his throat. "What are you talking about? What dance?"

"The information you need is right here." Grigg reached a hand into his pocket, then hesitated. He patted both pockets, searching. "Oh dear, I've misplaced it. I could have sworn I kept it somewhere around here. This is embarrassing."

He rechecked his pockets, Stoyan and Mira gaping at him, and Adelina couldn't help but join them. Then, as if lightning struck with the epiphany of the century, his eyes lit, and he jabbed a finger in the air. "Ah! Mira, you have it. If you would be so kind?"

All eyes turned to Mira. Mira blinked at Grigg.

Grigg pulled a pocket watch from his vest, eyed it, and replaced it in his pocket. "Any day, darling."

The poor woman continued to stare, this time adding a vague shake of the head and an intake of breath as if she were more than willing to speak, if she only knew what to say.

Grigg sighed. "You let everyone check out your décolletage, but I've heard self-examinations are important. Give it a look, would you?"

She glanced down, and all shreds of color fled from her features until she stood like a ghastly barefoot phantom in the room. Mira reached a hand down her corset, and when she brought it out, a folded piece of paper mocked them all from between her fingers.

The item he'd dropped down her dress earlier. Adelina shook her head. Control. Humiliation. Intimidation. His easy demeanor, casual insults—even the walnuts began to make sense. Like the apples on the rooftop, they were loud and obnoxious, and offered an air of complete and utter annoyance with the humanity in the room. How important must Grigg be—and how insignificant his audience—for a walnut to carry greater interest than those grappling for his attention?

Stoyan flushed beet red, but Grigg turned on him before he could speak. "You're going to reschedule your attack on the Carusos for three days from now, during the Lovers' Ball. In return, I'll leave the vault door open for you. You can clear it out and keep the spoils. When word gets out at what you've done, you can keep all the credit, all the fame, and all the glory."

Adelina arched an eyebrow. And all the heat, the blame ... the wrath of the Caruso family.

Stoyan snatched the paper from his wife, unfolded it, and read the contents. He glanced back at Grigg. "And if I don't?"

"Then you're dumber than your father and will die twice as

poor. I thought you were a man of ambition, Stoyan. Like I said, this is the best news you've heard all day and could quite possibly change your life forever, if you only grab it by the horns."

Stoyan's eyes narrow. "What do you get out of it?"

Grigg ran a finger along the edge of the writing desk and rubbed his fingers together, as if examining the furniture for dust. "The Carusos have had Smŭrttata in their grip long enough. And hey, maybe I like to root for the little guy. If you're ready to outgrow child's play, you know what to do. Good evening."

He dipped his head, acknowledging Stoyan and Mira one last time before grabbing Adelina's hand and heading out the door. She followed, heart in her throat, matching his fast pace as he swept from the room down the hall into the foyer and out the front door.

A chill breeze sent goosebumps running along her skin as they made for the horse still waiting for them with the guards outside. Grigg reached out a regal hand to help her up onto the horse. She took it and mounted. He swung up behind her without a word and kicked the mare into a stately trot off into the night.

As soon as they were out of earshot of the guards, Grigg leaned forward, his body pressed to hers, his breath tickling her neck as he spoke low into her ear. "Slavers, pirates, gang leaders, kings, princes, nobles. Do you know what they have in common? They all owe me favors."

CHAPTER FIFTEEN

The next three days came and went in a blur of training. Adelina had seemed to flip a switch—eager to learn, even joking, without much of the poking and prodding and trying to win that Grigg had seen from her at the beginning. She wasn't rash, and she didn't cheat. Instead, she listened carefully and followed instructions to the letter. Grigg didn't trust it.

He also didn't trust her to handle a meet with Nico Caruso to arrange for an invitation to the ball, just like he didn't trust Nico to manage such a meeting with particularly high ethical standards—which is why he'd sent written communication on her behalf instead of a having a physical meet. Adelina hadn't liked the idea, but she liked it better than going in person and seemed to come around since it was an excuse to get in the doors rather than an ironclad agreement that they would actually strike a deal. The Caruso estate had responded with an invitation for Adelina via Grigg's messenger, taking them one step closer to the Heart of the Stars.

Giovanna had been strangely quiet the past two nights as well, and he wondered if that meant she would reappear with a vengeance, and this was somehow silent treatment for his threat to make Adelina fall in love with him. Though, if it was, Giovanna needn't have worried. It was an empty threat, and though Adelina was cooperative, it was a far cry from genuine care for him. He was still her captor, after all, dangling her friend's life over her head.

Once, he'd turned his back to refresh the water in their glasses and turned around to find the living room empty. He'd panicked but hadn't heard the front door open or close. He'd found her in the bedroom. She'd said she was fixing something about her clothes and wanted privacy, but he'd sent her out and checked the egg just to make sure it was still there.

She was hunting. He could feel it. But the egg had been there, just as he'd left it. Except for the longer crack creeping around its side.

The pain in Grigg's chest was a deeper ache than it had been three days ago, but the flaring pain he'd experienced when he and Adelina had fought in the bedroom hadn't returned. Still, the black over his heart continued to spread, and the ache continued to worsen.

He was running out of time.

Adelina had mastered pickpocketing better than he could have expected in the time allotted, and it wasn't until halfway through their training time that he told her she wouldn't be pickpocketing at all. The practice was intended to train her in nuance and misdirection.

Pickpocketing was a great way to build those foundational skills, and when he had her build on that foundation with the vials and the potted plants, first distracting anyone watching, and then slipping the vials into the soil of the plants around the room, she'd done extremely well.

He'd made it a game where she had a certain period of time to drop them around the room without him noticing while they practiced other skills. He'd kept his word and let her show him her archery skills too, and she hadn't killed him, which he chalked up as a victory.

Her skills with a bow were unmatched. He'd never seen anything like it. She drew the arrow and let it fly, easy as breathing, and hit her mark every time.

"It's not much of a challenge if I'm not shooting from the back of a galloping horse or making the shot with my feet," she'd said dismissively.

"Duke's dowry, you were being serious about that? You can actually shoot a bow and arrow with your feet?"

She'd only grinned, and the light that had sparkled in her eyes had proved the smile was real. The amazed smile he'd returned to her had been entirely involuntary. The moment had held until at last Adelina reached for her glass of water, and Grigg looked away and adjusted his vest.

It was now the morning of the heist. He'd allowed the guards to bring Lucia up the night before, and let the women share dinner together, supervised, before returning Lucia to the basement and tying Adelina to the bedpost for one more night. Then he'd arranged for a hot bath for each of them, with guards watching over Adelina while Grigg washed, and Grigg and Boris facing away from her but still nearby to ensure she didn't try anything while she washed. The evening's event might call for many things, but dried blood and dirt caked under her nails were not one of them.

Now, the two of them sat side by side on the sofa, a blueprint of the Caruso mansion spread on a low table in front of them. Her hair spilled over her shoulders in lush waves, and she smelled like lavender and bergamot.

Grigg pretended not to notice as he pressed the edges of the papers down on the table and set his glass of water over one corner to keep it from trying to roll back up to how it'd been stored.

"They're calling the event Dance of Dusk 'Till Dawn, or Lovers' Ball. Their ridiculous cover story for the event is that anyone can fall in love, which means the divisions among us are meaningless. Connections can be made across families, across hier-archies—which is technically true, except that only the rich or important have been invited. It's a masquerade ball, with everyone wearing a mask. Of course, the event really allows for business deals between people who wouldn't normally be in the same room. It's a masquerade in more ways than one. The Carusos have connections to a copse of mercenaries, some of whom might be in attendance tonight."

"A copse is a group of trees."

Grigg shrugged. "It's almost like they grow on trees. Kill one, another pops up—one you probably hired to kill the first one. I admit it's a little messy with Stoyan and your little play for a deal with Nico. And Nico will, of course, be tempted to kidnap you. I generally don't get involved in plans with so many unknown vari-ables, but I'm in a bit of a hurry."

Grigg drew his finger along the entrance of the house. "Official guard posts will likely be here, watching the entrance at the windows on the second and third floor, here, here, and here. And in strategic positions inside the house with a flow of guests. If it were me, I'd put them in these positions." Grigg noted the spots on the page. "Now. There are two places where he keeps valuables. One is a locked vault, and one is a display room. We'll be hitting the display room before he shows it off to guests later in the evening."

Getting the itinerary had been a bit of a problem. The Carusos hired a coordinator for the event, who was frequently overruled by Nico's daughter, who'd decided without reason that she was the matriarch. The coordinator ultimately spilled the beans to Grigg's contact, and their plans now assumed nothing in the schedule had changed.

"Three of Nico's five children live in the mansion with him, along with six grandchildren, ages one to eight. The children's bedrooms are here, with windows facing the windows of the display room across the courtyard. A grappling hook or line between them would be a decent escape from the display room to the other end of the house for an exit without passing more guards, but—"

Adelina pulled back. "No, no kids. We don't touch their rooms, or I'm out."

Grigg cocked his head. He had no intention of getting close to the kids, and had been about to say so, but her sudden vehemence caught his attention. "I thought you only cared about girls. At least, that's the word on the street. And these are your enemy's sons and daughters."

Her lip curled in disgust. "They are *children*. It may be a tradition for the Guerrori to raise only girls in the jungle, but not all traditions are meant to live forever."

Her whole body went taut as if she herself were under attack. This was the most adversarial and firm she'd been in the last three days, and she just admitted she didn't like one of the strongest and most defining traditions of her people—of whom she was chieftess. Curious.

Fierce, protective. Over someone soft and gentle. Something that deserved protecting. Warmth filtered into his chest, thawing the sterile air between them. At least, on his end.

Grigg held up a hand. "What I was *about* to say is that we will *not* be using the children's rooms, or even the hall where their rooms are. But because I doubt Stoyan has the same qualms, I'm going to be bringing adhesive to lock the display room window shut while I'm in there, so that when they come after, they'll have a hard time getting it open and will have to find a different exit path just in case."

Her shoulders sat high, frozen, face still etched with tension. Her brow knit together as she considered him.

He lowered his head, leaned forward to look her straight in the eye, and searched her face. "No kids die. I'm sure you think I'm a monster, but even I have limits."

The harsh edges of her posture softened just a bit. He knew

she didn't have children. Did she want some? Had she seen some atrocity with dead children? Where had that visceral reaction come from? She took a breath and nodded.

Grigg laid out the rest of the plan. She would plant the vials of magna around the room, the magna in a powdered form that would suppress their powers when activated. At least, that's what he told her. He'd yet to find a way to make magna airborne.

Adelina was to accept any drink handed to her but never drink any glass that didn't come from Grigg, just in case someone planned to poison or drug her. Grigg lifted a pouch of powder. "This is an antidote for at least half the local poison varieties. If someone does poison you successfully, this should help bring you back around."

"And if it's one of the other poison varieties?"

"Then we're out of luck, and the evening ends rather horribly. Which is why you won't actually be drinking anything unless I hand it to you, so we won't need the antidote. If you keep Nico distracted in the ways we've practiced, I should be able to swap out any glass he gives you with one that I give you, and we'll be safe. *Should* being the operative word."

She swallowed. "Spectacular."

Grigg led her to the bedroom, opened the bottom drawer of the dresser, and pulled out a radiant floor-length gown. Even to Grigg, who'd seen his fair share of fancy elitists and exorbitantly expensive gowns, this piece was magnificent. Exquisite and entirely unique, the dress shouted for attention and looked as though the jungle itself had been transferred to fabric.

Shimmering green leaves laid on top of one another, almost like scales, reached up toward one shoulder, where the leaves melted into a transparent gauze. The other shoulder was left bare, and the bodice of the dress was fitted through the waist and flowed out to the hem. A network of sharp lobster-claw heliconia leaped off the jungle-green canvas in bright, bold shades of red, orange, and yellow, beginning mid-thigh and growing thicker and thicker toward the hem so that it nearly looked like the dress had caught flame.

He'd had it tailored to fit her more specifically just yesterday after gathering her measurements. The tailor had gotten it back to him only that morning. Grigg had to admit it was the most stunning piece of fashion art he'd ever had the pleasure of commissioning. Or even laid eyes on.

Adelina stared at the dress, speechless at its beauty. Or mortified by the dauntless statement of it. She wasn't often dumbstruck, and her expression didn't help him puzzle out her reaction. She blinked at the dress, her gaze moving across the way the light played in the satin leaves. It was a look of marvel. Wasn't it? Or did she hate it?

At last, she gestured at the piece. "What's this?"

"Thimbles and threads, it's a dress. I know you live in a jungle, but I hoped that much would be obvious."

She pursed her lips. "Yes, I can see it's a dress. But if we are so convinced that someone is going to try to kill me at this party, why are you wrapping me in a floor-length getup that I cannot run in?"

"Ah!" Grigg held up a finger and handed her the dress.

She held up the bodice to her body and glanced down at the dress with a skeptical eye.

Grigg grinned. "I anticipated you may have such a concern. I've built in a high slit. It serves two purposes. One, no one with eyes is going to be able to look away from you. Two, it'll keep you from being restricted around the legs, as the fabric will flow away from you to allow wider movement as you walk. You'll still have the skirts to contend with, so let's try not to get into any fighting scenarios, okay?"

She ran a hand down the fabric and lifted the cloth at the slit. Grigg moved the fabric away at the slit to show her form-fitting satin shorts ending at the very top of her thigh. It would be invisible with the skirt down, but he thought it might make her feel a little more comfortable in a completely foreign type of clothing.

"Look, I've even added short green trousers to match. No one will see them, but if you're worried about exposure while you run around or do handstands, they'll be there."

Not that she would be doing any of those. If she did, the evening would have gotten so far out of hand there might be little left to do to save it.

Adelina reached down to examine his embellishments to the dress, turning the cloth this way and that in her fingers. When she looked back at him, he couldn't decide if she was surprised by the strangeness of the outfit or grateful for his thoughtfulness over her comfort. Or maybe she just thought all of it was over the top and ridiculous. But he'd wanted a distraction, and by the gallows, this would give him one.

Grigg ushered her toward the corner to get dressed and turned around, facing the trunks in the same way he'd done before. She took the dress to the corner on the other side of the bed.

He fought the urge more than once to turn around. Images of her filed into his mind: her figure as she leaned forward to examine the map of the mansion; her walk as she strode toward him to distract him during their pickpocketing practice; her hand sliding down his chest ... her fingers brushing his pocket ... her lips red with fresh wine.

The curves of her body on the foot of the bed as she slept. Her, poised like a queen on a throne on the rooftop. Her smooth motion as she'd responded to Stoyan grabbing her and giving him exactly what he deserved. Her piercing eyes, so arresting that he couldn't help but look into them just a moment too long. She was magnificent.

He suddenly wanted very badly to see her try to shoot a bow and arrow with her feet. How would she balance herself? How would she have to contort to accomplish such a feat?

He cleared his throat. "Hurry up. How long does it take to put on a dress?"

"I'm not the one who made the dress. Calm down. I'll be done in a minute."

A rustle of fabric later, and she told him she was done. He turned, and every memory of her fled in favor of soaking up the vision of her now standing before him. Vibrant-green silken-satin leaves hugged her chest, waist, and hips, and her long dark hair fell like spring rain down her shoulders, lush as the rainforest, free as the wind.

The leaves reached up toward one shoulder and seemed to melt away as transparent fabric wrapped over her shoulder to join the leaves climbing up her back and melt again into the rest of the dress. Her other shoulder remained bare, allowing his gaze to trail the line of her neck, collarbone, and slender arms unimpeded.

The fitted bodice followed the curve of her body to her upper thigh, where the high slit he'd promised allowed the fabric to flow away from her like an unfurled red carpet when she moved. Flashes of the smooth bronze thigh and legs teased of a treasure more beautiful than gold as she walked to the foot of the bed, placing her neatly folded tunic and trousers on the end before turning to him again.

The gradually deepening heliconia embellishments down her skirt reminded him of her. Flames and flowers melted into one, sharp and arresting at once, intoxicating in the contrast of its sharp edges and soft petals. His mouth went dry as his gaze traveled up her dress and back to her face, where golden eyes watched him.

She stood like a chieftess, shoulders back, head held high. But it wasn't until she shifted her weight and absently twined a piece of hair around her finger that he realized she was waiting for something she hadn't gotten. She spread her hands and ran one palm over the surface of her dress.

Ferns and figs, she was waiting for *him*. Was it his imagination, or was there a question in her eyes? Uncertainty, a shadow of discomfort, anticipation as she waited to see if she was acceptable. But acceptable was an insult to the vision before him now.

He should be speaking by now. He could tell by the way she stared at him. When was the last time he'd been speechless? He'd hoped the thought would be rhetorical, but some part of his brain answered the question: *On the rooftop, with her sitting on your chair.*

His lips parted, and for a moment he forgot how words worked.

"Tongues of silver. You are mesmerizing. I'm not entirely sure I'm going to be able to pull off a heist with you in the room."

Her cheeks flushed with color, complimenting the red of her lips and the bronze of her skin more wonderfully than he could've imagined.

"One more thing." Grigg crossed once more to the dresser and returned with a sparkling diamond necklace strung on a gold chain. "May I?"

She hesitated, then lifted her hair up off her neck. Grigg stepped behind her and brought the necklace around her neck. The curve of her neck, the sweep of her hair, the softness of her skin as he fastened the clasp ...

He rolled his eyes at himself. *He didn't need to think about that.* And that was the end of that sentence, wasn't it? Grigg snatched a golden arm band from the dresser and slipped it on her upper arm, complimenting the golden yellows of the heliconia on her skirts.

He stepped around to examine her from the front and shook his head. "Maybe I should've told my tailor to wrap you in sacks instead. I'm going to look like a street urchin next to you."

She pressed her lips together, but her mouth twisted upward at the edges. The ache in his chest eased as she smiled, and in that moment, he couldn't think of anything more pleasant than the sensation that washed over him when she smiled at something he'd said.

Adelina nodded to him. "It's your turn. What are you wearing?"

He waved her off. "Nothing."

Her eyebrows shot up, and he choked on another verbal fail-ure. "Nothing like this, I mean. If I did go wearing nothing, that would certainly draw attention though, wouldn't it?" He grimaced and strode for the door, calling down to Boris to come up and watch her before he disappeared behind the closed door of his room.

Get a hold of yourself.

Five minutes later, Grigg returned wearing slim-cut black trousers, shining ebony boots, and a maroon vest embroidered with gold thread. Everything fit closer to his body than usual, save for his tunic sleeves—the black servant's jacket would have to fit over everything else, and button closed, before he shed it later in the evening.

He'd tamed his hair with scented oil, running his hands through his hair several times to adjust it, releasing pleasing notes of amber and sandalwood throughout the room. Except for the one lock of hair that always fell across his forehead, everything cooperated. The gold chain of his pocket watch draped just so across the front, complimenting the polished buttons and golden thread of the vest. He'd resisted the urge to roll up his sleeves, allowing the shirt to fit easier into the jacket of the serving staff he'd have to wear on top of the ensemble.

Adelina leaned against the arm of the sofa, waiting for him across from where Boris stood with his arms folded by the kitchen table. Her eyes swept over him, and now it was her turn to lose her words. She took him in slowly, as if he might disappear if she looked away.

But didn't she want him to disappear?

Also, had this been what it had felt like to her, waiting for a response from him?

But she didn't let the silence linger so long as he had. She shoved off the sofa, strode forward, and dusted lint from the shoulder of his vest before adjusting the tunic of his shirt at the nape of his neck where it'd caught beneath the vest. How had he missed that?

He watched her, allowing himself to pretend for a moment that he was just a man, and she was just a woman, and that such a man and such a woman might experience a life where they were free. Free to love or hate one another without any external pressures forcing the issue one way or the other.

What would it be like to have the love of a woman like Adelina?

But the thought skewered him to the core, turning his stomach the instant it entered his mind. Even if she didn't think him a monster, she'd never love him. Not really. And that was for the best, because the consequences of her loving him were catastrophic.

He would never be just a man. Not until the curse was broken.

And she would never be just a woman. She was the chieftess of an ancient tribe in a forbidden mountain. A chieftess he'd kidnapped and blackmailed.

Grigg offered her his arm, and she took it. "Let's go steal a star."

CHAPTER SIXTEEN

ADELINA

The three-story Caruso mansion sat atop a hill in the heart of the city, surrounded by half the city's nobility and more than half of the city's wealth. She'd seen it before from a distance, with its gaudy burnt-orange doors set in archways of royal-blue and dark-gray stone exteriors. She and Grigg had arrived nearby together before splitting up to enter the party at separate times. Grigg chose to enter first, but since he didn't have an invitation, he broke in around back with a servant's jacket over his evening attire. Once inside the party, he could later strip off the jacket. He wanted to be in place before her so he could observe how everyone reacted to Adelina and keep a wary eye on any drinks handed to her.

Adelina had no way to know if he'd made his way inside. What if he'd been caught? What if he was hanging upside down in a stable stall converted into a torture chamber? At this very moment, blood could be dripping down his body, while her own fine new noblewoman's shoes clacked on unpolished marble floors. The mask across her eyes did little to conceal her identity, even without the dress that practically screamed Guerrori by its bold theme. Her skirt swished against her legs as she walked, every step drawing a new pair of eyes toward her.

The guards had checked her for weapons briefly at the door. She felt naked without her bow and quiver, but Grigg had insisted she not try to hide even a dagger.

"If all goes well, you won't need it," he'd said. "And if all does not go well, then a knife won't have helped matters."

A shimmering deep-jade mantle draped her shoulders. She'd skipped the coat closet, pretending not to see the attendant as she swept through the foyer and down and through the double doors into the grand ballroom. The magna vials had been hidden in the thick fur lining. The guards hadn't found them, but she'd need to deposit the vials quickly around the room before someone accosted her to take her mantle. She could only pretend to be cold for so long before it would be obvious she was holding on to it when no one else was holding on to theirs. Given who she was, it was bound to be suspicious.

For all the Caruso's greed, Adelina had expected the ballroom to be grand, but she'd never been able to anticipate what lay before her now. Impossibly tall bronze doors opened into a great hall with ceilings soaring three stories high. Alcoves drifted out at the east corners of the ballroom, perfect for private business talks or couples sneaking off to kiss beyond the exposing light of the moon. Chandeliers hung over sparkling floors like crystal stars, a skylight letting in a pool of natural silver moonlight straight down into the center of the dance floor. White flowers dripped like icicles from the ceiling amid more vines and leaves strung across its length.

On the floor, pillars carved into the likeness of trees lined the long ballroom, greenery wrapped around them and dripping with flowers. Live potted trees interspersed among the carved pillars as if the mansion had brought nobility colliding headfirst with the jungle the Carusos so deeply craved.

Swirling dresses and flashy jackets with polished buttons oiled their way across the floor in all directions to the backdrop of stringed instruments played by musicians set up on the far side of the room. Servants in stiff black-and-white jackets and trousers moved between the guests with trays of hors d'oeuvres and drinks. Laughter chimed like doorbells, ringing of fake niceties, hollow compliments, and strategic connections between smiling faces of people who probably spewed vitriol behind closed doors.

Tressed-up women and already-drunk men paused mid-sentence to observe Adelina's entrance. Her stomach ribboned away into anxious shreds. The air in her mouth turned stale. For a moment, she couldn't breathe.

Most of the guests' clothing was in dark tones that complimented one another: respectable maroons, navy blues, amethyst purple. Grigg had overshot the standing-out feature by a million meters with her bold greens and bursting reds and oranges blossoming across her skirts. How could she ever plant the vials with everyone staring at her like this? And what did all those eyes think of her?

Adelina scanned the crowd. A gentleman bumped into her from behind as he entered the room. She startled and sidestepped out of his way to let him in.

She had to keep moving. Standing there stuck still like an idiot was certainly not the play if she wanted to even *pretend* like she could blend in. Adelina's gaze swept across the room a third, fourth time—still no sign of Grigg among the servants or amid the guests. She made for one of the servants carrying a tray and took a glass of wine to keep her hands busy before someone else could offer her one.

Adelina strode forward toward one of the pillars wrapped in vines, pretended to take a sip of wine, and worked the first vial out from the edge of her mantle with a practiced hand. She leaned against the pillar and slipped the vial into the greenery wrapping the pillar.

In all the commotion leading up to the evening, Grigg had failed to give her a last dose of magna, and she certainly hadn't mentioned it. If he forgot, she was going to let him.

Once the magna vials went off here, she wouldn't be able to use her power. But until that time, her fireblood ability would be at her fingertips again for the first time in days. It felt good. If she couldn't bring in outside weapons, keeping the weapon of her fireblood offered some small consolation.

Now she needed to quickly place the other vials before getting rid of her mantle and finding Nico. She hadn't seen any of the Caruso family yet, but the evening had only just begun. Guests were still arriving, and chances were more than decent that the hosts of the night would like to make a grand entrance.

Adelina moved through the ballroom with slow, measured steps, allowing herself to take in the general splendor so that anyone looking on might see her genuine curiosity and think that's all there was to her movements. Grigg had said that something he'd injected into the vial corks acted as a catalyst that would wear down into the vials and go off at the right time. He'd failed to say what the right time was, how long it would take for whatever he'd treated the cork with to let it slip into the vial and mix with the magna powder. But he had made it abundantly clear that she did not want the vials to still be in the lining of her mantle when that happened.

She'd considered placing them upside down so that the cork would drop out instead of into the powder, and the plan would fail. But there would be no reason to act out of spite to Grigg when that spite would only benefit the Caruso family, who was already planning her demise. Not to mention it would keep the Heart of the Stars in the Carusos' grasp and would probably get Lucia killed.

Adelina placed two more vials among the pillars and one in a potted plant, using all the nuance of misdirection skills she'd learned over the past few days to keep all attention away from the hand actually placing the vial. By the time she'd placed the first five vials, she was feeling a little more confident. Only one to go, with no hiccups so far.

An attendant appeared at her shoulder just as she was about to place the last vial. "May I take your mantle, my lady?"

Adelina turned to find a young female attendant in her upper teens, hair tied back, dressed in the same black-and-white attire of the other mansion servants. She had a sweet face, a soft, expectant expression, and her hand was outstretched to take Adelina's cloak.

Adelina flashed a smile. "Viper's breath. I must have forgotten I was wearing it." She winced at the curse she probably shouldn't have uttered in a place as fancy as this—though, on second thought, nothing owned by the Carusos really deserved delicate treatment. Exterior appearances were frequently only facades, both for buildings and for people. The real test was on the inside, and the Caruso family was rotten to the core.

She set her glass on the tray of another passing servant and reached up to undo the clasp of her cloak. But just as she undid the clasp of her cloak, Adelina also undid her necklace. It fell to the marble floors with a clatter.

The servant gasped in dismay.

Adelina brought her right hand to her naked neck where the necklace had been. "Oh!"

Her left hand ran along the rim of her cloak and drew the vial into her palm. Both women dropped to the floor to reach for the necklace. The servant girl got there first, and as Adelina reached for the necklace with her right hand, she slipped the last vial into the soil of the tree beside them with her left.

The girl held out her necklace, staring with open awe. "It's lovely, my lady. It brings out your eyes."

Adelina offered a meek smile. "Thank you for returning it. It must not have been fastened correctly. And thank you for the compliment. Here." She took the mantle from her shoulders and passed it to the girl, who took it gingerly in her arms. "Many thanks."

The girl dipped her head and was gone, just as the double doors to the ballroom opened again. The music changed to a stunning tune with the brightness and vigor of a welcome mingled with intense undertones, as if to whisper a final word of warning to the guests. Drinks stopped their clinking, laughter paused midgiggle, and speech dropped to a hush. A tall Morturi man in black from head to toe with a fringed jacket and towering traditional Morturi headdress stepped through the doors.

Looking at Nico, Adelina could see where Frederico got his broad shoulders and long legs, though Nico's rounder belly spoke of a life spent more in talk than in action as of late. Still, by all accounts, he could hold his own. The chief looked down his flat nose at his guests before spreading his arms like an entertainer and flashing a pearly white smile. He bowed and swept his hand behind him to acknowledge his entourage. Three more men and three women filed in, and the sight of the first man sent a tremor through Adelina.

Frederico. He wore a tunic with a deep "V" at the chest, exposing half his front, and the golden gauntlets that gathered billowing sleeves at his forearm matched the gold belt over his black trousers. His long dark hair was tied back, beard was as neatly trimmed as she'd ever seen it, and a large necklace of silver talons hung from his neck.

Nico smiled at his princeling son and spun to flash another smile at the crowd, who roared in applause over the music. Three more men followed, each with a woman on their arm.

Nico had never married and always walked in alone. It was said he claimed that his mother had been Guerrori and abandoned him, and that by blood he had rights to the jungle. If he had a Guerrori ancestor, though, his bloodline came from long ago. No respectable Guerrori woman would have slept with a Morturi man in recent history. And the idea of a merge between the two tribes had been just as detestable to the Morturi as it had been to the Guerrori for decades until now.

Adelina glanced around the room again. Whatever sort of operation the Carusos were running, they were making a killing on it and probably killing to get it. With such living in the lap of such luxury, why did they need the Nascosta? But just as the thought flitted across her mind, Frederico's dark eyes found hers. He stood a hair straighter, his chin lifted a little taller, and his focus swallowed her whole.

He wanted it because it was there. He wanted it because it was not his, and he was an entitled man caught square in the fist of supreme greed for power.

The music had stopped, and Nico was talking, but all Adelina could hear was the rush of her pulse and the hammering of her heart. Of course she knew Frederico would find her there, but she'd hoped it wouldn't be so soon—and from the looks of things, he wasn't in a good mood.

Nico said something else, and the crowd laughed. Frederico ignored them. When his gaze finally slid from Adelina back to his father, a vein in his neck bulged, and his hands balled into fists. He clasped them behind his back.

Adelina took a step back and tried to slide behind one of the pillars, but she caught Frederico's gaze flick back to check her position within half a second of her making the move. They were forty paces apart, but the large room had grown stuffy under that dark gaze.

Nico made another joke and glanced at his son. When he did, the levity on his face shattered. He followed Frederico's gaze to Adelina and took a casual sidestep between Frederico and Adelina as he spoke. "So welcome one and all to the Dance of Dusk 'Till Dawn, to the Lovers' Ball, where connections light the night like stars and the wine flows free as the rivers. Enjoy."

He clapped his hands and gave a bow and a wide practiced smile. The crowd erupted again in applause, and the musicians picked up a fresh lively tune. Guests converged into a crowd where they'd parted before in respect to their host.

Nico reached for his son's arm. His mouth moved, but Adelina was too far away to hear what he said. Whatever it was, Frederico wasn't interested. He shook off his father's grip without sparing him a passing glance and stalked straight toward Adelina, murder in his eyes.

Adelina ducked behind the pillar and scanned the room again. Where was Grigg? She never thought she'd be hoping for his face, but now there was no one she wanted to see more. Because if he wasn't there, it meant she was alone in a den of vipers who wanted her dead.

Three boisterous women with hair piled on top of their heads and linked arms swept past the place where Adelina stood. She half leaped from behind the pillar to walk on the other side of them, keeping their ridiculous tall hair between herself and the last place she'd seen the Morturi prince.

She'd set the vials. Part one was complete. But she was meant now to engage Nico to distract him—not Frederico. Frederico could die in a fiery hailstorm of arrows for all she cared.

A servant wove his way through the crowd toward the trio of women, stopping them to offer refreshment. They stopped to fill their hands with truffles from the tray, and Adelina dodged the servant, setting her eyes on a group of tall men three meters away.

If she could get behind them long enough to lose Frederico, maybe she could find Nico in the crowd and get to him before the prince found her. If she could get to Nico first—

"Have you decided to save the jungle?"

The low husk of his voice sent a recoiling shiver through her bones and set the hairs at the nape of her neck on end. Frederico was right behind her. She could pretend she hadn't seen him. He wouldn't want to make a scene, would he? In front of all these people?

Adelina ignored the voice and dove left between two men

gesturing with boisterous wild movements as they spoke of minerals and soil and mines. But the next thing she knew, a hand grabbed her elbow and tugged her to one side. She ripped her elbow free and whirled, half her mind set on combat, before she squared her shoulders toward the prince.

He arched an eyebrow. "I knew you didn't want to make a deal, but I never thought you'd go to my father."

Neither did she. It wasn't her idea, and she hadn't meant it. She wanted nothing to do with the Morturi. She swallowed. "It's a recent development. You broke the treaty your father signed, and I want a new deal. One with assurances. One I can trust."

His eyes narrowed. "And why would anyone make a deal with a liar like you? I didn't break the treaty. It was your women who broke it first, and your quakemakers who destroyed my outpost. It collapsed before we even passed the border of the jungle."

"My women were nowhere close to your tower." She hadn't known about the tower. If she hadn't done it, and he hadn't blown up his own structure ...

Grigg's cocky face burst uninvited into her mind's eye, and a grating gnawed at her gut. *I might like explosions, but do I use them for every single thing? No ...*

Frederico smiled a twisted smile that contorted his mouth but never reached his eyes. "Come now. This is a party. Why don't you let me get you a drink?"

Adelina's knees threatened to lock up as he hailed a servant from across the room. Grigg was supposed to swap out any drink she was handed. But he wasn't there.

Frederico turned back to her as the servant made his way over. "I told you today was the deadline for your decision, and here you are. If you do not accept my proposal by midnight, you and your women will die. Going to my father will not help you. He grows old, and he won't be chief forever. And he's not stupid enough to give up land when we should be gaining it." He stepped toward her.

She stood her ground and lifted her chin, as if splinters of ice were not impaling themselves into her chest with every word he spoke.

"Your hand, Chieftess, or your head. That's what I told you. But it seems to me you've already decided." He took her hand and kissed it. She gritted her teeth and snapped her hand back. He offered her a wicked sneer.

A servant appeared at his side, and Frederico took a glass of wine from the tray. He gestured at the people milling about them pretending not to watch the prince of the Morturi and the chieftess of the Guerrori facing off just off-center in the room. "Do you want these people to see you bullheaded and brash? Smŭrttata has put up with you for many years. What will happen when you lose the favor of the people completely?" He handed her the glass. "You're not at home, Adelina. Play nice or don't play at all."

Adelina's tongue stuck to the roof of her mouth. Her gut twisted as he raked his eyes slowly down her body and back up again. "Such a shame," he murmured, more to himself than to her. "I would have liked for you to be mine."

Revulsion roiled her insides like undercooked food. Then her mind trailed to how he'd phrased his words.

Would have? Because he knew she would never marry him, or because she was already past tense in his mind—because she was already dead?

Adelina's gaze dropped to the sparkling, blood-red liquid in the glass in her hand. She swallowed hard, then glanced up as a movement caught her eye just past Frederico's shoulder. A flash of ocean-blue eyes. Grigg. He was here, with a fresh glass of wine in his hand, sporting the stiff servant's jacket.

Adelina cleared her throat and lifted her chin toward Frederico. If she couldn't catch Nico alone, she would distract him and Frederico at the same time. A small price to pay for the smug expression to be wiped from his face by the end of the night. "I didn't come here for you. I came here for your father."

She turned on her heel and moved as if to stalk away through the crowd, but Frederico was there, hovering, following like a shadow. She knew he would, but a second man traced her movements from her other side. The man she'd been searching the room for the entire night.

Adelina turned as if to weave behind a couple standing close together on her left. Ocean-blue eyes never made eye contact with her as they passed, and neither of their feet stopped moving as they exchanged wine glasses in a smooth pass just out of sight of Frederico's harsh gaze. By the time the prince caught up to her, she held the new wine glass.

Nico stood twenty feet away, engaged in conversation with a couple sporting a matching dark-blue jacket and gown. Nico's back was to her. She could call out to him now. Once she had his attention, Frederico would have to either back off or confront his father directly. Likely an unpleasant thought for him, considering their disagreement on how to handle her and her tribe.

Frederico's fingers closed around her elbow. She ripped it free for the second time that evening and strode through the crowd toward Nico. Twenty paces. Eighteen. Fifteen.

"Adelina."

She ignored him. She would get just a little closer and call out. She would—

"Adelina, we didn't break the treaty. If you really believe we did, I need to know why. Perhaps there is someone beneath us in our organizations that we should be punishing. Presumably someone on your end."

It was an odd change of tactic, searching for common ground and cooperation after his usual dose of threats. Was he desperate?

She shook him off and strode forward. How could they both believe the other broke the treaty? Was he playing her, or was someone else playing them both?

Why had Grigg known Igor's name? Why had he used it the same night the man was supposed to be consulting with Nico

Caruso? Why had the breach occurred the same evening Adelina always watched the Palladinos?

A chasm of emptiness beckoned to take her in. *You are a fool.* Because Grigg was the only common denominator. He knew her routine. He knew the Carusos' lust for power and who they went to for advice. He'd known everything.

Her head whipped to one side, searching for the servant with the ocean-blue eyes. But the ocean was a lie—smooth and glassy just long enough for fools to drop their guard before the current ripped them out to sea. And she'd been dumb enough to be caught in the riptide.

Maybe she didn't need to get Nico's attention at all. Maybe she needed to leave this party right now, run to the jungle, corral her women, save Lucia, and deal with things her own way. Grigg—or whatever his real name was—was a liar. And not just a liar, but a liar in league with the mage who had cursed her.

If she got her women together, she could steal the Star, destroy the remnant of the mage's power, and cut Grigg off at the knees.

Resolve hardened in her chest. Adelina took another step toward Nico, then rotated ninety degrees on her heel and made for the double doors. She knew Grigg was watching, but she didn't care. She called to the fire. Heat flooded her palms. The magna had worn off, and she was in complete control again.

Grigg *had* made a mistake, and her patience had been rewarded.

She brushed past faceless guest after faceless guest, moving as if in a dream come to life; only the dream was a nightmare, and she couldn't wake in a cold sweat. She had to live it.

Her shoulder brushed a man to her right. The man swayed on his feet and collapsed. Adelina snapped her head and reached out on instinct, but she wasn't fast enough. The man hit to the floor, hard. He rolled to his back and began to convulse, choking on his own spit—or, more realistically, whatever poison had been in his glass. His hand dropped, and the wine glass shattered on the marble floor.

Feet rooted to the floor, Adelina stared down at his white face. It was Sebastian Palladino. Of course. He and his brother were the wine suppliers. Somewhere in the back of her mind, she'd known that.

Adelina dropped to her knees beside Sebastian, pulling at him to roll the man to his side, instead of his back, to keep him from choking, her mind still spinning.

The Caruso family would have schmoozed to get them here, inviting them to the party as a reward for their services. Access to important people. And now he was dying. But why would they want to kill Sebastian? Unless ...

She glanced up. Grigg stood at the fringes of the gathering crowd, a tray of wine glasses still balanced on one hand. What if he hadn't disposed of her glass after switching out the wines? What if he'd only placed it back on the tray for someone else to take? Someone like Sebastian. Which meant someone had tried to kill *her*. And though she lived, someone else would still die in her place.

And the killer would try again.

Red-hot fury built inside her as her eyes latched onto Grigg's steely, impassive ones.

"Help! He needs help!"

All eyes turned to the dying man on the floor, the chieftess bending over him. Frederico had halted mid-stride as the scene unfolded. Nico stopped mid-sentence and spun to see his guest crumple to the marble.

But it was Grigg Adelina wanted. Grigg had brought an antidote. And before Adelina killed the man, she planned to get it from him.

Grigg stepped forward slowly, set the tray on the floor, and bent over the body, taking Sebastian's pulse as his limbs jerked.

Grigg dropped his voice so low only she could hear, moving his hands as if examining Sebastian.

"Palladino. It's him, isn't it? You don't watch him to case the house. You're not looking to work with him or blackmail him. You love him."

Adelina reeled. How was this the most important thing right now? Who cared why she went to the house when a man was dying on the floor?

She'd never even met the man in the flesh. She couldn't deny she cared what happened to Sebastian. He was so good with his young nieces and nephews. He loved his family. And he had proved her mother was a liar. Sebastian, with soft eyes and strong arms he used only for tossing the children in the air and giving hugs when they fell.

He was hope of a life she wished were possible for herself. She couldn't let that die.

Her lip trembled. She blinked back unshed tears as her top lip began to curl into a snarl. A dangerous dark expression fell over Grigg's face as he watched the transformation in her face.

"Tick tock, Adelina. Let him go."

She clenched her jaw. "You killed him." The fire burned in her blood, begging for release, building into her glowing palms. Grigg grabbed her wrist and slammed her palm down on Palladino's chest, forcing her to retract the fire to keep from injuring him.

"I didn't kill anyone yet. I'm not the one who put poison in a glass. But if I don't get the Heart of the Stars by midnight tonight, I'll use the konnolan and kill anyone it touches."

Her head snapped up. "Konnolan?"

He read the question in her eyes and answered without emotion. "You heard me. You didn't plant magna in the room. You planted konnolan. They'll all drop to the floor like pretty little dolls."

Visions of Lucia vomiting on the open field, falling to the ground so weak she had to be carried into the house, filled her memory. Images of what that might look like on a grand scale shook her to the core.

But Grigg wasn't done. He ran his hand over Sebastian's chest, loosening his tight-fitting jacket and angling him further to his side as spittle spewed from his mouth.

"This isn't the kind of scene you were supposed to make. So you better make up for it with something good. Get everyone in the room watching you. Now."

She ran a hand over Sebastian's forehead and rolled him more fully onto his side as he convulsed, allowing the liquid in his mouth to spill out onto the floor instead of the back of his throat.

Grigg moved as if helping her to position Sebastian. His hand darted into his own jacket, then he turned the man on his back, and as he did, his fingers hesitated lightly over the man's open mouth. Something dropped inside. A tablet, maybe? She wasn't sure. But Sebastian stopped convulsing.

Relief swept over Adelina as color slowly returned to Sebastian's cheeks. Sebastian coughed and began to take in deep breaths, consciousness returning. The crowd roared in applause. Grigg clapped Sebastian on the back and leaned in toward Adelina.

"I did this for you. You owe me. You have two minutes to enrapture the entire ballroom. The konnolan is going off whether you like it or not, and I had better have the Heart in my hands before it does ... or they all die."

Adelina glanced up at the door. She'd been so close. But the room was full of people, many of them melders. It would be impossible to know how many out of those in attendance had powers. And though all the attendees were guests of the Carusos, some of them were innocent, like the Paladinos, whose only crime was serving wine at a catered event.

Sebastian coughed again. Adelina rubbed his back absently and helped him sit up. Frederico appeared on the other side of the man, offering him a hand and helping him to his feet. By the time Adelina looked around again, Grigg was gone.

Nico approached and glanced at Adelina.

Grigg reappeared at the fringes of the crowd. *Tick tock*, he mouthed.

Nico stepped forward, his gaze drifting between his son and Adelina. Had it been Frederico or Nico who tried to kill her? Perhaps Nico had decided his son couldn't make impulsive deals with the chieftess if she was dead.

Adelina swallowed hard. She gestured to Frederico to help her get the man up on his feet. Sebastian staggered, then stabilized with a wince. He glanced at her as though she were a fallen angel materialized out of thin air. Except that it was *her* glass that had nearly killed him.

"What—what happened?"

Frederico clapped the man on the back. "You had a seizure, sir. Thanks to the lady, you recovered quickly. And thanks to one of our staff."

Here Frederico swept his hand toward Grigg, just as he started to melt into the crowd. Frederico lifted his voice. "You must be new on my staff. I didn't catch your name."

Grigg dismissed his attentions with a wave and a courteous bow. "Georgi, at your service, sir. It was nothing."

Frederico's lips pressed into a flat line. He'd seen the two of them exchange words over Sebastian's collapsed body. And he hadn't been fooled. Adelina wasn't at the ball alone.

Adelina swooped to the floor to grab her glass—the one Grigg had given her—and lifted it in a toast. Her heart thundered in her chest, rebelling against the words she would utter next. "A toast!"

The room glanced at each other, then lifted their own glasses to mirror hers. Frederico swiped a glass off a tray, eyes fixed on Adelina's face, as if by just looking he could peel the skin from her face if she said the wrong thing.

Nico stood with his feet a shoulder width apart, glaring daggers at Adelina for having the gall to be alive in his ballroom.

And now, not only was she alive, but she held control of the guests in the palm of her hand with an upraised glass.

Adelina released Sebastian, stumbled forward as if she'd had one too many, and slurred her words just a little. "To health, to peace, and to healthy competition." She weaved her hand in the air, the wine sloshing against the rim of the glass.

The room echoed, "To peace, to health," in staggered mutters and confused glances, but none of them knew what to make of the last bit.

Adelina threw the rest of the alcohol down the back of her throat, gulping down the wine, and slammed the glass down into Grigg's hands as he stood at the edge of the audience. He stared at her as if even he was shocked by her sudden abrasive behavior.

She spun toward Frederico. "I wager my hand in marriage that you can't shoot better than me. If you can, I'll marry you, and you'll be the first man in hundreds of years to step foot in the Heart of the Mountain. If not, you give me one wish, whatever I ask for."

The room spun. Whether from the buzz of the drink, the rush of adrenaline, or the flurry of excitement that swept over the room, she couldn't say. Frederico and Grigg's eyes bugged out at her phrasing. *The Heart of the Mountain.* It was dangerous to say it out loud, but she'd gotten what she wanted. Confirmation they both knew about the real Heart of the Mountain, and they both wanted it. Badly.

She'd been right about Grigg. He was after more than the Heart of the Stars, and by showing her hand just a little, both men would come crawling to eat out of her hand like birds. *She* had the leverage.

If Grigg wanted a show, it was a show he would have. And not only would she have her fireblood, but her enemy was about to deliver a bow and arrow to her waiting hand. Frederico would never turn down the challenge, and Nico couldn't stop it so publicly without showing weakness in front of his guests.

A slow smile spread over Frederico's face until he lit ear to ear with a serpentine grin. "I accept."

CHAPTER SEVENTEEN

Grigg's fingers clutched at Adelina's empty wineglass. Okay, so subtlety wasn't her style. Sure, she could probably sneak up on any jungle animal. She could walk without making a sound. She could launch herself up walls and swing through the trees like a monkey. But put the woman in a room with actual, real live people, and the splashing wine on his shirt scenario was precisely representative.

Adelina stood like a regal queen in the hall of her adversary, surrounded by witnesses, calling for weapons and wrapping the whole situation up in the ribbon of a game. Judging by Nico's expression, there was no chance this competition would end well —especially not now that Adelina had said what she said: *the Heart of the Mountain.*

To be fair, Grigg had asked her to make a scene, and she'd come through. But this? Why not just carve *I know more than I should* into her forehead? Why not toss up a banner that said, *I have what you want, and I know why you want it,* and plaster it on the walls?

Perhaps when they rolled out the target, she could go stand in front of it. Maybe she could break whatever secret codes the Guerrori had for using the magic in the mountain and swear to use it against the Morturi—while surrounded by the Morturi leadership and their best warriors.

Frederico called for a bow and arrow. Grigg grimaced. She'd done exactly what he'd asked her to do. Guests circled. All attention was fixated on Adelina—save for Sebastian, who stumbled his way off into the crowd, presumably to get himself together and maybe douse his face with water.

As the guests converged around Frederico and Adelina, Grigg still stood at the fringes of the open circle surrounding the duo. Why was he still standing here? He had to disappear. With any luck, the competition would take some time, and Adelina would stretch it out, buying him more time.

Grigg sidestepped through the crowd, but didn't get three steps before a heavy hand landed on the shoulder of his servant's jacket. Frederico pulled him back with a strength at least equal to his own, a fixed smile painted across his face. "Please, after your heroics this evening, you deserve a treat. Stay and watch." Quieter, Frederico hissed, "You're not leaving my sight."

This wasn't part of the plan. He absolutely *would* be leaving Frederico's sight. Galloping gibbons, he should have let Adelina flounder on the floor with Sebastian. If he'd only let Sebastian die, Adelina would have made plenty of a scene on her own, and the dead man on the floor would have served as distraction enough for his getaway.

The next minute, two servants appeared carrying a target, as if the Carusos kept a room full of them in the foyer for just such an occasion. Two identical bows and one quiver of arrows were carried in next. Grigg hadn't noticed when the music stopped playing, but Frederico motioned to them now, and they picked up an intense melody with a beat on a drum like the final march of a dead man.

Grigg resisted the urge to shrug out of Frederico's grip. Better to let him think he was in control until the right timing presented itself.

His mind still spun. Why had he saved Sebastian? Because he didn't want Adelina to think he was a monster? Grigg's being a monster was a more honest assessment of who he really was. He'd told her so himself.

Did he not want her to see the truth about him, after all his threats, after constantly hammering into her mind what sort of man he was? What had turned him so soft? His moment of weakness was abominable and might ultimately get them both killed.

If he'd abandoned her like he was supposed to, perhaps he could have swept back and salvaged her from the ballroom after the konnolan went off. But if it went off before he got the Heart of the Stars—if he remained stuck in the ballroom—his escape window would close. He'd have to get the Heart and go. And if Stoyan didn't arrive before the konnolan went off, the room could be a bloodbath by the time he got the necklace.

Thinking of which, where *was* Stoyan? Grigg had to get to the display room and seal the window facing the children's rooms before Stoyan got there. Or maybe Stoyan wasn't coming, and no other distraction would appear. Maybe Grigg would be trapped here with a murderous man holding a bow and arrow and a father dripping poison into drinks.

Adelina shot him a look that, for the first time since she'd made her toast, said she would rather be doing anything than making this deal with Frederico. The whites of her eyes were larger than usual, her brows raised in that fearful expression of a wounded animal thrashing about in the snare. *His* snare.

For an instant, Grigg remembered how it had felt to be the one who made her laugh—that musical laugh that rang truer than all the bells this side of the sea. Now, he'd set a trap, shoved her into it, and set a fire.

Frederico jerked his head at Grigg. "Before we get started, I'm afraid I don't recognize you. As I said, I want to reward you for your actions if you're a hero."

A thick man with ears nearly big enough to fly with grabbed Grigg and yanked him backward, giving him his second thorough pat down in a week.

Frederico folded his arms as he scrutinized the process. "I'm sure you understand. Because if you're not a hero ... well, I can't let you stand so close to my future bride without knowing what sort of man you are."

Ear Guy plucked the money bag Grigg had lifted from Sebastian's jacket as he patted him down and handed it to Frederico. Frederico quirked an eyebrow.

Grigg grinned. "If you do get married, I'd love a back-row seat. Great view of all the pockets in the room, decent exit, not too close to all the kissing. I love a good kiss as much as the next man, but there's something repulsive about watching a guy as ugly as you contort the face of a beautiful woman like that." He nodded at Adelina.

Adelina's jaw dropped.

Frederico ripped his hand up from his waist, a dagger flashing from his palm as he did. The movement was so fast, Grigg hadn't noticed he'd unsheathed the dagger until it was in his hand. Grigg jumped back, only to find Adelina already standing between him and the Morturi prince. The corner of her lips twisted into the shadow of a smile, oozing a confidence that had not been there in her private look toward him moments before.

"Do you really want these people to see you bullheaded and brash?"

Color flushed the prince's cheeks. He clenched his jaw, but Adelina was moving. She crossed the open space, snatched half a glass of wine from a guest's fingers, and downed the drink in a swig.

"How can I marry a man without control?"

She sauntered toward Frederico with a walk that would have

struck Mira speechless, stopping only when they came toe-to-toe. Adelina tipped her head up at Frederico. "When I win ... you'll give me whatever I ask for."

Frederico grazed her cheek with the back of his hand. She stiffened at his touch, but to her credit, she didn't smash her elbow into his face. Though, blast it all, Grigg wanted nothing more at that moment than to slug the prince so hard he would fall and never get up. Considering Grigg had only seen him for a few minutes and already hated the man, he couldn't imagine the restraint this moment must have required for Adelina.

Frederico smiled. "Only *if* you win. Three shots."

"Five."

Somehow, she'd transformed back into the chieftess, fully in her element as she countered the terms. Five shots wouldn't give him much extra time, but it might be enough. A few seconds was all he needed, if only the opportunity presented itself to slip away.

Nico leveled the prince with a dark glare from the edge of the open circle. "Son."

The word carried authority, command, and warning in a tone that accused of insolence and demanded attention all at once. But Frederico wasn't interested in paying attention, least of all to his father. He grabbed the bow and quiver from the first of the attendants. He seemed to have forgotten about Grigg, at least for the time being.

"Agreed. Five shots."

Frederico stepped forward, notched his first arrow to the string, and pulled it back. *Thwip.* The arrow sang from the string and buried itself just a hair to the left of the center.

Adelina assessed the target and her opponent's shot with the steadiness of a jungle cat on the prowl. The problem now was Adelina herself. She had challenged Frederico, but she planned to win. He could see it in her eyes—in the way she had dropped into the calm space of a hunter stalking the forests rather than a woman in a ball gown she wasn't used to wearing. Shoulders back, eyes focused on her target.

The woman was all jungle and wilderness and fire, but if she won, Nico would have a fit of rage. He'd already tried to kill her once tonight, and chances were good he wasn't going to sit by and let his son promise to wed the chieftess. By a similar token, Frederico was arrogant. He was more likely to accuse her of cheating if she won than to abide by any agreement.

But the competition wasn't to show off. It was to buy time. He had to make sure that happened—the right way. Adelina had to lose.

Frederico nodded to the servant holding the second bow and arrow, but he himself stepped back so that he stood, bow in hand, behind Adelina. Adelina cast an annoyed glance over her shoulder before stepping forward to take stock of his position.

Adelina stepped forward to accept the bow and arrow from the servant. If she made a move, a room full of melders would act against her, not to mention Frederico himself. The prince had his bow, a full quiver, and a view of her back. *She* had only a bow and a single arrow.

Her gaze passed over Grigg, hesitating only an instant before moving on to face the target. The more attention she gave him, the worse things would get. She was playing her role well, even if the archery challenge was overboard on the theatrics. Then again, after the Palladino man fell to the floor, his demand that she capture the attention of the room in two minutes had been a bit of a challenge. He wasn't sure what he would have done differently in her place.

Grigg shifted his weight. The guard, with his hand clapped hard on his shoulder, gripped him tighter. He could try to wrestle his way free, but that would draw attention. He could wait for Adelina or Frederico to make more of a scene, or for Nico himself to put a stop to the challenge, but the chief stood now with his arms crossed, eyes on the chieftess, letting the situation play out. And still, Stoyan and his men weren't there. Without the konnolan affecting them also when it went off, which, according to his esti-mation, would happen in only a few minutes, a lot more people would die. His original plan had involved no deaths at all, although he'd been willing to allow one if someone really did try to poison Adelina, which they had.

And he'd wasted precious time saving that man. Like an idiot.

Adelina notched the arrow, drew back, and let fly. *Thwip.* Dead center.

She stepped back for Frederico to take his position, hardly bothering to examine her work. Grigg let out a slow, low whistle, which earned him a death glare from the prince. He didn't mind if the prince was rattled. Something about seeing the man sport an unpleasant expression was a salve to the soul.

Frederico's second shot was also dead center, rivaling Adelina's. Adelina's next shot hit just shy of her first, the arrowhead threat-ening to pierce the shaft of the one already buried in the target. If she didn't throw her shot soon, and Frederico missed his third, they might be in trouble.

Nico seemed to have the same idea as he exchanged a glance with a man in the crowd. Grigg followed his gaze to a man who slipped toward the front of the observation circle and dropped one hand to his waist, turning it subtly so his palm faced outward.

Frederico's third shot split the first arrow down the middle.

Adelina drew back her arrow. A whisper of wind wafted by Grigg's cheek as it stole toward the woman with the bow. The windcaller had sent out his rivulet of air too soon, to tug on the bow itself rather than the arrow. Adelina kept her hold on the weapon, arrow pulled back, and spoke loud for all to hear. "The air has shifted in a room without wind. We shoot fair, or not at all."

Frederico shot a glare around the circle. "No melders are to interfere. This is fair play. Hands down, all of you."

The rivulet disappeared, and Adelina took her next shot. By the time they'd each gotten to four out of five, the distances of the arrow shots were measured and the score was determined to be a tie. The next shot would be everything.

Frederico ran his hand along the smooth edge of his bow with a laugh. "I promise to be as much of a gentleman in our marriage as I have been in competition. I took it easy on you."

Grigg stifled a groan. The man had done no such thing.

Frederico called for a fresh target, and it was brought. "Whoever's closest."

Adelina wrinkled her nose. "Just like that? Standing still?"

Frederico snorted. "I can't very well bring a horse in here. This is my father's ballroom, and these are marble floors."

She shrugged. "Yes, but I thought your guests might like to be entertained. A final shot the same as all the rest is boring."

He shifted his weight and ran a hand across his chin. "What do you propose?"

"Set the target on wheels and use those windcallers who wanted so badly to be a part of our challenge. Let them send it rolling across the room."

A murmur ran through the crowd. Frederico scanned the guests and grinned. He spread his hands. "Set it on a cart."

Still no Stoyan. Still no escape route. Grigg glanced at the pillars where the vials had been stowed. No smoke. No popping sound. Nothing.

The cart came in from close to where Grigg stood, allowing him to adjust his position under the weight of the guard's hand on his shoulder, edging closer to where Adelina stood to let the staff member come through. Two servants strolled up to the front, set the target on the cart, and pulled it to one side. Frederico identified two women from the crowd and had them stand behind the target: windcallers. Neither had tried to cheat before, but Frederico had been no part of that. It was Nico's man who'd wanted to influence the game.

The windcallers lifted their hands, and a whoosh of air signaled the beginning of the challenge. The target rumbled across the marble floor. Frederico notched the arrow. The arrow hit dead center.

Had Grigg been imagining its trajectory? Hadn't it been off, just a hair? But no, the arrow hit the target so hard that most of the arrowhead was buried in the target. He'd cheated—or someone had cheated for him, driving the arrow in stronger and deeper than usual.

Which was all the better for Grigg. Because Adelina had to lose.

Nico's windcaller moved through the crowd until he stood at Grigg's shoulder on the other side of the guard, angling his hand but not yet acting. From Adelina's draws, if he didn't move fast, he'd lose his opportunity to make any impact at all, as the arrow would be in his target before the windcaller's air headed its way.

She could still tie with Frederico, forcing a tiebreaker shot.

Adelina pulled back the string in a smooth, fast motion of ironclad decisiveness. Grigg faked a sneeze and drove his elbow into the windcaller. He jumped, and a whisper of air hit Adelina's string just as she let go of the arrow. The target rolled across the space and the arrow hit a full hand's breadth shy of the center.

Grigg let out a breath. Crisis averted. She'd lost.

Adelina whirled on him. Fuming red blossomed in her cheeks. Rage crackled in her eyes. She stormed toward him, empty bow in hand, but Frederico wrapped his arms around her waist and swung her in a circle, catching her up off her feet.

"My friends!" He grabbed her hand and thrust it in the air with a shout. "May I present the future Adelina Caruso."

The room erupted in cheers and applause. Frederico grinned a slippery crocodile smile, but the chieftess beside him glared only at Grigg. If murder was a person, her name was Adelina. In that moment, as their eyes met, she looked like Giovanna had the split second before the mage had ripped his heart from his chest.

A rippling chill ran down his spine. Sure, he'd made her lose. But it was a competition, and it wasn't like she'd ever *actually* marry Frederico. Time on the vials was running out. She'd have to get over it.

A shout of alarm from somewhere further into the house interrupted the cheers in the room. A moment later, a guard rushed through the doors and gestured to Nico and Frederico, then whispered something into Nico's ear. The melder guard still held Grigg by the shoulder, but Grigg would bet his britches that was about to change.

And then it did.

Nico turned toward the guard who had Grigg, spoke to Ear Guy and the messenger, and jerked his head toward the door. Ear Guy nodded, and he and a second guard seized Grigg under the arms and dragged him out of the room.

Stoyan was here. It was time to clear out anyone who might be part of the attack, which included Grigg as a questionable character impersonating Caruso staff. He'd be placed in a holding cell in the basement, which was conveniently on the way to the display room.

Grigg didn't bother wasting energy fighting them, but he did drop his weight enough to wear them out, making them carry some of his weight as they lugged him from the ballroom and out into the hall. Once they rounded their first corner, the trio was alone, nearing the base of a grand staircase.

The first guard cursed. "Get up on your feet before I break them both."

Grigg wrinkled his nose. "What a thing to say. What would your mother think?"

With that, Grigg shot his right arm up toward the ceiling, free of the man's grasp, and rammed his elbow down into the man's nose. Ear Guy fell back, but not before Grigg threw his elbow again, this time hitting him straight in the temple.

The second guard yelled and seized Grigg from behind by the throat. For an instant, Grigg saw himself stealing the man's dagger from its sheath at his waist and stabbing it backward into the guard's gut. It would be fast, and it would be fatal. But he'd rather not kill anyone. Not if he could avoid it. Instead, Grigg stomped on the man's foot, shot his arm upward again, and spun, so that he trapped both the guard's arms in the crook of his elbow, immobilizing him.

Grigg fired off a punch to the throat and a knee to the groin. The man moved for a tackle, but Grigg spun out of the way, and the guard crashed to the floor.

The first guard gathered his feet and swung. Grigg blocked his throw, seized the man's face in his hands and brought his skull crashing down in a mighty headbutt that left a ringing against Grigg's hard head—and an unconscious guard slumped at his feet. Grigg grabbed the second man and threw a punch to the temple. The man crumbled like an overbaked cookie, joining his friend in dreamland.

Frederico still had Adelina, but that was fine. He could deal with her later. He had to get to the Heart of the Stars and seal the window shut before Stoyan came looking.

Considering Grigg hadn't even tried to get to the vault, much less left it open for Stoyan like he'd promised, Grigg could safely assume Stoyan would be less than enthused by his experience raiding the Caruso mansion. It was a night of making enemies, which was another reason he had to succeed on the first go. But if he failed, he'd be dead anyway when the egg broke apart and the mage destroyed him for good.

Grigg ripped off his servant's jacket, tossed it down the hall, and flew up the stairs three at a time, now wearing the embroidered maroon vest of evening attire. A clash of steel and a whoosh of wind from down the hall told him Stoyan had come in through the entrance. Anyone other than Nico would see the guards and assume they'd been attacked by one of Stoyan's crew.

Grigg reached the top of the landing and spun to his right, plunging down the hall with all his might. The words he'd mouthed to Adelina now taunted him. *Tick tock, tick tock.* It had taken him longer to get out of the ballroom than he'd expected, thanks to Adelina's stunt with the Palladino man. What was her obsession with him? Was she really in love with him, or was it something else?

He rolled up his sleeves as he sprinted through a grand hallway and tugged open one of the two bronze doors leading into the display room. A long room lay before him, carpeted in black and silver under vaulted archway ceilings of stone. Silver shields and Caruso family tapestries lined the walls, and statues of soldiers in armor bearing swords stood along both sides.

White marble stands held jewels, trinkets, and weapons standing out like stars against the deep contrast of the ebony carpet. Sculptures were arranged throughout the room between display cases and crystal figurines. Chandeliers bounced warm light off crystal displays. Two tall windows poured light in from either side of the room, one facing the children's wing across the open courtyard, and one facing the outer wall, with a single circular skylight overhead, letting moonlight shine down onto a circular white marble table.

He was so close to the Heart of the Stars, he could almost taste it. A network of diamond necklaces strung up in the air over a velvet tablecloth of midnight blue dotted the white marble circular table beneath the skylight. The moon and stars poured in silver beams of light, reflecting off miniature jeweled stars. But one central piece served as the masterpiece across the canvas of night.

The Heart of the Stars glittered within a crystal display case. The necklace hung on a rose-gold chain, the pendant the size of a medallion. A rose-gold ring formed the outer circle of the pendant, which was studded with diamonds on its rim. Inside, a polished fire opal served as the backdrop to a brilliant rose-gold star set with a moon on its left and the sun on its right. Another diamond star sat in the center. The larger rose-gold star exploded out beyond the edges of the diamond across the fire opal to the perimeter of the necklace on every side. It seemed to absorb the light in the room, pulling light toward itself, casting beams of rainbows around the display like a prism.

The chain hung from the top of the display case, the medallion dangling over the midnight velvet. The piece was stunning, a work of art in and of itself, but to think it also contained great magic ...

Grigg stuffed the thought down deep. First, he would save his own life by gathering the Hearts for Giovanna. Then he would find a way to steal it back and destroy Giovanna for good. In that order. The crack on the egg and the black on his heart were growing. He didn't have time for heroics, but if he could buy time, maybe—

A voice cut through his thoughts. "My brother doesn't have seizures."

Grigg had crossed halfway into the display room toward the Heart of the Stars. He jumped at the sound and turned.

Pietro Palladino stood in the doorway, shaking like a leaf, hands balled into fists at his sides. Jaw set. Eyes red. "I want answers. Now."

Grigg glanced from Pietro to the window he'd yet to seal, then to the Heart of the Stars. He looked back at Pietro. "Your brother was very nearly unfortunate collateral damage. The Carusos wanted to kill someone tonight. Sebastian wasn't their target, but they hit him instead by accident. What you need to know is that your brother is alive and well, and you need to get out and shut the door. I don't want anything bad to happen to you."

Pietro stalked forward, leaving the bronze door yawning wide in his wake as if to scream, *Here! We're in here with all your most treasured possessions, and your guards scattered to the four winds dealing with Stoyan and his goons. Storm right in and catch us.*

The man's voice trembled. "You knew he might kill someone."

Curse it all. Pietro wasn't supposed to see Grigg steal the Heart, but Grigg was running out of time. He ignored Pietro and strode for the Heart, rotating around the back of the table until he could see Pietro and the necklace at the same time.

"Are you really so surprised? The Carusos have a sordid, bloody history." Grigg examined the necklace's attachment to the corners of the crystal case, then glanced back up at Pietro. "My only job is making sure that the someone they kill isn't me or anyone critical to my own ends. On that note, I'd say the evening is going rather well."

Pietro's lip quivered. His face blanched to white and back to red in the span of three seconds. "That's about to change. You knew someone might die tonight, and it was almost my brother."

Behind the midnight tablecloth, out of Pietro's view, Grigg slipped the two vials from the heel of his boot. He drummed the fingers of one hand on the tabletop; the other held the two vials just out of sight.

"Careful, Pietro. Sebastian is only standing on two feet because of me."

Pietro let out a cry of rage and swung for Grigg. Grigg moved off the man's trajectory with ease, letting Pietro's momentum carry him past his mark. Grigg uncorked the first of the two small vials and dumped its contents on top of the crystal case before throwing a roundhouse kick at Pietro's leg.

"Pietro, please, you're a businessman. Have you ever thrown a punch?"

Pietro recovered his footing and threw another. This one was strong, but the man wasn't prepared for Grigg's counter. Grigg blocked Pietro's punching arm with the second vial closed in a fist, closed the distance, and smashed his elbow into Pietro's face. Pietro toppled over with a grunt.

Grigg stepped back, uncorked the second vial, and dumped it on top of the powder. A sizzle leaped from the mixture. Bubbling foam expanded across the surface of the crystal and sank into the fine clear surface as it ate away at the glass.

Pietro moved to get up, but Grigg dropped down behind him and captured the man's neck in the crook of his elbow in a rear choke. Pietro gagged and flailed his arms, but to no avail.

Grigg lowered his voice, keeping both of their bodies close to the floor and behind the table. "You're a good man, Pietro, but if you die tonight, the only part of you left for your children will be the stories. Stories of their father getting caught up with criminals over expensive baubles and a few acres of jungle. The moment you wake up, get up, dust yourself off, and run. Take your brother and run for your life. Go back to your wife and children and think about how much you love them and how much you have to live for until you forget that we ever met."

With those final words of warning, Grigg tightened his grip on the man's throat. Pietro thrashed, then slumped just as the hissing of the bubbling mass on the crystal stopped and a light *clink* sounded from over the table. Grigg jumped to his feet to find the display case still standing, the top of it burned away with a crack running down the side and the necklace lying harmlessly at the bottom, its chain free from its holdings.

Grigg reached in, plucked the necklace from the display case, and slipped it over his head. It took only moments to seal the window facing the children's wing, and he was out of the room sixty seconds later.

He already had the Heart of the Sea, and now the Heart of the Stars hung around his neck.

Only one more Heart to go.

CHAPTER EIGHTEEN

The doors of the ballroom slammed shut. A wave of people assaulted the doors on every side of the ballroom, their screams and fists enhancing the chaos. Stoyan had come.

Nico whirled on Adelina. "What did you do?"

She shook her head. "This wasn't me. I came to make a peace deal."

Okay, so she was lying about the peace deal. But she was telling the truth that this wasn't her. *She* had not arranged for Stoyan and his men to attack the mansion tonight. That had been all Grigg's doing. Just as the incited rivalry between the Morturi and Guerrori tribes had likely also been Grigg's doing. How powerful could a man without magic be?

A bald Morturi man in a sharp crimson jacket called to Frederico. Cassio, the man from the river attack. "They've blocked the doors. And they've got melders."

Crash. One of the metal doors beyond Cassio sunk half a foot into the cracked marble at its base. Cassio took in the damage and turned back to Frederico. "And at least one quakemaker, apparently."

Frederico spared Adelina only a moment's hesitation before abandoning her on the ballroom floor to take charge of the situation at the north doors. He was shouting orders and directing men and women in gowns and jackets, any who were not just invited guests, but Morturi members under his command.

"Quakemakers to the doors! Hold steady the foundations and the archways. See if you can lift that door back into place so we don't have to crumble it to get out. Windcallers, send air through the cracks and feel for bodies. Find out where they're standing beyond these doors and knock them off their feet. Crestbreakers, we may not have much water, but we have an awful lot of wine."

Cassio turned to a woman beside him in a silver gown. "Where are the Palladino brothers? Have them bring out any barrels of wine not yet poured."

Adelina spun. Where *had* the Palladino brothers gone? She couldn't remember seeing Pietro at all that night, and she'd last seen Sebastian stumbling into the crowd before the archery competition.

To her left, a group of firebloods banded around the west doors. To her right, a group of windcallers found a hole over one of the north door casings where the door had sunken into the marble floor. Three firebloods stepped up to shoot fiery missiles through the opening and rained down fire on anyone on the other side.

How many guests had stepped into one of the alcoves for a business meeting? What about the staff or Caruso family members who were in the mansion beyond the ballroom when Stoyan barricaded the doors?

Another thought struck like a gong. How long did they have before the konnolan went off? Grigg had likely thought she took her magna dose and expected all the melders in the room to be incapacitated except her, so she could leave while the rest of the guests were on the ground. But she *hadn't* taken magna. She could feel the fire flooding her veins even now. If the konnolan went off, she'd be down and out with the rest of them.

What if she hadn't placed it right, and it didn't go off at all? All these melders and Morturi working together could easily overpower and kill Adelina. Not to mention, if Nico got his hands on her, he could kill her now.

The poison hadn't worked, but the chaos would cover a second murder attempt just as well as anything else. And he might not get another chance. She had to find him before—

A thick hand seized her by the back of the neck and dragged her backward. Adelina swung, and a second hand caught her arm, jerking her around to face him.

Nico Caruso. "I'd know Stoyan Mironov's stubby fingerprints anywhere. Little puppy decided to make it big. And you're part of it."

Adelina ripped her arm free and shot off a series of blows—uppercut, uppercut, elbow strike. The man was thick, but more nimble than his frame would suggest. He absorbed the first two blows, blocked the third, and threw a front kick to her midsection, sending her rocketing backward across the slick floor in her stupid fancy noblewoman's shoes.

Adelina kicked off the shoes and struck out to sweep the leg of the chief and bring him down. Again, he evaded her, throwing a hammer fist at her skull.

Why wasn't he using a melder power? She'd never caught wind of which of the four elemental powers Nico had, but everything she'd heard indicated he had one. But he didn't reach for it, and neither did she.

Adelina darted out of reach and glanced to one side. Frederico's bow. It had gotten knocked from the hands of whatever attendant had been in charge of it, and two stray arrows lay scattered next to it on the glossy floor.

Nico took a flying leap forward and swung a powerful ridge hand down at her throat. "You want him to weaken us. You want a war."

Adelina ducked, spun behind him, seized him by the shoulders at his back, and drove her knee into the base of his spine. He whirled, but by the time he did, she had already thrown herself into a roll across the floor. When she sprang to her feet, Frederico's bow was in her hand, an arrow pulled back on the string.

Crackkkkk. Crash. The thunder of heavy demolished doors breaking apart reverberated across the room as quakemakers and firebloods worked together to split apart the doors and create an opening. A shower of dust and rock fell like hail on the melders standing near the opening.

On the other side of the room, the other set of doors fell with an echoing crash. Screaming guests and the ululating war cries of warriors flowed out beyond the bounds of the ballroom as a mass of humanity swarmed out, some looking for a fight, some hoping to escape whatever might come next.

She'd glanced away from Nico a fraction of a second too long. By the time she looked back, a dagger was already soaring through the air toward her heart. Adelina leaped to one side, nearly losing control of the arrow on the string as she did. She held it fast, but a searing rip of pain burned across her arm as his dagger sliced across the top layer of skin and buried itself in one of the potted trees between the pillars behind her.

Nico lunged for the final arrow on the floor. Adelina countered again with her footwork to stay beyond his reach. Why hadn't she let fly? Why hadn't she killed him? But that's not who she was. She didn't want to be a killer. Not if she could help it. If she could escape without killing him, she would. She was not an animal as he was.

But didn't some animals deserve to be put out of their misery?

Adelina shook the thought from her mind. Nico wasn't the

one who lit this fire. He truly believed that she and her women broke the treaty.

That's when she saw him. A man in a black-brimmed hat, easing his way through the crowd. He didn't run like a terrified guest. His hands weren't up to release melder powers. He stalked like a jungle cat, striding through the ballroom, invisible as breath, yet confident as an eagle. His sleeves were rolled to the elbow, the pressed shirt exposed beneath the gold embroidered maroon vest.

He was walking away from her, merging with the crowd. He'd already entered through the first set of broken doors and passed into the middle of the room. In a moment, he'd be swallowed by the crowd around the second set of doors, and he would slip out and be gone.

Breath left her body. He'd meant to leave her here.

Nico still faced off with her, but her eyes were no longer on the chief. The man in the hat kept walking, smooth as water, toward the bottleneck by the doors.

"Hey!"

No one else in the room seemed to hear her over the chaos of the shouts, the clang of steel, the whoosh of windcallers, and the crackle of fire in the hands of firebloods. But the man in the vest had heard it. He hesitated, standing frozen at the edge of the mass of people crowding his escape route.

Adelina angled the bow and arrow just a hair to her left, its target settling on the back of the man in the vest instead of Nico's chest. Grigg turned, eyes sharp as a knife off the whetstone, dark as the sea in a storm. And she knew. She knew it was all true. He'd planned all along to leave her here. He'd planned all along to abandon her with people who wanted her dead, an army of enemy melders hungry for blood.

He'd lied to her, used her, and now left her to die. Heat flared through her body. Pain ripped wide an old wound just barely scabbed over. Every tender moment between Pietro and his children, Sebastian and the Palladino family, shook and faded in her memory. Fracture lines splintered across the image of the face of Stoyan's guard lighting up at the mention of his child. The hope of good men flailed like a bird whose wings had been coated in tar.

Her mother had been right.

She released the string. The arrow shot forward. A perfect shot to center mass, the precise center of his chest.

Pop. Pop, pop, pop. Six pops in quick succession. And a weight like a sledgehammer slugged Adelina in the gut. A wave of dizziness rocked her. She swayed on her feet. Agony screamed through every muscle in her body, and her bones turned to ash as she lost her strength.

The empty bow in her hand clattered to the floor. Nausea rolled through her as another wave of dizziness sent the world around her spinning, a pounding in her head like a horde of galloping horses bashing in her skull again and again. Cold marble stone rushed up at her as she fell.

The stone was cool against her cheek, welcoming against the gash in her arm.

But why had she stopped falling? The room was still spinning. No, she'd already hit the floor. Why was everyone lying down? Well, most everyone. Everyone except perhaps a dozen—half a dozen—frantic, screaming people without powers, fleeing the ballroom like children who had just ripped open a hornet's nest.

Everyone except the man in the polished black boots and brimmed hat.

The man in the vest still stood on two feet at the edge of the sea of people. Only now, the sea of people was an ocean of bodies—crumpled, retching heaps.

How had he survived her shot? She'd launched the arrow before she heard the konnolan go off.

Her vision swam, and her eyes threatened to drift closed. When she opened them again, he was leveling her with an even gaze, two fingers tapping the center of his chest. That's when she saw it. The chain peeking out of his tunic, around the base of his neck.

No. She'd hit the Heart of the Stars under his shirt. Her one shot had become his final gloat as he got what he wanted and left her corpse in his wake, disappearing beyond her reach forever.

A wave of darkness swelled at the edges of her consciousness, promising to engulf her completely. Her eyelids fluttered half open, closed, and opened again.

One short meter away, Nico lay on the marble floor, facing Adelina. A vein popped out red in his forehead so prominently, Adelina wondered absently what it would look like if it ruptured right there on the ballroom floor. A wave of nausea rocked her again. Bile flew up her throat. She tried to move her arm but only managed to flop one arm forward like a fish.

Nico pulled himself toward her on his elbows. "You'll never keep the jungle," he rasped. "And you'll never get the third Heart."

Adelina's head lolled to the side on the floor, staring more fully into the chief's face. It was more pale than she remembered. Is that what she looked like? Pale, worn? Limp as a snake's skin discarded between the rocks?

Adelina begged her body to let in air. It came in short pulls and ragged gasps, mocking her.

Nico pulled himself closer to her again.

Adelina's heart surged to her throat, triggering another wave of nausea. She pushed herself backward along the marble, managing to squirm maybe a hand's breadth backward. Had he always held a throwing knife? Had there been one in his boot? How had he been able to retrieve it while she'd been lucky to pull in a breath under the influence of the konnolan in the air?

Slowly, the chief dragged himself forward on his forearms.

Adelina fought the nausea, the confusion, the black wave beckoning her into the void. She shoved off the floor with both hands. Dizziness swamped her, and she slumped to the floor.

Nico reared an arm back. He was within reach now. Adelina

fought to keep her eyelids open. She would not die in her sleep. She would die face to face with her killer. She would die with honor.

"You'll never get the third Heart," Nico said again. His lip trembled.

Adelina's brow knit together. Of course she'd never get the third Heart. The Heart of the Sea was lost to the sirens hundreds of years ago when they carried it off to the depths of the Aeian Sea. For all she knew, it had long since been destroyed.

But then, she'd thought the same about the Black Swan Mage. She'd thought the woman who cursed her was gone, and the egg destroyed. Until Grigg had turned up with it.

The hand with the dagger wavered in the air, and Nico stabbed down at Adelina. She lurched to one side late, as if she were drunk. But he was too disoriented, and his knife only stabbed the polished marble of his own floor.

Men were wicked. Men were deceivers. Men provided nothing but an endless well of pain.

This is what her mother had tried to tell her. Adelina had thought it was hypocritical of her mother to sleep with a man in hopes of a daughter, considering how close she'd have to get to a man to do it.

But perhaps the real curse on the Accardi women was not that the men who fell in love with them died, but that the women constantly tested the dangers of love to see if any man might break the streak of lies and agony.

Nico struck again. Adelina threw up an arm block, deflecting the attack, but the move winded her. It was only a matter of time before the konnolan wore off and the sea of enemies around her raced to end her life. She had to get out, but her body refused to listen. An ache seeped into her bones, deeper than the roots of the mountain, stronger than the oak, tighter than the strangler fig.

Adelina had been abandoned. And her mother had been right.

Nico swung once more, and Adelina rotated to deflect the

blow again, but a wave of dizziness and weakness sent her plowing into the marble without stopping the knife. The stinging pain of his blade ripped across her upper chest and glanced off her collarbone as a shadow fell over them both. A boot landed heavily on Niko's wrist, and the knife clattered to the floor.

Adelina fought through the haze to roll toward the owner of the boot. When she did, she rolled too far, flopping all the way onto her back like a wet noodle. A man with a hat and a vest and piercing blue eyes gored Nico with the glare of a thousand suns. He dropped to his knee, weight driving into the chief's arm, bringing his face closer to the older man.

"The next scratch on her skin, the next hair that falls from her head at your hand, and I'll chop off whichever limb did the deed."

Strong arms wrapped around her limp body. He smelled like sandalwood, amber, and long-forgotten childhood daydreams as he cradled her close against his chest. The world blinked black, then filtered in light from the room again. She caught her surroundings in snatches of bodies lying on the floor, fire burning through wooden furniture, crumbled rock around the doorways, as Grigg deftly stepped through, picking his way carefully to avoid jostling her any more than necessary.

Her lids fell again. Something told her not to give in—the warning in the back of her mind, the demands of her dead mother, the history of Guerrori warriors—but the warmth of the body around her, the strength of the arms holding her, the soft breeze against her skin as they stepped out into the brisk night air, whispered to her that she could shut it all out. Shut it all out and give in to the warmth.

She didn't notice when she'd actually given in, but the next thing she knew, she lay on her back on a bed of ferns and black orchids. Her hand brushed something soft and sleek with a smooth center line holding it all together. She lifted the object to her face. A black feather.

Which made no sense at all.

Adelina tried to sit up.

"Shhh." A soft voice came from some place nearby, in a low, soothing register similar to her own. "Rest now, love. You're hurt. What happened?"

Adelina tried to sit up again, but a hand pushed her back to the bed of ferns and feathers. The world was no longer spinning—at least not as badly as it had been. Her head ached, and the pain she'd felt on the marble floor remained, and pressure wrapped around her chest like an unrelenting boa. But she didn't feel in danger of pitching sideways at the drop of a hat.

She tested a call to the fire.

"That won't work here."

Adelina looked at the woman kneeling by her side. She looked to be in her sixties and wore a red collar and black animal hide decorated with fringes at the hem. Beads strung around her neck, and black feather earrings dripped from her lobes.

Adelina winced. "Viper's breath. I'm dead, aren't I?"

The woman shook her head. "No, love. Not yet. Tell me what happened."

Adelina scanned her surroundings. A canopy of trees strung with lights. No, *blooming* with lights. Blue and white flowers glowed in the darkness like a network of floral stars. She'd always loved the Nascosta canopy and thought it was the most glorious of ceilings, but this just might put it to shame.

Only the area right around her was illuminated, a soft glow of light falling in a circle right around Adelina and the older woman. Soft grass blanketed the ground, spreading out in all directions from her position on the makeshift bed. The woman still knelt beside her, hands folded neatly in her lap, eyes fixed on Adelina's face.

Adelina pressed her lips together. "Who are you?"

The woman smiled. "You are a guardian, yes? The guardian of the Nascosta, of the Heart of the Mountain. And should opportunity arise, guardian of the Hearts of the Stars and Sea as well. You can consider me a guardian as well. My name is Giovanna Accardi."

Adelina's blood ran cold as spiders of fear spread across her skin, leaving goosebumps in their wake and every hair standing on end. *Accardi.* This place—it was magical. And this woman was the mage who had cursed her. This was her mother's ancestor, whose emblem was emblazoned on Adelina's arm and every other Guerrori warrior. This was the founder of the Guerrori tribe and the first of the keepers of the Heart of the Mountain—who had passed on a sacred responsibility twisted with the curse of death upon all her daughters after her. Whose power had once been contained in a golden egg.

Adelina's mouth went dry. She couldn't tell this woman anything on the off chance that this was real and not a dream. If she was right about Giovanna, Adelina was in more peril now than she had ever been in her life.

Adelina's eyes narrowed. "Why are you here? Is it because of the man in the vest?"

Giovanna cocked her head. "What is this, my love? Who is this man?"

"The man with your golden egg. You're here because of him, aren't you? You're able to talk to me because he is close?"

All softness vanished from Giovanna's face. "How close?"

Adelina's head throbbed. With an effort, she propped herself up on an elbow, again struck by the odd bed she'd found herself on. She forced her brain to focus on the issue at hand. That must be it—her nearness to Grigg. If Grigg had the egg, he had the source of her power. A power that had been bound for decades. Was this why Adelina had never encountered her before? Did the egg have to be physically nearby? Had Grigg taken her back to the house where the egg was? Or was there another reason Giovanna was appearing now?

Giovanna leaned forward, so close that Adelina shrank back. "What is the man's name?"

Adelina didn't want to say. Perhaps because Giovanna had asked with such ferocity, making it not so much a question as a command. Perhaps because Adelina didn't like lying helpless on a bed on the ground with a powerful mage looming over her. The same mage who had ruined her life and the lives of every woman in her family. This Giovanna may have begun the Guerrori tribe, but she had stunted the happiness of every daughter related to her by blood. She had destroyed their freedom.

With an effort, she kept her voice calm and soft. Curious rather than adversarial. "What do you want with him?"

Giovanna took Adelina's hand and patted it with a tender touch, but her touch sent chills down Adelina's spine rather than comfort. The older woman's features softened, and Adelina wondered how hard it had been for her to create the gentler facade.

"There is a dangerous man close to you, child. He must be close. He is a liar, as all men are. You, of all people, should know this. I want to protect you." Her hold on Adelina's hand suddenly tightened into an iron grip. "You *must* live, but being close to this man has hurt you. And I will make him pay."

Adelina's hand hurt under Giovanna's inescapable hold. She tried to pull away, but the woman leaned down again, hovering over Adelina's body, until they were nearly nose to nose. She hissed, quiet as a dove, but with the edge of a serpent's tongue. "I need his name. I need to know for certain."

Adelina considered selling out the Carusos, saying it was Nico who had hurt her instead of Grigg, but no one deserved the wrath of Giovanna. If Giovanna thought she loved Adelina and had cursed Adelina into such suffering, what would she do to those she hated?

She shook her head. "Don't trouble yourself. I'll take care of it."

Giovanna frowned. "Nonsense. Don't be petulant, child."

Adelina set her jaw. No, she was not this woman's child. And she would not be sharing anything.

Giovanna let out a long sigh and picked up a feather along the bed. As she touched it, the edge of the feather's shaft grew and sharpened into a point at the end.

"Pain is important. It sharpens us. It disciplines us. It is in moments of pain that we remember those values to which we must hold most dear."

Adelina tried to inch backward, vines of terror wrapping her chest like seaweed climbing up through the ground. She wanted to tell this woman she was frightening her. That for someone who claimed to care for Adelina, Giovanna was acting a lot more like a creepy serial murderer than a protector. But her throat closed up, and her tongue stuck to the roof of her mouth.

Giovanna seized her hand again, this time wrapping Adelina's index finger in an unbreakable grip.

"It's for your own good, child. I need to protect you. This man is dangerous and must die. Confirm for me his name."

Tears stung at Adelina's eyes at the harshness in the older woman's face, the animalistic stone of her expression, the shadow of a snarl on her lips. Giovanna stabbed the razor edge of the feather shaft up under Adelina's fingernail. White-hot, searing pain shot up Adelina's arm.

A scream shattered the air around her. Her back arched. Her throat burned. Searing, cutting fire slashed up the nerves of her finger. She had only just registered the scream in the air was her own when another shot of pain exploded from the next finger. The razor-sharp feather tip never broke. Had the mage reinforced the feather somehow?

The feather was drawn back, and Adelina slumped back into the onyx feathers that now represented a swath of miniature torture devices. Giovanna ran her knuckles across Adelina's cheek. Adelina cringed back, a tear escaping her eye. The pain still radiated through her fingers and down her arm.

"All I need is a name, my love. Please. Please don't make me do it again."

Adelina met the mage's eyes, but instead of the hard stone she'd seen a moment before, pools of gold met her gaze, as if perhaps she did retain a shred of maternal instinct.

Another lie.

Adelina tried to pull free, but Giovanna only adjusted her grip on Adelina's hand, moving on to her third finger. She held Adelina's finger steady and raised the feather. Adelina shook her head violently on the fern and feather pillow.

Giovanna wiped a tear from Adelina's cheek with the thumb of the hand holding the feather, the edges of the feather sweeping into her hair.

"All I need is his name. I need to know if my nightmare has come true."

Adelina's lip trembled. Her body shook, her heart pounded. The fragile shreds of her life were unraveling. If Adelina was a keeper, but had been appointed by someone like Giovanna, was the mountain worth guarding at all?

Adelina had always thought that, though the curse was wrong, the purpose of the guardians of the mountain had been noble—had been right, had been necessary. But if Giovanna had been the one to institute it ... had everything she lived for been for nothing?

Pain sliced up again under her nail bed, cutting through the skin as if reaching to strike at her soul.

Adelina screamed.

Then her mouth was open, and she heard her own voice rasp into the night, answering the mage's question. "Grigg! I only know him as Grigg. It's not his real name. He's had a thousand. I don't know his name. I swear it."

It wasn't his real name. It wouldn't help the mage. It shouldn't. Should it?

Please, just please, make it stop.

Adelina fell back against the bed, chest heaving, tears streaming down her face. Dark clouds fell across her vision, spots blocking out the light of the glowing blossoms of the trees overhead. Could she black out in a dream when she was already blacked out? *Was this a dream?*

"Grigg," Adelina whispered, repeating the name. His name tasted like sweet wine on her tongue that left an aftertaste of bitter ash.

The instant an answer was given, Giovanna dropped the feather and covered Adelina's body with her own, wrapping her in a hug and rocking her against her body as though Adelina were a small child. Adelina was too weak to fight it.

"My child, my child," Giovanna murmured against her hair. "I'm so sorry. I'm so sorry he is still hurting us. But not for long. No, not for long." Giovanna pulled back, brushed Adelina's sweat-matted hair out of her face, and took her face in her hands.

"This is what I feared, my love. He's dangerous, like his father. He must die. If you can't kill him directly, you must make him fall in love with you. His death is the only way to ensure he won't double cross you."

She shook Adelina gently to call her attention to her. Reluctantly, Adelina looked up at the older woman. Giovanna ran a finger lightly across her cheek in a caress.

"To make sure he dies, gather the Heart of the Sea, the Heart of the Stars, the Heart of the Mountain. They *must* be together. As soon as you find the third Heart, kill Grigg and assemble the three Hearts yourself. It will keep you strong. It will protect us. Soon, I will be with you. I will help you restore our family legacy. I will make us the most powerful family in the world. You and I will destroy our enemies once and for all."

What legacy could there be beyond guarding the Heart of the Mountain? Beyond the curse passed down generation after generation? After meeting Giovanna face to face, the only further legacy Adelina could imagine her wanting involved more power and destruction—more of the same horrors, on a grander scale.

More than ever, the golden egg needed to be destroyed. But if it was cracking, was it already becoming destroyed? What if she attempted to destroy it, and all it did was unleash the mage on the world faster?

Adelina forced herself to be still, to be silent. No words came that would improve her situation.

But Giovanna had enough words for the both of them. "My love, everything I have done has been to protect you, but I beg you, do not give away your heart. It will not do any good. For the moment you do, it will come back to me. We belong together, and I wrote it in the terms of the original curse. I protected us from men like Grigg—from loving them. Do not cry for him. If you give your heart to him, it will return to me. You and I will be together forever."

Giovanna released her, and Adelina fell back into the orchids and ferns, trembling. No nightmare could live up to the horror of a reality trapped with Giovanna.

You and I will be together forever.

The last thing Adelina remembered was a swirl of black feathers and a black swan taking off into the night where the woman Giovanna Accardi had been.

CHAPTER NINETEEN

Grigg had nearly lost his hold on Adelina as her back arched and her body writhed at a level of agony he had never expected to see etched on her face. It had been all he could do to keep from dropping her when she screamed his name as they moved through the street to get to his horse.

Grigg had no particular love for his name. His first name was better than his last, and he hadn't heard his first name spoken aloud for many years before returning to Smŭrttata. But over the past few days, he hadn't minded hearing it on Adelina's lips.

Until now.

He'd managed to drape her over the horse, climb up, pull her limp body into a semi-seated position in front of him, and wrap one arm around her as they took off at a gallop for his second safe house. He'd only managed to secure two for this entire trip, so he sincerely hoped nothing had happened to it.

Throughout the ride, Adelina had drifted between conscious and completely blacked out. Once, she had whispered his name with a brokenness that had nearly torn him in two. How could the same woman say the same word twice in one evening, and each time spark such wild reactions within his own chest?

He'd gotten her to the location and wheeled the horse around as soon as he'd ensured she was safe and stable in the locked safe house, sleeping soundly. He didn't want to leave her, but he had to get to Nico before the konnolan wore off.

Dragging the larger chief off to the safe house had been a harder task. He'd been conscious, and tried to fight, until Greg's boot met the side of his head. But the man was *heavy*. When he finally managed to bring the chief back to the safe house, Grigg had smothered his mouth and nose with a concoction to put him to sleep and left him tied to a chair to return his full attention to Adelina.

Whatever was going on with her had not entirely been the konnolan's doing. The weakness, the dizziness, sure. The fury he'd seen in her eyes directed at him in the ballroom—well, that had been organic. He'd probably deserved it. Okay, so maybe more than probably. But the horror, the agony—none of that was him. And it wasn't the konnolan either.

He could only think of one person capable of creating that sort of misery in a person's unconscious. But why would Giovanna attack a woman? She had some sort of complex about women, as far as Grigg had gathered. She demonized men and exalted women in her mind. And she'd seemed genuinely concerned when Grigg threatened to make Adelina fall in love with him.

Grigg pressed the cloth against Adelina's upper chest, gently patting the cleaning solution over the place where Nico's knife had cut. If Grigg hadn't been there, Nico's next shot might have been strong enough to stab the heart, and those blazing golden eyes would have never opened again.

He shoved down the thought. She'd served her purpose, hadn't she? She'd done what he asked, and she would want to be done with him as soon as possible. She'd tried to kill him not three hours ago.

Grigg ran a finger over the Heart of the Stars, still hidden beneath his tunic and vest. It was a miracle she'd hit him precisely there—or, rather, a miracle that the necklace had been exactly in the center of his chest, not swayed one way or the other. Her skill with a bow was less of a miracle. He'd seen it himself.

The gash on Adelina's arm had been deeper than the one on her chest. Grigg refreshed the cloth in the bowl of clear cleansing solution beside him and pressed it to her arm.

For the first time since entering the safe house, Adelina moved. She winced, squeezed her eyes shut tighter, then slowly pried them open. She frowned. "Grigg?"

A wave of warmth shot through him from head to toe. Third time's the charm. She should get an award. He offered a stiff smile that was probably more disconcerting than comforting. "Long as I can remember."

Her brows knit together again. She started to push herself up, but grimaced as she put weight on her injured arm. Grigg shook his head and started to lower her back down. He moved his hand to lower her back to the bed, but she lurched forward and rocketed an elbow toward his face in a bold strike.

Grigg leaped back just in time to feel the wind from her blow across the bridge of his nose. She threw a punch next, and he backed away again, arms up, palms out, stumbling backward off his chair, away from the bed where she lay. The change had been so sudden, as if she'd transformed into someone else entirely. Sure, she'd wanted him dead in their last interaction, but when she'd said his name just now, it hadn't been in anger.

Then it hit him. It wasn't that she'd *become* a different person. It was that she'd *seen* a different person. In her nightmares. In her semi-conscious state.

"Adelina. I'm not her." He extended empty hands and dropped his voice low, slow, and hopefully reassuring. "Adelina, it's me. I'm not her. You're awake."

Adelina's sharp eyes scrutinized him, chest still heaving from exertion and adrenaline. She cast a furtive glance left and right, taking in the bare room. This one was underground with no windows, no lights except for the lantern on an end table beside the bed—the one he'd nearly knocked over in his haste to jump back from her attempt to bash his face in.

The bed was simple, a single mattress with a down pillow set over a basic wooden frame and a stone floor with nothing on it but an overnight bag tossed in the corner. No rug, no extra blanket beside the one on the bed on which he'd laid her. The side table with the lantern also held a couple of bowls of cleaning solutions, three small bottles of ointments, and bandages. The harshness in her eyes simmered to a skeptical side-eye.

"You're not *who?*"

Her question seemed to be a quiz rather than a shock.

Grigg gestured at the stool fallen over on its side beside the bed. "I was cleaning your wounds. May I continue, or would you like to keep trying to kill me?"

She hesitated, as if genuinely deciding whether his time on Earth should expire. After a moment, she gave a short, shallow nod and sank back, propping herself up on her uninjured arm.

Grigg gave a dramatic bow with a flourish. "Many thanks, my lady."

She rolled her eyes. She didn't have a bow, but she was still a fireblood. Once the konnolan wore off, she'd have access to that again, and he hadn't brought any magna to the safe house.

Had he really forgotten to give her the last glass of magna? He was slipping. A lot. How many slips had he had since meeting Adelina? It was unconscionable.

Grigg dipped his finger in the ointment and dabbed gently at the wound along her arm. "Have you seen her before?"

"Who?"

Grigg looked up from his work to meet her steady gaze. "Giovanna. Long black braid, beady eyes. Swan lady. She matches your tattoo. That's who you just saw, isn't it?"

To his surprise, she didn't meet the assertion with fire. Instead, her gaze drifted off to the bland, tan blanket beneath her. She picked at the pilling. "So *you've* seen her before?"

"More times than I'd prefer."

"Are you working with her?"

He grimaced. "We're not friends, if that's what you're asking."

The bite in his tone was stronger than he'd intended, and she looked up at him. He shrugged. "She's an unwanted connection I can't shake off, sort of like mosquitoes. They come and go, but you can never quite get rid of them, and they always seem to think there's too much blood in your body, and they need to take some."

Grigg placed the wet cloth aside on the table and picked up a clean bandage. He lined it up with the gash on her arm and pressed carefully and evenly. She drew in a sharp breath as it made contact with the wound.

What had Giovanna wanted with Adelina? But if he pushed her too hard, Adelina might shut down. It wasn't worth the risk. Not yet.

The good news was that Adelina's experience with Giovanna seemed to be a negative one, which made her less likely to want to team up with the mage. The bad news was that Grigg just thinking about what Giovanna might have done to Adelina was fueling a rage deep inside him that he couldn't let out. Because the minute he did, he would do something reckless enough that Giovanna would kill him, and Adelina would never be avenged.

If he was ever to give the mage what she deserved and live to tell the tale, he needed to take care of the Hearts first. *Then* he would destroy Giovanna.

Grigg picked up the long strip of cloth by the table, held it to the bandage, and began to wrap her arm, his fingers working with a ginger but firm care.

She watched him work for a moment before breaking the silence. "How long has she come to you?"

He shrugged. "She first appeared to curse my nights years ago, but more recently, it's been more nights than not. I guess she got bored with only cursing my days." He gave her a halfhearted, impish grin that faded almost immediately. All his facades were wearing thin, every nerve left in his body seeming to fray. What would happen when he came to the end of his rope?

Grigg tucked in the end of the bandage and reached for the second one, intended to fit over the cut on her upper chest. He reached for the ointment, dipped his finger into it, and drew it whisper soft across the broken skin.

When he looked up at her again, she was watching him closely, as if he were a puzzle and she was arranging pieces. Something in his gut twisted. Looking at her face had been a mistake. Seeing her looking at him with any iota of softness was a problem.

He couldn't afford to get close. And she didn't mean it that way anyway.

But when he returned his attention to the ointment just beneath her collarbone, he realized he'd already covered the area thoroughly. Twice.

Grigg snatched his hand back and wiped it on the wet cloth. He had to stop touching her. It was a bad idea.

He pressed his hand lightly against her forehead. Her hair was still wet with sweat at her brow, but her temperature was stable, and she didn't push him away. He cleared his throat and withdrew his hand. Had he not heard his own thoughts *just now* about how he had to stop touching her?

He cleared his throat. "Look, I know you don't owe me anything, and I'm sorry I had to kidnap you. I am. But if I kidnapped you and you helped me, I would let you go. And if I didn't get what I needed, I would die. So under the circumstances, I never expected you to understand, but ..."

Grigg trailed off. Where was he going with this? Why was he explaining himself?

He pursed his lips. "I guess I just wanted you to know that I never wanted you to get hurt. And if you'd had the magna, you wouldn't have been. You would already be free, gallivanting through the jungle by now. I wouldn't have held you. You held up your end of the deal. And I never break a deal."

She leaned forward and laid a hand on his arm. Her voice was soft, even. Genuine. "What does she have on you?"

Something pricked at the corner of his eyes. The edge of his mouth twisted in an incongruent grin. "What does she have on *you?*"

The ache in his chest lessened in the space of the silence that followed, replaced by something lovely and terrifying all at once. They sat there, staring at one another, searching each other's eyes —he on the stool and her on the bed, with nothing but the lantern light between them.

Well, that and her hand on his arm. And the almost tangible connection of finding someone with the horrific shared experience of Giovanna.

He'd never told anyone about Giovanna before. Who would believe him? And if someone *did* believe him, who wouldn't use it against him?

But with her, like saying his name, the truth had rolled off his tongue as easy as walking. He'd seen her in pain and wanted to mitigate it. And now, the way she looked at him, he could almost believe she wanted to help him with his pain as well. That she might care.

Grigg nearly toppled off his stool in an effort to back away as the thought surfaced. *No.* On the off-chance that Adelina cared about him as a human, the minute her generalized-kindness-to-a-fellow-human grew into something more—something specific for *him*—she would be in danger.

He wasn't convinced such feelings for him were even possible, but he couldn't take that chance. Not now.

After seeing her collapsed on the floor in the ballroom, he knew beyond a shadow of a doubt that he could never let that happen. She was too good, too kind, too strong.

He'd meant what he said to Nico.

How had Giovanna abused Adelina? What had she done to her? What did she *want* from her?

Adelina sat up, careful to avoid putting pressure on her injured arm as she did. "What's wrong?"

Grigg ran a trembling hand through his hair. "Nothing. I just—"

I have to get away. I have to make you hate me again. I could never make you hate me again. I need to be away from you right now.

The thoughts crashed over him in a tumbling wave, but none of them were suitable to say aloud. He cleared his throat. "I have Nico next door."

Her jaw dropped. "You *what?*"

"After I brought you here, I went back and got him and dragged him next door. He's tied up and locked in the next room over." Grigg jerked his hand toward the wall, indicating the space beyond. "I overheard Nico say something to you tonight about the Heart of the Sea. What *exactly* did he say?"

Adelina blinked at him for a moment, then shook her head. "I don't remember."

"Or you don't want to tell me." Grigg crossed his arms, then loosened them and adjusted the rolled-up sleeve at his elbow. "Adelina."

It was a beautiful name. It fit her. *Shut up, Grigg.*

He crossed his arms again. "I need to know. If I don't, it'll take me twice as long to get it out of him, and I don't want you to have to hear that."

She drew back as if slapped.

His chest tightened, and the ache seeped back in.

"He said I would never get it. The third Heart."

Because it was out of reach? Or because Nico already had his hands on it?

Grigg stalked toward the wall, spun on his heel, and stalked back. "What do you know of it?"

She shrugged. "I thought it was gone. It's been missing for hundreds of years. Lost to the sirens."

Grigg chewed his lip. "It was."

She leaned forward on the bed, eyes wide. "*Was?* As in, you have it?"

"I ... I know where it is."

Technically, he had it, *and* he knew where it was. He'd gone to the depths of the sea himself, struck a deal with a few renegade Iolani sirens, and brought it with him here to Smŭrttata. He'd stowed it along the river, hidden at the channel he believed might lead to the mountain. If he could get it there by water, he wouldn't have to lug it through the jungle, and he'd more likely pass undetected through Guerrori territory.

But the Guerrori had been a problem until now. He'd been waiting for an opportunity to incite the tribes against one another so they would be distracted when he got the Heart of the Stars and snuck into the Nascosta from the opposite end of the jungle.

Now, the Heart of the Stars hung around his neck, and the Heart of the Sea was waiting just outside the Nascosta. He just needed passage to the Heart of the Mountain.

Unless Nico had managed to steal the Heart of the Sea.

Pain swelled in his chest and rippled outward along the black lines beneath his shirt over his heart. Which, if his theory was correct, meant the egg's cracks were expanding as well. He had to know what Nico knew.

Adelina drew back. "It's here, isn't it?"

Grigg sucked in a shuddering breath. He had to get a hold of himself, but he didn't have the energy to lie. He clamped his mouth shut and spun for the door. In the doorway, he turned back to her. "Please stay here, no matter what you hear."

He wouldn't keep her locked up. Not anymore. Their deal was complete, and he'd meant it when he said he always kept a deal.

But two things reigned supreme on his priority list right now: getting away from Adelina and getting information out of Nico.

Grigg left the room and shut the solid door behind him, sealing himself into the dark of a small stone hallway. A staircase stood in front of him and a second door to his right led to the room that held Nico.

He screwed his eyes shut and ran a hand over his face. He had to be in the right frame of mind when he spoke to the chief. He had to have his head on straight to get the upper hand.

He felt like going in, daggers flashing, cannons firing, but that was the adrenaline talking, not reason. Grigg took a deep breath, as much air as he could, then sucked in another inhale when he felt his lungs were full and let it out slowly. He'd discovered the help of the breath when he was a teen, counting cards and scamming players at tables after talking his way into games above his pay grade. Not that he'd *had* a pay grade as a low-level street-urchin thief, but that's how he'd started out. He'd had to keep a level head through it all to keep from flashing anxiety signals like a banner waving over his head.

Grigg repeated the breath several times, stuck his hand in his pocket, withdrew a walnut, and rolled it between his fingers. It was time to go. Grigg pulled out a key, unlocked the door, and stepped inside.

The chief sat in the center of the room with his ankles bound to the legs of a wooden chair and his arms tied behind his back. Another lit lantern sat in the corner of the room, casting eerie shadows across the chieftain's face.

Grigg circled the man once to confirm his hands were indeed still tied behind him before grabbing the extra chair from the corner, spinning it around and straddling the chair backward with the casual feel of a chat between friends. He draped one arm over the back of the chair in front of him and popped the walnut in his mouth as Nico watched with cold, steely eyes.

Grigg chewed the walnut slowly, swallowed it, and pulled out another. A thousand questions surfaced. *Where is the Heart of the Sea? What do you know of it? How did you connect it to Adelina? How did you know it was here?*

None of those direct questions would get him far. Not yet.

Grigg rolled the walnut around in his mouth and cocked his head. If he were in Nico's shoes, what would he want to know? "You're wanting to know my weaknesses. I have three."

Nico's eyes narrowed. He hadn't expected this opening, which is why Grigg had chosen it.

Grigg fished another walnut from his pocket, tossed it in the air, and caught it. "I'm terrible at drinking games. I hate the taste of champagne. And there's no one alive I love enough to sacrifice myself for. I want to live, and there's nothing I will not do in the service of that goal. It seems to me you also have goals you won't compromise on."

Nico straightened in his chair—a small gesture, but Grigg took it as confirmation. The chief made no move to speak. Grigg rolled the walnut between his fingers, noting its ridges, taking a moment to savor the scent of it mingling with the dank stone of the underground room.

"Your son is smart, but too impulsive and arrogant enough to harm your tribe. You're getting older, and you want to know you can pass off leadership with confidence. If he won't keep himself from dangerous obstacles, you'll remove them for him. Like Adelina."

He paused for effect and checked the chieftain's face. The man remained stoic, so Grigg continued. "Frederico's temptation to conquer is too strong. You needed her out of the way." He spread his hands, indicating the bland stone room. "This isn't how you expected the evening to go."

Nico let out a short, raspy laugh. "You think you know me. You think because you spent an evening with Igor and appeared to my soldiers with a fake name that you'll escape my notice."

Grigg eyed the chief, but let the silence do its work. If he waited, the man might speak again.

And he did.

Nico leaned forward in his chair. "You come in here from out of town. No one has seen you before. And you shoot arrows into a flock of birds just to see them fly."

Grigg pressed the walnut hard between his thumb and forefinger, an effort to let out the sudden squeeze of anxiety in his chest without letting it leak onto his face. He'd underestimated the chief. Nico had gotten further in the last few days than Grigg had expected. For starters, Nico had ascertained that the man who'd appeared the night of the invasion claiming to be Igor was Grigg. It was less of a shock that Nico had puzzled that out, perhaps. But he'd also learned that Grigg had spent the evening with Igor prior to going to the outpost.

Could he have been followed? If so, perhaps someone saw him get the horse from the stableboy. But the boy didn't know much. And Grigg had only met with Igor several days ago. There'd been no reason for the Morturi to investigate Grigg until now.

Grigg turned the walnut in his fingers and glanced back up at the chief. "You think I'm a cocky young man with overinflated ambitions like Frederico. You think I'm a problem to be eliminated. You think if you tell me what you think you've learned about me that I'll be rattled enough to make a mistake you can take advantage of."

Nico said nothing, save for the glint in his dark eyes. Grigg couldn't trust him to tell the truth, but if Grigg got him talking, perhaps he could look for signs of stress, signs of deception that would lead him in the *direction* of the truth—whether Nico wanted to share it or not.

Grigg tossed the walnut up into the air and caught it. "Tell me about the Heart of the Sea."

Nico settled back in his chair, shoulders drawn back, as if he were lounging on a throne rather than tied as a captive in an underground bunker. "I know you need it more than I do. And I know you think it's safe. You think you're smarter than me. And that has served me well."

Even, steady breaths. Slow blink rate. No signs of anxiety or nervousness.

Not in Nico, anyway. Grigg's heart rate, on the other hand, had doubled in the span of three seconds. Grigg repeated the phrase he wanted Nico to elaborate on. "I think it's safe."

"Yes, you brought it here. But it's large and difficult to conceal and transport. So you rented a boat. You don't think I have ears? All across this territory, you don't think I have eyes like birds on every tree branch?"

Grigg popped the walnut into his mouth and nearly choked on it. The nut tasted like dirt plowed over by mightier men than he. It hurt to swallow, his throat too tight to allow it passage.

Nico knew about the boat, which meant he knew which body of water Grigg had rented it for. And if he knew Grigg was interested in the mountain, which he did since Grigg had incited the tribes to invasion, Nico would have a pretty good idea of where to look.

Nico grinned. "Is that our wordsmith out of speeches? A shame. I was hoping for another one."

If Nico really had gotten to the Heart of the Sea, Grigg was dead in the water. Probably literally. A corpse floating out to sea.

His chest burned and the ache in his bones intensified. If not for the chair he was sitting on, his knees might have given out.

Grigg folded his arms over the back of the chair and tried to level the man with an even stare, but he didn't believe himself, and he knew the performance was falling flat even as he spoke. "Tell me what you've done with it before I remove your fingers one by one."

Nico tilted his head as he scrutinized Grigg. "You know, a man is allowed to hate the taste of champagne. There's no shame in having a preference on drinks. I think your third weakness is that you're just as cocky as my son, but so desperate you've grown sloppy. Or were you never very good to begin with?"

The stone beneath Grigg cracked, and his chair toppled, spilling him onto the floor out of nowhere.

Kshhh! Another splitting, splintering sound assaulted Grigg's ears. By the time he looked up, it was too late. The wooden legs of Nico's chair were broken, and the man was free. The loops of rope around his ankles slipped from the wood. Nico leaped over his own hands to bring his bound arms in front of him, lifted the detached chair leg like a club, and swung it at Grigg's head.

Grigg rolled to one side, but as he did, the floor opened up and swallowed his right foot. The *stone* floor. Gallows. Nico was a melder after all—a quakemaker with power over wood and stone elements of the ground. And Grigg had captured him in a playground of nothing but wood and stone.

His heart stopped. The effects of the konnolan had worn off, and these walls would become Grigg's coffin.

CHAPTER TWENTY

ADELINA

Adelina stood in the narrow, dark hall, her ear pressed up against the cracked door leading into the room beyond.

"Tell me what you've done with it before I remove your fingers one by one."

Is that why he'd wanted her to stay in the other room? So she wouldn't hear him speak this way? But he'd all but dragged her along to threaten Stoyan and Mira, just to ensure she heard him do just that.

She'd followed pretty quickly after Grigg moved into the next room over, when she'd heard muffled voices and could be sure he was no longer outside of her own door. And despite Nico Caruso being a monster, Grigg hadn't started with a rough approach, but began the conversation cool, collected, and conversational.

But now, the air had changed.

Grigg wanted the Heart of the Sea, but he didn't just want it. He'd *had* it. And if he'd gotten the boat, it sounded as though he'd staged it just beyond Guerrori territory.

All the pieces clicked together in her mind. That's why he'd wanted the Morturi to invade. He wanted the two tribes so intent on taking one another out that no one would notice a lone, quiet boat sneaking up the river toward the Heart of the Mountain.

It was smart and probably would've worked if Nico hadn't figured out what he was up to. Adelina certainly hadn't caught on.

How could she have been so stupid? How was it that at every turn he seemed to be three steps ahead?

But Nico had trounced them both, and now he was gloating.

"... so desperate you've grown sloppy. Or were you never very good to begin with?"

Crrrrack. The sound was so loud, she nearly jumped out of her skin. She half expected the room to be caving in when she burst through the door. Instead, she found Grigg on the floor with one foot trapped ankle-deep in the stone of the floor itself. He twisted up toward Nico with his hand protecting his face as the chief swung a thick stick down at his head.

Not thinking, Adelina called to the fire. She didn't know when it had returned to her, but balls of flame shot from her palms straight at Nico's chest. A blaze caught what she could now see was a four-sided chair leg rather than a stick, turning his weapon into a fiery torch. With a flick of her wrist, she sent the fire shooting up the chair leg at Nico's hands.

Nico jerked his hand away from the heat, and the chair leg clattered to the gray stone of the floor. Her attack had shaken his concentration, and Grigg ripped his foot free as the stone moved where the chief had been manipulating it, but Nico didn't care. As far as Nico was concerned, Grigg was a flea. Adelina was another story.

She heard the crumble of rock half a second before the floor gave way beneath her feet. Adelina leaped for the shambles of a broken chair, planted one foot on its frame, and launched herself into a high arc over Nico. Adelina sent a blaze of fire raining down on Nico's head as she hurled herself up and over him. He threw up an arm to protect his face. Searing blisters rippled along his skin on impact.

He screamed and charged straight for the space where she would land.

Her feet hit the floor, and Nico slammed her body up against the wall. His thick hand wrapped around her throat. The stone wall rumbled at her back, and a burst of rock captured one wrist as she balled it into a fist, but the other hand wrenched free just in time. Adelina shot her free hand up to the man's face and let loose a torrent of flame at the same precise moment that the glistening edge of a knife blade protruded from the front of Nico's throat, dripping blood down his neck to soak his shirt.

Adelina yanked her arm back, and the man crumpled to the floor, face utterly disfigured by the burns, throat still impaled by a dagger from behind.

She snapped her head away from the horror on the floor and turned to find Grigg standing there, hand still extended from the throw of the dagger, blue eyes cold and hard. He stepped forward, bent over the body, and pressed a boot to the man's neck as he ripped the dagger free with both hands. Adelina flinched at the sickening squelch and fresh pool of blood that seeped from the gaping wound in Nico's throat. Grigg wiped his dagger clean on Nico's hand, closing the man's limp fingers around the blade to wipe off the blood.

Grigg straightened and looked at Adelina. "It seemed apropos. He has blood on his hands." He looked down at the body again, speaking to her as he glared down at the corpse. "I'd promised to cut off any limb that touched you again. I suppose that would be overkill now."

Adelina gaped at the body. She'd hated Nico. He was a violent slimeball, and he'd tried to kill her. Twice. But as much as she and her women trained for battle, they hadn't seen much of it in reality. Uneasy peace treaties and small skirmishes had been the extent of their dangers for most of Adelina's tenure as chieftess. But this—

Her eyes stung, and her throat burned. She blinked hard, fast, to gain control of herself. It was self-defense. He was going to kill her. She'd had to do it. And anyway, she and Grigg had killed him at the same time. It was hard to say whose blow had done it. Either blow on its own would have done the trick.

But the way he lay there on the floor, splayed awkwardly on the stone, his blood spattering behind him, his blood spattering on her, on her neck, on the front of her dress—her throat closed, and her mouth went dry. Her every muscle tensed, and her mind raced until it seemed to carry her away. It was almost as if she were watching herself standing in the room in a dream, her right wrist still trapped to the wall, encased in stone, the grisly death before her a figment of nightmarish imagination generated by some dark corner of her soul.

She wanted to look away, but all she could see was his face contorting in rage as the flame charred his face before her eyes. All she could hear were his screams, the crackle of fire—*her* fire. The smell of burning hair and flesh assaulted her nostrils. All of it, every sense mingled together superimposed over the corpse at her feet.

"Hey."

The voice was soft, and suddenly her view of the body was obstructed by gold thread and velvet cloth. The man in the vest. The man who'd proven her mother right. The one who'd abandoned her.

Yet he was the one standing between her and the nightmare now, his voice low and gentle, his hand light on her arm, ducking his head to search her eyes.

She looked up at him, choking on an unexpressed sob, swallowing the lump in her throat hard enough so it might not dare return. His eyes were a soothing blue, like waves falling into rhythm again after a storm.

"This isn't your fault. He tried to kill you tonight at the

mansion, and he tried again just now. He got what was coming to him—only slower than he deserved."

Adelina bit her lip and nodded, not trusting herself to speak. She was a warrior. What was wrong with her?

"You're all right." His hand ran down her arm to squeeze the fingers of her free hand. "Can you slip your other hand free?"

The question jolted her out of her daze. She'd clenched her hand into a fist just as the rock hardened around it. If she relaxed her hand—yes, she could just slip out. She winced as the rough rock cut against her skin, but after a moment, she wriggled free.

Nico's quakemaking to catch her arm had been sloppy. Whether it was from stress or lack of practice, she didn't know. Maybe he was still recovering from the effects of the konnolan. It seemed to affect people at different speeds. In any case, the rock hadn't encased her completely, and when she relaxed her muscles and her hand had some room, she found she could move it just enough to get out of its hold.

Adelina wrenched her hand free and rubbed it, running her thumb across the knuckles of the hand that had been trapped. As soon as it was out of the wall, Grigg took her by the elbow and swept her from the room before she'd had the chance to look back. But just as they passed the doorway, he left her in the hall and darted into the room with the bed.

Adelina followed in time to see Grigg snatch the bag from the corner of the room, toss it over his shoulder, and sprint past her up the stairs. Adelina took the stairs two at a time after him. "Where are you going?"

He didn't look back as he burst up through a trapdoor into a dark room above. "To save the Heart of the Sea."

Adelina flew after him. The trapdoor opened into what appeared to be a bakery storage room, with sacks of flour, apples, and other ingredients lining shelves on the walls. She hopped up onto the floor, closed the trapdoor behind her, and ran after Grigg through the only door, just as it began to swing shut—a back door leading out into an empty alley.

No. Not again.

Where had he gone?

There—the silhouette of his frame moved past a window with the light of a fire inside. She sprinted after him until they were side by side, and she matched his long, swift gait.

"What, that's it? You're just going to abandon me again?"

He didn't spare her a glance as he pursed his lips and set his gaze on some invisible point far off in the distance. "You only *thought* I abandoned you, but you really *did* try to kill me."

"You were going to leave me in the ballroom."

Grigg's pace quickened. "If I was going to abandon you, then why are you here?"

Adelina broke into a jog to keep up. "I don't know. Why *am* I here?"

He pressed his lips into a tight line. "You're out of the mansion because I got you out. You're here beside me now for reasons I cannot possibly hope to guess."

"Are you serious? A woman just tortured me in my sleep and turned into a swan in front of my eyes, and *you* knew who she was. I don't think anyone else would understand that, do you? No one else would be able to do anything about it, but together we might be able to fight her off. Oh, and then, when I woke up from that nightmare, the Morturi chief tried to kill me. Again. After trying to kill you first. You're welcome, by the way, for saving your life."

His steps faltered. They reached the end of the alley, and he made a left-hand turn. He avoided her gaze as he answered. "And you're welcome, too, for saving *your* life."

"I killed Nico at the same time you killed him. Maybe you were *going* to save my life, but I saved it first."

Grigg held up his hands in a defensive posture and met her eyes at last. "Fine. It was a tie." He grinned. "So, instead, you're welcome for saving you from the mansion—where you were only in danger to begin with because you apparently didn't take the magna."

"You mean the dose you forgot to give me?"

Grigg hesitated, then offered a grunt.

She took it as a concession and struck out on her next question. "How are you so sure that saving the Heart of the Sea is a good idea?"

He snorted. "Because without it, I die, and I think living is a pretty good idea."

She tried a new angle. "Why do you need the Hearts to live?"

He shot her a look. "Why do you need to know everything?"

Adelina rolled her eyes. "Viper's breath, there's not much I *do* know. I know I might be facing a coup when I get home. I know you promised me tools to fight the Carusos, and you've yet to hold up your end of the deal, though you've gloated that you never break a deal. I know that after you get the Heart of the Sea, you'll have two out of three, and you'll need the Heart of the Mountain—and that you don't know where it is. Not exactly. And I know that you're panicking, and people get stupid when they panic. And I know that you still need me, whether you know it or not."

Grigg took three steps in silence, then whirled on her so fast she bumped into him. "Why did you tell me about the coup?"

Adelina stared at him. "What?"

How could *that* be what he'd focused on out of everything she'd said?

He clenched his jaw. "That's personal information. It's a vulnerability. Why did you tell me that?"

"I ..." She trailed off. Why *had* she told him that? It wasn't critical to what they were doing right now. It was a personal sharing. Something she might have said to Lucia—whom, she remembered with a pinch of guilt, she still needed to save. "I don't know."

His expression darkened, playfulness replaced by hard lines and rigid edges. "Don't lecture me on making stupid decisions. If you had any brains, you'd stay as far from me as possible." His hands balled into fists at his sides.

It was such an odd thing to see him rattled. Not just about the Heart of the Sea but about having her along. About having her making good decisions.

"What do you care what kind of decisions I make?"

"Giovanna will kill you if you get involved."

Adelina lifted her chin. "No, she won't. Though I think I'd rather that she did."

He blanched at her admission. He hadn't expected it. Neither had she, when it came tumbling out.

After a moment's recovery, he tried again. "What reason could you have for traipsing into the jungle after the man you hate so much? A man who kidnapped you, used you, and is tied to a mage who tortured you."

Tied to a mage. Adelina considered the words. He didn't say he was serving her, that he wanted to work with her. He'd said before how he would die if he didn't. She thought about the curse on her bloodline, that men who loved her would die. Could she have cursed him too? Or threatened to kill him if he didn't do what she wanted?

Whatever Giovanna wanted, Adelina had to ensure she didn't get it. If Giovanna could torture her in dreamland while the remnant of her power was bound to the golden egg, what could she do if she were freed?

What if you have to kill Grigg to stop her? Are you strong enough to do what needs to be done?

She replayed his last words, then froze. She looked back at him. "Why did you say that? Why are you focused on what I think of you? I already told you, you're my only connection to figuring out the experience I just had with a woman who transforms into a swan and attacked me in my mind. You know I'm the guardian of the Heart of the Mountain, and you're headed there to do who knows what. It's my duty to protect it. I have every reason to follow you, and yet you want to know why I would follow a man you think I hate, and you listed your sins against me. You told me not to share personal information. You're usually careful with your words."

She thought of his open-mouthed gape on the rooftop when she'd been seated in his chair by the time he got back to the roof. The feel of his hand on her arm. The way he looked at her when he bandaged her wounds. His arms around her, holding her close as he lifted her off the marble floor and picked his way out of the rubble.

Adelina took a step forward, and he staggered back. "I'll ask you again. Why did you say that?"

His features flinched in the shadow of a grimace.

He likes you, a slippery dangerous voice nagged at the back of her mind. *You can use that. He's going to join the Hearts together, and it's going to free Giovanna. But if he falls in love with you first, it won't be you who kills him. It'll be the curse. It will be Giovanna. And isn't that a kinder way to go than an arrow to the throat?*

"I don't have time for this." His voice was tight, hoarse, as though speaking through a film. As though a part of him wanted to say something else but had been silenced. Grigg turned on his heel and stormed off down the street again, adding over his shoulder, "And you can't afford to care."

Adelina dropped into long loping strides beside him. "For all your bravado, I think you're a lonely man with an empty heart. Do you think if we collect enough Hearts you'll develop one of your own?"

A muscle in his neck twitched. "They say variety is the spice of life, darlin', but I think it's mystery. Don't you? The intrigue of trying to find out if I have a heart is far more interesting than the truth of the matter. I'll let you play the game. If I were gathering Hearts, why do you think I haven't gone after yours?"

Adelina spun in front of him and stopped, this time forcing *him* to come to an abrupt halt to keep from running into her. She tilted her head. "Maybe you have, and you're not very good at it, or maybe you're afraid—afraid to feel because you think that feeling is weakness."

His blue eyes cut to the quick, assessing her—sharp, keen, analytical. But in the space of the breath beyond, they melted into glassy seas under serene skies, drinking her in as if he thought she might be the last beautiful thing he ever beheld. Grigg ran a hand down her arm, his light touch whispering across her skin like the kiss of the night breeze. His other hand lifted toward her face—slowly, slowly.

She had every opportunity to block him or move away, but her feet were rooted to the spot. Her breath quickened. He trailed the line of her jawbone until his fingers came to her chin. Grigg tilted her face up toward him and leaned in.

Adelina froze. He was going to kiss her.

Could she let him kiss her? If he did, did it mean he had genuine feelings? Would it be the start of the end of his life?

But nothing about the man was real. One kiss did not love make. One kiss did not create love. Who knew how many other women he'd kissed without a second thought? But as he brought his face to hers, it didn't feel like pretending.

What would his lips feel like? What would it be like to have his arms wrapped around her, here under the stars, against everything screaming in the back of their minds that the kiss was forbidden? She could allow herself just one kiss, couldn't she?

He hadn't cared for her at all just days ago. He couldn't really be in love, so the kiss wouldn't kill him. And even if it stirred feelings, they didn't have to mean anything. She still had time to decide what to do with Grigg. This one small moment wouldn't kill her.

At least, that's what she told herself, as a longing beset every fiber in her body to entwine herself with him and let him take her by the mouth. Her lips parted, and she leaned into him just a hair. His nose brushed hers, and she thought she heard his breath catch.

And then he halted, so close that his lips touched hers when he spoke.

"Or maybe I just don't like you as much as you think I should." His hands dropped away from her, and he stepped back with a shuddering breath he tried to hide. He took another deep breath in and let it out, and when he did, the stoic cheat was there, and the man who'd threatened to chop off Nico's limbs for touching her was gone.

"You're right, I do need you. You're alive because you know where the Heart of the Mountain is. And you're going to take me to it."

CHAPTER
TWENTY-ONE

Threatening Adelina that she would lead him to the Heart of the Mountain probably fell flat, considering she'd already told him she wanted to be there and intended to follow his every move as he entered the Nascosta.

Grigg swung back by the house with the rooftop to instruct Trifon and Boris to release Lucia in one hour, leaving Adelina at the door as he did so, and then he swung by the stable where the young boy had brought out a horse tacked and ready to go each night for the past week in case he showed up.

Of course, the last horse Grigg had taken from the boy had not come home—or at least had not come home quickly. He didn't know what had happened to it, though it was possible it had made its way back to the stable the next day.

He worried at first that the stableboy might have gotten in trouble for losing a horse, feared for his job, and broke their deal, bribe be hanged. But as they approached the stable, there he was, holding the reins to a chestnut mare. Grigg tossed the boy a golden coin, took the reins, and led the horse away.

Adelina followed, never but a step behind him over the last hour and a half as they had wound through the streets.

He couldn't believe how turned around he'd become, because she was right. He *had* essentially asked her what she thought of him, presuming that she had stayed with him based on something between them, when in reality she had plenty of other, more important reasons to be there.

Grigg had strategic reasons of his own to keep her close, like having a guide to get to the mountain, and it was suspicious that he was pushing her away. It broke baseline from how he'd acted when they were training before the ball.

But when they'd stood there in the alley, standing close enough for him to breathe in the lavender and bergamot scent from her hair, feel the warmth of her skin, the graceful lines of her body, and a look in her eyes he never wanted to forget, it had been all he could do to tear himself away. His chest had felt lighter than it ever had in recent memory, like soft salve replacing miserable jagged edges.

But his stomach had flopped and soured at the same time. If she was faking what she'd felt in that moment, Adelina was a better actress than any he'd ever seen. But if it was real, though he'd almost begun to want it, that would be the worst outcome of all.

And the moment they'd broken eye contact, the ache was worse than ever. The black across his heart.

She held out a hand. "Dagger, please."

The corner of his mouth twitched. "Baron's backside, you really expect me to hand my only weapon to a fireblood?"

Adelina shrugged. "It's not my fault you aren't better prepared. And I'm not riding a horse in this." She gestured at the heliconia-decorated floor-length skirt still billowing about her legs.

The slit did provide both greater movement and an excellent view of her long legs, but he had to assume it would be a hassle to ride in.

He unsheathed the dagger and handed it over. "You should know that defiling a dress like that should be akin to murder."

She grinned. "Duly noted."

Two minutes later, the bulk of the flaming heliconia skirt had been cut free of the dress and stuffed into a grain barrel behind the stable. Her one-shoulder green dress was fully intact at the top, accented now by the white bandage over her upper chest, and another white bandage wrapped around her upper arm. The skirt cut away at an angle from the slit halfway up her thigh on one side to just above the knee on the other, creating an asymmetrical view of her figure that was not at all unpleasant.

Next, they'd squabbled over who would take the reins. It was a stupid argument because Grigg knew where the boat was and she didn't, so he won without much of a fight. But as he got to steer, she got to choose where to sit. She opted to sit behind him rather than in front. He'd arranged the bag with the egg in it so that the strap went across his torso, but the egg itself was in front of him, and they were off. Adelina held herself upright with only the muscles of her legs as the mare took off with a trot. But as the animal dropped into a canter and both riders leaned forward to accommodate the motion and higher speed, Adelina wrapped her arms around his waist. He tried to ignore the feel of it.

The most important thing now was that Grigg reach the Heart of the Sea before Nico's men did—unless they already had it. Maybe the chief had been bluffing, but if Nico had had men scouting it out, they might have found it and given word to Nico during the ball. If that was true, Grigg might already be hours behind.

And he wasn't just racing against Nico's men, but against the ticking clock of the cracked golden egg. Stopping to save and bind up Adelina may very well have cost Grigg his life as he wasted precious time when he should have proceeded immediately to the Heart of the Sea, and on to the Heart of the Mountain before the egg split open and killed him.

It took another hour to ride to the edge of the river where Grigg had stashed the Heart of the Sea on a little fishing sailboat barely significant enough to have earned a painted name on the side: *The Wandering Heron*.

And finding the mooring post would have been a relief, except that *The Wandering Heron* wasn't tied to it.

The Heart of the Sea was a life-size statue taking up the bulk of the bed of the fishing boat. He'd had to remove two seating planks just to fit it into the little vessel, and he'd tied it down to the boat to keep the statue level so it wouldn't capsize the *Heron*. The sheet he'd tossed over the statue had done little to conceal what it was, and he'd had to rely on the spot hidden behind thick brush and around a band of trees to keep it from being found. But he hadn't expected anyone to come looking, either.

No. Grigg urged the horse along the riverbank and turned his head to speak to Adelina. "This channel leads to the Heart of the Mountain, right?"

"Why would I tell you that?"

Grigg let out an impatient breath. "Are you more afraid of what I would do with control of the mountain or what Frederico Caruso would do?"

She paused. "Yes, it leads to the Heart. We're close."

His hypothesis had been right. La cascata vivente, the living waterfall, connected to this channel and drew its supposed healing power from the Heart of the Mountain. He'd known they had to converge somewhere. Grigg kicked the mare, and they carried on along the riverbank.

Adelina pointed. "There."

Grigg squinted in the dark. Aside from the crackling brush of leaves and twigs snapped under the horse's hooves, and the whistle of wind through branches, there was little he could hear or see. The water glistened black in the starlight, black like the onyx of a glassy lake in his nightmares with Giovanna. Moss and underbrush grew thick on the bank as the horse's hooves stepped into the boundary of the jungle of Dead Man's Folly, but beyond that, there was little to see.

The more time he spent here, the less he liked the name. And the more accurate it seemed.

Weariness tugged at him. He rubbed his eyes. How long had it been since Giovanna had let him have a full night of restful sleep? Not to mention it was nighttime right now.

"What are you looking at?"

She glanced at him and shook her head. "No, not on the far side of the bank. Just there, two meters off. The reeds are broken. The Morturi were careless."

"They're traveling along the bank?"

"Looks like it. How big of a boat is it?"

"Ah." He sucked his teeth. "It's a little fishing boat. The thing would only have fit maybe three people beyond the statue and the sail."

A stroke of luck at last. If some of them were on the bank, it meant they'd have to move at the pace of those going by foot.

Adelina slipped off the horse and crept forward along the grass. "They're probably using crestbreakers to move the boat upstream."

Pressure squeezed around his heart as she stepped away, half melting into the darkness. What if she left him? What if she ran off, found her tribe, and came back to kill them all? He wouldn't mourn the Morturi, but he'd definitely mourn himself.

But a moment later, she pushed flame into her palm—just enough to illuminate the area in a small meter diameter around her, as she examined the brush. She nodded at the bank with a pinched expression that hadn't been there before. "They're here. This way. We should dismount and go in quietly."

"What's wrong?"

She chewed her lip. "Three of the tracks are women. Morturi don't use female scouts and rarely use female warriors."

Grigg's brows rose. "Your women are working with them?"

Her eyes flashed. "If they are, they're not *my* women, are they?"

Grigg dismounted, tied the horse at the edge of the jungle with a nice patch of grass, and followed Adelina as quietly as he could manage. Judging by the looks she sent his way, he wasn't doing a very good job.

Adelina extinguished the flame in her hand, and after Grigg stumbled three times about as quietly as steel beaten on an anvil, Adelina grabbed him by the wrist and pulled him behind her. He did his best to mirror her footsteps, though he felt a bit like a big bulky carrion bird trying to imitate the movements of a hummingbird.

They traveled another hour on foot, but the pain in Grigg's chest grew worse with every step. Each footfall fell heavier than the last, each breath more of a fight to draw in. He shouldn't have been this worn, this exhausted, but the ache—the fatigue—none of it held a candle to the razor-sharp pain gnawing at his heart. It felt like a hundred piranhas had made their home in his chest and were gnawing their way out, suddenly unhappy with their accommodations.

Lub-dub, lub-dub. Lubbb. Dubbb. The pounding of his heart rang louder in his ears, but slower than it should have been. He stumbled and fell, his knees crashing into the brush. He wasn't going to make it.

It had all happened so quickly. His decline from the effects of the cracking egg should have been slower. *Should have been* being the operative phrase, apparently. There had been no rules presiding over a standard, a steady progression of decline.

Lub-dub. Lubb-dubbb.

Adelina's hand touched his shoulder. The movement both warmed him and sent a spike of pain through his chest. He waved her off, half-frozen in place where he'd crumpled to the jungle floor.

He had to see it.

He had to know.

"What's wrong?"

Grigg waved her off again. "I'm fine. If you think it's safe to speak here, is it safe to light a fire as well?"

She hesitated. "I could manage a short glow, but nothing that would light much of a path."

He nodded. "That's fine. Do it."

Adelina dropped into a low crouch at his side. "What's happening to you?"

Grigg shook his head. "Doesn't matter. Knowing what it is won't fix it. Give me a light."

He couldn't afford anything that would make her feel sympathy for him. Things were bad enough as they were.

Grigg grabbed the satchel in front of him and ripped it open. He didn't care that Adelina was there, he just had to see it. He had to know.

Adelina knelt beside him and lifted a hand, a soft glow illuminating her palm and shining warm light on the glistening golden egg. Except, it wasn't as gold as it had been before, and it had light of its own as he pulled it free of the bag. The two main cracks had widened, the lines of the fissures glowing from something inside the egg. A hundred tiny splinters worked their way across its surface, and three more major cracks wrapped around the egg.

She sucked in a breath. "What—"

He waved her off again, and she fell silent. Grigg turned the egg in his hands. The largest of the cracks crawled up the shell as he watched, until the edge of the crack was mere centimeters from the edge of the crack on the opposite side. The light glowed from within so brightly, Adelina extinguished the glow in her hand.

Grigg crumpled. No, he couldn't fall. Not now. They had to keep going. They had to get to the Heart of the Sea.

"The egg." Adelina chewed on a fingernail. "You're connected to it. When it cracks, you feel it somehow."

He took his time drawing in three long breaths before he

answered. "Very astute, darlin'." Grigg shoved the egg back in the satchel, its mild glow working its way through the fabric of the bag. "Let's go."

Grigg struggled to his feet, and Adelina caught his elbow as he nearly fell again.

"What happens when it breaks apart?"

He gave a sour laugh. "What do you think?"

They moved in silence another couple of meters before she spoke again, her voice low, almost a whisper. "You know that if you do what she wants, she'll probably kill you anyway once she's done with you."

He resisted the urge to roll his eyes. More because even that would take up too much energy than for any other reason. "Again, how astute of you."

Grigg wavered on his feet and threw out a hand to stabilize himself against a tree. "That's why as soon as I'm free of her, I'm going to kill her."

And then the world tipped, and he toppled to the ground.

And found himself at the edge of the despicable lake with a reprehensible mage, his feet immovable as a scarecrow whose stake was driven into the ground.

Giovanna grabbed the front of his tunic and ripped it open with a strength ten times what he would expect of a slender woman in her sixties.

She stepped back to examine her handiwork with a smile. The black spot over his heart was too expansive to properly call it a spot. It took up the entire left side of his chest, with its outward, long-reaching greedy fingers wrapping up and over his shoulder and across his torso in every direction, even extending down his left arm to the elbow.

Her eyes sparkled. "Does it hurt?"

Grigg gritted his teeth, but it was all that he could do just to keep upright, even in the dream. "More than you know."

Giovanna stepped forward, her crocodile smile splitting her

face in the widest grin he'd ever seen. She waggled her eyebrows at him. "Are you in love?"

He winced against the raging burn in his chest. "Falling in love doesn't hurt me. Not physically, anyway. It only hurts the women who love *me*."

The mage clapped her hands and practically bounced side to side. He'd never seen her so giddy. It sent bile up the back of his throat.

"You think you know so muchhhh." Her voice came in an eerie sing song. "Oh, he thinks he loves a girlll. Oh, he loves a girl! Grigglor Frizzletwerf, son of the man who never loved at all."

Grigg shook his head. *Son of the son of the son of the ...*

He didn't have the energy to clarify it for her anymore.

"I didn't say I was in love. Only that, if I was, it wouldn't hurt me if I was. But if she's a problem, I can kill her now. I have a dagger. And she has nothing."

Not entirely true, of course. She was a fireblood with superior combat skills. And he could barely stand on two feet.

A guttural moan of pain ripped from the trees to the side of the lake behind Giovanna. Grigg snapped his head up in the direction of the groan, and Giovanna herself staggered back and turned toward it.

No living thing had ever appeared in the nightmare visions except Grigg and Giovanna herself, either in human or swan form. No birds. No frogs. Nothing. This was new.

Giovanna left him standing on the bank, transformed into a swan, and flew into the trees. Grigg wrenched his feet off the ground. They felt secured there as if his shoes were trapped in mud and tar and molasses all at once, but he tripped his way after her just the same.

If Giovanna was surprised—if she was *distressed*—there was something in those trees she didn't want him to see. And he intended to see it.

His heart burned in his chest, weighing him down like boulders. Once, he fell, twice, but he kept moving until he broke the line of the trees with the white-and-blue glowing blossoms—and nearly fell over dead at the shock of what he found.

Adelina lay curled in a heap on a bed of black and green fern leaves, some sort of black-petaled flower, and—were those feathers? The black swan hovered over Adelina and materialized into Giovanna's human form, hands fluttering over the younger woman, whose face was screwed in pain. Adelina clutched at her chest and moaned again.

Giovanna's eyes were wild, hands flitting to and fro, but never quite landing anywhere, as if unsure of what to do next.

Adelina rolled to one side and braced herself with her hands, shoving up against the feathers and flowers. She ignored Giovanna and instead turned her golden eyes to Grigg in a broken look that nearly ripped him in half.

Giovanna did have a weakness: she cared about Adelina. It wasn't just that they were part of the same tribe, it was something more, and as he saw them there together, he could see it. The same lips, the same deeper vocal tone, the same body structure, high cheekbones, dark hair.

Six hundred years ago, Grigglor's ancestor Sergei had fallen for —or pretended to fall for—Giovanna Accardi. And six hundred years later, Sergei's descendant Grigglor was falling for Giovanna's descendant, another Accardi woman.

He hadn't meant for this to happen. And he'd never dreamed a woman like Adelina would feel anything for him but loathing. No one who knew the real him ever *should* feel anything for him but loathing. But somehow, something deeper had connected them that he could never have anticipated. They were both bound by magic—she to the guardian life, and he, a bug under the mage's boot—prisoners of separate dungeons, beset by the same dungeon master.

Was this what Adelina had meant when she said Giovanna would never kill her, though Adelina might wish that she would?

Adelina hadn't had as much time with Giovanna in the dream world as Grigg had, but that interaction, combined with whatever legendary information and oral tradition she carried from the Guerrori warrior tribe, and her family line, told her all she needed to know: being loved by Giovanna would be just as dangerous as being hated by her.

The Black Swan Mage shook Adelina. "I'm here, I'm here, my love. The time is almost over. You *must* gather the Hearts, now more than ever. Once I am free, I can save you. I can save you ..."

Adelina's eyes rolled to the back of her head, and she collapsed to the jungle floor, sagging out of Giovanna's hold.

Grigg tripped forward toward the place where Adelina had fallen, but Giovanna blocked his way, suddenly standing before him.

She slapped him across the face. "You did this."

Giovanna lurched forward and drove her hand deep into Grigg's chest, through flesh, through muscle, through bone, to seize the beating organ of his life force. She ripped it out.

His mouth opened in a silent scream. Agony exploded from every nerve he didn't know he had, a wave of pain so mighty he might have crushed his heart in his hands himself if only he'd had the means. His physical heart glowed with a mingle of blood red and cursed black in her hands.

Her fingers clutched his heart and squeezed. "You will not do to her what he did to me."

Grigg fell to his knees, his body buckling under the pressure of the heart she held in her white-knuckled hand. Her eyes were wild, her face pale, hands trembling.

Grigg chanced a glance at Adelina, but she wasn't lying with her eyes rolled back anymore. She still lay in the position she'd fallen, but her breathing was even, and her eyes were fixed on his face.

She'd faked it? Brilliant.

Giovanna had swallowed the facade hook, line, and sinker and left Adelina alone to turn on Grigg, freeing up Adelina to soak in any information Giovanna spilled. But Adelina had no weapons here, and neither did Grigg. Fighting back directly within the dreamworld would be useless, no matter what they learned.

Giovanna lifted Grigg's heart in front of his face and shook it at him. "She can't give her heart to you, because once it's fully yours, it returns to me. You can kill any number of girls, Grigglor, but you can never take her from me. She is mine forever, as are all of my daughters."

Again, Grigg's gaze drifted from the mage's face to meet Adelina's eyes. They glistened with unshed tears, the cage of prison walls etched into the sorrow of her face. He swallowed hard against the lump in his throat.

"I may be a miserable man, with more vices than there are arrows in the world, or grains of sand at the sea. But I see now that my sentence is too light. I only wish that I could trade my sentence for hers, for hers is a fate worse than death—to be trapped with you forever."

Giovanna's lip curled into a sneer. "You have until daybreak to gather my Hearts until I can kill you myself."

With that, she shoved his heart back into his chest and threw him out of the nightmare and back onto the riverbank.

CHAPTER TWENTY-TWO

Adelina wrenched upright as Grigg vanished. Just … *poof*, into thin air. What did a poof mean in dream world? Was this Grigg real, or an imaginary version?

But she dismissed the idea of an imaginary Grigg immediately. Adelina clearly was not in control of these dreams, and if anyone was in control, it would be Giovanna. But Giovanna had been just as surprised to find Adelina here as Adelina had been to arrive there. Something linked them and opened the door for this meeting differently than before, in a way neither of them could have expected.

Which meant the man in this dream had been the *real* Grigg, and she was the real Adelina, and Giovanna had truly ripped his heart out and shoved it back in like she'd plucked the wrong spice bottle from the shelf.

"What did you do? Did you kill him?"

Giovanna turned on her heel from the place where Grigg had stood to pivot toward Adelina on the bed of ferns and feathers.

Giovanna crouched on the ground beside her, drilling her with a cruel stare.

"Why would I take that away from you, my love? You should be the one to do it. Do to him what I was not strong enough to do to Sergei. He doesn't really love you, but he could. He could love you just enough. He doesn't have to fall all the way in love to be weakened by the curse. Just the beginnings will do."

Adelina gathered her feet and staggered back. Kill Grigg? An ache claimed her chest and exploded outward through every fiber of her body. She shook her head. "I won't."

Giovanna rose and smiled, offering a small sympathetic smile. "Don't you see? He's already at the door. All you have to do is open it. He's already sick. I can feel it. His heart will fail."

Adelina took a step back, but Giovanna closed the distance, stretching out her hand toward Adelina's chest. Adelina tripped over her feet in an attempt to get away, memories of Grigg's heart in Giovanna's hands flashing before her eyes. Her back struck the harsh bark of a tree, but Giovanna kept coming. The older woman's hand spread over the top of her chest and over her heart, where the bandage should have been in reality. The cut was there, but the bandage wasn't, and neither was the cut-up evening dress —Adelina wore tribal animal skins similar to Giovanna's.

Giovanna's hand pressed hard into Adelina's chest. She tilted her head. "But why is yours weak?"

Adelina swallowed.

Giovanna seized her face in both hands, eyes suddenly sharp as needles, hands strong as dungeon bars holding her in place. "You're falling for him. You're *dying*. Any woman who loves him will die. You must kill him before he kills you, or assemble the Hearts so that I can do it for you. If you are not strong enough, I will be your strength. Make him weak. But don't let yourself fall."

Adelina's world spun. What had he told her when she accused him of feeling something for her? He hadn't said she was wrong. He'd said, *You can't afford to care.*

He'd confirmed that the mage had cursed him, but he'd never shared the terms of the curse. She'd been right that Grigg was cursed as well. The two of them didn't just share nightmares of Giovanna. They had almost identical curses cast by the same mage. The men who loved Adelina would die, and the women who loved Grigg would die. But now, they were both falling, and the two of them had begun to die together.

Any woman who loves him will die.

But the moment the words were out of Giovanna's mouth, Adelina knew it was already too late. If only the beginnings were enough to be impacted by a curse, she was already there. She had tried to avoid it, to deny it, to stuff it deep down. But things had changed when he'd put a blanket over her on the bed. When she saw the way he looked at her when she'd put on the ballroom dress. When he carried her out of the mansion and tended to her wounds.

She hadn't known enough to fully appreciate the gesture in the moment. But he'd sacrificed precious time to care for *her* when *he* was dying, not only from her curse, but from his link to the slowly shattering golden egg.

Things changed again when he'd stood close enough to share a breath, his hand at her chin, his eyes fixed on hers, and she realized she wanted him to kiss her.

When he told her he had vices but would trade his sentence for hers.

And now, she was convinced beyond all veils of doubt that his apology had been genuine. He hadn't wanted to hurt her or scare her. He hadn't wanted to take her to secure her help.

And once he'd come to know her better, he'd begun to trade time for her, risking his expiring life every time he chose her over the mage's call, over gathering the Hearts.

Like when they'd stood in the alley, and he stopped to challenge her instead of forging ahead for the Heart of the Sea. He'd pushed her away then, denying the evidence that he cared. But now, knowing the curse he bore, every time he pushed her away only served to drag her deeper into danger, into the danger of falling victim to his curse.

Surely, it would've been easier to get her on the hook and let her fall. To weaken her. He was a cheat, after all, wasn't he? A criminal? But if he really cared ...

If he really cared, he wouldn't want her to fall. Just as she didn't want him to fall.

Moments ago, when he'd said he wanted to trade his sentence for hers, the look in his eyes had been unconscionable. Pained, sort of stretched. A steady resolve reigned in his eyes as if she were the anchor to his tossing waves, even when he knew it would drag him under forever.

"Weaken him, Adelina. I'll be with you soon."

But the voice felt wrong somehow, far away, as if filtering in through thick fog. By the time it lifted, she was back in the Nascosta with leaves and twigs under her as she lay on the jungle floor. A cool breeze whisked across her skin. Light danced across her closed eyelids—more light than there should have been.

Had she slept all night? What if it was midday? What if Grigg had left her there? What if—

Adelina snapped her eyes open and jerked upright. Grigg stood in front of her, back toward her, hands up, palms out in a defensive posture. He turned his head to check on her as her movement rustled the underbrush.

"Hello, darlin'. Good news. We've found the Heart of the Sea."

Half a dozen Morturi surrounded them. Two were firebloods with flames in their palms lighting the area—probably the light she'd seen with her eyes closed. Cassio stood to one side, palm stretched toward Grigg and Adelina. Grigg had positioned himself between Cassio and the firebloods, and Adelina. Off to either side, two archers had arrows on the string, pulled back and aimed for Grigg's chest.

Another man leaned against a tree just beyond Cassio, arms

crossed, dark eyes taking in the scene. He was still decked in his party attire. His lips twisted into a sneer. Frederico. "You just can't stay away from me, can you?"

A woman to his right scowled. Adelina's gut wrenched. Caterina. She skulked just behind him along the riverbank, glaring at Adelina. Behind her, the silhouette of a fishing boat stood out in the shadow of the firebloods' human-hand torches. A massive sheet fell over a lumpy object half the height of the mast inside the little boat.

Three more melders, two Morturi and one Guerrori woman, held their palms toward *The Wandering Heron*, keeping it upright through windcalling and crestbreaking abilities. The Guerrori crestbreaker held her hand out toward the water. But as her hand stretched toward the fishing boat, her neck craned around Caterina and Frederico to catch a glimpse of Adelina. The girl's eyes were wide, her face ghostly pale in the eerie shadows of the flickering flames.

Letizia. She'd been the one to say Adelina should never have let the Morturi claim land so close to the Nascosta borders—that they should have struck first. And now, she was ready to get into bed with the Morturi?

How many of Adelina's women felt this way? Had she lost all of their trust?

Adelina returned her gaze to Frederico, but spoke to Grigg, ignoring the Morturi prince. "Not bad for a couple of hours' work. We found the Heart of the Sea, and our enemies were kind enough to save us the trouble of tracking them."

Grigg bobbed his head in casual agreement. "I bet they'll even take it where we want it to go."

Frederico's sneer widened. "Oh, we'll take more than that."

He signaled two of his men and jerked his chin toward Grigg. Caterina lifted one hand and blasted Grigg to the ground with a gust of wind. Grigg fell like a rotten tree.

Adelina rushed to catch him, but a debilitating pain in her

heart twisted around her chest like chains, and her knees buckled. Cassio stepped forward to stop her approach, but ended up catching her instead as her knees gave out.

Was Grigg really sick because of her? Because he loved her? Was she really sick because she was beginning to love him?

The only thing she knew for sure was that agony seared through her like a brand. And that mere hours ago, she'd shot an arrow at Grigg's chest with full intention of killing him, but that now she just might stand in front of an arrow to protect him.

Adelina blasted a ball of fire at Cassio. It had taken half her energy, only to have Caterina launch a wall of wind to meet Adelina's flame. The fire hit the wind and dissipated in a shower of sparks. Cassio yelped and smacked at a flaming ember catching on the edge of his tunic before wrenching Adelina's hands behind her back and shoving her forward toward Frederico.

She whipped her head back to check on Grigg. Two of Frederico's goons seized him by the arms and hauled him up, as Caterina kept a steady current of air against his chest to slow any attempt at retaliation. From the looks of him, he would hardly have been able to walk on his own as it was, just as Adelina's limbs barely managed to carry her weight.

As Cassio had to drag her forward, so too Grigg's body seemed to fail him. He breathed in laborious breaths, shoulders bowed under the strap of the faintly glowing bag still holding the egg swinging in front of him.

The men shoved them forward toward Frederico until the two prisoners were nearly abreast.

Grigg met her gaze with an adamant surety he didn't look like he should've possessed. "Don't look at me like that, darlin'. It's not worth it."

You can't afford to care.

A burning, tearing sensation seized Adelina at the ribcage, as if the talons of a hundred buzzards were tearing away at her flesh.

Cassio shoved her forward another step, and she struggled to stand.

"You're lying. Because you don't want me to die."

Grigg blanched white and sagged in his captor's arms. Had it been her words that created more pain? Or the shock that Adelina knew the terms of Giovanna's curse? Or maybe the egg was breaking further, and the timing was a coincidence.

"Shouldn't you worry more about you?" Adelina called to the fire from Cassio's grip, but his own hands went hot at her arms in answering threat, and the energy of the summon drained her. They were nearly to Frederico now, but she didn't care. Her eyes were locked on Grigg. "Your time is almost out. Why shorten it?"

Grigg laughed. It was a shallow, choking sort of sound, like echoes in a hollow chamber. "I don't have the energy to fight it. If I'm going to die anyway, I don't see as it makes much difference. I've got nothing left to lose."

Unless ...

That single word poured fuel on the embers of Adelina's despairing soul.

Unless there was a way to keep Grigg alive without the weight of the curse. If she could combine the three Hearts, it could slow Grigg's dying just long enough for Adelina to get Giovanna's attention. If Adelina could pull Giovanna's attention off Grigg and onto herself, she could threaten Giovanna.

If Giovanna wasn't at her full power *now* but believed she *would* be when the egg broke apart, Adelina had to combine the Hearts before the egg broke. If Grigg was right, doing so could stop the time clock on Grigg. The remaining risk were the two curses of love placed on them, but Adelina had no way to know for sure how much of Grigg's weakness was related to his link with the egg and how much was related to the curse on Adelina.

But if she could make a bargain with Giovanna, if she could find a loophole ...

Grigg's voice dropped to a low growl, just loud enough for her to hear. "Whatever you're thinking, it's a bad idea."

Frederico stared between the two of them and clapped his hands. Adelina jumped. He flashed a crocodile smile. "What a nice surprise. Not that you're here. I would've been disappointed if you didn't show. But tonight, I learned that Guerrori women haven't sworn off men like the legend implies. In one night, one of you promised to marry me, and another nearly begged to take her place and be my wife. And then my fiancé is found traipsing about in the woods, fawning over a criminal. Perhaps, Adelina, it wasn't that your standards were too high, but that they were too low. No one in Smŭrttata was low-life enough for you to consider. Until this man waltzed in."

Adelina bit back a retort.

Grigg laughed. "I kidnapped her and forced her to guide me to the Heart of the Mountain. You think she's stupid enough to want anything else from a guy like me?"

Adelina's stomach plunged to her toes. The ache nearly swallowed her whole. He'd taken the heat off her, trying to bait Frederico into focusing on him instead of her.

Frederico's gaze flicked between them. Adelina ripped her eyes from Grigg to Frederico.

The corner of his mouth twisted up. "Yes, that's exactly what I think."

Grigg tilted his head toward the fishing boat. "Careful with that. You wouldn't believe the trouble it took for me to find it, much less retrieve it."

"Oh, don't worry. I've made plenty of assurances." He gestured to the bag around Grigg's torso, still glowing from the light of the egg inside. "What's this? Did you bring me a prize?"

Caterina stepped forward and ripped the bag open. The glaring gold of the egg shone from the bag like a beacon, the cracks all but exploding with barely contained light. Frederico's face lit with the golden tones from the egg, its splintering light reflected in his eyes. He stepped toward it, reaching out a hand, then snatched it back. He gave Caterina a nod, and she reached for it. If it was going to kill someone, he had no problem letting it be Caterina.

The moment Caterina touched it, the network of fractured cracks all around its shell seemed to shatter. A piece of the top of the egg fell to the dirt as thick fissures expanded and cracks met. Grigg cried out and dropped to the ground, the two men holding him stumbling forward under the surprise of the extra weight.

Adelina's hands lit with fire, but Cassio lit his own palms around her arms. The shock of the burn jolted through her body. She tried to wrench free of his grasp, but to no avail.

Frederico seized Grigg by the shirt and hauled him up, muscles straining with the effort. He bored Grigg with eyes ablaze, lip curling in a snarl. "You're going to tell me everything I want to know. But first, you're going to pay for what you did tonight."

CHAPTER TWENTY-THREE

GRIGG

The list of things Grigg had done that night that Frederico might want to rip him apart for was somewhat extensive. For one, he'd killed Frederico's father. Adelina seemed to have taken credit for it before, but Grigg would accept it as a tie. Unless Frederico found out about it, in which case Grigg definitely killed him.

But there was no way for Frederico to know that Grigg had killed Nico, or even that he'd kidnapped the man. When Grigg had gotten back to the mansion, there were quite a slew of people still on the ground in the ballroom just beginning to move, but Frederico was not among them. If scouts had found the Heart of the Sea and reported the location to Nico and Frederico during the event, it's possible that Frederico would have dealt with Stoyan and made a beeline for the river before Grigg managed to return to the house. This was the most likely scenario, considering that Frederico had also managed to meet up with the two Guerrori women, find the boat, and move it along the river before Grigg and Adelina showed up.

On second thought, maybe Caterina had been the one to find the boat, and she'd used it as a bargaining chip with Frederico to sway him in her favor for negotiating terms over the Nascosta.

Either way, Frederico didn't know about the worst thing Grigg had done that night. Which left several possibilities that he would now be punished for, including impersonating Caruso staff, breaking into the house, and stealing from a dying man—which had been a ruse to make it seem he might have been there just to lift coin, but was an infraction nonetheless.

He'd also been working with Adelina, which Frederico might be jealous of, drawn Stoyan and his men to the mansion, and he'd stolen the Heart of the Stars. Oh, and exploded a chemical that temporarily rendered nearly everyone useless.

The question now was whether Grigg could shove aside the torture of his physical heart, which felt as though it'd been tossed on a butcher's block, long enough to catch the swirling thoughts running through his mind. He had to be at the top of his game, but if the game was a chessboard, Grigg didn't think he was even on the board. He felt more like the dust off the player's shoes that had been scuffed on the floor beneath the game.

He forced weight into his legs to stand in front of the Morturi bully. The motion sent shockwaves from hip to foot as though the butcher had started flaying his limbs layer by layer. "If you're worried about your marble floors, I think you should talk to your own people. There was quite a scuffle this evening, and your melders were overzealous at the doorways."

Frederico laughed and sent a fist straight to Grigg's gut. Grigg folded at the waist until the guards' hold kept him from moving further. It probably would've hurt more if his chest wasn't an all-consuming suffering.

The prince ran a finger across his knuckles and clenched his striking hand into a fresh fist. "I know what you did to our towers. I know you started a war. Two of our men died in the collapse, and one of the Guerrori women died in the invasion. And tonight, more deaths. And there you were again, right in the middle of it all."

Adelina spit on Frederico's boot. "You never should have entered the Nascosta. Are your men really so dull that they would take the word of a stranger to charge into the jungle?"

Frederico seized Adelina by the face. Grigg wrenched sideways toward him, but to no avail. The men held him fast. His body betrayed him, and he sagged. But he learned he could force himself to move within the pain. If he had to, if he shored up his strength ...

Frederico spared Grigg only a satisfied scoff at his pitiful state before turning back to Adelina. "Don't think I'm done with you. Death is too good for you. Maybe I'll still marry you after all. You promised, remember?"

Adelina glared back at him. "If you do, Caterina will kill you. It'll be one thing the two of us can agree needs to happen."

Frederico released her face and wagged a finger back and forth in her face. "I'm affronted, Adelina. I'm a man of my word, and I've promised to marry you both. But who's to say I can't have you both? Or I can marry you, and then you'll have an unfortunate accident, and I'll marry Caterina next. It's time to turn the tables on the black widows, don't you think? And there are so many lovely Guerrori women to work my way through."

He'd said the last half low enough that Caterina and the other woman couldn't hear, but loud enough for the Morturi guards holding the prisoners to hear, which earned him a rumbling laugh.

The prince grinned. "Who knew? All this time, all we needed to become more powerful was weak leadership in the Guerrori chieftess, and someone in common for the two tribes to hate more than each other. Thanks to the two of you, we've been graced with both."

Frederico spun back to Grigg. "Stoyan is dumber than a fly against a window. But you ... you're smart enough to try something of a more elegant stupidity. You consider yourself a puppeteer, but you're out of your depth. You got caught."

He curled a single finger at Grigg in a beckoning motion that sent bile up Grigg's throat. What he wouldn't give to send a twin dagger into the throat of the son as he'd done to the father.

The melder guards shoved Grigg forward. Frederico grabbed Grigg's dagger from its sheath and sliced his tunic open from the neck down. "We'll start with a good old-fashioned whipping. I'll make you wish—*what is that?*"

All eyes fell on Grigg's blackened chest. The unnatural charred-coal color spread across his heart, deeper and darker than ever before. But it wasn't a modest little spot anymore. The center, over the place where his heart lay, was pitch black as a soulless void that even light was afraid to touch.

Hungry fingers reached out from it in all directions, completely encompassing his left shoulder and running down his arm to the elbow. On the right, it reached out for his shoulder and down toward his waist. He couldn't tell for sure without seeing himself, but based on the horrified looks, he wouldn't be surprised if it had started crawling up his neck.

Every last one of them stood stunned. The guard on his left dropped him in his haste to back away, leaving the man on the right to try to catch his falling weight. Grigg forced weight into his legs to stabilize himself as best as he could, using the guard as a counterweight to help him stay upright.

This was his chance to create value for himself, and he intended to make the most of it. He needed Frederico to take him to the Heart of the Mountain, rather than dump him off somewhere or toss his carcass to the buzzards.

The Heart of the Stars glittered from around his neck, all the brighter for the charcoal skin canvas behind it. Frederico's initial horror at the mark of the curse on Grigg's skin twisted into a gleam of hunger for the magic of the Heart.

Grigg laughed. "You've never worn the Heart of the Stars, have you? It's only been strung up under a barrier. Your father was smart to protect it, but it's not only that *it* needs protecting. *You* need protection *from* it. Last night, my skin was clear as a baby's. Now, if I don't get the Heart of the Stars to the Heart of the Mountain, it will kill me. And it will do the same to anyone who carries it. Taking possession of the Heart of the Stars is to take responsibility for returning it home. Why do you think so many people have died over it throughout the years?"

Frederico's eyes widened, so shaken he seemed to forget about punishing Grigg. Or perhaps he only wanted to wait until his victim was more alive. It wasn't much fun killing someone who was already mostly dead.

Adelina slumped to the jungle floor beside him with a stifled cry of pain. Cassio kneed her in the back to keep her upright, but her knees were weak. Grigg wasn't a melder, but he'd known enough of them to know it did expend some energy to call to whatever element one had power over. Adelina was straight out of energy.

Caterina glanced at Frederico and put a hand on his arm. "Enough. They're not strong enough to try anything."

Frederico remained staring at Grigg, his gaze moving from the cursed skin to the magical necklace and back again.

Grigg mustered a small smile. "Why don't you kill me and take the Heart of the Stars yourself, all the way to the Heart of the Mountain? It's too late for me, but maybe you'll get to it in time, and the damage will be reversible for you."

Frederico grimaced. He didn't look positive about Grigg's story, but neither did he seem anxious to test it. He gave a nod to Caterina. "Help get them in the boat. We're bringing them with us."

The guards took up their charges once again. The two men assigned to Grigg stumbled to hold him while still trying to avoid touching the blackened parts of his skin. And then half his weight just ... lifted. A blanket of air rose from beneath him to lighten the load on the men as Caterina raised her hands and ordered gusts of air to buoy the prisoners. Together, Caterina and the guards half carried, half floated Grigg and Adelina down the bank to *The Wandering Heron.*

The statue took up the entire front portion of the boat. The men paused to unload a couple of crates of counterweight on the other side to make room for Adelina and Grigg before they bound Grigg's hands and dumped him on top of two barrels and a crate. His head hit the side of the boat as he fell awkwardly into the small space opposite the statue of the Heart of the Sea, still concealed under the sheet. They tied Adelina's hands and chucked her in next, and she toppled into him, her arm crushing his face and her head lolling over the side of the little fishing vessel.

The ridge of a metal band around the barrel cut into Grigg's back, and the rough side of the boat crushed his right arm. On his other side, Adelina's weight pressed in on him. The half-dozen Morturi and two Guerrori women followed the boat on the bank, leaning on the crestbreakers and windcallers to move the boat upstream with its cargo.

The Heart of the Stars still hung around Grigg's neck. They were headed toward the Heart of the Mountain, and the Heart of the Sea statue stood proud in the boat.

He was so close.

Grigg gathered his strength and shifted to one side, just as Adelina seemed to do the same, wrenching herself further into the boat so her head could lean against the rim. Her weight shifted beside him rather than on top of him, their arms pressed together, their heads touching as they rested on rough-edged crates and barrels and against the edge of the *Heron.*

Now that the others were on the bank, they were far enough away that they would not be able to hear anything spoken quietly in the little boat.

Adelina dropped her voice low. "You told a good story about your heart."

Grigg took a breath. His lungs burned. "When stories are all you've got, you make the best of them."

"How long have you really had the mark?"

"Since I was born. Six hundred years ago, when Giovanna had a falling out with one of my ancestors, she cursed him and all the males in his bloodline after him. But it used to look almost like an ugly birthmark. After I got the egg, and the egg started to crack, it started to expand."

It was weird answering questions so directly, but the truth had slipped out smooth as melted butter. Adelina was cursed too, both of them suffering under Giovanna's thumb. They were both in the same boat.

Grigg let out a little laugh at that.

"What's so funny?"

"We're in the same boat."

She snorted, and he could almost picture her rolling her eyes as they lay there, side by side, staring up at the sky, and branches reaching out over the river above them.

"You're ridiculous."

"Says the woman stupid enough to get caught by my curse." He shook his head grimly. "If I were a better man, maybe I'd understand it."

"Says the man dying by two curses at once. Or haven't you fallen for the curse placed on me?"

She wanted to know if he really loved her—for the curse only impacted those who were falling in love. There was no other reason for her to be sick than for her to have started falling for him. But Grigg had the added curse of his link with the egg to contend with.

Grigg swallowed the ache of his body as much as he could until it dimmed to a chronic background of misery. Though going through horrible shared experiences may have bound them together somewhat, Grigg and Adelina hadn't known each other long enough for the depth and breadth of love depicted in stories of old. They certainly didn't have the robust foundation of trust some relationships seemed to have—that stern stuff upon which decades of commitment were built. But when he'd seen her on the rooftop ...

When he'd taught her about pickpocketing with the scarecrow jacket, and he'd watched the fire in her eyes over demanding the bed ...

When he'd watched her give up an escape for Sebastian ...

She was funny and smart and bold, brazen one minute, challenging the next. The blaze in her eyes demanded his attention. He never wanted to look away.

They didn't have a love story. Not really. But at least for him, he knew he'd already begun to fall, and fall hard. He'd already given up time for her—his most precious commodity as the clock on the cracking egg ticked.

When he'd told Nico he would cut off any limb that touched Adelina, he'd meant it. He hadn't felt an ounce of remorse to follow through on his threat to protect her when he threw her up against the stone wall. And now she was here, by his side, after he'd given her permission to go. She'd even had the decency to laugh at his stupid joke in the midst of the pain they shared.

But if she asked him if he was falling in love, did she *want* him to be falling for her? If he said yes, would his confirmation make her love him more? Would she die faster?

He shook his head. "I can't answer that."

She shifted beside him, her forehead turning against his as she angled toward him. "You can't? Or you won't?"

"Both."

Morning light fell in a blanket of soft haze over the river, signaling the end of the night. But for Grigg, the feel of the darkness didn't lift. Birds began to chirp as the sun poured its light on every living thing down below, on Morturi and Guerrori alike, man and woman, human and beast.

The boat continued down the river, moving against the

current, and they fell into silence. The water rippled away from the smooth cut of the fishing vessel, harmonizing with the soft creak of the boat. A light breeze wafted over them, just before it bumped up against the wind barrier, catching the sail with windcaller gales.

Grigg found himself hoping Adelina would speak again, if only to hear the voice of a friend as they traveled up the river. Did he really consider her a friend? In any case, he couldn't initiate a conversation. Not when he'd ended their last exchange the way he did. But the talk had also distracted him from the pain.

She may have had the same idea, as eventually she broke the quiet tension between them. "My mother always told me men were greedy and selfish."

His experience with humanity hadn't been much better. "Wise woman."

If anything, her statement had been too limiting. Giovanna, for example, took the cake on evil people he'd encountered, and she wasn't a man.

Adelina ignored his comment and continued. "My mother believed all men were evil, at the core, no exceptions—only facades and trickery, luring women to believe differently. Most Guerrori have felt the same for decades. It's in our blood."

She hesitated. "I might have believed it more fully had I not started sneaking off to visit my grandmother as a child. My father's mother. She told me stories of her late husband and her son, my biological father. Those two men served as proof that mother lied. Dead proof, but they held a sort of hope. I still visit my grand-mother when I can. She has such a gentle optimism—a view of the world that promises light on every morning.

"My mother had interpreted that to mean the light would draw you in with its beauty and burn you when you got too close. I've been looking all my life for evidence that my gentle grand-mother was right, and my harsh, unforgiving mother was wrong."

By and large, the world was harsh and unforgiving. But perhaps Grigg's experience was skewed. He'd met some optimists in his day—a matronly baker in Vodkra. An old shoemaker in Radha. A princess who'd led him to Ghosts' Gorge. They'd all looked at the world differently than he had.

"What did you discover?"

Adelina's shoulder twitched against his arm, which he interpreted as an attempt to shrug. "Men really are greedy and selfish and evil, but so are women. And yet, there are pinpricks of something else. Little moments small enough we might not notice if we're not looking for them. Moments that tell a different story. Some people show it more than others, but it's there. I see it in an older man who buys extra fruit and hands it to small children in the street. I see it in a mother holding her crying children with a tender hand and a comforting smile. I see it in ..."

She trailed off.

"In what?"

Adelina sighed. "In the Palladinos, Pietro with his wife and kids, playing games. Holding his wife when she cries and kissing her every day when he comes home. I see it in Sebastian, too, in the way he cares for his brother and his family."

Grigg's lips parted. "*That's* why you go every week to watch them. To see if that softness is real. To see it behind closed doors and know if it truly exists."

"Yes. I went to learn about family. To see if it could be real in the way the old tales describe. I wanted it to be real, but it seemed too good to be true."

Grigg had often wondered what it would have been like to grow up with parents who loved each other. Specifically, parents who loved each other and stayed alive long enough to enjoy it.

Then a thought struck him, and his stomach dropped. She'd shared a deep, critical moment in her life. Insight about herself. A wordless pressure to reciprocate settled over him, but he couldn't share what he was really feeling. Not with her. Not now.

He'd likely take it to the grave in the next few hours.

He could withstand such gentle pressures for a few small hours.

But was that really how he wanted to go? Still, again, he couldn't hasten her death. But he couldn't leave her with nothing either.

Thoughts strung together in his mind, tumbling over each other in flashes of memory. The scent of medicinal herbs, and the sound of heavy doctors' footsteps, and a father's furious scream. His mouth went dry.

"The first girl I ever loved fell ill when I was twelve."

He couldn't muster the words or the courage to say more. It was enough of an explanation. And if it wasn't, it would have to do anyway.

She waited for him to go on, but he didn't, and she didn't press.

The light of the sun grew brighter as they continued upriver, but whether the sun would illuminate their way or burn them when they got near it, Grigg couldn't say. Perhaps it was enough simply to be grateful to see it one more time before he passed away. What was the span of life but a sprig of spring green pushing up through the earth, weathering wind and rain, and withering by nightfall?

The weight on his chest doubled as though someone had thrown a new slab of marble on top of him as he lay there in the boat. But he found that if he accepted the pain rather than fighting it, giving in to the reality of it, he could breathe just a little easier.

One hour passed.

Two hours.

Three.

He couldn't help himself. He leaned his head gently into Adelina's as they lay on their backs in the bottom of the boat, staring up at arms of far-reaching jungle branches stretching out over the boundaries of the river. The two prisoners in the boat listened to the crunch of footsteps on the bank, the whistle of wind, the flap of the sail.

Against every sane thought, he moved his hand just enough to brush hers. For a moment, he thought she would move away, but she never did.

They lay like that until at last Frederico's voice barked out an update. "We're here."

CHAPTER
TWENTY-FOUR

They'd made good time along the river. No doubt Caterina had provided all the directions, which was more than likely at least half the reason Frederico had put up with her for this long. Adelina didn't know if Frederico really intended to marry Caterina, but he would certainly use her for every last utility she could provide.

From what Adelina had gathered from snatches of conversation and the sounds of blades on brush, the foliage had gotten so thick on the sides of the river that Frederico's crew had been forced to hack a path through for the melders as they guided the little boat. Finally, Frederico himself had made stairs in rock outcroppings rising up on either side until the group reached a landing once again.

The blue sky mocked them overhead with its frivolity and warmth as the boat bumped up against the patch of rock and sand at the base of the arch of the Great Tree. Strong arms reached in, seized Adelina and Grigg, and hauled them from *The Wandering Heron.*

The ground here was sacred—or at least, they'd always been *taught* that it was. Adelina wasn't sure what she believed anymore. But because it was sacred, they only traveled here once a year to perform a ceremony that Adelina, as the chieftess, presided over.

Only Adelina could open the Great Tree of the Heart of the Mountain. Caterina knew that. Did the woman believe if she took control of the Guerrori tribe, the Tree would open for her without a proper passing of authority? Or had she known all along Adelina would be necessary for this part of their plan?

But if Caterina told Frederico their Guerrori secrets, perhaps that was the real reason Frederico hadn't yet killed her.

Thick jungle filled out the scene behind her with vibrant green and overhung the place where they stood at the approach to the soaring rocky arch at the base of the mountain. The pure blue of the river flowed from beneath a network of rock and tree bark, the bark moving up a sheer cliff into the majestic Great Tree.

Tall rock formations formed walls on the other side of the river like a narrow hallway, ensuring none who dared come here made an easy escape. The only way in was by the river—one way in, one way out. Unless one brought a quakemaker, like Frederico.

The rocky arch soared five stories high in a perfect massive circular structure. But it was the sight of the tree that stilled her heart every time she saw it.

It would have taken fifty people hand in hand to wrap around the perimeter of its trunk. It stood proud and tall, filling the entire space of the arch, and the mountain climbed up from it, up, up, up as far as the eye could see. The trunk of the Great Tree curled this way and that as if it had swayed in a breeze here, bent to a wind there, and became frozen in time as its long green branches spilled upward and outward. Its great canopy spread like the feathers of a mother eagle, reaching to cover the whole of the archway, its twigs and leaves even growing up and around the stone boundary at the top of the arch that stood at the base of the trunk.

Thick roots flowed over the rocky slope in a tangle of twisted tresses thick as her thigh in the most impressive display she'd ever seen, magnificent and powerful, with a sort of wild grace that struck the heart with awe. The edges of the roots glowed with crystals that grew out from them throughout the interlocking system. The crystals stood out like blossoms made of pure amber, not in the branches above but in the foundations of the Tree below.

"Kill him, Adelina."

The voice was a hiss in the back of her mind. At least, she'd thought so. But then Adelina saw her—Giovanna, walking on the other side of Grigg as his guard bore him forward. But though she was there, Giovanna had a shimmering quality about her here. Something non-corporeal.

Like she wasn't really there, maybe. Or was only partially there?

She eyed Grigg, and her gaze slid over to lock onto Adelina. "Making him fall in love is taking too long. You're a fireblood. Boil his blood and kill him now."

If she were going to kill anyone, Frederico was a decent probability. Giovanna was only spared from the top of her list by the fact that Adelina wasn't entirely sure how to do the job. Adelina also hadn't considered that she could boil someone's blood. But even if that were true, she didn't have the strength to pull it off.

And what did Giovanna mean by *it was taking too long*? Grigg looked like he could fall over dead any minute.

She shook her head. "I can't. My strength is gone."

Cassio, who had again been assigned as her guard, shot her a look. "You don't have much of a choice."

But she hadn't been talking to him.

Giovanna's walk transitioned from a leisurely stroll to a predatory stalk. It was something in the way she carried herself, the way she looked down at Grigg, and back across at Adelina, as Frederico and Caterina led the group to the rock wall with the network of roots cascading over it.

"Why does he want the Heart of the Mountain? Why does he want the Heart of the Stars, the Heart of the Sea? Don't you get it?" Giovanna's lips twisted down at the corners. "Fool. He's not here for you. He's here for power. He's here for the jungle, for the secrets in the wood. He's here for everything you've spent your life protecting."

She jabbed a pointed finger toward Grigg's chest. He didn't react. He didn't see her. "He's here to destroy you."

Adelina clenched her jaw. Giovanna was trying to break her feelings for him so she would escape the curse and be strong again, but she didn't want to believe it.

What if, as backward as it all was, Grigg was the evidence that her mother had lied? What if what he felt for her was real? What if —if it weren't for the curse—it could last?

Even if it was all a lie, she didn't want to be trapped by Giovanna forever. As Grigg had said, it was a fate worse than death. She could take a chance on Grigg or live in the fist of the tyrant mage.

Still, Grigg was there for the Heart of the Mountain. He'd never even pretended to be there for anything else. He'd said he was here as a thief, and he'd been true to that purpose. He'd stolen the Heart of the Stars and had intended to use her to find the Heart of the Mountain, and here he was, at just the place he'd sought. But whose fault was it all, really, when Giovanna was the one who'd cursed him?

What would Adelina do to break her own curse that Giovanna had placed on her? Her chest swelled with roiling, mingled emotions. She wanted to shout at Giovanna, tell her the mage had already destroyed Adelina. That of the two of them, it was Giovanna that Adelina hated the most. But everyone around her would hear if she spoke. She clamped her lips together and focused on every step forward.

Giovanna followed her, coming around from Grigg's side to appear at Adelina's shoulder. "Everything I've done has been to protect you and your mission. You've done well. The Heart of the Mountain has remained secure until now. It's time to complete your assignment. Grigg is dangerous. So are all the men here with you. But if you combine the Hearts first, before they do, you won't need protecting. You will have the power to fight back the Morturi on your own. To fight back Grigglor Frizzletwerf. To fight back everyone."

Adelina blinked. Was it true? Whoever assembled the Hearts would gain power?

If Adelina had this power, could she sweep back the Morturi and maintain control of the jungle? Could she put Catarina in her place and save not only the Nascosta, but all of Smŭrttata from the greedy fingers of the Morturi tribe?

What else could she do? If she had this power, perhaps she could destroy her ancestral mother forever. She could destroy the curse herself.

If combining the Hearts restored Giovanna to her full power, and Giovanna would grant Adelina that same power for being the one to put the Hearts together, maybe she just needed to play along long enough to gain that power.

If Frederico combined the Hearts, he would rule with an iron fist. He would be a tyrant.

If Grigg combined the Hearts, he would—

Adelina hesitated. She wasn't exactly sure *what* he would do. What would he be without the curse on his name? Had he ever had other goals or ambitions? To be something other than a cheat? To do something worthwhile and meaningful with his life?

Would he become something she couldn't recognize? How well did she really know this man? Who was Grigglor Frizzletwerf? Perhaps he didn't even know the answer himself.

Realization dawned on her. "Grigglor. Grigg is a nickname."

It was a small sort of epiphany, and one she'd hardly realized she'd said out loud. She'd never known his full name, first or last.

But Giovanna knew it. Another reminder that Giovanna had afflicted Grigglor as long as she had afflicted Adelina.

Grigg and Adelina were both cursed by the same person. *This* person. The Black Swan Mage. The person most responsible for her suffering wasn't Grigg, or even Frederico or Nico. It was Giovanna.

But if destroying the egg directly only served to break it apart faster, Grigg would die. And whatever shattering the egg would do, Giovanna wanted it to happen. And Giovanna's power was already growing. She'd never appeared to her in full consciousness before.

The egg was crumbling further, and here they were at the source of a mighty skein of magic, the Heart of the Mountain. Which meant Adelina needed to be the one to merge the three Hearts. She needed to gain this power from her ancestral mother.

No one but Adelina would be protected from Giovanna's wrath. If Giovanna came to full power, would she kill all the men here at the Heart of the Mountain the moment she came to physical form?

Adelina glanced at Giovanna again. The woman watched her sharply, a small smile creeping across her face. She saw Adelina come to a decision but misjudged it. She believed she'd won Adelina over.

Grigg looked at her with a quizzical brow, confused and concerned. He didn't see or hear Giovanna, but Adelina was acting strange. And she'd just pronounced out of thin air that the name he'd provided her was a nickname.

His eyes narrowed. "How do you know that?"

Adelina ignored him, fixing her gaze on Giovanna, then turned to Frederico. He stood beside Caterina at the base of the lattice of roots, his finger drawn along a glowing crystal protruding from the system. He turned to look at her.

She pulled her shoulders back. "What must I do?"

Frederico would hear the question and assume it was directed at him, but Giovanna would know it was meant for her.

Giovanna placed a hand over Adelina's heart. She didn't feel flesh and bone from the contact, but a tingling sensation pricked at her skin.

The mage smiled. "I will let you borrow some of my strength. It will help you to last until the Hearts are merged. This is what you must do."

CHAPTER TWENTY-FIVE

GRIGG

How had Adelina known Grigg was a nickname? And what did his name have to do with anything?

In the span of that small realization, something in the air had shifted. Adelina was different. She stood suddenly taller, stronger than before, lifting her chin as Frederico answered her question.

"What do you think? I need you to climb up and open the Heart of the Mountain. Bring it to me."

Adelina glanced at her bound hands. "You expect me to climb with my hands tied?"

Caterina snorted. "It won't be a problem for you."

Adelina shot her a look, then shrugged. "Fine. But once you have the Heart of the Mountain, you won't need the Nascosta. You can leave us alone."

Frederico's lips twitched. "We'll see."

The terse exchange sent eddies of anxiety twisting through Grigg's gut. He was supposed to remain calm in every situation, unmoved, unflappable. He'd been close to death lots of times. It was a miracle he'd survived this long leading the sort of life he'd led. But this time, death crouched behind a shroud of golden egg shell. And her name was Giovanna.

And there was someone in the world whom, try as he might to avoid it, he now cared about.

Grigg glanced up at the towering canopy of the massive tree. He wasn't even sure it could still be called a tree at that point, but what else could it be? The monstrous thing towered over them, its roots working their way down over the rocky formation and deep into the water of the river. The soft morning light gave an ethereal quality to the scene, shining on the sparkling golden crystals, outgrowths from the roots, both above and below the water. But the roots themselves were nearly two stories high to climb.

Three minutes ago, Adelina had hardly been able to walk. Grigg had managed to force his body to move, but the idea of expending enough energy to climb anything was as outlandish as him trying to fly.

He shook his head. "You can't climb that."

Cassio rumbled a low laugh. "She climbs it, or she dies."

"If you need her to open it and she dies, where will you be left then?"

Frederico gave him a long look, then jerked his chin at Caterina. "Go with her. Make sure she doesn't fall. Windcallers on alert, and catch her if she slips."

Adelina held his gaze. "I'll be fine."

What had happened to her since getting out of the boat? Maybe she'd realized caring about him was too costly. Maybe she'd reflected on the sort of man Grigg was and realized—realized what, exactly? That she'd only begun to love the idea of him, rather than him as a person? Or that he was as awful a human being as she'd first thought. Maybe she'd come to her senses and shaken off the curse organically. But why had she said Grigg was a nickname? Did she know something about his family? It sounded almost like—

But no. Giovanna only appeared to the unconscious mind, and here, they were fully awake.

Adelina stepped up to the root system, and Cassio let her go. Caterina gestured for Adelina to start first, and even with her hands tied, the chieftess spidered up the wall with more strength or agility than he'd ever seen. Her movements were sure and familiar. She knew every branch and root, every cleft in the rock, all the best places for footing. She made adjustments here and there for her tied hands, and two times Caterina caught her elbow as they climbed together up the roots.

She hadn't put up much of a fight to Frederico's asking her to retrieve the Heart of the Mountain, but it wasn't the *getting* of the Heart that would be a problem so much as what to do with it once she had it in her hands.

The Heart of the Stars still hung around Grigg's neck, nestled against his bare, curse-riddled chest. Frederico would let Adelina retrieve the Heart of the Mountain and let Grigg hold the Heart of the Stars until the last moment—just in case Grigg's lie about the holder of the Heart was true.

The unstable part would be once Frederico got the hearts all together in his possession. Then all bets were off as to what would happen or who he would kill first.

Three-quarters of the way up the cliff of roots, Adelina stopped climbing upward and worked her way sideways along the face until she neared the center. Caterina stopped and watched from a distance, no longer following.

Frederico stepped forward for a better look and called up to them. "What are you doing?"

Adelina ignored him, but Caterina called back down. "The Heart isn't at the top. It's here. It's a sacred place, and only she can open it. I won't go closer."

Adelina closed her eyes and pressed both palms on the roots. Her lips moved, but he couldn't make out any words she might be saying. The instant she finished, every glowing crystal shone in brilliant golden glory, flashing bright as the sun as the Great Tree received her words. The roots around where Adelina stood rearranged themselves into an elegant archway with a glowing passage beyond it, inviting entrance for the chieftess. Adelina disappeared inside.

What if there was another way out? What if she could escape? *Would* she escape?

If she did, Grigg would die. But if she returned with the Heart of the Mountain and gave it to Frederico, that would get Grigg killed, too.

How sentient was the tree? What if the tree was angry that she'd brought outsiders and decided to kill her for her betrayal?

Grigg fixed his gaze on the empty arch where he'd last seen Adelina. Two minutes passed. Five. Frederico began to pace, this way and that, plucking at the crystals of the roots.

Caterina spoke only once, chastising his disrespect. "Don't touch that."

He shot her a sour look but kept his hands to himself and continued his pacing.

Grigg lifted one shoulder to scratch at an itch on the side of his face where a trickle of sweat had trailed down. With his hands still tied behind his back, his shoulder only barely reached his cheek. How long had it been now? This was a bad idea. He wasn't precisely sure what they could've done instead, but surely whatever was going on inside the tree wasn't meant to take this long. Even Caterina peered anxiously at the archway every few seconds, and Letizia shifted her weight back and forth.

If the Guerrori felt it was taking too long, something must be going wrong. The Morturi felt it too. Several checked the position of the morning sun in the sky, and again moments later.

And then a figure stood in the door of the Heart of the Mountain. Adelina reappeared on the ledge, her long dark hair flowing behind her, looking for all the world like the queen of the jungle in the cut-off formal gown from last night. She still wore the green dress with its overlapping leaves wrapped over one shoulder, fitted through the bodice, but slashed in the skirt just as the heliconia had begun, cut off mid to low thigh, showing off long muscular legs. Her wrists remained tied, but within her palms she cupped something round, circular, and glowing jade green.

Adelina lifted her voice to the half-dozen waiting people down below.

"I've got it. But I can't climb down with my hands tied without crushing the Heart. We need to be gentle with it. Caterina needs to untie me, so I can hold it in one hand and climb down with the other."

Frederico shook his head. "Not a chance. Jump."

Grigg snapped his head toward the idiot prince. The root-covered cliff dropped beneath Adelina to the river just a couple of paces off from where the fishing boat now floated, but sharp rocks jutted up from the water.

"Are you insane? What if she cracks her head open? What if the Heart is destroyed?"

Frederico rolled his eyes. "We've got windcallers and crest-breakers. We'll catch her." He turned back to Adelina and repeated his order. "Jump."

Adelina hesitated, weighing her options. Then, in a sudden move, she took two long leaping strides forward and launched off the ledge. Her body shot out straight as an arrow, the Heart captured in her hands.

Caterina threw out a hand, as did the melders on the bank. A blanket of air shot up and around her as a wall of water from the river rose up to meet it, a safety net in case the wind failed. Adelina hung suspended in midair over the waters of the river flowing around the rocks below.

Caterina slipped on the wall. Her concentration broke. Adelina plunged, but in the next moment, the other melders stabilized her in the air, and Caterina regained her footing. They floated

Adelina over *The Wandering Heron* and back to the ground in front of Frederico.

Idly, Grigg wondered why they hadn't used the melders to get her up on the wall to begin with. Perhaps it was a power move to make Adelina climb, or he wanted to save the melders' strength as long as possible. Either way, it didn't sit right.

Adelina alighted on the ground beside him like a bird on a branch. Grigg stared at the glowing object in her hands. It was round and smooth and pointed at one end, the shape of a seed and the size of a large rock or a human heart filling the full palm of her hand.

Grigg's aching heart quickened. The Heart of the Stars burned against the skin of his chest. The hearts were together. Now if only Grigg could somehow be the one to merge all three ...

Frederico lurched forward with hungry hands and snatched the green glowing Heart of the Mountain from Adelina's hands. He held it up, turning it over and over, vindictive victory sifting across his wide-eyed face.

The prince sidestepped and snatched the Heart of the Stars next, ripping it, chain and all, over Grigg's head so that he held one Heart in each hand. Frederico laughed a light, giddy laugh and glanced between the prisoners, eyes bright. "I've waited all my life for this." He turned to the statue still standing in *The Wandering Heron.* "And now for the third."

Grigg resisted the urge to clutch at his chest as a wave of agony stabbed through his heart and splintered outward to every crevice of his body. He was getting worse. He cast a glance sideways to look for the egg, but it had been plunked off to the side against the root wall, still glowing from within its bag.

Frederico strode forward, stepped off the bank and into the boat, and steadied himself on the single mast. He looked up at the sheet draped over the statue of the Heart of the Sea, then back down at his hands. He couldn't remove the sheet while still holding everything. Frederico grinned again, placed the Heart of the Stars over his own neck, and reached up with his free hand to pull the sheet free.

A collective gasp went up from all eyes watching from the bank. It was impossible to ascertain of what exactly the statue was made. The ethereal shining surface looked much like an abalone shell but seemed to glow with a light all its own. Soft as mother-of-pearl, radiant as firestone opal, it depicted a siren with long hair flowing from a crown placed on her head.

The siren held up her hands before her and just above her eye line, so that she looked up at a pure, shimmering orb the size of a millstone. The siren's unflinching gaze was fixed on the orb. Her face, both delicate and fierce, was stunning to behold in all her majesty.

Frederico fell back a step, and the guard holding Grigg lost his grip at the sight of her. Grigg toppled to the ground with a grunt, unable to support his own full weight.

Frederico didn't notice. He stared at the statue. She was stunning, and she was the last Heart he needed to bring the three back together once again. Frederico took a deep breath and moved forward again, slipping the necklace from his neck and lifting the Heart of the Stars and the Heart of the Mountain up toward the orb of the Heart of the Sea.

He touched the items together. Nothing happened. He tried again, this time placing the two other hearts close to where the physical heart of a siren would be. Nothing.

The prince glanced at Grigg. "I'm pretty tired of games. You're going to tell me how to combine these hearts."

Grigg wrenched himself upright. "Or I could just do it for you. I know you hate to get your hands dirty."

Frederico raked his eyes over the statue of the siren. "There's nothing dirty about this. I'll be the one to merge the Hearts."

Grigg sighed. "To be honest, I'm not sure why it's not working for you. Maybe you have to have an actual heart to combine these three." He wasn't being honest, of course, but that hardly mattered. "Seeing as you don't have a heart, perhaps you've been disqualified."

Frederico pursed his lips. "Says the thief who started a war and caused multiple deaths. You just want power. I want a rightful inheritance. We are *not* the same."

The man stepped out of *The Heron* and transferred the Heart of the Stars and the Heart of the Mountain into his left hand. "I could use my powers to crush you in the rocks, to swallow you alive. But nothing makes me feel more alive than a good old-fashioned beating." He snapped his fingers at one of his Morturi melders. "As you said, it's been too long since I've gotten my hands dirty, right?"

The Morturi man passed Frederico a short whip. Its handle was the length of a dagger's blade, with multiple strips of braided leather twice that length attached to the top.

Grigg's eyes followed the trail of the skin-ripping end. "I didn't say that. I don't know how long it's been since you've gotten your hands dirty. And hey, why start now? As a person who also hadn't gotten my hands dirty until recently, I'll tell you it's not good for your supply of clean shirts. I can't tell you how many excellent pieces of my wardrobe have been ruined just in the last week."

Frederico jerked his head at the guards, who seemed to know what he meant. Considering jerking his head at people was his primary mode of communication, it was somewhat amazing they always guessed correctly. Two of them seized Grigg, ripped the tattered remains of his shirt off his back, and threw him forward to the dirt-dusted stone.

Every element was readily available. Water in the river, rock in the cliffs and along the ground, air in the wide-open jungle, and fire straight from the palms of the firebloods. If he ran, they'd only crush him. If he stayed, he might die by scourging. And his strength was barely enough to stand as it was.

He searched for Adelina's face as the first blow fell. Cassio was back at her elbow, long spindly fingers wrapped around her arm.

Her brow knit together, her muscles tensed like a cat about to spring, and she leaned in toward the beating. But it was her eyes that held him, golden pools of a tenderness sprouting protective thorns. There was fire and there was concern—for him—though he deserved none of it.

A piece of him broke inside at the thought, but as it did, another part of him rose up to take its place—a part fueled and bound up by genuine affection he desperately desired.

Searing pain cracked across his back, lighting his skin on fire. He could almost see the red welts in his mind's eye exploding up and down his back. The whip crashed down again, and Grigg's knees gave out below him. He crashed his cheek into the rough cut of a stone as he landed.

"Stop! Gallows, stop! I'll tell you." Grigg spat to one side. "The ritual requires the sacrifice of an arrogant pig. So kind of you to volunteer."

If he was going to die anyway, if he had one last good thing to do in this world, it would be keeping this information from Frederico.

Frederico let out a feral cry and threw the whip down again. Grigg's back split open, and he couldn't stop the scream that ripped from his throat.

Frederico reared his arm back again for another blow. He stepped and flung his arm. Grigg braced for another impact. Then from the corner of his eye, he watched as Adelina threw an elbow into Cassio's gut, wrenched free, and threw herself to the ground over Grigg, covering him with her body before the last whip fell.

Frederico pulled back at the last moment, staring down at her in consternation. Grigg shut his eyes, as if to block out reality. But with Giovanna torturing him by night, and Frederico by day, there was nowhere to run. And now it was not only him, but Adelina in the crosshairs.

Grigg struggled to sit up beneath her, and she helped him into an upright position. Each movement shot pain down every fiber of his body. He leaned into her support but dropped his voice low. "Stop acting like you care about me. It's bad for negotiations."

Whether she truly cared for him or not, it really *was* terrible for negotiating. Because the truth was, whether she cared for him or not, he cared for her. Now Frederico knew it, and by the twisted grin creeping across Frederico's face, it was too late.

Frederico ran a hand down the leather strips of the whip and rubbed his fingers together over the smear of Grigg's blood that came off on his hands as he did. Frederico flashed Grigg a pearly white smile, tossed the Heart of the Mountain up into the air and caught it. "New deal. Instead of hurting you, I hurt her. Until you tell me how to combine the Hearts."

Fury destroyed a dam inside a deep well within Grigg's body, heat fueling his every move. Grigg's wrists were still bound, and the weakness of the curse still pulled at him like tar. But he lurched upright anyway. He staggered, but the next moment, straightened, and planted himself between Frederico and Adelina. It was a miracle he managed to keep his feet under him as he shot a white-hot glare at the Morturi pig.

"The last man who touched her is dead with an incinerated face and a knife through the trachea."

"Is that so?" Frederico curled his lip into a snarl. "I don't care."

He waved a hand, and the ground beneath Grigg's feet pitched, knocking him off balance and back to the ground. Grigg whirled in time to see Adelina throw a beam of fire toward Frederico, but she should have saved her energy. She fell the moment the flame left her palms.

Caterina and the other windcallers knocked Adelina flat on her back with a wall of wind, pinning her to the ground as Frederico stalked forward, seized her by the throat, and hauled her up. "I think that idiot really loves you. He must not know you very well."

Frederico spun her around and shoved the chieftess' face forward into the dirt, her hands still bound in front of her. Frederico lifted the whip and slammed it down over the place where Adelina lay.

Crackkkkk.

But it wasn't the sound of the whip.

Light.

Beams of blinding light were everywhere.

The black over Grigg's heart surged down across his entire torso, down to his forearm, and up the back of his neck. He could feel it hot along his skin, as if his heart planned to gnaw its way through his chest.

The egg rolled out of the bag where it had been set along the wall of roots. Spears of light pricked through the shell on every side. Its gold flashed, and the egg itself vibrated and rose up off the ground of its own accord, hovering in the air.

The man holding Grigg fell to the ground behind him, dropping his bow from his opposite hand. Grigg's arms wrenched this way and that, his body flailing on the ground as though somehow the tie between himself and Giovanna let him feel the anxious writhing of the mage, striving for freedom.

Four warriors covered their faces from the light. One blasted the egg with a wall of air and found himself flying backward into the cliff instead. Another shot an arrow. The arrow *plink*ed uselessly against the shell and dropped to the ground near Grigg's feet. The archer turned tail and fled, using the makeshift rock steps Frederico had created on their way in to run back along the cliff the way they'd come.

Adelina twisted back toward the egg from her place on the ground, her hands still tied at the wrist. Frederico still stood near her, but the light of the egg consumed his attention.

"Grigg."

Their eyes met. She looked at the bow that had fallen near her, and Grigg glanced at the arrow at his feet. Understanding shot between them.

Instead of collapsing, Grigg felt a surge of strength. He wasn't sure where it had come from or if, as the mage began to escape her confinement, he had a short burst of reprieve before the final blow would take his life.

Grigg snatched up the arrow and tossed it to Adelina. Adelina grabbed the bow and the arrow with her bound hands. Grigg threw his bound hands around the neck of the nearest guard, yanking backward hard. The man flailed, striking at Grigg, but he held firm. The guard made a choking sound and collapsed, strangled by the bonds he'd used to tie him up.

Grigg glanced back at Adelina. Adelina's body was contorted, her hands planted on the ground like a handstand, head up toward her target, torso twisted backward so that her rear nearly touched the back of her head as one foot held the bow and the other pulled back an arrow on the string.

Thwip! The arrow hit Frederico, and he dropped like a stone.

Grigg snatched the dagger from his victim's belt and sliced Adelina's hands free. She plucked a fallen quiver from the ground and notched an arrow to the string before Grigg had collected the two hearts from Frederico's limp hands.

The egg still blasted light like a sunset that didn't know when to die.

Seconds remained on the clock of his life.

He ducked under a ball of fire thrown by a Morturi fireblood and hurled himself over the side of *The Wandering Heron*.

CHAPTER TWENTY-SIX

ADELINA

Adelina reached for a fresh arrow from the quiver at her back. She'd nabbed it off a fallen Morturi warrior moments ago, and not a moment too soon.

Thwip. An arrow to the throat.

Thwip. An arrow between the eyes.

Thwip. The third arrow was caught in a firestorm burst from Cassio's palms.

Cassio threw another blast at Adelina, but whatever this Black Swan Mage had done to Adelina provided bursts of energy at intervals. Adelina lifted her palm and shot a blaze of fire of her own. The fire met Cassio's blast, forming a battling blaze between the Morturi man and the Guerrori chieftess.

Adelina notched another arrow and shot through the inferno as though through a fog. He never saw it coming. Cassio's form toppled to the side, an arrow protruding from his chest, the fireball between them dissipating in a shower of embers.

Letizia stared at the fallen man, turned, and fled along the steps of the cliff face that Frederico had created. The band of Morturi she'd attached herself to was falling one by one, and Caterina was not strong enough to save her if Adelina turned on her. The tide was changing. Caterina was already gone. Another Morturi followed suit, though she couldn't be certain he wouldn't return along the top of the cliff and try to attack from above, or gain enough distance to use melder powers from behind better cover for himself.

Cassio's body stared up at the sky five paces from the place Frederico had breathed his last, both with her arrows still protruding from their bodies. Five or six corpses littered the ground, but enough of them had escaped that Grigg and Adelina couldn't take their time here.

Both sides would return with reinforcements.

What Adelina needed most now was to get to the Heart of the Sea. She couldn't let Grigg complete the ceremony and combine the hearts on his own. Giovanna had told her what to do. *She* should be the one to do it.

Adelina threw herself into a low roll and hesitated on the ground, hidden from Grigg's view by the side of *The Wandering Heron.* The step in the ritual that Frederico hadn't known was the telling of secrets. According to Giovanna's instructions, the sphere the siren held represented the hoarded secrets of all who came to treat with her, and she required one new secret for each Heart absorbed into herself at the combining of the hearts.

What would Grigg's secret be?

She couldn't see him, but neither could he see her. If she burst over the side now, she might be able to stop him from offering up the Heart of the Stars, and then she'd have to fight him for it.

And she'd never know his secret.

But Adelina had hesitated too long, and the choice was made for her as Grigg's voice floated on the wind, whisper soft, to her waiting ears.

"I have loved only once in my life. Her name was Sofia Isakov."

The words hit like a blow. Her stomach turned sour, and breath refused to come. She'd been played.

But of course she had. He was a cheat, and he'd played plenty of roles before. He'd been her hope of good men, but not only good men. He'd also been her hope that *she* was lovable, that she could be loved by a man in the way the fairy tales spun their stories of sunshine. That something legitimate might thaw the frost of bitterness that had taken root and grown generation to generation in the tradition of her people.

But even if such a love could exist, why would she look for it in a man like Grigg? He wasn't a good man. He was a swindler. A liar. A man of a thousand faces and only one heart to give.

But for whatever reason, she hadn't wanted to feel something with anyone else. She had come to hope that something about their interactions was real—and, as ridiculous as it may have been, somewhere along the way, she'd begun to love him.

Adelina's chest constricted as she thought of his arms around her, the way he looked at her on the roof, his laughing eyes as he teased her.

No matter. She had to stop him before he added the Heart of the Mountain. He'd lied about everything, and she would have time to process her stupidity later.

But then, he'd never *said* that he loved her. He'd avoided saying it. He hadn't really lied, had he? He'd just let *her* fill in the gaps, let her think that he was protecting her from his curse. But then why had he gotten so sick? Why had he—

She shoved away the tirade of thoughts and rose from her place, but Grigg still stood, his back to her, facing the Heart of the Sea statue. And in his hands, he held not one, but two hearts. His hand pressed the Heart of the Stars against the heart of the siren in the statue, but nothing happened. Grigg sucked his teeth and let out a breath.

He tried again.

"I have only ever loved *two* women in my life: Sofia Isakov years ago, and Adelina Accardi, even now."

A glow burst from the core of the statue. Sapphire blue, the glow seemed to shove forward through the statue, wrap around the Heart of the Stars, and suck it in so that the necklace absorbed into the same substance as the statue—no longer gold and opal, but with the same abalone look as the rest of it. The entire statue began to pulse with a lightly emanating blue hue.

For the second time in the space of a minute, Adelina's breath caught as if someone had ripped the ground out from under her. The statue had rejected Grigg's first secret, because it hadn't been the full truth. Perhaps a month ago, Grigg could've said he'd only loved one woman in his life, but that statement was no longer accurate.

He really had begun to love her.

A strange, involuntary warmth spread across her scalp and down her body in a ripple of soul-salve that promised safety and requited love.

Grigg stared at the statue, then looked down at the last Heart —the Heart of the Mountain—glowing jade green in his hands. One more secret, and all three hearts would be combined.

But even if he did love her, she couldn't let him combine the Hearts. Just because he loved her didn't mean he would do something good with any power he gained from combining the hearts.

Adelina vaulted over the side of the fishing boat. Grigg spun and shot a fist at her head before he realized who it was, and Adelina ducked and caught his hand as she came up again. Long, thick veins like black oil oozed their way down his arms and had begun to wrap around his hands. Adelina glanced over her shoulder. The egg on the ground still poured out light so bright it hurt to look at. Any moment now, it would finish its work, and Grigg would die.

Why wasn't he dead already?

Perhaps if he did combine the hearts, he would gain enough

power to survive whatever the mage had in store for him. But if Adelina had a part in it as well, maybe she would have enough to keep in check whatever errant thing Grigg would choose to do with that power.

Adelina released his fist and instead put her hand over his open palm where the Heart of the Mountain lay. She looked up at him.

"Together."

Something in his face tugged at her heart as his ocean-blue eyes searched her brown ones. They were not the hard, calculating eyes of a man accustomed to threats, nor the mischievous glinting eyes of a liar whose line has been believed. They were pools of endless softness, and a hint of surprise that she might receive any of the tenderness he found he wanted to give.

He nodded. "Together. Two secrets for one Heart."

Adelina and Grigg moved their hands to the orb, their fingers interlocking as they pressed the Heart of the Mountain to the siren's orb of secrets. But as the Heart bumped up against the sphere, their eyes left the siren and instead found each other.

Adelina swallowed hard. "I'll give two secrets—one for the Heart of the Stars, and one for the Heart of the Mountain, just in case. I'll go, then you go, then I'll go again."

Grigg dipped his head, and a black tendril shot up around his neck. He winced. "Hurry."

She cleared her throat. "I am Adelina Accardi, daughter of daughters of Curser of Souls—Giovanna Accardi—and guardian of the Heart of the Mountain."

Was it enough? Her tribe knew she was guardian, as were all Guerrori women. They didn't know about the curse, but Grigg did. Better to be safe and add something no one knew. She bit her lip. "And I no longer trust or believe the tenets of my mother's line about our sacred purpose or about their teachings on men."

The pulsing sapphire-blue glow intensified. But the statue did not merge with the Heart.

Grigg pressed his lips together, then spoke as much to her as to the statue.

"My curse is twofold: any woman that loves me dies, and I can never keep anything I earn. Businesses go bankrupt, supply catches fire, coin disappears. But I found if I stole it, it was a workaround. My father discovered the same loophole and lived that way for years until he fell in love with my mother. She died when she started loving my father for real. I was five, and I hated him for taking her from me."

It was the most open he'd ever been. He'd become a criminal as a means to provide for himself when no legitimate career would be productive for him. What would it have been like to live in his shoes, destined for failure, with a father he hated and a beloved mother dead?

A burst of blue-and-green light confirmed the truth of Grigg's words. The statue melded with the Heart of the Mountain, but not completely. The seed sunk into the orb halfway and stopped.

It was her turn.

Her mouth went dry. She didn't want to say it. But she couldn't think of another secret. It felt wrong, somehow, to offer up something so delicate. Something so insane.

She swallowed. "I have begun to love a man named Grigglor Frizzletwerf."

The words burned her throat on the way out. But through the thickness of her throat, the strangeness of the words, somehow there was a sweetness to the sound of them. Grigg's hand tightened beneath hers, and as the orb absorbed the Heart of the Mountain into itself, he twined his fingers through hers and stepped toward her. He slipped his free arm around the small of her back. He was going to kiss her. He—

The statue flashed blue and green and white.

And then shattered into a million pieces.

CHAPTER
TWENTY-SEVEN

Shimmering abalone-colored shrapnel exploded outward from the statue in every direction. Grigg pulled Adelina into his chest and turned his back on the statue, shielding her from the blast. But just at that moment, as he lifted his eyes beyond the edge of *The Wandering Heron* to the egg on the shore, the last of the shell broke apart, and in the last of its light, a swirl of ebony blackness formed the silhouette of a woman.

Pieces of shell fell to the ground, all light lost from their fragments as the Black Swan Mage took bodily form and stepped from the bounds of her dungeon.

But Grigg did not die. The egg had been destroyed. What had gone wrong? Or ... right?

The beady eyes of the dark mage bored into his soul as she took in the sight of Grigg with his arms wrapped around Adelina. But just as quickly as her eyes had fixed on Grigg, Giovanna's gaze tore from Grigg and Adelina and shifted to where the statue had been behind him.

Grigg turned to follow her gaze and nearly fell to the bottom of the boat. The siren had shaken off the bonds of the statue and come to life. But far from the tranquil beauty of the statue, the creature before him now lived and breathed in a vision as glorious as mutiny and as stunning as perfectly crafted steel blades beset with gold filigree.

Green-and-gold gauntlets glistened over the blue-tinged skin of her forearms, her upper arms bare until the skin ran into a form-fitted emerald breastplate. A magnificent sparkling jade tail fell from her waist, with a belt of gilded emerald wrapped around her hips. Her features were glorious but sharp, her hair white but streaked with blue, her eyes an eerie pupil-less blanket of shining green.

The orb in her hands had materialized into what still looked like a large pearl, but radiated with every color under the sun, eddies of black and red smoke swirling within it, working their way through the brighter colors like poison.

Water surged into the little fishing boat, buoying the siren aloft in its tower. The siren lifted the orb with one hand and skewered them all with a soulless gaze of green as she looked down her nose at the mage on the bank and the two humans standing in the boat.

The crawling darkness along Grigg's skin splintered outward, spiraling down his torso. He could feel it like rope twining around his arms and legs, the pressure in his chest threatening to bash in the bones of his ribcage at any moment. He wasn't sure why he was still alive if the egg had broken apart. But he seemed to still be victim to Adelina's curse, just as Adelina was victim to his. How long would it take before they both succumbed to Giovanna's pair of curses?

"You swore fealty to me, Giovanna." The siren's voice cut through the air like a knife.

Giovanna fell to her knees. "And I am faithful, Your Majesty. I have been bound for six hundred years, but without me, you never would have been freed. I have used these two as servants. I demanded your freedom before I demanded my own."

The siren eyed Grigg and Adelina, then looked back to the

mage. "The lover's curse you placed on them—has it turned out the way you had hoped? Has my gift of power been stewarded well?"

"Yes, Your Majesty. All has been well, and the Heart of the Mountain was protected because of me. My line guarded the Heart until now, the first opportunity to bring the hearts together again to free you. Now imagine how better I could serve you if my full power was restored, Your Majesty! Reward my service with the gifts you had begun to give me before your unjust imprisonment, and I will beat back your enemies."

Grigg glanced between Giovanna and the siren. Adelina stared. The statue really had been the siren, imprisoned or frozen. And the siren was more powerful than Giovanna. *She* was the one who had bestowed on Giovanna the power to curse Grigg and Adelina in the first place.

"You ask for more power, and yet the two you have cursed have ended up together. They freed me of their own accord. Perhaps they want a reward of their own rather than to do your bidding." Pale-green eyes assessed Grigg and Adelina with a harsh glance.

Grigg's skin crawled under her sharp gaze.

The siren looked back at Giovanna. "Six hundred and fifty years is far too long to wait. You let me rot for fifty years *before* magic was put to bed."

The siren held out the orb toward Giovanna. "Give me a secret."

Giovanna rose and lifted her hands in front of her, palms up. "My secret is this: I lied. Sergei's seed doesn't need any of the three hearts to break his curse. As you know, the three hearts were meant to break the imprisonment on you, Queen of the Sea, placed there by the King of the Wind and the Jester of the Fates. But the man believed he was saving himself. He didn't want to free you—he believed combining the hearts would break his own curse."

Grigg's mind spun. All these years ... all this time ... he had assumed the mage was telling the truth about the terms of the curse. How could he have been so stupid? But what other information did he have? The egg had cracked, and the black on his skin had expanded each time it did. Perhaps it had more to do with the link with the mage's growing power, and as the egg fell apart, the curse grew in power, which would eventually culminate in his death. She spun the evidence like a spider spins a web and sold him a story he swallowed hook, line, and sinker.

She'd played the game and won.

He'd never stood a chance.

Adelina lifted her chin toward Giovanna. "That's no secret. The egg is broken, and Grigg didn't die. Obviously, there was more to it. And even if it was a secret to us, it's no secret to Her Majesty. We didn't know Her Majesty existed, but you insult her by offering trinkets instead of real secrets."

Smart. Adelina's phrasing exalted this Queen of the Sea, whoever she was, while looking down on Giovanna, playing off any tension between the two of them. The siren peered down at Adelina with interest.

Giovanna's lips curled into a tight-lipped smile, but her eyes were dark as death. "Another secret, then." Giovanna strode toward her, transitioned into a swan, flew forward, and reappeared as a woman two paces off inside the fishing boat. "No one knows the true terms of the curse on Sergei's line but me. The real way to break the curse on Grigglor is with the Heart of Hearts and the blessing of the mage's blood. But he could never win the Heart, and he will never receive my blessing."

She turned icy eyes on Grigg, derision rolling off her in waves. "Did you really think I had any intention of letting you go?"

The black vines of the curse over his heart cinched around him tighter and tighter, squeezing the breath from his lungs. Grigg thought of the strangler fig crushing the life from the victim tree, so that only the shell of the curse would remain when his body was crushed. The curse pressed into flesh and bone, reaching up toward his face, cutting through every piece of him.

Excruciating pain shot down his body from head to toe, then localized in the ripping sensation of a heart turned inside out. She would destroy all hope of life, all hope of love, all shreds of humanity left in his charred soul until nothing but a shell would find its way to his grave.

Her gaze intensified the power of the curse, as if the queen's coming to true form in the flesh had brought the curse to completion. He withered beneath her iron glare as the vines of the onyx curse choked out the last of his life force.

And then he was falling.

CHAPTER
TWENTY-EIGHT

Adelina

"N o!"

The scream ripped from Adelina's throat like a cracking whip. She lurched to catch Grigg, but Giovanna grabbed her by the arms and tugged her away.

"Come, my love. Come with me. It's done."

But it wasn't done. Grigg had collapsed in a heap in the bottom of the boat, but his body was convulsing, blue eyes rolled back. The black cords around his skin nearly covered him, with ribbons of normal skin tone peeking out from beneath the curse's chokehold.

But convulsing meant movement. And movement meant life.

Adelina drove her elbow back into Giovanna's face and flew to Grigg's side. But just before she got there, the Queen of the Sea reached down and shoved her hand into Grigg's chest—the same way she'd seen Giovanna do in the dream state.

What allowed a person to reach through people's chests? Was it an innate ability? Was it an intention? A specific power?

Adelina had played a role in restoring the Hearts for the Queen of the Sea, whether or not she'd been aware of what she was doing at the time. Could she have earned this power? Or, as the daughter of the mage, could she have inherited it?

But Adelina still stood on the borrowed strength of the Black Swan Mage. Without it, she surely would've dropped to the bottom of the boat as well, dying of Grigg's curse just as he died from hers. Granted, he was dying of two curses at once—his link to the mage, and his love for Adelina.

But what if ...?

The Queen of the Sea held up Grigg's heart between her long pale blue fingers. Somehow, it still beat. The heart emitted a soft red-and-black glow, vines of shadow swirling around it like the curse on his skin. And a flicker of gold.

Giovanna held out her hand toward the queen, no longer focused on Adelina. The heart of the man she hated stole her focus from the daughter she supposedly loved. "Let me finish this."

The queen examined the heart, turning it over in her hands. "Interesting. The love is not fully grown, but just the beginnings are enough for the curse to take hold. But the link you formed with him when you cursed him, Giovanna, gives him more resistance to other curses."

"I ..." Giovanna stared at the heart in disbelief. "A mistake I will not make again."

The queen snapped her head up toward the mage. "Nonsense. Every curse has side effects. They are not always predictable. Your desperation makes you overeager and willing to make promises you cannot keep."

Adelina could keep silent no longer. She hovered over Grigg's body, holding his head in her lap, stroking his face as his body thrashed. Tears burned hot in her eyes.

"Your Majesty, Giovanna did not restore the Hearts. Grigg and I did. She has not earned any reward you planned to give her. And

I do not ask for anything so significant as your power. I want protection from Giovanna and life for Grigg and for me."

Giovanna laughed. "Idiot girl. You sound just like I once did. But you will learn."

"Giovanna." The queen dragged a finger absently down the side of Grigg's heart as she eyed the mage. "What you wanted was power to destroy Sergei and his line. I gave you that power on the condition that I would have your allegiance, and you did not come to me in my hour of need."

Giovanna gaped at the queen. "Your Majesty, no, I was prevented, I couldn't, I—"

The queen held up a hand. "I might question your general competence for a curse to take six hundred years to take effect, but your curse fell victim to the mitigating effects of the confinement of magic. It was muted by those who feared melderblood abilities —by those who believed melderblood abilities were all that magic had to offer. Silly people with narrow minds. What were you off doing while I was imprisoned? Making love to men who did not love you in return? I was behind enchanted bars for fifty years before being made into a statue. I gave you power that I was unable to use. And you abandoned me."

Grigg's convulsions began to slow, his thrashing still severe, but less constant. Adelina tried to hold him steady. Was he aware of the pain, or had his mind already gone? A tear dropped from her face to his.

She glanced at his heart, still captured in the queen's grasp. The beat of his heart had slowed. And that flicker of gold ...

What had Giovanna said?

The real way to break the curse on Grigglor is with the Heart of Hearts and the blessing of the mage's blood. But he could never win the Heart, and he will never receive my blessing ...

Adelina froze. What if Grigg didn't need the mage's blessing? He only needed the blessing of the mage's *blood.* Or blood *line.* The blood of an Accardi.

And though Grigg might never win Giovanna's heart, he had already won Adelina's.

The mage had said if Adelina gave her heart away, the heart would return to Giovanna. Which meant it was possible for Adelina to give it away. But what if she'd meant it literally?

Giovanna edged closer to Adelina, eyes still on the queen. "The man will die, Your Majesty, and you are returned to us. My work here is done. Give me my daughter and my next task. I will not fail you."

The siren flashed pupil-less green eyes at the Black Swan Mage. "This is my final gift to you. Complete what you began. Kill him, and be done with it."

She threw the heart.

Threw.

The heart.

It was as if the world slowed to infinitesimal segments. The black-and-red heart cut through the air toward Giovanna's waiting hand. Grigg's back arched, and his mouth opened in a silent scream. Once Giovanna crushed Grigg's heart, she would take Adelina. But Adelina, too, would die. Didn't she realize it? There was no forever for Giovanna and Adelina if Adelina was dead.

Was she willing to let Grigg die if it meant Adelina would die too?

No matter. Adelina couldn't wait for Giovanna to do the right thing and lift the curse. She'd have to do it herself.

With the Heart of Hearts and the blessing of the mage's blood.

The heart bearing the mage's blood, freely given.

Adelina called to the fire. She wasn't exactly sure why, except that the fire was her doorway to magic, her access to power. She let the power pool in her palm, sizzling in currents along the skin of her hand without bursting into flame.

And she thrust her hand into her own chest. She gasped, but no air came. Her hand closed around a living, thumping, solid organ, bypassing ribs and muscle and every filament obstacle.

Adelina yanked it free and shoved it into Grigg's empty chest before she'd fully registered what she'd seen.

The heart—*her* heart—had been gold. Like the fleck of connection between Giovanna and Grigg, marking his black-and-red heart, only hers was not a fleck. Hers was pure gold, like the dragon's treasure in fairy tales.

That was odd.

And then she was falling.

CHAPTER
TWENTY-NINE

Crushing weight. Strangulation. Strangler figs. Figs. Jungle. Adelina.

Pain. Blinding, searing pain. Blinding light. Golden egg. Giovanna. Adelina.

"Did you really think I had any intention of letting you go?"

No, he supposed not. His life had been a series of tragedies from the start, with a few hiccups of criminal success tossed in to spice things up in his wretched, meaningless life.

Setting eyes on a woman like Adelina, and experiencing the privilege of coming to love her, and be loved by her in return—if only a little, and for only for a short time—could easily be the highlight of his miserable existence.

Weight.

Agony.

Screaming.

Writhing.

Blackness.

Nothing.

Nothing but nothing.

Until an unidentified something came crawling out of the abyss, seizing him by his hollow chest and wrenching him from the claws of death and back into the light.

Grigg squinted into the light. He was lying on his back in the fishing boat, staring up at a blue sky. To his left, a stray breeze whispered against his cheek. To his right, water bumped up against his side, soaking him to the skin.

Flashing scales glinted from within a tower of water on his right, the powerful tail of a siren—not like the metallic tones he'd known in the Iolani, but bold and green as an emerald.

And something was lying across his feet.

And someone was screaming. Someone who wasn't him. That was new.

Grigg sat up. The pain was gone. He looked down at his skin. It was clear. His hand flew to his chest. The mark over his heart. Gone.

Completely gone.

But ... so was his heart. Wasn't it? He'd seen it, he—

Then it all registered at once. The scream was from Giovanna. Her wild, open-mouthed cry rang like the screech of bats impaled alive. Her form hunched over Adelina, whose body had been the weight he felt on his legs. Her eyes were closed, her body slumped.

"What's wrong with her?" The pitch in his voice rose fever-high. "What did you do?"

Grigg reached for her. Giovanna smacked his hand away with a closed fist. Something was in her hand. A shell? An apple?

No. A heart. *His* heart. But then how could ...

"She threw her heart into your chest, you fool!"

She'd done ... *what?!*

Giovanna's hands moved frantically over her daughter's—descendant daughter's? Eventual daughter's?—still form. The Queen of the Sea lifted a hand, and Adelina's unconscious body rose up into the air, suspended as if by invisible wire.

Giovanna wrung her shaking hands, fumbling Grigg's heart in

the process. The Queen of the Sea snatched it out of the air, turning it over in her hands.

The mage barely noticed. Her lip quivered. "She isn't supposed to be able to do this. Her heart should return to me, it should ..."

Rrrrriiiiiipppppppp.

Oh no.

Grigg's heart was in the queen's hands, but the rogue heart in his chest was making its way out. Grigg had no idea how he wasn't dead, but something told him being twice without a heart wasn't good for survival rates. And he didn't have long.

The mage would never help him. His one and only chance lay with the mysterious Queen of the Sea.

The one who'd let her vulnerabilities slip when she'd spoken to Giovanna earlier. She had enemies. Enemies who had imprisoned her before and could conceivably do it again. What had she called them?

The answer slammed into him like a blessed splash of cold water in the scorching heat.

He whirled to the siren. "You've got enemies, and I've got skills. How would you like to hit the King of the Wind and the Jester of the Fates with a blow they never saw coming?"

Hardly had the words left his lips than a golden heart pulled free of his chest and flew to Giovanna. But the heart that had been in his chest was not the black and red he had seen of his own, but pure gold. What did it mean? Why was Adelina's heart gold?

Giovanna seized the heart and shoved it toward Adelina's chest as she floated, suspended in the air. But the heart did not return to Adelina's chest. And Grigg did not die.

The Queen of the Sea cocked her head. "Interesting. Her body rejects her own heart."

Giovanna snapped her head to the queen. "What does it mean? Why would it do that?"

The queen narrowed her gaze at Adelina's chest, her green eyes glowing, then receding as she looked back at Giovanna. "The girl gave a gift she never intended to take back. Her heart has stronger resistance to magical interference than other hearts—as do all the women in your line, because of the protections you put in place for your daughters. Hers is the blood of a mage."

"*I* am a mage." Giovanna's lip curled and trembled as she spat the words at the queen. "And I am far more powerful than she."

"Yes, and it is *your* power and *your* affinity for the use of magic that you have passed to her."

The siren twirled Grigg's heart in her hands. Goosebumps fled up and down his arms to see her so casual with his life force.

Neither Grigg nor Adelina had a heart in their chest, but neither was dead either. Which meant something was keeping them alive. Giovanna might have the power to sustain Adelina for a short time without her heart, but if she had a long-term solution, she wouldn't be so frantic to get Adelina's heart back inside. And Giovanna clearly did not want Grigg alive, yet here he stood—which meant only one person present might still find him valuable.

He had to seize the opportunity before it disappeared.

"You say you have more work for Giovanna to do, Your Majesty, but can you really trust her to do it? She says she told me to gather the Hearts for you, but not only did she fail to gather the Hearts herself, when she *did* have opportunity, she let you rot. As for me, I didn't just—"

"How *dare* you!" Giovanna stepped toward Grigg, but the Queen of the Sea held up a hand toward the mage, eyes fixed on Grigg.

Grigg swallowed hard and continued before his confidence failed. "I didn't just combine the hearts. I went to the depths of Ghosts' Gorge for you. I have seen Chieftain Makuakan and his rival, Limakau, and I know of the underwater prison lined with skulls and bones. I ferried naïve young royalty across the sea—stupid maladroits as they may have been—and turned them into heroes. I indebted rebel Iolani to myself, and some of your own outcasted people played a role in getting me the Heart of the Sea. But they didn't believe you were truly the Queen of the Sea. They saw the statue merely as a superstitious relic. But tell me, are sirens known for their trust and collaboration with men, or is that an accomplishment that comes only once in a millennium?"

"You speak quite highly of yourself for so young a person." The queen held onto the end of the word *young*, dragging it out as she tasted the word.

Grigg shrugged. "If modesty would save my life, Your Majesty, perhaps I would employ it."

"Arrogance could get you killed just as fast."

Grigg gestured to the heart in her hands. "You hold my life in your hands, and you bear an orb of secrets that tests for truth. What have I got to lose, and how could I dare to lie to you?"

The Queen of the Sea pulled at the water around her. The river sloshed further into the boat, the small fishing vessel rocking from side to side. A wall of water slammed into Grigg, catching him in its current, and dragged him forward in icy cold, covering him from the neck down and pinning his arms.

Three paces off, the mass of fresh water slammed into the mage, and Giovanna grabbed the mast of the sail as she treaded water, holding on to the mast with one hand and Adelina's unconscious body close with the other.

The queen tossed the orb up into the air, and a tower of water caught it, suspending it there above their heads as water continued to rise over the boat. She drilled Grigg with a long stare. "The King of the Wind is not like other royalty."

In a flash of green, the queen was gone.

Grigg's heart stopped—or at least, it might have, if it had still been within his chest. He hadn't seen how the queen may have preserved it, but if she was done with him, he would be dead, wouldn't he? His mouth went dry. Who was this Queen of the Sea? What was this Queen of the Sea? If she accepted a deal, what would that mean for him?

A trail of scales snaked across the back of his legs. An involuntary creeping shiver shot down his spine at the feel of a long, cold fish bumping up against him in a watery cage he could not escape. Panic welled in his chest as he searched the water for her. He glanced again at Adelina, still unconscious, in Giovanna's arms—her golden heart clutched in Giovanna's hand as the mage struggled to hold the mast, the heart, and the girl all at once. What would happen if Adelina's heart dropped into the water? Would it be destroyed?

And then the Queen of the Sea swam up just in front of him until the two of them were nearly nose-to-nose. She seized him by the face, one hand on either cheek, long icicle fingers of pale blue shooting spears of terror through his skin.

"Tell me a secret."

His mind went blank, his thoughts suddenly fuzzy as if a fog had descended, imprisoning his defenses and leaving only stripped-down, barren, childlike truths. "I'll do anything."

He didn't want to say it. This wasn't how good deals were made. This wasn't how negotiation was supposed to work.

But with her hands on either side of his face, and the fog encroaching on his mind, he'd felt as though he might crumble to dust if he didn't say the words.

When he did say them, they rang truer than he'd anticipated.

She smiled and released him, just as abruptly as she'd taken hold. "It's your lucky day, Grigglor Frizzletwerf. Is that what you like to be called?"

His tongue grew thick in his mouth, and when he swallowed, it hurt. "Grigglor is fine, Your Majesty. I'm not a fan of my last name."

"Understandably. It's the ugliest surname I've ever heard." The queen lifted her hand, and in it she held a deck of cards—shining, shimmering, luminescent-blue cards. Aside from the gauntlets on her forearms, the crown on her head, the Heart of the Stars around her neck, she wore nothing. No bag, no purse. No pockets.

How had she produced the cards?

The queen flashed three face cards in front of him from the deck. The first depicted a mighty dragon with fire in his eyes and mouth, power in his wings, and judgment in his jaws. The emblem of air marked the card for the King of the Wind.

She shook her fingers, and a new card flashed before his eyes, this one with the emblem of water. A warrior siren held a regal ornamented staff in her hand and was adorned with the same crown, gauntlets, and breastplate she wore now. "Queen of the Sea, wartime siren of sirens." She grinned. "Yours truly."

Her fingers flashed again, and a third card faced him. This was the strangest of the three. It didn't have an elemental emblem representing a suit. Instead, it was wild—the joker card.

The creature looking back at him from the card was human from the waist up except for curved horns coming out of his head and what looked like goat ears flopping out beneath brown wavy hair. From the waist down, he transitioned to animal hair, two hooves, and a tail to match the goat ears. His face was painted with an impish expression, and in his hands, he held a flute.

"Jester of the Fates, the shape-shifting satyr. If you can retrieve for me what I need from them, you and your love will live."

Grigg's mind spun. He'd never even heard of these individuals before today. It was still rather a shock to have seen a statue come to life and be talking to someone who called herself the Queen of the Sea.

Giovanna adjusted her grip on the mast. "Your Majesty, do not stoop to a fool like him. I can get you everything you—"

The queen cut Giovanna a dark glare. "Speak again and die."

Giovanna snapped her mouth shut. Heat flooded her cheeks, but the look in her eyes as she turned her glare on Grigg was murderous.

The queen slapped Grigg on the face, and Grigg jerked his gaze back to the queen. "Don't look at her, look at me. Or did you want to make a deal with the mage?"

Grigg shook his head. "No. Only with you."

"That's what I thought. Now, you're a thief, aren't you?" She twirled her body in the water. Rippling white foam rolled over her shimmering scales and blue skin in the wake of her movement. She came again in front of him, necklaces, rings, and gem-studded armbands sparkling on her body. "Steal from me."

CHAPTER THIRTY

Adelina

Dark. The color of death. The color of curses.

The color of the nothingness she knew in the abyss.

CHAPTER THIRTY-ONE

Grigg blinked. "Your Majesty—"

"If you cannot steal from me, you'll never stand a chance against the King of the Wind and the Jester of the Fates." The queen's mouth curved into a devastatingly arresting dark smile. "So. Steal from me."

Grigg resisted the urge to glance at Adelina. She was still unconscious, but Giovanna would keep her head above water. At least for now. But would the mage really let her daughter live if it was a life apart from Giovanna?

He took in a steadying breath. The hold of the water around him eased, and he was free in the water. But the queen had just asked him to steal. What could he take that she wouldn't expect?

In one hand, the queen held the deck of cards. In the other, Grigg's own heart, a twinkle of gold flashing amid the swirl of black and crimson. She held it beneath the surface, but a pocket of air protected his heart from the river. Over their heads, a tower of water still buoyed the orb of secrets aloft. He needed to do something bold, something surprising, something impressive.

Grigg held out a hand as he treaded water before the queen.

"I've never bowed to a queen while in water before. Forgive my fumbling, but would you do me the honor?"

She tilted her head, eyes skeptical, but offered him her hand—the one with the deck of cards in her palm. He took it, his thumb brushing her knuckles, the edges of his fingers bumping up against the shimmering cards as he bowed his head and lifted her hand to his lips.

He lowered her hand and tugged lightly to pull himself closer to her in the water. "The thing about sirens, particularly any that look like you do, is that you're used to holding power over men. The other problem is, you're expecting me to steal."

She kept her eyes on him, but didn't pull away. She wanted to see how he'd play the game.

Grigg ran a hand up her arm, his fingers grazing over the treasures on her arms. "What could I take that you wouldn't expect?"

He let his eyes travel up the lithe curve of her tail, her bare waist, and the glistening metal of her curved breastplate. He could feel the heat of her gaze on him, and he let her soak up his attentions as he moved his gaze to catch her unnerving green eyes. "The best con is the long con, but you haven't given me much time."

Slow and steady, he moved his right hand to linger at the edges of the gauntlet on her left arm, as if contemplating how to remove it without her notice, and he brought his opposite arm to rest on the gilded belt snug against her hips—where her human form transitioned into a tail. His fingers dug in around the belt and pulled her close. He could see his heart burst into a frenzy of activity as her body bumped into his.

She held up his heart between them and arched an eyebrow. "Careful, young man. Have you forgotten the challenge?"

He pulled her in with his left hand, his right drifting down to the rings on her left hand. He squeezed her hand in his and fastened his gaze on her green eyes. "Not at all. What is more challenging than to survive an encounter with the Queen of the Sea?

What is more remarkable to steal than a kiss from the most deadly creature in the ocean?"

"And what do you think your unconscious love will think of this when she wakes?"

Grigg could feel the strength of her tail keeping them both aloft in the water as his hold on her waist kept his head above the surface.

He let a mischievous grin twist at the corners of his mouth. "I think I meant it when I said I would do anything it takes."

Grigg reached his left hand from her waist to the back of her neck and leaned in. At the last moment, she pulled away, flicked her tail, and tossed his heart up into the air.

His heart soared up in a tall arc over their heads, and the queen seized the hand that had been at the back of her neck. She pulled the Heart of the Stars from his fingers where he'd unclasped it from her neck, coiled the chain in her hand, and caught his heart in the same palm as the organ completed its arc and dropped into her waiting hand.

A burst of light flew over the surface of his heart as the Heart of the Stars made direct contact with his life force. An exhilarating tingle rolled through him from head to toe.

She stared down at it as if she herself was taken aback by a mysterious effect. What had it meant? What had just happened?

The queen shrugged it off and tilted her head at him. "Indelicate and obvious, young man. You don't have what it takes."

Grigg lifted his other hand and flashed her a shimmering blue rectangle. "But did you know I took this?"

The queen jerked her other hand up, the deck of cards still nestled in her palm. She began leafing through the cards. He bowed with a flourish and handed her the card he'd stolen.

"I believe this concludes our challenge, Your Majesty."

She stared at him for a long moment. With a flick of her wrist, the deck disappeared. She refastened the Heart of the Stars around her neck and rolled his heart between her hands. "Very well, you have yourself a deal. But it will come at a price."

Of course it did. Deals always came at a price.

Grigg steeled himself. "What will you have me do?"

The queen ignored him, as if they weren't in the most critical portion of the middle of a conversation, and turned to Giovanna. She gestured her hand, and the waters receded until the river swirled only waist high and Grigg's boots touched the bottom of the boat again. Giovanna, too, landed with her feet in the boat, her arms still wrapped securely around Adelina's floating form, a hand still clutching the golden heart that should have been in the young woman's chest.

"Excellent news, Giovanna," the queen purred in a voice gentle as iron. "Your daughter will live. For now."

Giovanna swallowed. "You're making a mistake. There must be another way."

"*You* made the mistake when you failed to rescue me with *my* power that I gave you." The Queen of the Sea held out her hand.

Giovanna hesitated, then passed her the golden heart.

The siren now held Grigg's heart in one hand and Adelina's in the other. "Adelina's body refuses to take the entirety of her heart back into her chest. She's healed Grigg of his curse but traded herself in the process." The queen inspected the hearts. "Pure gold, and flecks of gold. Darkness of the curse, and darkness of the soul. With the curse lifted, will the darkness spin into a greater abyss? Or be eradicated?"

Darkness of the soul? So the blackness *wasn't* all from the curse?

"The two of you have only the beginnings of love. But what I need from you will require more. A commitment to each other that is unbreakable."

The queen smashed the two hearts together. Grigg doubled over as if punched in the gut, and Adelina's frozen body jerked in the water. The queen pressed and pressed as if molding clay. And as she separated her hands again, she had two hearts—each a combination of the two distinct ones she'd held moments before. Gold and red and black.

"These hearts have been bound together. You'll find this comes with side effects." The queen lurched forward and shoved the hearts into Grigg and Adelina's chests at the same time. Grigg stumbled back, and Adelina's body jolted once more. Cold and warmth tumbled over each other in his body as the strange new combined heart took up residence in his chest.

He looked at Adelina. The heart had been placed. Her body accepted it. She should wake.

But she didn't.

Grigg turned to the queen, but Giovanna spoke first. "She should wake. What's wrong with her?"

If the queen had had pupils and irises, Grigg was pretty sure he would have seen her roll her eyes.

"Patience, Mage. I've just combined their hearts. The pair of curses they've lived with up until now dictated that if they loved each other, they would die. Now, they live and breathe as one. They will share more now than any two humans ever have. Contrary to the curses they were under before, now, if they do not protect each other, they will die. But to begin this bonded life together, they must start not apart, but close. He will kiss her, and if she feels the same, they will live."

Giovanna's eyes blazed with fury. "If Sergei's seed dies, Adelina dies?"

The queen sneered a wicked smile. "I'm glad you've been paying attention, Giovanna. Yes, that's what I said."

Giovanna lunged. She wrapped her arms around Adelina and yanked her away, shielding her from Grigg, eyes ablaze as she turned them to the queen. "You've made her weak. Love is *weak*."

The Queen of the Sea lifted a finger, and vines of river water wrapped around Adelina and pried her from her ancestral mother's arms. "These two survived your elementary curses because the beginnings of love are enough for its work to take effect. The man says he will do anything for her, but these are only the beginnings. Feelings such as these are subject to change. I need to be certain he will *always* do anything for her, so that his allegiance to me remains true. Your little agendas mean nothing, and I will make the deals I choose to make."

The queen floated Adelina over to Grigg and deposited her into his arms. "Go on, boy. Seal our deal."

Grigg wound his arms reflexively around Adelina's body. Her eyes were closed, her perfect lips just slightly parted. Head leaned back in her suspended state, her long neck arced with her lithe body in a frozen perpetual fall. If he did this—if he kissed her now—there would be no going back.

He didn't know what side effects the queen might mean, or if she even knew them herself. After all, she'd said magic could be mysterious, and he still didn't know what it meant that the Heart of the Stars had pressed upon his heart. What he knew for sure was that the queen hadn't done any of this to benefit *him*, but only as a means to *control* him further.

She hadn't even told him yet what she would require him to do with the King of the Wind and the Jester of the Fates.

But he also knew he would do anything to save Adelina.

His gaze drifted to her closed eyes, and he realized suddenly how deeply he wanted to see them again. How he dreamed of kissing her lips and holding her close, dreamed of what it would be like to be loved by Adelina without the risk of her death.

He'd never had the chance to even attempt to love and be loved before. Not really. And there was no one with whom he'd rather fumble through love with than her.

Grigg slipped an arm around Adelina's waist and another around the back of her head, his fingers twining in her long dark hair. He pulled her to him and leaned his forehead against hers, not knowing what waited on the other side of this kiss. His new heart galloped in his chest like a stampede of chariots.

This was the quiet before the storm. The softness before the threats fell.

But darkness and storm awaited him either way. None of that was new to his experience. The only new thing was the tender shoot of hope sprouting up through the fresh soil of a curseless life. Hope of someone who might stand by his side, of someone who might see him as more than a thief. Hope of Adelina looking deep into his eyes and finding a man worth loving—a man he could strive to become.

Grigg was under no delusion that he was currently a man worth loving, but he could spend the rest of his life becoming that man. Someone worthy of her affection, someone worthy of her respect. Because she already had all his.

And in that moment, he could wait no longer. He pulled her in and pressed his lips to hers, tender and velvet soft at first, then deeper as desperation took hold.

It wasn't working; it wasn't—

And then her lips were moving against his. A jolt of lightning shot through his body, and he came alive.

Her arms flew around his neck, pulling him in tighter, tighter. She clung to him and he to her as if the world consisted of nothing but shared breath and satisfied longings. Her fingers worked through his hair and pulled him into a deeper kiss, her lips parting in invitation.

He wanted nothing more. She was alive, and she was here, and she wanted him—wanted *him*. Whatever it took to get here had been worth it.

He would do it again a billion times.

Relief fell like boulders rolling off his bowed back. A thrill ran through him as he held her close, unwilling to part from her. But enemies still stood watching.

At last, they parted. But the moment they did, iron fingers wrapped around Adelina and hauled her back by the hair.

Giovanna. She'd waited for Adelina to be brought back to life, but the queen hadn't said Adelina and Grigg had to be *together* for her plan to work.

Giovanna's long fingers transformed into claws, dragging Adelina backward out of the boat. Grigg launched himself over the side as Giovanna began to transition into a swan in flight. Adelina's feet dragged along the shore and trapped the handle of a fallen dagger between her toes. Giovanna hadn't seen it. Her long black neck elongated into the swan, impossibly large, strong enough to carry off a human.

He couldn't lose her like this. He would chase her down to the ends of the Earth. But what would he chase if she were dead?

Grigg sprinted after them, but already Adelina's feet were as high as Grigg's head and too many paces off.

Adelina passed the knife between her feet up to her hand and thrust the blade up into Giovanna's belly as she flew. A swirling shower of black feathers obscured the woman and the swan. The last image Grigg saw of her was Adelina's back arcing in agony, her mouth open in a scream, and Grigg's own heart, now combined with hers, bursting with pain.

Searing horror ripped across the space between his shoulder blades at his back. He stumbled, but then the pain was gone, and a thrill washed over him that he didn't understand.

Grigg looked up just in time to see Adelina emerge from the swath of black falling feathers with massive wings spreading out from between her shoulder blades. But she wasn't transforming from woman to swan—she was a human with enormous black wings like those of a swan, swooping down and alighting on the ground beside Grigg.

He gawked at her. What had just happened? Had Giovanna's power been transferred to Adelina—but differently? Or incompletely?

Was she really okay?

Adelina still held the dagger, crimson blood dripping off its blade.

The Queen of the Sea approached on her tower of river water, arcing the deck of cards between her hands as she did. "Congratulations."

Grigg tried to step between the queen and Adelina, but Adelina took his hand and shook her head. She seemed okay. And she could handle herself; he knew that. It was just that the idea of the queen directing her wrath on Adelina shot bile up the back of his throat.

Still, Adelina was right. A strong, united front was better than a protective one. He relented and stood at her side. She squeezed his hand, and the two gave their attention to the queen.

Pupil-less eyes drifted between them. "You have killed my most recent servant. The two of you share a heart, and the two of you together will take her place. Let's hope your usefulness is higher than hers, and your ending is more ... favorable."

She lifted a hand, and the tower of water holding up the orb moved to bring the sphere to her. The orb rested in her hand, and she held it before them. "Your new abilities, whatever the extent of them turn out to be, will serve me well. But you'll need more than a few parlor tricks to steal secrets from the King of the Wind and the Jester of the Fates."

New abilities? Grigg shot another look at the sleek black wings protruding from Adelina's back. She was a fireblood, in the line of a mage, with a mysterious golden heart and massive black swan wings.

He was a melderless swindler who got by largely by the aforementioned parlor tricks, a silver tongue, and the skin of his teeth. And whatever the Heart of the Stars shenanigans had been when it touched his heart. And whatever effect came from blending his heart with Adelina's.

The Queen of the Sea produced two crystal vials strung on a chain and draped them over their heads as necklaces. "Your affinity for secrets is high, Grigglor. You will be able to see valuable secrets in colors and chase the threads you might want most. But you must be in physical contact with the subject to gather the secret into the vial—one secret from the King, and one from the Jester."

Grigg's brow furrowed. "Is that what the Heart of the Stars does? Give me some way to see secrets?"

"No. My specialty is secrets, so that comes from me. The Heart of the Stars houses healing magic that burns away infiltration—poisons, mind influence, anything that pushes into your mind, body, or powers. Seeing as you have no natural, physical magical powers, I have no idea what it may have done to you.

"Perhaps you thought you killed an enemy in Giovanna and made me a friend, but this is not the case. You are servants, and you would be wise to remember it."

The queen smiled a mirthless smile. "The Jester of the Fates will destroy you. And if any portion of you is left after that, the King of the Wind will kill you. If you surprise me and live, you will be rewarded. You will gather two secrets from each of them or die trying—because if you fail, I won't need to kill you. They'll do it for me."

THANK YOU FOR READING!

Continue the adventure with *Oath of Odds*...Turn the page for a sneak peek at chapter 1!

Thank you so much for reading *Heist of Hearts*, book 1 of the *Heist of Hearts Series*! I hope you enjoyed reading it as much as I enjoyed writing it.

If you did, would you be willing to leave a review? Reviews help enable authors to continue doing what they do, and help other readers to find books best suited to them.

If you'd like to leave a review on Amazon, scan the QR code.

Oath of Odds

Chapter 1

Adelina

Gazing over rolling hills and green farmland was a nice way to pretend she hadn't exchanged a deadly curse for a deadly deal. Adelina breathed in the scent of pine and oak and kicked up dust as she looked out over grassy fields with grazing flocks of sheep on one side and soaked in the lowing of the cows on the other. She ran a hand over Velocina's ebony neck. The mare tossed her head in acknowledgement.

Blue sky spread endlessly over the farmland, the edges of a lake twinkling in the distance down the slope to her left. On the other side of the road, by the cows, a man rolled a wheelbarrow into the barn in the distance, and Adelina wondered what it would have been like to live a life like his—one marked by hard menial labor, measuring out grain for animals, and sleeping deeply at night with an ornery cow or a rusty door hinge serving as her only troubles.

There was more to farm life than old hinges and obstinate cattle, of course, but compared to her old life as chieftess and guardian of a magical tree with the power to restore full abilities to a dark mage and free an evil siren queen, it certainly sounded simpler. Grigg had tried to tell her that if they wanted to understand the Queen of the Sea in order to find her weaknesses, they couldn't think of her as evil. They had to get inside her head, and the queen surely didn't think of herself as evil.

What did the Queen of the Sea hope to do with the secrets she demanded they gather from the Jester of Fates and the King of the Wind? Who were the jester and the king, and why were the three of them emblazoned as the face cards in a card deck in the queen's possession?

Grigg hadn't had any better answers to those questions than Adelina when he insisted they not think of the queen as evil if they wanted to get into her head. But considering that Adelina's ancestor Giovanna—the Black Swan Mage who had cursed Adelina and Grigg in the first place—had gotten her power from the Queen of the Sea, and the Queen of the Sea neither mourned Giovanna's death nor hesitated to force Grigg and Adelina into a magically binding deal leveraging their lives as collateral, Adelina thought *evil* was a pretty appropriate term.

Grigg rode beside her on Spavento, the flighty gelding he'd borrowed to barrel into Guerrori territory the first time they'd met. The horse had spooked and thrown Grigg off its back, where he hit his head and woke up surrounded by Adelina and her warriors. He'd planned to get caught, though she hadn't known it at the time. But he hadn't planned to get knocked unconscious.

Buying the gelding had not exactly been his first choice, but they'd been in a hurry. The horse had been rattled from its experience in the jungle, what with the fire, blasts of wind, and quaking earth beneath his hooves as the two rival tribes had fought. Spavento had wound up spooked and, as a result, cheap. The owner wanted to be rid of him, and was one of the few willing to make a sale with Grigg by the time they were ready to leave. Spavento wasn't nearly as honorable a steed as Velocina, but he could manage basic travel from point A to point B with only moderately annoying hindrances.

Adelina ran her thumb over the smooth stones of green agate and polished crystal of her mother's bracelet at her wrist. She hadn't worn it until leaving home, but somehow, despite her mother's lies, she'd wanted more of her history with her as she left the jungle. As reminders of who she was, and what she was leaving *for*. But as they rode from place to place, she'd found herself playing with it and wondering if her mother had done the same when she wore it, and what she would think of Adelina being in possession of it now that she'd given up the chieftess role and the purpose of the tribe had crumbled.

Grigg nodded to the town up ahead, its stone buildings with dark wood beams criss-crossing along their exteriors, giving the buildings a unique character beneath their sloped roofs. Flowers spilled out from window boxes overlooking stone streets, as the dirt paths of the farmland outside the town transitioned to cobblestone up ahead. The stonework was cracked, and grass grew between some of the stones where the dirt met the cobblestone, but the condition of the road improved the further in they got.

"We're here."

Adelina shot a sideways look at Grigg as he surveyed their destination. His body rolled lazily with the movement of his horse, his mop of dark wavy hair rustling in the light breeze. The shadow of facial hair stubble shaded his face beneath high cheekbones, and his ocean blue eyes matched the glory of the open sky. He'd steeled himself to trade out pressed white shirts for an off-white tunic, still rolled to the elbow as always, but missing his signature velvet or embroidered vests.

"No need to flash around my wealth," he'd said. *"We don't know much about Eversacht, but it doesn't sound high-end. We want to fit in, not stand out."*

Traveling together had been strange since their meeting with the Queen of the Sea. Adelina had shoved her heart into Grigg's chest to save him from his curse, and he'd cut a deal to save her in return—one that resulted in both of their hearts being ripped in half, and melded together again half and half with one another, each of them now bearing a heart that was half Adelina's and half Grigg's. The kiss—*his* kiss—had saved her life and sealed their new deal with the Queen of the Sea.

Adelina could hardly think of the memory without her stomach flip-flopping. She didn't know what she'd expected her first kiss with Grigg to be like, but that moment had surpassed it. Still, neither of them had ever lived without a curse before, and they hadn't quite known what to do with each other once they were free.

Magically linked together? Check.

Feelings of what the Queen of the Sea had described as *the beginnings of love* floating around between them? Check.

Electricity like crackling lightning when they touched or looked at each other? That too. Except for other moments, when he'd crack walnuts between his teeth too loud, or she would crack her neck for the third time in an hour. Those moments didn't result in particularly loving glances.

But they were free of the curse, and still doing nothing about it. Her love wouldn't kill him. His love wouldn't kill her. So why did everything feel so...

He shot her a look, and her insides squirmed and exploded in a burst of drunk butterflies bumping into the walls of her body.

The corner of his mouth twisted up. "You know I can feel that, right?"

She grimaced. "Feel what?"

It was a stalling tactic for time to think. A bad one.

Instead of answering, he turned in the saddle to fix his full attention on Adelina as she rode the glistening black mare beside him. She'd braided her long dark hair and let it trail over one shoulder, though escaped wisps from the braid after half a day's riding probably didn't do her any favors. The sun warmed her bronze skin, and she'd opted for a fringed animal hide top that felt a little more like home in the jungle, and paired it with trousers and a lightweight sage green mantle.

She'd had to customize all her shirts after acquiring a portion of the Black Swan Mage's power. Pitch black swirls of abyss marked her skin in ovals out of shoulder blades and long lines branching out toward her shoulders where the massive black wings of a swan could burst free at a moment's notice when she called for them.

The mage could completely transform from human, to swan, to human again. Adelina couldn't do that. And though she hadn't been able to make the marks go completely away, she *could* transform the marks on her back into wings, and back to marks.

Since then, Adelina had needed to amend her wardrobe for backless clothing so that her clothes wouldn't be ruined every time wings sprouted from her shoulder blades. But, she also needed a way to cover her back to keep her freakish secret. Hence the long mantles she'd become accustomed to wearing. Additionally, except for the beaded fringes falling down the front of her top, swaying with the wind, her tops had needed to be made form-fitting to keep the shirt firmly in place to keep it from shifting and interfering with her wings if she called for them.

Grigg and Adelina agreed it would be best save her energy and keep a lower profile, keeping this particular secret close to the vest, using her ability sparingly and strategically.

He turned in the saddle to look at her more directly, taking in the messy wisps of hair around her face, her sun-kissed skin, the awkward shift she made in the saddle under his unrelenting gaze. His eyes bored into her, steady and unyielding, but the longer he stared into her eyes, the softer they became—hard edges smoothing over like butter melting into a steaming roll.

Or maybe she was just hungry.

She wanted to look away, but a new sensation rolled over her. No, not a sensation. Not entirely. Her own emotions were there—

confused, conflicting, and tumbling over one another—but something else was there now, too, inserted from the outside in like a foreign body. Only now it infiltrated the seat of her emotions, and her own heart raced to match the thundering beat of a swell tearing through not her own chest, but Grigg's. Her chest tightened, a burning longing bound in a cage. She wanted to reach out and touch him, wanted to reach for him, but something held her back.

Had it been *him* that wanted to reach for *her* that she was experiencing? On the one hand, there was a settledness, a rootedness in his emotion when he looked at her. But side by side with it came a parasitic, uncertain anxiety. The magical link between them from bearing combined hearts allowed each one to feel strong emotions from the other. But though she could experience his emotions, she couldn't identify *why* he was feeling them.

Was he unsure if he wanted to be with her? Unsure if he wanted to kiss her? Unsure on whether or not to be upset about their magical link?

It occurred to her, not for the first time, that perhaps he felt the same cascade of emotions when he experienced *her* feelings. He felt uncertain, and he could feel her uncertainty. Perhaps that was why he hadn't kissed her since that day in the Nascosta when their hearts had been combined.

Or maybe he had come to his senses, regretting making a horrible deal with a despicable, powerful being ten times as bad as the mage had been, and didn't want to get any more attached than he already was in case she died.

Or in case he found a way to leave her. Though with the current situation in place, she couldn't yet conceive of how he would manage it. And if she died, he too would die, and vice versa. That was how the Queen of the Sea had ensured she could forever blackmail one of them with the safety or torture of the other. She hadn't trusted their novice love would last without some magical assurances, and without the two of them in love, she couldn't dangle the other's safety over their heads. Now, with their combined hearts, if Grigg and Adelina didn't get the secrets the queen required, they would die. Her gut twisted at the thought.

Grigg swallowed and looked away. "Does that answer your question?"

Adelina resisted a flinch as the softness in his eyes withdrew like a slap, the conflicting emotions of tenderness and gentle uncertainty replaced with a dark swirl of resistance and guarded rejection. He pulled into himself and refocused on the village up ahead, but his heart still raced, hers sprinting to match its pace—their tangle of emotion only spiraling further as they pretended not to want to look at each other.

But the gut wrench he'd felt from her hadn't been at the thought of him caring for her, or him having conflicting feelings for her. Those were both confusing and comforting. It was at the other, intruding thought that had been the culprit behind her sudden dread. The one about getting the secrets or dying. The part about being bound to a sinister siren queen with untold power, dancing their lives over their heads like bread crumbs over a mob of beggars.

Had he misread her dread as a distaste for *him*?

And so things had gone, since four weeks ago when they'd set out from Smŭrttata.

She could try to apologize, but that could be misread just as easily. And when he shut down like this and pulled into himself, he didn't like to talk. Currents of bitterness, anger, and emptiness would swirl like eddies, and anything she did to bring attention to the fact that she could feel those emotions made him shut down further. He would change the subject or crack a joke and try to stuff whatever it was deep enough down that she could no longer feel them through their link.

But that was ridiculous. Because whether he wanted her to or not, she *could* feel what he felt, and if they didn't talk about it soon, she was going to explode.

Adelina pursed her lips. She wasn't going to let him ignore this. Red hot jagged edges took up residence in her heart. She opened her mouth to speak, but shards of annoyance slit into her from Grigg, and he cut her off.

"I'll find us a place to stay and stable the horses as soon as we get there. Why don't you walk around and get a lay of the land?"

His voice was even and controlled, even if she knew the rest of him wasn't.

"Fine." The word came out too harsh. She cleared her throat and tried again. "That's fine. I'll start near the residences and work my way toward the market."

He almost smiled, and a twinge of bittersweet warmth interrupted his ire. She clamped her mouth shut tight to keep from a biting comment or retort for whatever he was thinking.

She liked residential areas. It gave a taste of a town, a feel for how families lived together, a sliver of culture. Sure, maybe when she lived in the jungle with her warrior women, she had snuck off and stared in the windows of one particular family, spying on them in a vain attempt to spark hope that families could live peacefully together. That joy was real, and mothers and fathers could live together and love their children. To dream of a life she could not live, because her father was dead, and her mother and entire tribe had hated men.

And sure, maybe she did have a fascination with watching families live their ordinary lives. Maybe it offered a slice of normalcy to give in to a daydream now and then. Maybe daydreams were as close as she'd ever get to having such experiences for herself. But there was practical utility in it too, which is what she reminded Grigg every time they passed through a new village or town or city, as she did the same thing: start with the residential areas.

The horse's hooves moved from the soft *pthhh pthhh* against dirt paths to the rhythmic *clip-clop* against stone as they passed through the outskirts of Eversacht and wound their way further into the town. Green grass and flowers sprouted from any place beyond the cobblestone streets. Colorful clothing hung from lines strung between the houses a street down from the cobbler they were passing now.

Grigg nodded in the opposite direction, northeast from the direction they'd come. "There's a nice tavern there by the lake. Waking up overlooking the water doesn't seem so bad."

She nodded absently, scanning the windows of the homes on the west side of the street. "Sure, that works."

He laughed and steered Spavento further to the west, nudging Velocina closer to the homes Adelina so enjoyed getting to see. Once they reached the end of the row, Grigg nodded at the houses. "Go explore. I'll take care of the horses and find us a place to stay."

She checked the saddlebags with her bow and quiver and packs of supplies. Everything was just as organized as it had been that morning. There was no reason for it not to have been. She hadn't touched them since.

Adelina nodded and slid down to the ground, passing Grigg the reins. "Take care of her."

"She's survived this long, hasn't she?"

Adelina ran her hand down Velocina's nose and scratched behind the mare's ears. After a moment, she dropped her hand.

"Okay."

She gave a long lingering look to her bow and quiver, but no one they passed wore visible weapons. It seemed that was an unusual daily wear item for this place, so it might be odd if she wore her bow.

Grigg gave her an encouraging nod. "I'll come find you, like usual."

She nodded back and turned toward the houses. Finally— peace and quiet, walking on her own two feet, shaking off the stiffness of the saddle. Staring at homes and lives and people instead of field after field and meter after meter of endless road. She nearly skipped away from Grigg and into the rows of houses.

Adelina only made it down the first row of houses before she saw something that stopped her in her tracks: a carving of a satyr over the door. From the waist up, he was a man, save for the curled horns and long ears; from the waist down, he was a goat, dancing on two hooves as he played the flute in his hands.

The Jester of Fates.

THE BLOOD & FLAME SAGA

This explosive new dragons and assassins series is about to become your new addiction.

Are you ready to ride dragons and unravel the mysteries of a land steeped in magic and betrayal?

Scan the QR code to start reading.

THE MELDERBLOOD CHRONICLES

Shadow and Bone meets *The Selection* in this addictive, fast-paced fantasy adventure series.

Princess Aviama's world has been steeped in chaos ever since long-dormant magic returned – and came alive in her blood.

Scan the QR code to start reading.

About the Author

Author of *The Forgotten Stone* and the *Blood and Flame Saga*, E.A. Winters loves making herself a cup of chai tea and delving into creating epic fantasy worlds for you to enjoy.

Erin lives in Virginia with her husband and two boys. When she's not writing, Erin is spending her time with her family. She loves playing board games and reading, whenever the elusive "free time" opportunity arises.

- Website and newsletter: eawinters.com
- Facebook: facebook.com/eawintersnovels
- TikTok: @eawinters
- Instagram: @e.a.winters

ALSO BY E.A. WINTERS

BLOOD & FLAME SAGA

Complete at four books, the Blood & Flame Saga is a fast-paced, no-spice YA fantasy, following an assassin raised by a dragonlord who must choose between the only family she's ever known and the kingdom she was trained to destroy.

Book 1: Dragon's Kiss

Book 2: Broken Bonds

Book 3: Noble Claims

Book 4: Crimson Queen

THE MELDERBLOOD CHRONICLES

In a palace of gowns, secrets, and betrayal, one princess walks the tightrope between duty and death... while magic simmers beneath her skin.

Book 1: Melderblood

Book 2: Shadow Caste

Book 3: Wraithweaver

Book 4: Reaverbane

HEIST OF HEARTS

If he loves her, she'll die. If she loves him, he'll die. But only by working together can they stop a vengeful mage from rising again—and lift the curses that bind them both.

Book 1: Heist of Hearts

Book 2: Oath of Odds